I remembered the days when Tony and I were an inseparable item and everyone on the street knew it. Days of discovery and promise, when the excitement in Bensonhurst was as high as the girls' teased hairdos. . . .

Chosen by *USA Today* as one of their "New Voices" of 2011, Suzanne Corso makes her unforgettable literary debut with

Brooklyn Story

"Corso gets the Brooklyn dialect pitch-perfect and keeps the pace brisk."

—*Publishers Weekly*

"Wonderful. . . . You're hooked from the first sentence."

—Olympia Dukakis, Academy Award–winning actress

"Tragic yet triumphal . . . a must-read."

—Lorraine Bracco, Academy Award–nominated actress

"This story explores the mind and heart of a young girl struggling for her identity in a soulless world. Heartbreaking and sensitively written. A very unusual coming-of-age story."

—Armand Assante, Emmy Award–winning actor

This title is also available as an eBook

Brooklyn Story

SUZANNE CORSO

G

GALLERY BOOKS

New York   London   Toronto   Sydney   New Delhi

G

Gallery Books
A Division of Simon & Schuster, Inc.
1230 Avenue of the Americas
New York, NY 10020

First Gallery Books trade paperback edition November 2011

GALLERY BOOKS and colophon are
trademarks of Simon & Schuster, Inc.

For information about special discounts for bulk purchases,
please contact Simon & Schuster Special Sales
at 1-866-506-1949 or business@simonandschuster.com.

The Simon & Schuster Speakers Bureau can bring authors
to your live event. For more information or to book an event
contact the Simon & Schuster Speakers Bureau
at 1-866-248-3049 or visit our website at www.simonspeakers.com.

Designed by Esther Paradelo

Manufactured in the United States of America

1   3   5   7   9   10   8   6   4   2

Library of Congress Cataloging-in-Publication Data is available.

ISBN 978-1-4391-9022-7
ISBN 978-1-4391-9023-4 (pbk)
ISBN 978-1-4391-9024-1 (ebook)

To the three women who made me who I am today:

My Grandma Rose
My Mother Judy
and The Blessed Mother

If you keep thinking "That man has abused me,"
holding it as a much-cherished grievance,
your anger will never be allayed.

If you can put down that fury-inducing thought,
your anger will lessen. Fury will never end fury,
it will just ricochet on and on.

Only putting it down will end
such an abysmal state.

—*Sunnata Vagga,*

from *The Pocket Buddha Reader,*
edited by Anne Bancroft (2001)

PROLOGUE

June 1982

Some people lived in the real world and others lived in Brooklyn. My name is Samantha Bonti and of course I was one of the chosen. At age fifteen, I was seduced into a life that shattered my innocence, a life that tore at my convictions and my very soul, a life that brought me four years later to the sunlit steps of the courthouse in downtown Brooklyn.

Now, at age nineteen, I stood below the stone facade, watching strangers come and go with purposeful strides; I paused to contemplate how I got there. The dark events of my recent past replayed in my mind in an instant, while thoughts about my disadvantaged beginnings and a lifetime of struggle flooded my consciousness. It had been no small blessing of Providence, I knew, to be born without deformity, to be endowed with a fierce determination to make my own way in the world, and to be favored by His hand, which worked through others as I matured.

My mother, Joan, tried her best to give me a better life filled with possibility. But she was scarred by her own past, poisoned with cynicism and shackled by addiction and poor health. Mom was a striking woman on the outside and a frail one within. Her beauty was obvious from a distance, but up close one could see that her bottle-dyed, wavy auburn tresses covered

deep lines in her face. A witty woman who had had the potential to be brilliant and used to be full of life and spunk, Mom
had been beaten down by an abusive husband.

Vito Bonti was a Catholic immigrant from Italy and as
hardheaded a Sicilian as there ever was. A Vietnam vet who
owned a pizzeria, he did nothing for Mom and blamed her
for his bitter disposition. After all, Mom was nothing more
to him than a poor Jewish girl from Brooklyn and he never
failed to remind her of that. Despite her willingness to forgo
her own faith and take up his beliefs and his customs, he
cheated on her with other women as often as he could steal
away. When Joan and Vito were alone in their apartment, they
argued long and loud enough for neighbors to hear. In a fit
of rage one month before I was born, he threw a car jack at
my mother's pregnant belly. The hemorrhaging forced her
into premature labor and she was rushed to the hospital. The
doctors said if I was lucky enough to be born, I would most
likely have severe brain damage from the impact of the blow,
or, even worse, be a stillborn. Fate achieved, fear stepped aside,
and I survived. Then Vito abandoned her. He never sent a
penny for support and never came around. I saw him once by
chance when I was six years old when Mom pointed him out
in the neighborhood. He was a nice-looking man with long,
black hair and a scruffy beard, who wore a brown shirt buttoned to the collar that had pink flowers on it. I ran to my
father and hugged his legs tightly. He pulled away, and I never
saw him again.

Maybe it was better that way, I thought. Mom had it tough
enough as it was, living off Social Services and living with dis-
ease that visited her weakened body; she didn't need more of
Vito's physical abuse on top of her hardships. Mom may have
felt that having a daughter was one of them, but she never
said that to me. And although there were moments when I
knew she loved me—when she wouldn't let me hang out in the

streets with neighborhood kids and when she kept me away from boys—I only heard her say those words once. Instead, she criticized me at every turn and picked fights with me without any provocation on my part. She would never say I was pretty, but would prove it in other ways by sticking up for me which were flat-out embarrassing. Like walking into the bathroom in elementary school with gold spandex pants yelling at the other girls who were talking about my chipped tooth. My nickname was "Razor Tooth" until Mom saved up enough money to fix it two years later. Mom, of course, set them straight. They never said a word again to me until eighth grade.

Mom's only comforts were cigarettes and going unconscious with drink, prescription meds, and the recreational drugs she used on occasion. Sniffing glue was what she did because it was cheap—alone, or with seedy friends or even my friends. Over time, illness drained her body and addiction poisoned her spirit. To her credit, Mom kept her worst habits and her demons from me as best she could and told me now and then that there was another way to live.

Grandma Ruth reinforced that message daily. She never made excuses for her daughter's shortcomings and never missed an opportunity to take charge of my upbringing. The last straw was when Mom had come home with crabs that she contracted from some man she had been sleeping with for a supply of glue. After a long night in the emergency room, tossing all of our bedding and sleeping on just a cold mattress, Grandma had seen enough and moved in. She then quit her job when I was seven, after Mom and Grandma got robbed at knifepoint when we lived in the projects by Cozine Avenue in Brooklyn. They soon realized it was best to change locations, my mom opting for an Italian neighborhood. Grandma just wanted away from this place.

Grandma arose every morning to cook my breakfast and send me off to school, letting Mom get a little extra sleep. With a larger-than-life aura, this short, big-boned Jewish woman had sinewy, arthritic hands, rounded shoulders, and burning bunions on her tired feet. Grandma was a steadfast woman who remained true to her religious and social convictions, but her overbearing opinions came with a heart the size of an ocean. Her wisdom, which I had learned to depend upon, was such that she allowed me to make my own choices and make my own mistakes while she remained a constant source of encouragement as I strove to better myself. Grandma was the loudest, most opinionated silver-haired lady you could ever meet, and I loved her completely. Flawed as we three women were, we were family.

Others came into my life as I sought to escape from the Brooklyn that enveloped me and my contemporaries. Father Rinaldi preached to me as much with his serenity as with his measured words; without speaking, his countenance told me that an inner peace was real and attainable. His neighborhood church, Our Lady of Guadalupe, which I visited for the first time after months of seeing happy people leaving it as I walked home from school, was as constant a presence and as sturdy as my grandma, and was a haven from the confusing, turbulent, and sometimes harsh world I lived in. The church's solace, mystery, and promise of knowledge that could help me lured me back on occasion. I never told Mom or Grandma about my stops there, or about the saintly priest who welcomed my infrequent visits and my inquiries, drew parallels between biblical parables and my ordeals, and offered an ear and guidance without any strings attached.

Mr. Wainright, my high school English teacher, looked with soft eyes upon my first, clumsy attempts at creative composition. He extracted and held out to me the kernels of aptitude buried within my clutching words and awkward phrasing as motivation to continue my efforts. He believed in my talent as one believes in God—with scant tangible proof.

I had met my best friend Janice Caputo on the bus to New Keiser High School when I was a freshman and she a senior, and although she was older, she had taken me under her wing. Janice told me later the reason she had done so was that I wasn't like other girls and she liked that about me. It hadn't mattered to her that I was poor and didn't have the trendy clothes and accessories that everyone else seemed to have, and she sought no pleasure as other classmates did in making fun of me—sometimes to my face. Janice was a constant companion on my circuitous path to a life that was different from the Brooklyn one we knew, the one she accepted for herself but that I longed to leave behind. Corralled in the community of my ancestors, I longed to cross the Brooklyn Bridge into Manhattan and flee the destiny that was assumed for all in our outer borough. Janice's generosity of spirit encompassed my writing passion even though she wouldn't share the world it represented and the reduced closeness it portended. Janice soaked up every word I wrote and nudged me along as we endured the normal growing pains of adolescence and the additional slings and arrows endemic to a self-contained Italian community. Janice stood by me and suffered along with me as I was swallowed up by circumstances that threatened the attainment of my lifelong dream of becoming a writer.

That some people lived in the real world and others lived in Brooklyn was an understatement. Most of the others were content to stay there and be a member of the group that was appropriate to their station. Mobsters molded their women like Jell-O and controlled everything else in the neighborhood, from gambling, hijacking, robberies, drugs, and prostitution to social conduct. They even exerted a measure of influence over the local cops, who often looked the other way.

The wannabes—young and old—idolized the mobsters and sought to impress them with their willingness to reject the straight life and engage in anything illegal. Wannabes patterned their mannerisms and activity after the mobsters, orbited as close as possible to them, and celebrated those who were taken into the fold. And then there were the nerds. Young ones buried themselves in their textbooks and their hobbies, and had nothing to do with anyone. Older ones worked in honest, middle-class jobs and honored values that the mobsters and wannabes gave lip service to but disdained.

Less than a handful of people I knew intended to leave Brooklyn. But I always did, starting when I first learned from books and movies that there was a lot more than the narrow minds and narrow visions of those around me, to that very moment in front of the courthouse. I stood there, beneath the words "Justice" and "Equality" that were etched in the large stones of the facade, and I thought about how the Brooklyn Bridge had always represented freedom and the way to a new life for me. Don't get me wrong, Brooklyn was a beautiful place for most, but to me it had become a past I had to flee.

That famous span, far from my family's humble apartment, was foremost always in my thoughts. Its two massive towers and intricate web of steel cables were a combination of strength, tension, and balance, and the bridge stood as a symbol of how my own life should be fashioned. I needed to be strong, I needed to stretch myself, and I needed to counterweight the life I was born into with the pull of what lay on the other side of the East River, in Manhattan.

I thought about the bridge's origins. The vision of one man, John Roebling, was realized by his son more than ten years later and that meant a lot to me. Dreams could survive generations and come true. The bridge proved that, even if John and a score of others died during its construction. I felt the power of the bridge each time I gazed at it, and it inspired me to look beyond the confinement of my Bensonhurst neighborhood and the humiliation of poverty. I vowed to get past the stereotypes and the welfare checks, food stamps, waiting on line for a block of cheese, only to get there and find them to be gone. The secondhand clothes, and dinners of toast or, on special occasions, Kraft macaroni and cheese.

I never lost the desire to construct my own bridge to my own future. I knew that wouldn't be easy for a girl like me, just as building the Brooklyn Bridge had been fraught with hardship, peril, and sacrifice. And although others were there to help, I knew that in the end it would be up to me to endure the trials and setbacks, and to overcome each and every obstacle as the Roeblings had done. I found out just how hard building and crossing a bridge would be.

An Adonis named Tony Kroon, five years older than I, swept me off my feet when I was a teen. The moment I saw him, when I was starting my junior year of high school, I was captivated by his thick blond hair, stunning blue eyes, and defined jaw. I was flattered by his immediate interest in me and felt an immediate bond with him because his Dutch-Italian heritage mirrored my Italian-Jewish one. In our Bensonhurst neighborhood, being anything but pure Italian was a distinct shortcoming. People like us didn't belong entirely to either culture and had to endure the prejudices of both. That was the subtext for me in my home, and for a wannabe like Tony, acceptance by his fledgling mob associates was a constant issue.

I empathized with Tony's struggles and was smitten by his increasing attention to me. I overlooked his thinking only about himself, high living, and his standing among his contemporaries, the Brooklyn Boys. Like them, he forbade independent thinking in his chosen woman, so I kept my hopes and dreams from him. The wannabe boys of Brooklyn kept their "business" away from their girlfriends, who learned from the start not to ask imprudent questions. Tony lived in secrecy the way all his Italian contemporaries did, and treated me the way they treated their women: with minimal information, with impossible demands delivered over a clenched fist, and with clothes and jewelry that had fallen off trucks. I was supposed to remain quiet, feel honored to be on his arm whenever he wanted, and support the decisions he made for both of us, decisions that took me farther from the Brooklyn Bridge that I had been determined to cross.

It wasn't as if no one had warned me. Grandma had told me more than once not to trust Tony. "*Bubelah,*" she would say, using the Yiddish term of affection for a child, "don't go with that Catholic half-Italian piece of crap. He's a real charmer, just like your father. He'll steal your dreams. Find yourself a nice Jewish boy." But I didn't listen to her, nor to Father Rinaldi or Mr. Wainright, who tried to gently steer me away from what they also knew. I followed my heart instead of my head, and my heart told me I was in love.

I had powerful feelings for Tony then and I had powerful feelings for him as I climbed the stairs to the imposing court-house. Locked in a holding cell beneath the court, Tony would still be thinking about himself, I knew, but his thoughts would be different this day. At the age of twenty-four, he faced a long stretch behind bars if the jury delivered a guilty verdict. He'd be cast into the monstrous world of hard-core criminals with their daily frustrations, rages, and lusts.

I pulled the handle of a heavy wood door and entered the building where Tony's fate was to be decided and I would confront my past. The courthouse lobby, with its high ceiling, marble floors, and musky, stone interior reminded me of Father Rinaldi's church. A different kind of praying took place here, I thought, and I took the elevator to the ninth floor. None of the souls who had risen silently in the lift with me had had any inkling of what I would face there or why I had to be there.

The tall, dark-stained courtroom door closed behind me

without a sound. I squinted in the glaring fluorescent light of a large chamber with walls and a floor that matched its entry doors. The judge's raised bench and the jury box were vacant. A low hum wafted through the sparsely filled room as lawyers huddled around massive desks beyond a wood railing and spectators milled about or sat whispering with tilted necks. The prosecutors looked upbeat. I slipped into a seat in the last row and felt as though I were on trial, too, for all of my lies and deceptions—to everyone, including myself—of recent years. I looked at the spectators up front who had played their parts in bringing me to that judgment day.

The Kroon family occupied the front row as if they were at a funeral. Pamela, Tony's mother and aging wannabe bombshell with multishaded dyed blond hair, sat erect in a dark, tight-fitting designer pantsuit. Philip, his father, wore a short-sleeved cotton shirt and his head was bowed between his hunched, slight shoulders. Tony's fourteen-year-old chubby sister, Katrina, bobbed in her seat as if she was enjoying the spectacle. Vin Priganti, known to everyone in Bensonhurst as "the Son" of local mob boss Tino Priganti, fidgeted in a chair behind the Kroons. Vin took occasional beatings from his father's heavy fists along with the wads of cash he slipped into his son's hand. Vin ran the crew to which Tony and his friends belonged. Richie Sparto, a crew member and Tony's best friend, sat alone three rows farther back.

All of these people lived in the Brooklyn that stifled my dream. None had lifted a hand to help me. None cared if I made it across the bridge that stood a few blocks away from the courthouse. Truth be told, they probably preferred that I never tried or, even better, never thought to do so in the first place. In my own backyard, they were as far from me as the life on the other side of that bridge. They hadn't seen me come into the courtroom, just as they had never seen who I was.

The door beyond the jury box opened. All eyes were on

Tony's stoic face as he was led by the bailiff to a chair at the defendant's table, and he sat down without looking directly at anyone. Although his shoulders no longer stretched the silk material of his custom-tailored suit as they had when I first met him, I couldn't help thinking that he was still much too good-looking for prison. But for a half-breed wannabe like Tony who honored *omerta*—the mafia code of silence—that was what he confronted as everyone looked on.

I sighed, and remembered the days when Tony and I were an inseparable item and everyone on the street knew it. Days of discovery and promise, when I had had those different feelings about everything and when the excitement in Bensonhurst was as high as the girls' teased hairdos . . .

August 1978

"C'mon, Sam," Janice said as she reached down and took my hand. "Sorry I'm late."

"That's okay," I said, rising from the stoop in front of the three-story apartment house where I lived on the top floor with my mother and grandmother. The building on Seventy-third Street was indistinguishable from the dozen others it was connected to on the long block, save for the fire escape that was affixed to the front of the structure instead of the rear and its arched entrance that reminded me of the stained-glass windows at Our Lady of Guadalupe and the Gothic towers of the Brooklyn Bridge.

Like most multifamily residences in Bensonhurst, mine had a postage stamp–sized patch of grass in front, surrounded by a low wrought-iron fence that was tended by the old people, who provided meticulous care. Together with them, I cherished those strips of green and the few narrow-trunk trees, struggling to rise amid the concrete that lived and breathed and changed with the seasons.

"It's a beautiful day to be outside," Janice said.

"That, and getting away from my mother."

"Sumthin' happen?"

"Just the usual." I adjusted my red tube top and low-waist

jeans and swept my long, raven hair behind my shoulders with my fingers. "Gave me a load of shit about my hair and what I'm wearin'," I said. I glanced at the statue of the Blessed Mother that Mrs. Moretti, who lived on the first floor, had set upon the small lawn. Many neighbors and other Bensonhurst faithful did likewise with the icon of their choosing, and I always thought these icons watched over me when I walked by.

"Forget about it," Janice said. "Let's go have some fun."

I always have fun with Janice, I thought as we headed toward Eighteenth Avenue and the bustling retail district in the heart of Bensonhurst. Janice and I went to all the new movies and visited the local pastry shops and pizzerias on a regular basis, where we were often served at no charge. I used to think it was because we were two young girls, but I came to understand that there was another reason for the way we were treated. Janice's father, Rocco Caputo, owned Cue Ball, the pool hall above a row of stores on Eighteenth Avenue, and the bar downstairs named after him. Mr. Caputo was well respected in the community, particularly by those who mattered most—Italians connected with the mob. I never asked my friend for any details about her father's connections, and she never offered.

Janice treated me as an equal even though she was three years older and in a different league than I was. She shopped all along the avenue at stores run by women who were connected to mobsters or dated one or wanted to date one. Janice's boyfriend, Richie, bought her the kinds of things I could only stare at through display windows. She lived in a private corner residence far away from Eighteenth Avenue and the elevated subway line known as the N train on New Keiser Avenue. I loved going to her house and hanging out in her large bedroom with all its frilly appointments. I felt safer there than I did in my own home.

Janice and I seldom included other girlfriends in our get-togethers. We weren't standoffish, but we felt most were petty, competitive, and jealous, and we preferred not to bother with them. On occasion, we did go to parties in nice homes or joined the groups who gathered at Outer Skates, the local rink, where macho Italian boys rented skates for the girls. Those times were enjoyable but they paled in comparison to those when Janice and I were alone together. We were at ease with each other, shared everything without reservation, and couldn't be closer if we had been sisters.

"How do ya feel about summer bein' almost over?" Janice asked as we walked.

"The sooner I get back to school, the sooner I'll graduate," I said.

"Can't wait to get across that bridge, huh?"

"Nothing's changed," I said.

Janice turned toward me without breaking stride. "We'll see about that."

We made our way past the well-kept homes all along my quiet block. I couldn't help thinking that very little had changed in the neighborhood across a few generations. Janice and I knew that, just like in the rest of Bensonhurst, most front doors would be unlocked and they and the windows that were open would remain that way at night. Italians in this neighborhood had nothing to fear because the local mobsters enforced their own code and thieves stayed out of the area. If they knew what was good for them, they plied their trade elsewhere.

Most residents had no direct involvement with the Mafia, but they knew about everything it did and subscribed on occasion to its services, especially gambling and hot merchandise at can't-say-no prices. Residents benefited from the Mafia's unofficial law and order and were grateful for it every day. It protected their families, which were everything to them, and protected their way of life of hard work and simple pleasures.

Janice and I reached Eighteenth Avenue and Randy

Crawford's "Street Life" played in my mind as we joined the throng strolling on the sidewalks:

> *You dress you walk you talk*
> *You're who you think you are*

I knew who I was, I thought, and who I was going to be someday. Someone very different from the girl who had to walk past every store because she had no money and lowered her head with shame whenever she saw a proprietor because of a mother who was known for shoplifting and a dissolute life. I cringed as I recalled, as I often did in the retail district, the humiliation of being caught by Mr. Conti with a bottle of shampoo that my mother had forced me to slip into my schoolbag. After scowling at my mother, who was standing outside his store, Mr. Conti let me go. He had left it up to Father Rinaldi to chastise me, and my humiliation was soon revisited when the good priest mentioned my sin during our next impromptu chat in his church.

As Janice and I ambled along the crowded sidewalk, I touched the Blessed Mother pendant ever-present around my neck and thought some more about my mother. Mom never practiced her adopted Catholic faith, and never sent me for formal religious instruction, but she had given the pendant to me when I was six and always made references to Jesus and the importance of faith in Him, especially his Mother. She said even when she's not around anymore, I will always have a mother. Whether she truly believed or was just rebelling against my Jewish grandmother, I took it to heart from that young age.

"Let's grab a bite at Sally's," Janice said as she took my hand and led me across the avenue to the local coffee shop. A Greek establishment that was accepted in an Italian neighborhood because of its specialty, Sally's offered fountain items and served the finest coffee, feta cheese salads, hummus with pita,

and other Greek selections, and the best fried chicken sand-
wich for miles around.

We squeezed past diners exiting the narrow restaurant and
headed for the row of booths beyond a line of stainless steel
counter stools with red leather cushions where customers faced
glass displays showcasing donuts, pies, and Greek pastries. Janice and I giggled as we always did when our heels clicked on the
worn black and white ceramic tiles, and then we slipped into
a booth across from each other on leather that matched the
stools.

Janice grabbed two menus that were propped up by the con-
diments and handed one to me. "Order whatever you want," she
said as she started to scan the offerings that made my mouth
water. "My treat." Janice almost always paid the way no matter
what we did, and she never made me feel embarrassed whenever
she did so. But I always squirmed at such times.

"I have some money, Jan," I said.

"No ya don't," she said. She was right, of course. Any time I
had three dollars in my pocket—which wasn't often—I felt rich.

"I will," I replied, "as soon as I turn sixteen and get that job
in the bookstore."

"Then you'll be saving for college," Janice said, and looked
up. "You can pick up the tab at those fancy places in Manhattan you'll be taking me to when you're a big shot." There was
never any doubt in her words when she referred to the dream
that I had always shared with her.

"I'll just have a Coke and some fries," I said.

"Nonsense," Janice said, and she opened my menu. "I'm
starved, and I'm not goin' to eat alone." I knew that there
would be no point arguing with my best friend once she had
made up her mind. And what I really wanted, anyway, was some
of Sally's moussaka. "Besides," Janice added, "we have a lot to
talk about."

"That guy you mentioned?"

"I had to check it out first with Richie. He's okay with it and Tony's available."

I repeated the lie that had escaped my lips when Janice first hinted at an introduction a few weeks before. "I already told you I wasn't interested."

"Your mouth says no but your eyes and budding breasts say something else," Janice said with a knowing grin. There was no point arguing with her about that, either. "But let's order first. Then we'll discuss your raging hormones and that Italian passion that's just screamin' to get out."

After Grandma, Janice knew me best. Despite my yearning to leave Brooklyn, I had the other, insistent yearnings that any young girl had. And I knew I would have to live in Bensonhurst for some time before I was able to move on. The possibility of having a boyfriend excited me.

Janice placed our order with the waitress and then excused herself to go to the ladies' room. She went as often to fuss with her makeup as she did to relieve herself and I never had a problem filling the time she was away with my own thoughts. When she left, my mother's experiences when she was my age weighed upon me. Mom had been sexually active, had gotten pregnant several times, and had undergone abortions. But she had never confided in me about such things; Grandma did, when I was old enough and had to hear them—for my own good, Grandma always said.

"I don't know," I said to Janice when she returned. "Maybe I can't handle a relationship on top of schoolwork and dealing with everything else at home."

"Who's kiddin' who, Sam? You're dyin' for a boyfriend. Besides, ya need a love interest for that book you're writin'." Although I had had a couple of boyfriends, there hadn't been anything serious and I hadn't progressed much beyond kissing and holding hands. Anything more serious than that was confined to the imaginings of a fertile mind.

"That can wait," I offered.

"Bullshit. I've read your journals." Janice was the only person who had read everything I'd written. And she asked regularly if I had anything new to share with her. She never looked down upon my thoughts or my striving, and any criticism she offered was heartfelt. She was generous with sharing her own feelings and experiences and never resented when they informed my writing. Grandma was the tower of the bridge I needed on this side of the East River; Janice was the one closest to Manhattan.

"Okay, it's your party," I said as the waitress delivered our food. "I'm listening."

"I swear, Sam," Janice began, "Richie and his friends are so cool. Not like the nerds." I didn't think nerds were all that bad; their lives didn't revolve around the goings-on in Bensonhurst. I kept that to myself as my best friend continued. "An' lemme tell ya, Sam, Tony's a real hunk!"

"There are a lot of hunks around," I said.

"Not like him."

"What if I don't like him?"

"Oh, you'll like 'im, all right. He's the perfect guy for ya."

"What makes you so sure?" I asked as we started to eat.

"Becuz ya have a lot in common with 'im."

"I also have a lot of writing to do and places to go. I don't know anyone around here who shares those."

"I don' mean that. Tony isn't pure Italian. His family useta live in the neighborhood but they had a hard time fittin' in," Janice said.

"I know how the greaseballs are, but my family never felt we had to leave Bensonhurst."

"It's diff'rent for guys. Ya know, how they carry on about blood and loyalty and all. How a man has ta make a livin'."

I thought about how mixed parentage was looked down upon where we lived. Prejudice about ethnicity and race was

just beneath the surface for certain Italians who exposed it in
ugly displays of their supposed superiority. A Black man walking in Bensonhurst was enough instigation for many of them
to glower or give voice to their contempt. Such bigotry often
came as a shock to the innocent, myself included. Giorgio at
Davinci's Pizza had taken a liking to me after I started going
there when I was twelve. He used to give me slices and wanted
his son to date me when we started high school. When they
found out I was half Jewish, the freebies stopped and his son
gave me the cold shoulder. Tony and I would have something
to share right from the start, I thought, and that might be a
good thing. "What else can you tell me about him?" I asked.

"The guy's pretty exotic, Sam. I'd date him myself if I
wasn't so tight wid Richie. Just wait 'til ya see 'im."

"What makes you think he'll like me? I'm no Farrah Faw-
cett, you know."

"Have you looked in the mirror lately?" Janice asked.
"You're a knockout, Sam. Your hair alone is enough to capti-
vate him."

For as long as I could remember, my hair that reached
below my waist had always been my prized asset, which everyone knew. When Janice said that, I couldn't help remembering
when my mother, in a fit of anger, had cut my hair above my
shoulders when I was nine and permed it, to teach me a lesson
about who was in charge in her household. But after such battles, I often thought about how my mother had tried to show
me love by bringing little things to me—notwithstanding how
she had acquired them—and with her halting attempts with
words, and her heavy-handed decisions meant to keep me from
suffering a fate similar to hers. Janice wouldn't be the only one
I'd treat to some good times in Manhattan someday, I thought;
I looked forward to improving Mom and Grandma's lot at the
first opportunity.

"What if Tony likes short hair?" I asked.

"I don't know any Italians who do."

"Maybe it's the Dutch part," I chuckled.

"Well, we're gonna find out real soon what he likes."

"I haven't agreed to anything yet, Jan."

"Look. I've arranged the perfect setup," Janice said. "Everybody will be at the feast next week and we'll bump into him there. If ya don' like him we'll just walk off together."

"You sure Richie won't mind not being with you?"

"Trust me, he won't. He spends more time with Tony now than he does with me," Janice said as the busboy cleared our plates. She looked toward the front counter. "Now we're gonna have some coffee and baklava."

"Since it's your treat," I kidded. Janice always went first class and I couldn't wait to bite into the walnut puff pastry. All I got at home—and it was once in a blue moon—was prepackaged Entenmann's from the Key Food supermarket. Grandma swore by that baker—"He's a Jew," she had said more than once.

"So how old is he?" I continued.

"Twenty. Same as Richie," Janice said. I frowned. "That's not old, Sam. My mom is ten years younger than my dad. They get along great. Besides, ya don' care for guys your age, anyways."

"Maybe I just haven't found the right one."

"Fine. In the meantime, what's the harm with meetin' Tony?"

I had already come to the same conclusion. "What does he do?"

"He's in construction. Some union job."

"There's money in that," I said.

"There's money in a lotta things," she said. I didn't need to ask Janice what she meant by that. Italians had their fingers in numbers and other gambling activities, and in other vices that most thought were illegal only because the government said so. Whether or not people participated, vices were accepted. That was Bensonhurst.

But that wasn't necessarily Tony, I thought. After all, he was half Dutch and maybe he just wasn't involved. "I'll check him out," I said. "So long as I'm with you."

"You won't be sorry," Janice said as the dessert arrived.

"With Tony or the baklava?" I cracked, and we both giggled.

"And when we're done eatin', I'm dyin' to show you the heels I picked out at Sugar that Richie is going to buy me," Janice said. Two-hundred-dollar shoes were just one of the many things that were out of my league. I couldn't imagine owning a single pair, let alone the dozen or so that Janice had. And what are such heels if not accompanied by the clothes and jewelry to match? I thought. Janice wore the finest designer jeans, form-hugging tops, and slinky dresses from Italy. Her clothes may have been "Brooklyn chic," but they were expensive nonetheless. And she had enough gold and diamonds to open her own store. It would be some time before I could contemplate having such things. Until then, I decided, I would be grateful for the thrift clothes that Grandma tailored for me with her sewing machine.

We finished eating and made the detour to Sugar before parting under the N train nearby. A stretch of local streets, which were conveniently located under the train tracks. They were nicknamed early on "under the N."

"I've got to get home," Janice said. "Richie's gonna call." We hugged and Janice headed for the staircase while I turned to walk the fifteen blocks home.

On the way, I decided to make a detour of my own. Our Lady of Guadalupe was just a few blocks out of the way and I hadn't stopped in for a while. Although I didn't understand much about the saints and Catholic rites—Mom didn't know enough about them, didn't attend services, and couldn't afford to send me to the Catholic school that was adjacent to the church—I always felt good there and always felt that the more I learned about faith, the better off I'd be.

The warmth of the church's desert-sand brick and Spanish tile roof embraced me as it always did when I approached. I bowed my head at the ten-foot crucifix outside the entrance and went inside.

I dipped my middle finger into the holy water that was on a stone pedestal and crossed myself as I'd seen others do long before. A handful of parishioners who were spread out in the cavernous, dimly lit church sat or knelt in silence. In the sanctuary, at the other end from where I stood, a woman shuffled around the raised altar, tending to flowers and the items that were a mystery to me. I took a few steps on the checkered marble floor and sat down in the last pew, as was my custom.

My eyes scanned the chapel. I thought about my hopes that were as high as the beamed ceilings far above my head. I'm building a bridge, I said to myself. Piece by piece. The towers were in place, and people like Father Rinaldi and Mr. Wainright were the support cables for the road I was building that would take me across.

My eyes came upon the Blessed Mother statue to the left of the altar. *Hail Mary, full of grace. Our Lord is with thee. Blessed art thou among women, and blessed is the fruit of thy womb, Jesus. Holy Mary, Mother of God, pray for us sinners, now and at the hour of our death. Amen.* She's supporting me somehow, too, I thought.

2

The annual Feast of Santa Rosalia, a large outdoor street fair during the last week of August, was Bensonhurst at its best. Natives showed up in droves at sunset on the Saturday night of Labor Day weekend and strolled with broad smiles up Eighteenth Avenue from Sixty-sixth to Seventy-fifth Street. They stopped at crowded sidewalk stands to eat heros, pizza, Italian ices, and cannoli, and to drink cheap Chianti. Women who lived in the apartments above the stores stood in their doorways and tried to be heard over the music playing on loudspeakers and the street noise as they gossiped and nagged their kids. All along the avenue, old men with leathery skin sat on rickety folding chairs and had wrinkled brown paper bags at their feet and Cuban cigars clenched between their stained teeth. Beat cops mingled with the crowd and ignored minor infractions, anticipating a contraband cigar and a sip or two of whiskey as a clandestine reward when the evening came to a close. Live and let live was everyone's motto. The cops and *italianos* had been sharing this territory for many years. As long as the residents didn't bother anyone as they pursued their pleasures, they would be left alone.

The corner of Sixty-eighth Street was so crowded, Janice and I had to watch where we stepped as we squeezed through the crowd. The heat of the sun still radiated from the dark macadam that seemed to have a perpetual oil slick on it, sort of like the hair on most of the local guys. That was just one of the many things endemic to Bensonhurst, I thought, as was the smell of diesel fuel, the vibrations of the elevated subway, the tattoos on chests and arms, and the sound of screeching cars.

As Janice and I made our way along the avenue that had been closed off for the feast, we inhaled the aromas of sausage and peppers on hot, crispy Italian bread, and of family-recipe tomato sauces that steamed over bowls of spaghetti and meatballs, bracciole and stuffed ravioli. The mixture of so much garlic and onions made my mouth water.

Italians liked eating better than anything in the world, but then again, so did Jews. Food is the one thing that both cultures are equally enthusiastic and insatiable about, I thought, and it probably was the only thing that my Jewish mother and Italian father didn't argue over during the years he was running wild with his friends.

Food bonded me to Grandma Ruth, too. We talked whenever I helped her prepare ethnic specialties such as potato pancakes and blintzes. Grandma always had plenty to say, and our conversation always revolved around the same topics.

"That no-good Italian ran out on your mother," Grandma had said. "What could she do? I tell you, my Samelah, you marry a Jew, you hear me?"

"Oh, so a Jewish guy will never leave me. Right, Grandma?" I replied.

"Right. They stay with the family. Look, now you have no father. He punished you, too, see?"

"Yeah, well, I'd rather have been abandoned by him than learn firsthand who the hell he really was."

"Watch your mouth," Grandma chastised me then. "Don't get like your mother, always swearing and cursing through the house. Consider yourself lucky to have better prospects." After she said that, Grandma Ruth looked at me with tender eyes. "So, *bubelah,* any boy got your heart yet?"

"I'm waiting for the right one, Grandma."

"Good. You don't want to do what your mother did. Don't be in such a hurry and give milk without making them buy the cow first." Grandma wiped her brow then. "*Oy!* Your mother, she never listened to me and look where that got her!" She fumed silently for a minute as she always did after bringing up bitter memories, and then switched to our favorite subject as she stirred the potato pancake mixture. "Did you write today?"

"Yes, Grandma. I did," I responded. I made notes in my journal every day and often used the portable typewriter Grandma had given me on my fourteenth birthday to write poems and stories.

"*Mechayeh.* I'm proud of you. Write yourself out of this story and into a better one." I glanced at the ceiling and sighed when I heard Grandma's words. That's exactly what I intended to do.

"I wish Grandma could give you some money to bring to the feast tonight. I'm dying for one of those sausage-and-pepper, give-ya-heartburn heros, but my gallbladder would just act up again," Grandma had said as she started making patties. "Maybe another time, sweetheart. You go and have fun. But run your mother's bath first. She's *feelnish git.*"

Mom seldom felt good. Our humble circumstances would have been easier to take if she didn't exacerbate her poor health with her cigarettes and alcohol and drug addictions, and if she and I had a normal mother-daughter relationship. Like when I was five years old and she had a man waiting in the other room and came in to quiet me. I was still in a crib at this point, go figure. I see it ever so clearly, her putting a cigarette out on my arm. I am constantly reminded of that night when I gaze upon my scar. Don't really know what made her do it, but I do know she never did something like that again. To get back at her, I began a nasty habit by the time I was seven. I hated when my mother would bring home different men and, for spite, I would pee on the carpet in her bedroom. After a while we all noticed the weird smell, until I got caught in the act by one of mom's suitors. All I wanted was her attention, her love. To notice that she had a daughter who was trying to love her. I didn't want other men around her. I wanted her for myself, but she didn't feel the same. It was what I had to accept. I often wondered as I grew older what it would have been like to have two normal parents, although one could wonder how I would have turned out.

"Hey," Janice asked as she shook my arm at the feast. "Where are you?"

"Right here," I replied.

"Like hell you are. Off in your writer's mind again?"

"Sorry. Let's get some zeppoles."

We worked our way to a makeshift counter and I parted with a couple of precious dollars. A black-haired, thin woman with dark, sunken circles around her eyes grabbed hot, greasy balls of dough with a pair of tongs from a deep fryer. She tossed them in a brown paper bag and sprinkled them with powdered sugar before handing the bag to us. God, were they good! They always reminded me of the funnel cakes at a carnival when I was a little girl. I bit into the piping-hot dessert treat and smiled broadly as grease saturated my napkin in a few seconds. My grandmother's blintzes, as cheesy and light as she made them, did not match a zeppole for taste.

Giggling and talking with our mouths full, Janice and I licked our fingers and made our way through the crowd, waving to friends along the avenue. This was such a tight-knit neighborhood, held together by a shared culture, the Catholic faith that was almost universal there, and the mobsters who provided security as they went about their clandestine business. Everyone knew everyone and kept a watchful and sometimes critical eye on one another. News about every event, whether significant or trivial, spread rapidly through an informal grapevine made up of inhabitants who gathered day and night in small, impromptu groups on their stoops.

The Feast of Santa Rosalia was a public celebration of a common heritage Italians felt in their hearts and expressed in their homes every day. They reveled in their traditions and the opportunity to display their pride together. Whatever differences and disputes that existed within and between families were forgotten during the week that united all.

Janice and I shuffled between the happy people who stood and gesticulated on the crowded avenue. Father Rinaldi saw us through the crowd and waved, signaling us to join him in front of the church raffle booth. The priest stood out in the throng, and it wasn't just his black suit and white collar, I thought. He was tall and lean with a full head of perfectly cut dark hair, and his broad smile exposed teeth that were as pure as his soul.

"It's a shame such a hot-looking guy isn't available," Janice said on our way over to him.

"Tell me about it," I said as we neared the popular clergyman. I could never understand why a priest couldn't love God and be married at the same time.

"I could do him," Janice whispered.

"Janice!"

"Wouldya blame me?" She giggled and I couldn't stop myself from doing likewise.

"You girls enjoying yourselves?" Father Rinaldi asked.

"Sure," we replied.

"How's your mom, Sam?"

"So-so."

"I'll keep her in my prayers."

"Thanks, Father."

He placed a hand on my shoulder and looked me in the eyes. "Haven't seen you in church in a while."

"You missed me a few days ago, Father," I said. "I'll be back soon."

"Good," Father Rinaldi said, and he slipped a raffle ticket into my palm. "Now go have some more fun."

"We will," Janice said. She took my hand and we melted into the crowd again.

"I guess Tony's not here yet," Janice said when we reached the corner.

"Maybe you missed him in this wall-to-wall crowd, Janice," I said.

"Not a chance," she said. "Believe me." She took my hand and led me across the street to a coin-toss game booth that was manned by her mother's best friend, Rose Gallo. A tossed nickel, landing and resting in the center of a glass ashtray, would win a stuffed animal like a spotted giraffe, a huge black bear, a lion with a fuzzy mane, or a gangly legged zebra with a yellow bow tied around its neck that hung high up on the side wall. The coin toss was popular and the guys lined up to nab a prize and be a big shot for their girls. We stood behind the boys as they played, Janice in a red halter top and khaki chinos and me in tapered lime green pants and an off-white tank top that covered my modest breasts and tiny waist. I grabbed my hair in my hands and held it off my neck to cool my skin in the heat of a muggy late-summer evening where there wasn't a breeze to be had.

"Ya don' have to show off, Sam, to attract these guys," Janice teased. "They'll be all over ya anyways." Janice knew that I took great pride in the mane that framed my brown, almond-shaped eyes and kewpie-doll lips and cascaded down my slim body almost to my hips. I had been told more than once that my hair was just like Cher's, which had made me proud. After all, who had better hair than Cher? I wondered. As if the DJ had heard my thoughts, her voice boomed from the PA system,

Half-breed, that's all I ever heard
Half-breed, how I learned to hate the word

Janice wrapped her arm around my waist as we sang along with Cher with a few others who were doing likewise. As the words I knew so well flowed from my mouth, I thought about how music was a large and constant part of Bensonhurst life for both young and old. Sinatra and Bennett were mainstays for our parents' generation and we didn't look down upon their style as we embraced contemporary artists such as Donna Summer and the Bee Gees. We loved to dance in time with the upbeat tempo of a new sound and we knew every word to every popular song.

Janice let go of my waist when the song ended and stood with her shoulders back and her head high amid the celebratory crowd. She knew how to carry herself in any situation and I just loved her inherent classiness. Janice never exhibited the awkwardness that most young women did; instead, she presented herself with the confidence that I shared but kept to myself for the most part.

Janice's looks matched her sophistication. Her hair was the same color as mine but shorter. Her round, brown eyes looked intelligent, as if she actually stopped to think before she gave an opinion—a rare quality in the passionate, outspoken, and aggressive Brooklyn neighborhood where Janice and I had been born and raised. I knew that she judged herself as too overweight, but I liked my best friend's developed body, with her mature breasts and rounded butt, that got every guy's attention when we walked the streets of Bensonhurst.

Janice had gone steady with Richie Sparto when she was a junior in high school and that continued after she had graduated in June. I had dated a few boys but hadn't gone steady with anyone yet. Even though I had other interests like reading and writing, when groups of girls got together every now and then, it was all about boys as we spent afternoons or evenings giving ourselves facials, dyeing and teasing our hair, and doing one another's nails. Girls compared boyfriends and talked about other guys—which ones were exciting, which ones were dangerous, who was a nerd, who had brains, who was cheating on whom, and who was the most likely to make a good husband. I always enjoyed those free and easy hours and I was sure all the girls did, especially those like me who had questionable relationship role models and a bickering home. Life could be hard in Bensonhurst, particularly for families that scratched to make the rent each month. I lost myself during those primping sessions and dreamed of luxury and sweet times with the "perfect" man.

The Bonti family's two-bedroom apartment, within walking distance from Janice's, was less than modest. Mom had a small bedroom to herself while Grandma and I shared another. There was one bathroom that had balky plumbing, a tiny living room, and a narrow kitchen. It was there that we huddled around a horrible black Formica dinner table with tubular metal legs to eat and kibbitz next to the stove, on which a pot of tomato sauce and a pot of chicken soup often sat side by side. Over time, cooking aromas infused the kitchen's walls, and although broken furniture was taped and glued rather than replaced, it was home and there was love there. Despite my disadvantages, I did have a place to call home.

Janice tugged at her tight slacks as we walked onto the next block. She may have needed to lose a few pounds, but she looked bigger than normal beside my tiny frame. I mean, I couldn't have weighed more than ninety-five pounds, soaking wet. Janice vowed that by the time I graduated, she would lose enough weight to fit into a slinky white dress for my ceremony. But that was three years off, I thought, so what difference did an extra cannoli make right then?

"Look, there's Dara," Janice said as she pointed to her

classmate Dara Celentro, a voluptuous blonde (from a bottle, of course, where many otherwise dark-haired Bensonhurst women also found the shade they felt attracted and pleased men) with light brown eyes and high, teased hair, and wearing jeans so tight it was a miracle she could walk. The word on the street was that her pants were down more than they were up, so walking wasn't a priority for her. Known as the biggest slut on the block, Dara was dating "the Son," who was, in three words, tall, dark, and sexy. Not to mention powerful. Dara wouldn't be taking her pants down for anyone else as long as she was with Vin, and no guy would dare mention he had slept with Dara before Vin hooked up with her. For the previous six months, Dara had fallen under Vin's spell, becoming more and more withdrawn and reclusive because he demanded that. Occasional black-and-blue marks on her arms and chest (she swore she tripped or fell down some steps or walked into a door or got hit by an errant baseball) suggested the method Vin used to keep her in line. Everyone knew Dara was being battered, but nobody interfered because of Vin's dad, Tino Priganti. Mom and Grandma made me promise that I would never go with a guy who did not respect me. They also made me promise I would never, ever date a man who was associated with the mob.

I started toward Dara to say hello but Janice held me back. "Not yet," she said. "You know how Dara flaunts it and I want you to meet Tony on your own."

"What's the matter?" I asked as we walked on. "Aren't we hot enough?" We laughed and then stopped at a booth that had a large punch bowl filled with deep pink–colored liquid on its counter. Lyrics to a Rolling Stones song wafted through the streets:

Brown Sugar, how come you taste so good? (A-ha)
Brown Sugar, just like a young girl should

Rick Romano, a friend of Janice's dad, ladled the alcoholic concoction into small paper cups, fifty cents a drink. Janice leaned forward, her cleavage a couple of inches above the wood counter. "How about some for us, Mr. Romano?" she asked with a teasing edge to her voice. "We won't tell."

"She's fourteen," Mr. Romano said after glancing at me, and after his eyes had traveled from Janice's chest to her eyes.

"Fifteen," Janice said. "Goin' on sixteen."

"Still too young," Mr. Romano said.

"C'mon," Janice pleaded, batting her eyes. Mr. Romano looked around and then slipped two half-filled cups to Janice. "I don' want no trouble. Youse be cool 'boudit," he said.

"Are we ever anything but?" Janice said, and giggled as she handed me a cup. "Bottoms up," she said, and gulped down most of her drink. Janice laughed as I sipped mine and then she finished the last of her punch. She leaned across the counter toward Mr. Romano and tried to talk him out of one more. I wandered back to the coin-toss booth and watched a neighborhood guy named Angelo as he tried to win a zebra for his timid girl. I thought I'd seen them both around but couldn't quite place where or when. Angelo tossed coin after coin that ricocheted off the ashtrays onto the wood floor of the booth. He cursed each time he lost and then pulled another nickel from his pocket. I finished my punch and considered my appetite while I watched.

What I really had a taste for was a Papa Tucci calzone, the best in town, but I didn't have enough money for one. Come to think of it, steamed clams in broth with drawn butter sounded even better. Papa Tucci made that, too. Someday, I thought, when I was a successful author, my friends and I would dine at Mama Leone's in Manhattan—the second location after the one on Coney Island, the famous amusement area that had seen better days—whenever we felt like it, order whatever we wanted, and I would pick up the tab without having to consider how much it was.

By the time Angelo had dropped a couple of dollars in nickels with no results, he had gotten so agitated that Rose Gallo asked him to leave. "You're drunk, Angelo," she said. "What would your mother say? She worked hard all her life. Go run a hose over your head and come back when you're sober enough to see straight."

Angelo stared at her for a moment as his face turned deep red. "What the fuck did you say to me?" he thundered.

His girlfriend grabbed his arm. "C'mon, baby," she whispered. "Let's just go."

Angelo shoved her with both hands and sent her stumbling backward to the sidewalk. A man rushed to pick her up. "Look what you did, you asshole," he said.

Angelo got in the man's face. "Mind your own business," he gritted. The man let go of the girl and clenched his fists. I had seen this kind of thing many times before in school and in the neighborhood. It always started with something trivial and always ended in bruised egos and bodies.

"Break it up, you two," a strong voice that came from behind them commanded. A tall, blond, muscular young man appeared, clutched one of their arms with his massive hands, and separated the two would-be combatants. He stood with legs planted in his tight-fitting Adidas jogging outfit, looked from one to the other, and then whispered something that only they could hear. After hesitating, the two men shook hands for a moment without much enthusiasm. "Now go take a walk," the blond man said to Angelo. Angelo grabbed his girlfriend and took off down the block muttering to himself.

I felt as though my breath had been taken from me the moment I saw that dashing young man. It was out of a movie. He had a look, a way, an aura. He was Steve McQueen, only live and in person. I stared in awe at this blond hero who had just broken up a confrontation with a simple whisper. What had he said to these men, I wondered, and who was he, anyway?

Janice hurried to my side and squeezed my elbow. "See what I mean?" she cooed with excitement. "Didn't I tell ya? Was I lyin' about this guy, or what?"

"That's Tony *Kroon*?" I asked.

"Kroon," Janice said. "Better not get his name wrong. That'll really piss him off. I mean it."

"I won't," I said quietly. Ever, I added to myself as I looked Tony Kroon over. He was well built and slim with soft, blond hair—no grease—and a pair of deep blue eyes that could stop traffic. Or at least a street fight or two. His arms were long and muscled, his hands were wide with thick fingers, and his waist was thin. Tony Kroon would definitely be my choice for the Hunk of the Year award.

"What's with the blond hair?" I whispered to Janice.

"I already told ya. His Dad is Dutch. His mom is Italian. He came out pretty good, don'tya think? Imagine running your fingers through that hair!"

"Mm-hmm," I agreed, mesmerized by this uncommonly good-looking man with the unwavering self-confidence. As if this were all a dream, Hot Chocolate sang out on the PA system,

> *I believe in miracles,*
> *Where you from, you sexy thing?*

No one was supposed to be that handsome, I thought. And he was a half-breed like I was, I thought, and wondered how that got in his way and made his life chaotic at times, like it did mine. He'd already had to move to a new neighborhood because of his nationality, I remembered.

My own household had been hopelessly divided since my Jewish mother had converted to Catholicism to rebel against my grandmother, as she had by taking an Italian-Catholic husband and giving me a Christian name. The problem was, although my father was never religious and didn't live with us, and Mom wasn't observant, either, my Christian upbringing had made Grandma Ruth clutch her Star of David around her neck and pray in Hebrew—for the rest of her life. My mother wore the crucifix. Sometimes I would wear both to keep the peace, along with my Blessed Mother.

The battle was on each and every day.

Maybe Janice was right, I thought. Maybe Tony and I *were* meant for each other. I was going to find out about that real soon, as the blond young man with the glowing aura swaggered toward where Janice and I were standing.

"Howya doin'?" Tony asked Janice after eying me up and down.

"Good, Tone. Real good." Janice was almost stuttering. "We saw what ya did. Pretty impressive."

"Ah, it was nuttin'."

"But ya was so cool, Tony," Janice said. She couldn't stop fawning over him, and I couldn't take my eyes off him. "Right, Sam?" Janice asked. I just nodded.

Tony gave the expression "drop-dead gorgeous" a whole new meaning. I really could understand how a girl could forget herself, even a girl who was going steady with a guy she said she loved. Tony looked at me with probing eyes as Janice made the introductions. "Tony, this is my best friend, Samantha Bonti. Sam, Tony Kroon."

I put out my hand. "How do you do?" I asked.

Tony laughed and shook my hand. "So formal," he said. He didn't take his eyes off me. "She's a real kick, Janice."

Janice looked pleased with herself. "I told ya she was sumthin'," she said.

Tony didn't respond to Janice. "Where ya from?" he asked me.

"The neighborhood. Coupla blocks from here."

"Nice, quiet area," Tony said.

"Where *you* from?" I asked.

"Around. We just moved, but this is still where I hang out. It's friendlier."

"It wasn't so friendly a few minutes ago, Tone," Janice said. "That is, until you showed up."

Tony ignored Janice once more and kept his attention on me. "Whatcha doin' out here tonight?" he asked.

"Nuthin'," I responded without hesitation. A girl needed to be a little bit mysterious; I remembered Grandma had told me that.

"Ya wanna walk wid me, Samantha Bonti?"

I stopped myself from looking as flattered as I felt. I knew better than to let on how attracted I was. Especially with this guy. Heaven only knew what I could do with someone like him. "Well, that sounds okay," I said, "but I gotta meet up with Janice later."

Tony waved his hand. "Forget about her," he said. "I'm here now." He put an arm around my shoulder. "Ya got a guy?"

"Not at the moment."

"Good," he said. "Unless you're some kind of lesbian or sumthin'. I mean, 'cause ya don' have a guy."

"No. I'm just real picky," I said.

"Good," Tony said again. "Me, too."

"Don't you have a girl already?" I asked.

"None that matters," Tony said, and he narrowed his eyes toward Janice. She stepped back.

"Hey," I protested. "I came with Janice."

"She don' mind. Do ya, Janice?" Tony asked without looking back at her.

"'Course not, Tone," Janice said. "I gotta go find Richie, anyhow," she added, trailing off in the opposite direction.

Tony and I walked side by side and made our way through the crowd. A thin brunette wearing less than was decent waved at Tony and shot me a dirty look. What the hell had I done? I wondered. I was just walking with the guy. The neighborhood was full of that kind of girl who always gave another pretty girl a look, as if it wasn't fair that she would have the local hot guy on her arm. Well, if he wasn't already taken, then honey, why aren't you with him? I thought. From the looks of things, Tony was available, but the truth at that moment was I did not even know for sure if I wanted him. I would go with the flow and wait for it to unfold like Grandma had taught me. Tony ignored the brunette while I smiled and looked straight ahead. "I came with Janice, you know," I repeated, somewhat uncomfortable walking beside this outrageously handsome man who was getting looks of admiration from women of all ages every step of the way.

"Fuhgeddaboudit," he said. "I'll make sure ya get home okay. You can count on me."

"How do I know that?"

"You saw what I did wid dem guys. Janice sure was impressed."

"So what'd you say to them?" I asked. "'Cause I never saw two guys so upset who shook hands so fast."

"It was nuttin'."

"Had to be sumthin'."

Tony smiled. "I just told them if they laid a hand on each other, dey'd hafta answer ta Vin Priganti." I knew nobody wanted to be on "The Son"'s bad side.

Tony pointed to a couple up ahead at another punch stand. "Hey, there he is, wid Dara. How do ya like dat for timin'?" Tony waved to Vin and shouted, "Hey, Vin. How's it hangin'?"

Vin turned toward Tony. "Hey man," he said, grabbing at his crotch. "Hangin' low." His crudity turned me off, as when other Brooklyn Boys acted that way, but Dara held Vin's other arm close to her. "Seeya later, right?" Vin asked, his dimpled chin visible from fifteen feet away. "'Bout that thing." Tony nodded as we passed the couple. "Later," he said.

I was curious and wanted to know what "that thing" was,

but I knew better than to ask. All the Brooklyn guys liked to strut around like peacocks and act tough. Was it just an act? I wondered. There was something different about Tony and I just could not put my feel around it, but I just knew it in my gut, as I concentrated on the warmth I felt on my right side, where he was walking beside me. With his Nordic looks, he was practically a god compared to the other neighborhood guys, I thought. I wasn't sure why, but my body felt tingly, uncomfortable in a needy sort of way, and I had trouble getting any words out.

Tony, however, had no trouble speaking at all. "That Dara," he said, shaking his head.

"What about her?" I asked.

"I don' know. She's really been around. What I'm tryin' ta say is, she ain't no virgin."

"Yeah? How do you know? You dated her?"

"Fuck no. I like my women real pretty and, well . . . innocent."

"She might still be a virgin," I said.

"Tell me another one," Tony said, laughing. He stopped walking and looked at me. "Ya don' really think that, do ya?" I knew all about Dara's history. Everyone did.

I pursed my lips and then shook my head. "Not really," I replied. "But it isn't her fault."

"Whose fault is it, the boogeyman?" Tony asked, laughing again. I couldn't help chuckling at his crack but felt sad about a girl who was like so many others in Bensonhurst.

"Dara had it pretty bad when she was a kid," I said.

"Well, anyways," Tony continued, "she ain't like you. Right?"

"She's pretty enough."

"I meant the innocent part. You are innocent, aren't ya?" Tony asked. It was none of his business and I didn't respond. He seemed to sense the truth, anyway, and changed the subject. "Janice tells me you're a half-breed, huh?"

"Like Cher. My mom is Jewish and my dad is Sicilian."

"I don' know 'im."

"Join the club. I don't, either. He left when I was born."

"Aw, jeez," Tony said. "What kind of a Sicilian man leaves his kid? Sorry." His sympathy seemed genuine, but I didn't really know this guy, I thought. Janice knew him, though, didn't she? Didn't that stand for something? Richie was a regular in the Bensonhurst crowd, and according to Janice, he'd taken to the Dutchman right away. Tony's association with the Prigantis wasn't the best of things, but I knew the way it was for the wannabe Bensonhurst guys. It didn't seem fair to hold it against Tony, and there didn't seem to be any reason not to enjoy the interest he was showing in me.

"Your mom has a tough go of it, huh?" he asked.

"She manages to get by."

"What about you?" Tony asked.

"I'm like everyone else. Goin' to school and hangin' out."

"That's not what I hear."

"And what, exactly, have you heard?"

"Not a lot. Just that you're different, is all."

I looked into his eyes. "Maybe."

"Ya sure look different. Not a lot of makeup or teased hair," Tony said. "I like that." A warmth rose in my body. "What about you?" Tony asked. "What do ya like?" His blond hair and blue eyes had my head spinning.

"I like the way you look, too," I said.

"No, I mean what do ya like to do? Besides hangin' out."

"Stuff."

"What kinda stuff?" I wasn't sure I should tell him about my aspirations. Anyone who wanted more than the pastimes and cliques that Bensonhurst offered wasn't looked upon favorably. But I figured if he couldn't handle it I might as well find out sooner rather than later. "I like to write," I said.

"Really," Tony said, and pondered that for a moment. "What about?"

"Anything in my life," I said. Tony reached for my hand and it felt comfortable, natural, in his.

"Well, ya can write about me now," he said. His eyes continued to stir my insides. "So, Samantha Bonti, you wanna walk some more with me?"

I loved the way he said my full name. "Okay," I agreed.

We sidled through the crowd and Tony exchanged slaps to the shoulder or slight nods with the men he knew. We stopped at a few game booths and then Tony bought Papa Tucci calzones for us. I wish I could've taken some home for Grandma. We talked some more while we ate, standing across from the kiddie rides at the entrance to the next block.

"Ya like kids, Tony?" I asked.

"Wid da right woman, sure."

When we finished the calzones, Tony took my hand again to walk up the avenue. "I'll get you a cannoli or an Italian ice later," he said.

"I'd like that."

"I'm sure you'll like a lotta things," Tony said. "Wait here a sec." He walked over to a whirligig to help a young mother take her twins off the ride. The woman kept her eyes on Tony as she strapped the children into a stroller while he ambled back to where I stood.

"The hero comes to the rescue again," I said. Tony smiled broadly and put his arm over my shoulders as we started off again, serenaded by cries of glee from children on the amusement rides. I looked at all their happy faces and sang quietly along with the Beatles, who warbled from every loudspeaker,

Ooh, did I tell you I need you ev'ry single day of my life?
Got to get you into my life . . .

"The kids are sure having a lot of fun, aren't they?" I asked Tony.

"Everyone can have their fun here," he said. I certainly could, I thought.

When we reached the next corner Tony led me into a side street. He stopped next to a parked van and nudged me up against it before pressing his body into mine. "I need ta tell ya sumthin'," Tony whispered. That had happened so fast my mind was spinning. Who is this person? I wondered. I don't even know him and yet I allowed myself to be taken by his charm, his persistence, his . . . way! I looked into his eyes, which were so close to me I could hardly breathe. I felt perspiration form on my forehead.

"Ya shouldn't be hangin' round here alone at night," Tony said. "Nice girl like you."

"Oh yeah?" I asked as I wiggled for some more room between us. "Why's that?"

"'Cause I like ya and ya can get into trouble out here," he said. "Make yourself a bad name like 'Donkey Dara.'"

"That's not very nice," I admonished. "Anyway, I can take care of myself. Been doin' that a long time now." We looked at each other for a moment. "Besides," I finished my thought, "I wasn't alone. I was with Janice, and right now it looks like I'm with you."

"Yeah," Tony said, smiling. "You're in luck tonight." I'd let him act like a big shot if that was what he wanted, and said nothing. "I been around some," he said with a laugh.

"So have I," I fibbed.

He must have sensed the truth again and laughed. "Ya ever been kissed?" he asked.

I stiffened. That wasn't any of his business, either. "I ought to slap your face for asking that."

"Well, have you?" Tony persisted. I looked him in the eye.

"Are you asking if you can kiss me?"

"I don' hafta. I can jus' do it if I want." He leaned close to my face and grazed my ear with his lips. I edged away and giggled nervously.

"No you can't," I said. "I don't even know you."

Tony leaned close again, and my eyes couldn't help focusing on the large gold cross that swung out from under his black T-shirt and swayed gently back and forth. I felt drawn to his eyes. They bewitched me and held a strange power over me. What was it? I wondered. The scent of Brut engulfed my nose as Tony's mouth found my lips. I closed my eyes. His lips felt soft and I placed my small hands around his waist. "Now you do," Tony breathed after our lips parted, and then he moved softly with precise motions, kissing my cheeks and my chin with tenderness. I felt as if I were melting into him. Was I really sharing this kind of intimacy with such a great-looking guy, a stranger whom I was getting to know real fast? Tony brushed my lips with his, pressed both sides of my head with his hands, and then thrust his tongue deep into my mouth. I was startled, but my mouth drew him in. I had never been kissed like that before, I had to admit, and I had to admit, too, that it felt good. I liked that feeling and felt as if he was talking to me without saying any words. I also felt privileged that Tony, the great blond gladiator whom everyone showered with admiring eyes, was kissing me. Poor, no-father, sick-mother me!

I relaxed a little and he kissed my neck and ears. I shuddered and turned my face completely toward him, asking for more as a John Paul Young song, muffled in the distance, wafted through the branches to where we were:

And I don't know if I'm being foolish,
Don't know if I'm being wise . . .

He wanted me and no one else, I kept telling myself. I allowed my tongue to probe his mouth and felt a familiar moist heat between my legs. There was something about Tony that made me tingle all over. With his body pressed so close to mine, I felt a man's hardness for the first time and my body stiffened again. Tony seemed ready for anything but I wasn't. The kiss had been fine but this was way too fast for me. I pushed his shoulders away a bit, took a deep breath, and smiled at him. He backed off.

"You're a natural, Samantha Bonti," Tony said, "since this was your first kiss and all." Did he really believe I'd never kissed another boy in my whole life? I wondered, my pride somewhat dashed. But I knew it had never been like what he had just done. And I knew I sure as hell wasn't going any further than kissing.

Tony leaned toward my ear once more. "I want ya ta know that I really like ya, Samantha Bonti," he said. I just loved the way he said my name. "And that's a pretty big thing in a girl's life, when a guy like me falls for her. I know we just met and all, but there's sumthin' about ya that I could get used ta . . . if ya know what I mean."

The things he had done and what he was saying both excited and scared me. I was glad he hadn't forced himself completely on me and that I would have time to sort things out. I wanted to find Janice and go home. "I have to go, it's getting way too late for me to still be out."

"Yeah, at your age an' all. Ya should be home in bed," Tony said with a narrow smile. "Gimme your number. I might wanna take ya out to Angelo's sometime. What do you think of that?"

I thought enough of going to *the* place in Manhattan's Little Italy to open my purse and take out a tube of black eyeliner. I grabbed Tony's hand and wrote my number on his palm. He reached into a pocket and handed me a piece of scrap paper with his name and phone number written on it. "Take this," Tony said, "an' call me when ya wake up tomorrow. I wanna hear how ya sound first thing."

"Yeah, okay," I said, taking the paper from him and staring at it before putting it in my purse. "What do you do? Carry those around in case you meet a hot girl?"

"You're already breakin' my heart, Samantha Bonti." Mine fluttered as he led me back to the avenue. "Let's go find Janice so's you two can hold hands on the way home."

I walked beside Tony, searching for my friend at every food and game booth that we passed. I saw her at last, hanging on Richie's arm and munching on a cannoli. I smiled at the two of them together and then rushed over and hugged my friend. "Hey, Richie," I said after I separated from Janice.

"How ya doin', Sam?"

"Not too bad," I answered, blushing. Tony came up and they exchanged hellos. "Want one a doze?" he asked me as he pointed at Janice's cannoli. "I better not," I said as I looked at Janice and tilted my head to the side and back quickly.

Janice turned to Richie. "I gotta walk Sam home," she said.

"Okay," Richie said, "I'll call you later."

Janice and I disappeared into the crowd and headed for my street. "So, was I right, or was I right?" she asked.

"He was pretty cool," I said.

"'Pretty cool'? Is that all you have to say?"

"He gave me his number and asked me to call him in the morning."

"I knew it!" Janice said. "Now we can be a foursome."

"Not so fast," I said. "I haven't decided for sure to call him yet. He's pretty pushy."

"They're all pushy," Janice said. "Trust me on that one. And trust me, you'll be calling him. There's no way you'll ever find a hotter guy than Tony Kroon. Everybody wants him and you got under his skin. I saw it. But he won't wait around. He don't need to."

Janice was right. I *had* gotten under his skin. And he had gotten under mine.

3

Sleep eluded me the night I kissed Tony Kroon.

If I'd had my own room, I would have turned on the light and written in my journal about the feelings that were coursing through my virginal body, but I didn't want to wake my grandmother. She would soon be seventy-five and insomnia plagued her; I often heard her rustling the sheets during the night. She slept soundly that night, her chest rising and falling so rhythmically that, as much as I wanted to write or talk to her about Tony, I didn't have the heart to disturb her.

I dropped off to sleep after hours of tossing and turning. When I awakened, still a little groggy, Grandma was already in the kitchen. I could hear the pots and pans and smell the aromas of scrambled eggs, lox, onions, and bagels, our usual fare on Sunday mornings. We did not keep a kosher home, but ever since my father had abandoned us, bacon was banned from the frying pan and lox became a satisfactory replacement.

After I inhaled the wonderful smells coming from the kitchen, I grabbed the telephone. Tony really ought to be calling *me*, I thought. I mean, he had to know that. But I had promised to call him when I awoke and I always kept my word. "Without your word, *bubelah*," Grandma always said, "what do you have?"

I closed my eyes and felt Tony's kiss again, the way it had made me melt, and then I looked at the slip of paper he had handed to me. I said hello a few times out loud to test my voice before I dialed the number. It rang a few times—I almost hung up—and then a woman answered the phone.

"Hello?" she mumbled.

"Oh, hello. Is Tony there?"

"He's sleeping. This is his mother. Who's this?"

I hesitated a bit before I spoke. "Samantha. Can you ask him to call me when he wakes up? He has my number."

"Yeah, sure," she said, and hung up the phone. I guess she's used to annoying phone calls in the morning, I thought, like Tony had numerous girls calling him and she knew the drill. Would she give Tony the message? I worried. If she didn't, he would think I hadn't called and I didn't want that. But there wasn't anything I could do except wait.

It was time for breakfast, and if I could get into the kitchen before Mom did I could have a private talk with Grandma about Tony. Grandma was less reactive and much more level-headed about things that young girls cared about—although the topic of dating Italians sure challenged that. I preferred not to keep secrets from my mother; I had been taught to be honest at all times, and instructed in a code of ethics that was supposed to get me through life and avoid trouble. That meant telling the truth and dating boys who were honest, too. Janice tried to live by the same code. She had gone out with a guy once who rented a limo to take her to a very expensive restaurant in Manhattan. When the check came, he asked her to wait in the car while he took care of it. It was not until they'd sped down the street and across the bridge that the guy told her he had cut out without paying. She never dated him again, and he couldn't understand why she had been so pissed off.

"Sam?" my mother called from the hall outside her bedroom door. A private talk with Grandma would have to be postponed, I thought, and I slipped Tony's number into a drawer in my bedside table, threw on a nylon robe, and went to hug Mom. Her familiar scent of jasmine bath salts made me feel cozy.

"Did you sleep okay, Mom?"

"Not really. My pressure was acting up. I heard ya come in late last night."

"Not very," I said.

"No matter. Ya know the rules."

I nodded and we went into the kitchen. I put my arms around Grandma's waist and squeezed. She was a lot heavier than she used to be and her flat breasts sagged against her body. "Morning, Grandma," I said. Mom and I sat as Grandma handed me a glass of generic orange juice. I was accustomed to the no-name stuff in my household.

"I heard ya talkin' on the phone," Mom said.

"I met a guy last night, Mom," I said, wide-eyed. "At the feast. He told me to call when I woke up."

Mom pursed her lips and shook her head from side to side. "He did, did he? And ya just did it?" She lit a cigarette, pulled her thick auburn hair back, and tied a rubber band around it before eating or drinking a thing—her morning ritual. Puffs of smoke circled that once-lustrous hair I had loved and the break-fast table as it always had, that was when she wasn't off dyeing it every different color under the sun. I swear one day it would be jet black and one day it would be platinum blond. When she got really bored she would hit the box of dye, hard, her modest splurge besides drugs here and there. The blond-in-front-and-black-in-back look took the cake. I preferred the auburn strains. They were safe and that's what I wanted so badly for her.

Grandma and I said nothing. Mom had grown deaf to our protests and concern for her health long before. "I told ya that boys are supposeta pursue girls. They won' respect ya otherwise."

"It was just a phone call, Mom." I looked to my grandmother for support but she kept her eyes glued to the frying pan.

"So what did he have to say?" Mom asked. "Did he remember ya name?"

"He wasn't awake yet."

"It's ten thirty in the morning!" Mom shouted. "What the hell is he doin', sleepin' his life away?"

"Mom, it's Sunday. Everybody sleeps in on Sundays."

"Unless they're God-fearing people that goes ta church," Mom said.

"You don't go, so who are you to preach?"

Mom's eyes narrowed. "Don't crack wise with me, Sam."

Grandma turned her head and her eyes met mine for an instant before she resumed cooking. "Sorry, Mom," I said. "I don't know about church, but he does wear a cross."

"That doesn't prove anything," Mom said. "Plenty of creeps, your father included, wear medals."

I lowered my head. Grandma changed the subject while she stirred the eggs. "What does he do, Samelah?"

"Well, I can't say exactly, but it's important. Everbody's real respectful of him."

"Respect him?" Mom asked. "How old is he?"

"Around twenty."

"Chrissakes, Sam! He should be wid someone his own age."

I didn't answer. It was no use arguing with my mother. She was bitter about her life and that she had gotten sick, and sometimes directed her resentment toward me and Grandma. Mom battled with her mother over not wanting to be Jewish and the kind of men Mom hung around with, and she never dealt with her demons in a healthy way. The older I got, the more I knew her weak condition had stemmed from an unhealthy lifestyle and addictions that weakened her immune system. It was sad, but over time I had been able to accept who she was. I felt terrible because I did know in my heart that Mom wanted to be happy for me. It was just too hard for her.

Grandma put a generous helping of eggs and lox on our plates and sat down at her place. She and I started eating while Mom stubbed her cigarette and then pushed her food around. Her appetite was often suppressed by a load of meds she had to take for her various complaints. She put her fork down and looked at me. "Don't forget the welfare check today," she said. I cringed. "It's on the nightstand and I need you to refill some of my pills."

I hated cashing the checks and living on welfare. But I knew Mom needed my help, especially on the days when she just didn't feel good enough to go out. She had made friends with the local check-cashing guy and he would give me the money without asking for a matching ID. Mr. Weissbaum was one of the nice men whom Mom could have dated, but didn't.

The welfare checks and food stamps were an ugly reminder that we weren't like most other families. Standing in line at that check-cashing joint with a bunch of other people, ashamed as I was, staring at the floor, was pure torture. No one could imagine how humiliating it was to be in the checkout line of the supermarket, ready to pay with food stamps, while kids I knew from school were one aisle over, laughing at me. I would pray to God and then rationalize my situation. At least I was able to eat and buy clothes, I would think at those times. I felt that I was the one who was paying for my mother's mistakes, but knew I had to help her as much as possible. If that meant cashing a check or two, so be it. It wasn't until I got much older that I realized that those other kids were idiots, and their smirks and remarks weren't important at all. Surviving takes its toll but makes you strong, I learned.

"Well," Mom said, "now that you're callin' boys first thing in the mornin', I hope ya won't forget your family."

"Jeez, Mom, all I did was call a guy on the phone. Don't make a federal case out of it."

Mom softened. She lit another cigarette and sipped her coffee. "I jus' worry about ya, Sam. Who is he?"

"His name's Tony."

Mom grunted. "Half the men in Bensonhurst are called Tony."

"He's got Italian blood but his last name is Kroon."

"Never heard of them. They must not be from around here."

"Janice and Richie know him."

"That should make me feel good?" Mom clucked from deep in her throat. "If Richie knows him that means this Tony knows Vin Priganti. I won' have ya takin' up with Italian trash like Janice did." I fumed at Mom's comment about my best friend. Mom knew how good Janice was to me and I felt she didn't deserve to be dragged into the conversation. "God knows I had enough of that in my life and ya don' need it in yours."

"I'm not you," I said. Mom screwed her face and dragged on her cigarette. "What kind of a name is Kroon?"

I looked at her through the smoke. "Dutch. He's a half-breed, like me."

"Don' talk like that," Mom snapped.

"But I am," I said.

"Let's slow down a little, Joanie," Grandma said. "You're jumping all over Samelah and maybe he's a good boy."

Mom smirked. "Maybe not," she said.

"Mom, I told him I'm gonna be a famous writer and he liked it. Told me to write about him."

"So now it's all about him," she scoffed.

I knew my mother's painful marriage and abandonment by her husband soured her on men. If only I could do something to make her feel better, I often thought. God knows how I tried every day. When I got my first book deal, I decided, I would take the advance money and buy her a real bed to sleep in with beautiful, exotic Italian sheets. What a dream that would be! A string of pearls would look real nice on Grandma, too, and that would only be the beginning.

We continued eating our breakfast in silence; it was no use trying to make idle chatter when Mom was crabby, which was more often than not. She must have been in some kind of pain last night to be in such a bad mood, I reasoned.

When the phone rang. I jumped up, grabbed the kitchen extension, and said hello.

"Samantha?" Tony asked. "Is that you?"

"Yeah," I said, twisting the curled black cord around my fingers. Colored wires showed through where it plugged into the wall, but a new phone cord was at the bottom of the Bonti shopping list. I wished my mother and grandmother would leave the room but they sat where they were. I turned my back to the table.

"I hear ya called at the crack a dawn," Tony said.

"Ten o'clock, if you call that the crack of dawn."

"What're ya up ta?"

"Mom, Grandma, and me are havin' a little breakfast."

"That's real nice. I like ya havin' breakfast with your family." Too bad they hadn't heard that, I thought. "What about you?" I asked.

"I'm wakin' up. You sound good this morning, Samantha Bonti. I'm comin' over."

"No. Yes. I mean, if you come by at two, that'll be good." I figured I could cash the check and have Mom's medications back home well before then.

"Hey, you seein' someone else?" he asked.

"'Course not. I told ya last night and I don't lie."

"I like that, too," Tony said. "Hey. Ya ever been on a motor-cycle?"

My stomach fluttered. "You got one?" I asked, and felt my mother's and grandmother's eyes glaring at my back.

"Shit yeah," Tony said. "A Harley."

"Wow." I glanced over my shoulder and saw my mother's

raised eyebrows. I knew that I could never let her or Grandma know about Tony's bike.

"See ya at two," he said.

"I'm not sure, Tony."

"What'ya mean? Ya just said it was okay."

I bent my head and lowered my voice. "I mean the ride. My mom . . ."

"Don' worry. I'll meet ya at the end of the block," Tony said. I hesitated.

"Okay?" I squeezed the receiver. "Sure, Tone," I said.

"Good. Get ready for the time a ya life. Ya scared?"

"Should I be?"

"Nah," Tony said. "See ya later." I hung up the phone.

"What's goin on?" Mom asked as I sat down.

"Nuthin'. We're goin' out later."

"He calls, and you just jump?" Mom asked.

"It's just a casual date, Mom."

"Yeah, well, that's how it starts. School's startin' soon and I don' want ya gettin' tied up with some punk."

My face reddened. "He's not a punk!" I blurted.

Grandma intervened again. "Sam, if you're finished with your breakfast, go get the check. Mom needs her pills."

Grateful to be given an out, I ran into my bedroom to dress. Thank God for my mother's sake, Mr. Weisbaum's place was open on Sundays. Jews celebrated on Saturday; Sunday was for Catholics.

I was surprised at how easily I had lied to my mother without thinking twice, and I didn't feel good about it. I didn't lie. I wondered if that was what bad boys did to you and whether Tony was one. Did bad boys turn you into a liar before you knew what hit you? I decided to get that out of my mind. It wasn't really much of a lie, anyway. I was just going to have some fun. I pulled on a pair of jeans and a sweatshirt.

No matter what I'd told Tony, I was plenty scared.

4

"How come you're wearin' a skirt?" Tony asked, straddling the idling Harley with his arms crossed after I had rushed to the corner. "I told ya we were takin' a ride on a bike."

"I don't know," I said, catching my breath. I felt like a total fool. I knew I should have kept my jeans on, but I had wanted to look feminine. "I wanted to look good for you."

"Don' ever wear a skirt if I ask ya ta ride wid me again," he said.

"Want me to go back and change?"

Tony picked at a hole in the knee of his blue jeans. "Nah. I'll let it go this time." He grabbed the handlebars and gave the powerful machine some gas. The bike roared under Tony's body, itching to start rolling.

"So where we goin'?" I yelled.

"Sheepshead Bay," he responded, and then looked at me intently. "Now I'm gonna tell ya what ta do and be sure ta listen. I don' need some dumb girl fuckin' up my ride."

I put my hands on my hips and looked him in the eye. "I'm not a dumb girl," I said.

"Prove it," Tony said, and then he explained how and when to get on, how to hold on to him, what to do when he turned corners, and how to get off. I listened hard, determined to show him. "Keep that skirt down, unless you want some horny guys lookin' at your underpants."

"What if I'm not wearing any?" I teased.

"Ya better be."

I swung my leg over the bike, tucked my skirt under my legs, tightened my arms around Tony's leather jacket. I felt the engine vibrations all the way up my spine as we took off around the corner in a roar of thundering horsepower. I tried not to forget what he'd just told me. "Lean into the turn, not away," he'd said. It was thrilling! I didn't want to topple the prize bike, but each time he made a turn, I felt like we were about to fall. I was a quick study.

By the time we pulled up to Vincenzio's Restaurant, a local dining spot on Avenue U, I felt like I'd gotten the hang of motorcycling. Although it had been frightening, I had reveled in the freedom I felt with the wind in my face and Tony's warm body against me. Then Tony freaked me out by popping a few wheelies in front of the restaurant. After holding on for dear life, I was shaken and breathless when Tony stopped at the curb. I inhaled his cologne. That was really living! I thought. I could never tell my mother, but wondered if someone had spotted us on the bike and would blab to her. All hell would break loose if that happened, that was for sure, but I didn't care at that moment. I was with Tony and I felt good.

When he turned off the engine, Vin and Richie came out to the curb to ooh and aah over Tony's Harley. I could not have felt prouder as Tony took my hand and helped me as we got off the bike. Damn, he liked to be on display, and I had to admit that I liked it, too. I patted my skirt down while Tony and his friends knocked fists together.

I looked behind Richie. "Hey, where's Janice?" I asked.

Richie looked at Tony and cleared his throat. "She wasn't feelin' so good."

"What's wrong with her?" I asked. "I talked to her this morning and she was fine."

"Flu. Came on suddenly."

"I ought to go visit her, I guess," I said.

"Nah," he said. "She's sleepin'. Doctor said she had to get lots of sleep."

"She saw the doctor? Jeez, she must be in bad shape."

"I jus' told ya," Richie said through clenched teeth, "she's okay. She got disoriented and fell down. Just leave it alone."

I stared at Richie's face. Did Janice have the flu or had she fallen down? It was obvious to me that Richie was lying, but I didn't know why, and it was pretty clear he wasn't about to tell me. No matter what he said, I'd visit her after Tony brought me home. I turned my attention back to my boyfriend, who made me feel special, like neighborhood royalty. I was the Queen of May as I walked into the restaurant with the coolest guy in Bensonhurst.

Vin directed us to where Dara was sitting. We joined her and Tony ordered a lemonade for me and a draft beer for himself. I hoped it wouldn't affect his ability to ride the bike, but I refused to let anything break the spell. I could always walk home if he got too drunk, I reasoned.

Dara wasn't in a good mood and said a brusque hello. I was afraid she might do something stupid like Janice told me she did the last time she was crabby. Dara had picked a fight with Vin and ended up sprawled on the floor. She had to limp home that day. I tried to perk her up. "Ya look nice, Dara," I said. "How's it goin'?"

"Okay," Dara said with a blank face as she looked me over. "The ride must have been fun. Too bad your hair got screwed up, though." I reached up to smooth my windblown mane.

When the waitress arrived with the drinks, Tony ordered a pizza for the two of us. He hadn't bothered asking me what I wanted; I would have ordered a plate of baked clams because the establishment near the water was mainly a seafood place and Mom rarely splurged on fish. On the rare occasions when

I ate out with schoolmates, I rarely ordered the hamburgers and fries and Cokes like everyone else did. I'd have salads and salmon and vegetables instead. I had done research on food after reading about proper nutrition in the grown-up magazines I'd peruse in the school library. It confirmed what I'd always suspected about Mom's Kraft macaroni and cheese, Weaver Chicken, and Rice-A-Roni, which she'd buy when the welfare check came in. Even though it wasn't my preference, it was still really tasty.

The pizza arrived and I ate my share of the pie and looked around the family-style restaurant, brightly lit with large tables, as the guys talked. Vincenzio's was one of the places where Brooklyn Boys took their girls to eat and chat and talk about whoever wasn't there. I'd been there a couple of times, but never with a guy like Tony. It gave me status to be seen with him and I liked that. His great looks didn't hurt, either. But those weren't the main reasons I was into Tony. What turned me on the most was how interested he was in *me*.

I swallowed a bite as the conversation about matters that were foreign to me went on. "It's all set, then?" Tony asked Vin.

"Yeah," Vin replied, "Tino took care a everythin'."

"Good," Tony said. "Weez can make da rounds later."

I had no idea what they were referring to and didn't care. I was looking forward to making my own rounds around town with a new boyfriend, one who excited me. I couldn't wait to be on his arm everywhere.

Tony only had one more beer and within an hour we were back on the Harley. I felt like an old pro, except when he popped wheelies again before we sped off. I hoped he wouldn't do that on my block. I squeezed his midsection as we rode into the wind, inhaling the fresh air and taking in the scenery. We were a unit of two, roaring our way through a world of sensations that rocked my body and mind.

"Didja like it?" Tony asked over his shoulder, his blue eyes sparkling, when we stopped at the end of my street. "Sure did, Tony," I said. I didn't mention how I had felt about the wheelies. What if he got offended and decided I wasn't tough enough to be his girl? Then I looked at him with eager anticipation. "How'd I do?"

"Youse was great. Did you see the looks in the guys' eyes? They were jealous as hell." He helped me off the bike, set me on the sidewalk, and remained straddled above the hot metal.

"Dara didn't look real happy," I said.

"Donkeys are always unhappy. Next thing you know she might even bray. Wouldn't that be a hoot?"

I didn't think so but didn't have time to respond. Tony pulled me close, arching my back, and kissed my lips. He let go of me, smiled, and sang a few lines from a Diana Ross hit:

Upside down you're turning me
You're giving love instinctively
Around and round you're turning me . . .

"Not bad for a tough guy," I said.

Tony crossed his arms. "Hey, we're all goin' to the movies later," he said. "Wanna come?"

"Who's we all?" I asked.

"Vin, Dara, Richie, Janice. Ya know, the gang."

"I thought Janice had the flu."

"Oh yeah, I forgot. Vin, Richie, and Dara. So we on or not?" I hesitated. "Don' worry," he said. "I'll pick ya up in my car. I'll even come in and meet your mom and grandma. Parents love me."

I still didn't say anything. There was nothing I would rather do than go to the movies with Tony, but I didn't want him to see my home. The furniture was threadbare, so worn-out we had thrown white sheets over the ratty material. Being poor sucked, I thought, as I had countless times before. Would I have to keep my boyfriends at bay and never let them see my surroundings until I walked down the aisle? I wondered. I thought if Tony had the rescuing gene, like it seemed he did, it would work in my favor. If he didn't, he might be history.

"What's the matter, Sam?" Tony asked. "Any girl in Bensonhurst would be glad ta be wid me."

"Nuthin'," I said. I really wanted to go out with him whenever and wherever he planned to take me. And I felt I was a catch, too. Tony and his buddies knew the difference between good girls and bad girls, the so-called sluts in our neighborhood. I was a good girl, every Brooklyn Boy's dream—young and innocent enough for a guy to mold into what he wanted. That's how it went down in Brooklyn. I decided Tony would have to see the worst sooner rather than later. My life was what it was, I reasoned, and I had to be proud and grateful for what God had given me, I decided. "I'll come," I said. "What's playin'?"

"Whatever. Whatcha gonna do now?"

I smiled. "I gotta go wash my hair and do my nails and all that kinda stuff," I gushed.

Tony's face darkened and his eyebrows furrowed. "Who ya gotta look good for? Tell me and I'll break his face."

"Jeez, Tony. It's you." His question hadn't made any sense, but I felt flattered nonetheless.

"All right. But I need ya ta know if anybody tries ta get next ta ya, I'll break his face."

"I know you will, Tony."

"Good. I'll pick you up at seven. Wear sumthin' hot."

Mom and Grandma were taking naps when I stole into the house. I changed my clothes, ran a brush through my windblown hair, and set out for Janice's. I should have called first but the truth was I wanted to see for myself what was going on. Why did I feel so uneasy, like I was on my way to the dentist?

When I walked up Janice's driveway and rang the bell, her mother came to the door. "Hello, Sam," she said softly, eyes lowered.

"Hi, Mrs. Caputo. Is Janice here? I heard she has the flu."

"Right. The flu," Mrs. Caputo snarled. "Come in. I guess you don't know."

"About what?" I asked as I entered.

"That asshole Richie. I swear I'll kill him if I ever see him again." Her hands turned into fists as she held them by her sides.

"What do you mean?" I asked.

Mrs. Caputo motioned toward the rear of the apartment. "Go in her bedroom and see for yourself."

I headed to the familiar place where Janice and I had had so many sleepovers together, talking all night long about our dreams and giggling, too, about boys. We had done our hair there and let cucumber masks dry on our faces, and concocted harmless pranks and schemes, like the time we climbed out her window late one night into a tree and ran around the neighborhood with no purpose other than to see if we could get away with it.

I opened her door and saw that the windows were shut, the blinds were lowered, and the lights were out. A place that had always been so joyful seemed like a funeral parlor to me. I could barely make out Janice's form, huddled in her bed. I reached for the light. Janice turned away from me onto her side. "Janice, it's me," I said. "What's going on?" She didn't move and didn't respond. "Geez, it's hot as hell in here," I said, and opened the window next to her bed without taking my eyes off her. "Janice," I said again. She turned slowly and I gasped. Her face was black-and-blue and one eye was so swollen it was almost closed. "Oh my God!" I shouted, and rushed to her side. I wrapped my arms around her. "What the hell happened?"

"I thought I was so smart," Janice wailed. "I guess he really got me this time." She made a sound like she was trying to laugh and in the next moment she was sobbing.

"How could he do this to you?" I demanded.

"It was my fault, Sam. I shouldn't have talked back to him in front of Vin last night. I know that. I just hate it when he acts like he owns me." She sat up, grabbed a tissue, and dabbed her eyes. "Ow!" she cried. "Everything hurts so bad."

"Your father know about this?"

"No. He's out with his friends. I begged Mom not to say anything. With the people he knows, there's no tellin' what he'd do."

"He'll see for himself when he gets home."

"No, he won't. I'm not comin' outta this room for a coupla days."

I steamed. Where did Richie Sparto come off, doing this to her? "He had no right," I said. "Wait'll I tell Tony. He'll take care of this."

"Sure he will," Janice said. "Richie's his best friend. Do ya really think he doesn't know?"

"You think so? But how could he go along with it?" I asked as I looked at my friend's bruised face. Tony couldn't possibly know the extent of it and do nothing, I thought. Tony was a peacemaker. "I'm gonna go tell him right away and you'll see. Richie'll never get away with this."

Janice grabbed my arms and glared into my eyes. "Ya can't!" she begged. "If ya do, Richie'll never speak to me again. Ya don' know how it is," Janice sobbed. "Please don' ruin it for me, Sam."

I could hardly believe my ears. It was already ruined, as far as I could see. Would Janice really just go back and be with Richie again after what he'd done? I wondered. I stroked my best friend's hair.

"Don't worry, Janice. I won't say a thing. To anyone." I also wondered if Tony would ever do something like that to me.

5

The doorbell rang at a quarter to eight Sunday evening. I had been ready for an hour but I stayed in my bedroom while Mom went to the buzzer. Although waiting had made me nervous, I was glad Tony was late because I needed the extra time to try on every outfit in my closet. Although I did not have a lot of great choices among my mother's hand-me-downs and discount store items, I managed to pull something together. I was poor, there was no denying that, but I always made what Grandma called "a suitable presentation."

I had settled on a royal blue dress gathered at the waist and I checked myself in the mirror one last time. I fluffed my hair and ran my hands across the $1.99 number that Mom had purchased for me at our local St. Jude thrift shop, a favorite among the welfare recipients in the neighborhood. I looked pretty damned good, I thought. I wore a touch of light pink lipstick because I didn't want to give Mom and Grandma any ammunition against my new boyfriend. I'd apply a dark red shade on the way to the movie theater.

I glanced at my makeshift desk and my portable typewriter. Even though I had a lot of new material in my head, I had been too excited and preoccupied to write anything that afternoon. I'd catch up with my journal later, I decided, and then Grandma's booming voice filled the apartment. "So you're Tony," she shouted.

Everyone knew Grandma was hard of hearing, something she never admitted. She refused to wear a hearing aid, which made her talk even louder because she couldn't hear herself all that well. It was funny how she yelled the loudest when she was meeting new people. It was as if she figured they'd all hear better once they got to know each other. The elderly woman's eyes were so soft and loving, everyone was smitten with her.

When I walked into the living room, I saw Tony wedged between Mom and Grandma on the couch. I stifled a laugh. He looked trapped, but he was smiling politely and answering a question and they smiled in return. He really knew how to handle himself, I thought. Tony was the kind of guy, I guessed, who could sweet-talk parents until they stretched the curfew, reassuring them that their daughter would be in good hands. One look at Mom told me that she was being charmed. Thank God her female instincts had overtaken her biases for a change, I thought. Tony looked toward me. "Wow!" he exclaimed. "Ya look real good, Sam." His head swiveled between Mom and Grandma. "Doesn't she?" he asked them.

"My *bubelah* is one gorgeous girl," Grandma shouted. "She's a smart one, too." Mom just nodded and then Grandma frowned as she stared at the huge cross on Tony's neck. She so desperately wanted it to be a Jewish star, wanted me to marry a Jewish boy. She had reservations about Italians, Sicilians most of all, and said they were sneaky, stubborn, and control freaks. I couldn't blame her for feeling that way after what my father had done to her daughter. Though there was plenty of other evidence around us to support her views, I wasn't inclined to make such sweeping judgments. Tony was different, I felt. He stood up and took my hand. Grandma's eyes narrowed. "You take good care of her, now."

When we got outside, Tony helped me into the passenger

seat of his 1972 black and beige Toyota. I knew my family would be watching from the third-floor window and that they'd appreciate seeing me being treated like a lady. This guy would never do to me what Richie had done to Janice, I thought.

When Tony got in the car I opened my mouth and closed it again. I was dying to say something about Richie but remembered my promise to Janice. Instead, I thought of something casual to say as we drove down the block. "Hey, do they really have dikes in Holland?"

"Ya mean lesbos?"

"No, silly. I mean that story about the boy who put his finger in the dike to hold back the water."

Tony grinned. "Musta been pretty smelly," he said.

"Don't be so gross, Tony," I said.

He laughed for a second and turned serious. "But it ain't funny," Tony began. "I ain't never hangin' wid no queers." The veins in his neck bulged as his hands twisted around the steering wheel. "None a my crew would put with that very long."

There was silence for a long minute and then I changed the subject. "So what took you so long to get here? I was ready at seven."

"Good. I like a woman who listens."

"So where were you?"

Tony looked straight ahead. "I hadda, you know, do some stuff with Vin and Richie," he said. He jangled the rosary beads that hung from his rearview mirror. All the guys in Bensonhurst had some sort of religious artifact on the mirror or dashboard to protect them. Mom had told me that Saint Christopher was the one who watched over you while you drove, and there were plenty of his likenesses in Bensonhurst cars.

"What kinda stuff?" I asked.

"Bizness. I was takin' care a bizness," he said.

"On a Sunday?"

"Listen, Sam. I'm in business for myself, kinda. Me and the guys."

"No kidding. What do you do?"

"Loan dough to dems that need some, and we're in the used radio trade, too," he said.

"Oh. You some kind of entrepreneur?"

Tony grinned, sat back, and drove on with one hand as his other arm hung outside his side window. "I knew you were a smart girl," he said. "That's exactly what I am. A ontra-pa-noo-er."

I looked at his powerful hand on the wheel. "I thought you worked construction," I said.

"Yeah, that's right. Union shit. But me an' the guys have some things on the side."

Everyone knew that many Italians, especially those connected to the Mafia, had *gumadas,* or mistresses. I hoped that business was all that Tony had on the side. I stared at him while he drove and looked forward to another date. "So what movie are we seeing? I love movies. My favorite is *West Side Story,* especially when Maria sings to Tony. *Tony, Tony,*" I sang out like a fool, giggling at myself.

"Oh that," Tony said. "We're not goin' to the movies."

"But Mom and Grandma think I'm at the flicks."

"What they don' know won't hurt 'em," Tony said.

"I don't like lying."

"Ya want 'em to think *I'm* a liar? They'll never let ya see me again." Tony glanced at me with a smirk. "But if that's what ya want, I can turn around and take ya back home so you can be honest."

My lips tightened. "No, that's okay," I said.

"Good. You wouldn't really want to miss goin' to Platinum, would you?"

"You're taking me to Platinum?" I asked, my voice cracking. The thought of being at one of the hottest nightclubs around thrilled me. The Harley ride had been excitement enough for one day, and now this!

"I was gonna, but if you'd rather be with your mommy, that's fine with me."

"'Course I want to be with you, Tone. I was just surprised, is all." I paused for a minute. "How'm I gonna get in?"

Tony reached into his pocket and handed a driver's license to me.

"Who's Priscilla Montiglio?" I asked.

"That's you. You're twenty-two."

"I don't look twenty-two. And she has short hair."

"Don' matter. I know the bouncer. The fake ID is just for show. Ya hand it to 'im when I tell ya."

After Tony parked the car, he took my hand and led me past the long line of anxious clubgoers waiting to get in. When I handed the fat bouncer the fake ID, he smirked at Tony and then unhooked the velvet rope. Tony grabbed Priscilla Montiglio's ID back from the bouncer and tucked it away in his pocket after we entered the club.

Holding tight on to Tony's hand, I let my eyes adjust to the lights above the dance floor, the surrounding darkness, and the cigarette smoke, and my ears to the overwhelming din. The place was jumping as a young crowd gyrated on the dance floor. Everyone boogied to "Love Machine" by the Miracles:

(I, I,) I'm just a love machine
And I won't work for nobody but you

Boys in tight pants and nylon shirts that were half unbuttoned undulated to the music with girls whose breasts bulged out of short halter tops. I wondered how they danced in the high-heeled platforms they wore. I would topple over, I decided, and was glad I wore low wedge sandals.

Tony guided me past the bar and along the dance floor to a

restaurant area. A hand went up at one of the tables along the dance floor. Tony smiled and nodded toward Richie and Vin. We made our way to their table and sat down. In front of a club that was so alive, I felt like a queen again.

Dara sat slumped beside Vin. I smiled at her and eyed the large-breasted girl sitting next to Richie who had a grin plastered on her face. "Meet my cousin Gloria," Richie said to me. "Gloria, this is Samantha."

I nodded to her and wondered at the same time. If she was Richie's cousin, then why was he practically sitting on top of her? Kissing cousins was more like it, I concluded. If I had despised Richie for beating up on Janice, I detested him now. His flaunting another girl made me feel sick to my stomach and I looked at Tony with a narrow smile. This was my first visit to Platinum and I wanted to have fun, but guilt gnawed at me. How could I enjoy myself when my loyalties were to Janice? I decided to make the best of it. What could I do about it, anyway?

Tony poured a glass of pink champagne for me from a pretty bottle. I tasted it and wow! I could get used to that, I said to myself. I felt good. Despite my reservations, I thought it was time for me to have a little fun. "So," I said after another sip, "I hear you guys are in the radio business."

Vin chuckled. I didn't know what was so funny. "Yeah," he said, and glanced at Tony. "Well, we don' exactly buy. We kinda sell. Ain't that right, Tony?"

Richie exploded in a guffaw and he spilled some beer on his lap. I frowned as Gloria, his so-called cousin, patted him dry, her napkin lingering on his crotch. I thought of Janice, depressed and alone. Richie's delight irritated me beyond belief. I would have enjoyed seeing him drown in a vat of beer right then. Good thing I knew better than to open my mouth again, about radios or cousins or best friends.

Dara excused herself to powder her nose and I took a

moment to study Vin Priganti. Everyone knew about the Priganti family, who oversaw underworld activity in Brooklyn. Tino, Vin's father, had squashed all rivals years before and had risen to the top of an empire built on gambling, theft, loansharking, and prostitution. Sicilian through and through, Vin's family lived by the rigid code brought over from the old country.

Local people heard all the stories about the mobsters in their midst and talked in hushed tones about how Tino kept his two sons in line the same way he controlled his hired muscle—with the back of his hand and the barrel of his gun. Everyone feared him enough to do anything he asked. Vin's older brother, Joe, however, would not be following in his father's footsteps. Sensitive and less ambitious than Vin, Joe had a stooped posture and a retiring nature that were unsuitable for leading a crime family, and he would never take over the reins. Vin, a strong, silent type who didn't have a conscience and wasn't afraid to take action, was the favored son. He would take over for Tino when the time came. His cohorts knew it, and that gave Vin special status in the neighborhood. Everyone jumped at his command, too.

Dara wobbled back and almost fell onto Vin when she took her seat. She looked around the table. "Where's my drink, Vin?"

Vin handed her a Coke. "Ya had enough already. Drink this and shuddup."

"Who the hell da ya think ya are?" Dara slurred. She pushed the drink away and it toppled onto the table. Vin rose without saying a word, clamped a hand around her arm, and pulled her out of the nightclub while she kicked at him from behind.

"Shit," said Richie. "She's a real loose cannon, that one. Wonder why he keeps her?"

"That ain't all that's loose about Dara," Tony said, and the Brooklyn Boys guffawed.

I felt sorry for the girl. Sure, Dara might be a pain in the ass and hard to like, but the guys didn't have to treat her like that. Tony tapped my shoulder and motioned toward the animated bodies under a rotating, spotlit globe. B. J. Thomas sang out,

> *I'm hooked on a feelin', high on believin'*
> *That you're in love with me.*

I slid onto the wood floor and danced with Tony, self-conscious at first. When we got into a groove, everyone in the packed crowd disappeared as Tony and I just looked at each other. Thoughts of Janice and Dara faded away as the song played on:

> *I got it bad for you girl, but I don't need a cure.*
> *Keep it up girl, yeah you turn me on.*

I closed my eyes and my mind floated to a place beyond the night.

6

At two in the morning, I closed the door to my apartment without making a sound, took off my sandals, and tiptoed into my home without turning on a light. I thanked God that Mom wasn't semiawake in one of her hazes on the living room couch. She sure as hell would have picked up where she had left off Sunday morning about my no-good boyfriend, I thought, and at that hour, her wrath would have no doubt been doubled. I made my way down the hall with the aid of the glimmer coming from a streetlamp and eased into my bedroom.

I hardly breathed as I undressed and then slipped into bed, worried that my pounding heart could be heard around the room. My head hit the pillow and I closed my eyes.

"Did you have fun, Samelah?" Grandma punctured the silence in a subdued voice that nonetheless sounded as loud as usual to me in our dark, still room. I caught my breath and rolled over to face her. "Yes, Grandma. A lot."

"I can see your smile in your voice. That makes my heart feel good."

"Sorry it's so late," I said.

"That's okay, as long as you're home safe."

"I wish Mom would feel that way."

"She doesn't have to know what time you got in."

"What if she heard me?" I worried.

"I'll tell her it was midnight. She drank a bottle of Thunderbird before she went to bed and won't know the difference."

"Thanks, Gram."

"So? What about your date?"

I propped my head on my arm. "Tony's the best, Grandma. Took me to Platinum," I gushed, and then regretted my slip.

"At your age?"

"It's no big deal, Grandma."

"You're not supposed to be in the clubs, Sam. You didn't have any alcohol, did you?"

"Of course not," I said without hesitation. "We just danced and talked a lot."

"He's a nice boy?"

"You saw for yourself on Sunday."

"I didn't spend much time with him. He seemed all right for an Italian."

"Half," I reminded her. "And you'll be seeing a lot more of him soon."

"You like him a lot, huh, Samelah?"

"Tony's a real catch, Grandma. All the girls drool over him. But he only looks at me."

"Did he get fresh with you?"

I paused a moment. "He's a gentleman, Gram."

"Good. Can't have some greaseball botherin' my granddaughter."

"None of those guys would think of coming near me as long as I'm with Tony."

"You shouldn't be anywhere that kind hangs out."

"I can take care of myself," I said, but questioned whether I could do that any better than Janice could. I decided that Tony wasn't Richie, and I wouldn't have to cross that particular bridge.

"It would be better if you didn't run into them at all," Grandma continued.

"Oh, Grandma, they're all over Brooklyn."

"Not in the temples," Grandma said, her voice slightly raised. I knew her lips would be pressed together.

"If I met a nice Jewish boy, I'd go out with him."

"I wonder," Grandma sighed. I doubted what I'd said, too. Jewish boys tended to be nerds, and although I shared some things with that neighborhood group, the pull of being a part of the in crowd was too strong. And I belonged with Tony, I felt deep inside. I knew that I would continue to keep my writing to myself for the most part while I explored the exciting avenues that Jewish boys never traveled.

Grandma's bedsprings squeaked as she shifted her position. "There would be nothing to wonder about if you had gone to shul like I wanted. Instead, your mother sent you to public school and filled your head with Christianity nonsense."

"That's just a different path to the same God, isn't it?" I asked.

"Well, some paths are better than others," she grunted.

"Maybe you're right," I placated her. I reclined on the bed once again. "'Night, Grandma," I said.

"Good night, sweetheart," Grandma said. "I love you," she added after a prolonged exhale.

"Me, too," I said as I slipped a hand under my pillow. I clutched the rosary I always kept there and drifted off to sleep.

I awoke late Labor Day morning refreshed and full of energy. Grandma was already up as usual, and I sprang out of bed to join her in the kitchen. I was relieved to find that Mom wasn't there to interrogate me but then I worried about her. "Mom's not up yet?" I asked Grandma.

"No."

"I hope she's okay," I said.

"She's fine. Snoring away when I looked in on her. Let me fix you something, Samelah."

"I'm starved, Gram. And then I have a lot of writing to catch up on."

"I'll keep your mother occupied when she gets up so you can concentrate on your work."

"That'd be great. I don't plan on coming out of my room for a while," I said, and smiled the whole time Grandma fussed with my breakfast.

The words poured out of my mind as I sat at my desk, and my fingers had a hard time keeping up on the typewriter. Pages filled with fresh thoughts about my mother, about Janice and Richie, and, most of all, about Tony piled up next to my portable Smith-Corona. His musk energized me and our budding relationship informed everything I wrote.

Although Mom's experience with my father had been awful, I wondered if she had ever felt about him the way I felt about my new boyfriend. Or if she had ever had anyone else that caused her stomach to turn flips like mine did when I even thought about seeing him, let alone actually being with him. I wondered, too, what Mom's hopes were before she was swallowed up by circumstances—some of which, I knew, could have been avoided if she had been strong enough to resist. Mom had never even hinted about any of her hopes, so I could only guess what they might have been. I never considered the possibility that she had never had any, even after she'd scoff at me, "You're a dreamer, Sam," when I'd share mine. I'd felt that it was her frustration talking at those times. Her encouragements to seek a better life, though infrequent and further apart as time went on, reflected how she really felt, I had decided, and I vowed to remember them more than anything else she said or did. As I typed, I imagined how horrible it must have been for Mom to have her hopes beaten out of her by my father.

I wrote about that as I had before and explored what it was that made someone stand for that. As Janice had. Was her need for acceptance so great that she would suffer physical abuse, along with mental torment, for it? It didn't have to be that way, I knew. Janice was well-off and she wasn't unappealing. She had other options. And yet she stayed with Richie and feared losing him. It didn't make sense, but that was how it was in Bensonhurst and I wrote about it.

And I wrote about Tony. About the excitement of discovery, of motorcycles and champagne and dancing in his arms. And about his kisses that lingered still in my mouth. Exploration and sharing, along with interest in and attention to the other person, was what a real relationship was all about and my mind formed the words that came alive on the page.

I didn't kid myself about the kind of guys Tony hung around with. How could I? Vin Priganti was the son of a man who had left his mark—literally as well as figuratively— all over Bensonhurst. And Tony spent a lot of time with Vin, and with Richie, and they hadn't thought twice before striking their women. I didn't kid myself, either, that Tony wouldn't exhibit some of the mannerisms that Brooklyn Boys had, but I was certain that he was above that kind of behavior. Tony was different, better than those creeps, I wrote. He might do what he had to do to belong, but he wouldn't be poisoned by those other guys. I just knew it. Tony had a softness underneath the tough exterior he displayed. His kisses proved that.

I hoped that Tony would want to go with me across that bridge I was building. Surely he wanted to get away from Brooklyn, too, I thought, away from the prejudice and discrimination and limitation. He must, I concluded, and I wrote about the yearnings I imagined he would have for something more than what Bensonhurst offered to him. Our future would be different, special. I couldn't wait to live it with him.

✧ ✧ ✧

Hours of writing exhausted me, so I went to bed right after dinner, which was just as well the night before the first day of school. I awoke early and fussed more than usual about how I looked before heading into the kitchen to grab something on my way out the door.

Grandma was in her usual place at the stove, but I was surprised to see Mom, more haggard than usual, sitting at the table with her customary cigarette between her lips. A full black plastic ashtray sat beside her empty plate. I hated always smelling like smoke, plus inhaling it.

"Mornin', everyone," I said. "You're up early, Mom."

"Never went to bed," Mom said, surrounded by smoke.

I glanced toward Grandma before responding. "Sorry to hear that. Not feeling well?"

"Since when do I?"

I pointed to the ashtray. "Those don't help."

"Don't lecture me, Sam," Mom said before taking another drag.

"No lecture. Fact."

"Just the same, I don't need to hear it from you."

Grandma turned to both of us. "Let's not start anything today," she said. She came over to me, put her arm around my waist, and pulled me close. Grandma looked at me with soft eyes and then faced her daughter. "This is Sammy's first day of junior year. Before we know it, she's gonna graduate high school, Joan."

Mom pulled on her cigarette, tilted her head back, and blew smoke toward the ceiling before looking at me. "Let's hope she can keep her mind on her books instead of that new boyfriend."

"She will," Grandma said, and then she looked at me. "Right, Samelah?"

"Of course," I said. I gave Grandma a peck on her cheek and turned toward the doorway. "Now I've got to get goin'."

"But you haven't eaten," Grandma said. Mom stubbed her cigarette and lit another.

"No time, Gram. Gotta catch the early bus," I said, and I grabbed a banana from the bowl on the counter before leaving the kitchen. "Bye, Mom," I shouted before the apartment door closed behind me.

There was a bustle of activity outside New Keiser High School as I exited my bus in front of the brick building with iron bars on its large windows. Students gathered in their small cliques and observed everyone who arrived, either by bus or the N train, which was next to the school, or by car, which the most privileged did. I could only imagine what it would be like to get out of a parent's Cadillac as some did, or own a Mustang or other hot car as some other students did.

I wasn't close to any of my classmates and wished that Janice was still in school. I felt sad that she had graduated and I wouldn't have her to lean on. As I made my way across the oval track to the entrance, I felt critical eyes on me. At times like that I feared my thrift store clothes revealed the welfare secret that I labored to conceal. My red three-quarter tight pants and white cotton scooped-neck T-shirt were passable from a distance, but I didn't think they'd stand up to close inspection. I was glad when I got inside and melted into the throng that was ebbing and flowing in the hallway. I squeezed through the crowd to my assigned locker.

"You have something good for me?" Mr. Wainright asked from behind as I opened the narrow, vented metal door.

I turned my head. "You bet," I said. He smiled and squeezed my shoulder before he moved on and disappeared down the hall. I couldn't wait to turn in the stories I had written over the summer and looked forward to my English teacher's appraisal.

As always on a first day of school, there seemed to be a newness about everything: fresh paint and polished floors, some faces I'd never seen before, and a different class schedule with an extra free period. Posters announced football and cheerleader tryouts, and clubs and other extracurricular activities looking for participants. I would write for the newspaper as I had since freshman year and forgo everything else, not because I had no interest in them but because I couldn't afford the few dollars it took to participate.

The novelty of a first day made the hours fly by. But as exciting as everything was to me, I missed Tony, especially during lunch and the other free times when I had time to think. The muffled rumblings of the elevated trains nearby reminded me that there was a world outside waiting for me. And Tony was a part of it.

When my last class was over, I packed my bag and reveled in being able to leave. I looked forward to getting a jump on my homework. Every completed assignment would bring me closer to that world across the Brooklyn Bridge I knew. I bolted out the front door and headed for the row of buses along the curb.

A distinctive roar that reverberated under the elevated subway platform stopped me in my tracks and then a motorcycle jumped the curb ten feet from where I stood, frozen. Tony switched the engine off, straddled the bike, crossed his arms, and grinned from ear to ear as he had on my corner two days before. I blushed, sidled over to him, and cradled my book bag.

"You look hot, Samantha Bonti," he said. "Howz about a lift?"

I looked away for a moment. "I've got to get home, Tone," I said.

"Sure ya do. But we'll hit Sally's first." I didn't move. "C'mon, I'll get ya there before the bus would, anyways."

A bike ride and a snack at Sally's with Tony sounded like the perfect way to celebrate my first day. "Okay," I said, and hopped on. His cologne filled my nostrils.

Tony started the Harley and turned his head back toward

me. "We're gonna have to do something about you takin' buses," he said. I had no idea what he meant, but other days didn't matter at that moment. Tony rolled the bike to the street, gunned the engine, and took off for Eighteenth Avenue.

I squeezed his midsection and knew I had made the right decision.

7

Tony and I repeated our rendezvous after school every day that week. He picked me up with his Harley or his Toyota and it didn't take long for my schoolmates to notice my hot new boyfriend. That didn't change my interaction with them, but it seemed I had gained newfound respect in record time.

Sometimes, Tony would drive me straight home, and other times we'd make a stop at Sally's or a fast-food joint. We parted every time with a lingering kiss. Friday was one of the days when he wanted to take me somewhere. He picked me up in his mother's white Lincoln Continental with a red leather interior and said we were headed for Belmont Park when we jumped into the front seat.

After I closed my door, I looked into the rear, where silk dresses hung along a tension rack that was spread above the seat. "You in the garment trade, too, Tony?" I asked as he pulled away from the curb.

"I know sumbody," he said. "Pick sumthin' nice out for yaself."

I turned around on my knees and riffled through the row of dresses. "Jeez, Tone," I gurgled, "I'll take this lavender number, if you're sure it's okay."

"Take whatever ya want." Tony beamed.

I rolled the dress and put it in my bag after I turned around, and thought about all the new things I was experiencing with Tony. The Harley, Platinum, an expensive dress. Not to mention the kisses, I thought as we sped along the Belt Parkway. We were on our way to another place I'd never been and I was sure there would be many others with Tony.

Although the racetrack was on the border of Queens—one of the outer boroughs of New York—and the suburbs that were almost as densely packed as Brooklyn was, it seemed like the country to me when we pulled off the highway. A couple of miles to Coney Island, on Brooklyn's southern edge, a few times during summers was the farthest I'd ever gone from home. Tony swung the car up to the unpaved curb in front of the clubhouse and tossed the keys to a valet who ran toward him. Tony took my hand and whisked me inside.

The concourse reminded me of Grand Central Station. People—almost entirely men—hustled to and from the betting windows or pored over forms and newspapers at counters and high tables. TVs hung all along the ceiling, and a race announcer boomed from loudspeakers. Tony led me through the crisscrossing bettors to a Plexiglas window that was nearly opaque from grime and smudges. He peeled off a few hundred-dollar bills from a wad he took from his jeans pocket, handed them to the clerk, and turned to me. "Ya gotta fav'rite number?" he asked. "I like three and seven," I said, wide-eyed. Tony leaned toward the small holes that had been drilled into the thick plastic that separated him from the clerk. "Box the one and two and give me a quiniela on the number three and five, twenty times, and put a yard on the fifty-to-one," he said. He took his slips and put them into his other jeans pocket and then grabbed my hand again. "I'll take ya outside," he said, and led me to the grandstand.

"Geez, Tone," I started as we sat down and looked at the race taking place on the far side of the track. "That's a lot of money you laid down, isn't it?" He craned his head toward the galloping horses. "I never put the milk money unda the window," he said without looking at me. "It's jus' entertainment dough." He leapt to his feet, as did the rest of the sizable crowd. I stood and followed everyone's eyes, which were focused on the finish line. A few people cheered raucously at the race's end and the rest tossed slips of paper away in disgust. Some walked up the aisles while others returned to their seats.

Tony and I sat down. His face was expressionless. "Did you lose?" I asked.

"Nah," he said as he slipped an arm behind me. "I wuzn't in that race. The next one."

"Oh," I said. "You come here often?"

"Here'n there."

"How do you do?"

"I'm up, usually."

"It seems like fun, but I don't know the first thing about it."

"You'll catch on. And ya know what else?" Tony said as he breathed into my ear. "I'll take ya ta AC someday, too. Then you'll see what real fun is all about." I wondered how thrilling it would be to go to Atlantic City, and who Tony knew to get me into the casino to gamble with him. And then I wondered how I'd ever get Mom to agree to let me go. I don't think I'll ask her, I said to myself.

We did make it to the movies Saturday night, even if it wasn't what I wanted to see. Bruce Lee's bone-crunching blows and kicks were not my idea of a good movie. I liked lighter fare like *American Graffiti* or *Bananas*.

"Why does he keep doing the same stuff all through the movie?" I asked Tony. "Doesn't he ever talk?"

"Shhhhh!" came a voice from the seat behind me.

Tony turned around. "Shut the fuck up!" he growled. Great date, I thought. Tony's cursing and I have to share him with other couples again. I couldn't wait to get out of there. At least I had told my mother the truth that time, I thought; we *had* actually gone to the movies. I cringed and looked down the row at Vin, Dara, Richie, and Janice. Despite her mother's objections, she had forgiven Richie after he gave her a gold rope necklace. I guessed it was a perverted sort of war medal, a Purple Heart that was supposed to take the sting out of the damage. It wouldn't have worked with me, I was sure of that, but Janice seemed content.

I felt guilty that I hadn't told Janice about Gloria, Richie's "cousin," but what good would that have done, anyway? They were back together and I would only have gotten in trouble with Tony for spilling the beans. I supposed that Janice had been right when she told me to forget about ratting on Richie to Tony. The guys stuck together no matter what.

When we left the theater, Tony and the guys tapped fists with each other, their customary neighborhood handshake. "Later," Tony said as he and I headed in a different direction.

They were always meeting up somewhere "later" and I'd heard from Janice enough times that they never told their women exactly where that was. The girls knew it would be someplace like Scoundrels or Spades, nightclubs where they could drink and talk business. A lot of the girls worried that their guys did other things there, too, with other women. But not me; I knew Tony wanted to be with only me.

Tony led me down the street to the Rainbow Ice Cream Parlor. We sat in a booth with a pink plastic tablecloth and he ordered a hot fudge sundae with extra fudge. I recalled all the times when I could only look into the parlor's windows and watch couples sharing triple scoops with whipped cream and wafer cookies. I was one of them at last.

When the sundae arrived, I dipped my spoon into the white ice cream and fudge and savored the treat. It was really something, I thought. I dipped in again but hesitated before bringing the spoon to my mouth. Even though it seemed Tony didn't mind, I was not acting very ladylike. Maybe I should slow down, I thought.

"What's the matter?" Tony asked. "Don't you like pistachio?" The truth was that it wasn't my favorite and I wished Tony would ask me what I liked *before* he ordered. "I like it okay," I fibbed. "I just thought they were pecans and I was surprised."

"You mean walnuts."

What was it about Brooklyn guys? I wondered. Why did they always have to be right? "No. I mean pecans, Tony. Like in vanilla pecan."

"Whatever," Tony said.

We ate as we continued talking. "Hey, Tone," I said, "I decided to write somethin' about you."

"Yeah?" he asked, breaking into a grin. "Hope your readers can stand to read about such a handsome, cool guy." I laughed and drank some ice water.

Tony put his spoon down. "What's so funny?"

"Nothin'. Just you," I said. He looked upset. "Hey," I said, "I wasn't laughin' *at* you. You just make me laugh sometimes."

"See? That's just it," Tony said. "Any other girl laughs at me like that, fuhgeddaboudit. She's history. But with you, I don't know, you just . . . I feel sumthin' for ya." Tony reached for my hand. "And I don' want nobody else near ya."

"Well, I'm not seein' anybody else."

Tony smiled. "So what're ya writin'?" he asked. "Sumthin' romantic? Making me a hero?"

"Wouldn't you like to know."

"I don' want my girl embarrassing me," Tony said. "Anyways, when you get it finished, lemme know. I know a guy in publishing, a sales rep. He owes me a favor."

I stopped eating and gazed at Tony with wide eyes. "You know someone in publishing?" I asked when I had caught my breath. "Is that true?"

"Ya callin' me a liar?"

"No way, Tony. I just never dreamed . . . Is he in Manhattan?"

"You think he's in Timbuktu?"

I could not wipe the grin off my face. "I mean, Bensonhurst's okay and all," I said, "'specially now that I met you, but I know I'm meant to be across that bridge."

"After you graduate, I'll set you up a meetin' whenever you're ready."

"For real?"

"Sure. Just make me look good in your book."

I looked out of the window next to our booth. "Writers have to be honest, Tone," I said.

"Then it should be no problem. Right?"

"Right," I said without looking at him. I could barely contain my racing thoughts and my excitement about getting a real chance to fulfill my dream. Mr. Wainright had cautioned me several times that it was hard for a writer to get her work seen and that I shouldn't get frustrated. But I would have a connection as soon as my book was finished!

Half the sundae was melting in the bowl when Tony and I left the ice cream parlor. He didn't go for sweets all that much and the very idea of meeting a New York publisher had distracted me. Tony opened his car door and got behind the wheel as I let myself in on the other side. He didn't start the engine and just stared at me.

"What is it, Tony?" I asked. "Is everything okay? I liked the pistachio, honest. I just got full and—"

"Fuhget the ice cream. Ya look fantastic, Sam," Tony said. He leaned over and licked my ear. I pulled back. "Whatsa matter?" he asked. "Ya don' like that?"

"It just startled me, is all," I said.

Tony leaned close to my ear again. "I just keep thinkin' about ya, and that's unusual for me. I wantya so bad, Sam," he whispered. "I can hardly control myself. Lemme try that again." I didn't move. Tony licked the edge of my earlobe and then I turned my face to him. Our lips almost touched. "You're killin' me, Samantha Bonti," he moaned, and he kissed me while his hands traced my breasts over my white blouse. Ripples of pleasure shot through my body. He collected some of my hair, kissed it softly, and whispered to me again. "Sam, you're so beautiful tonight. Ya got the softest skin I ever felt and you're makin' me crazy." I didn't resist as his fingers stroked my naked forearms. That feeling I had up against the van the night of the feast came back and I squirmed in my seat as I felt the warmth and moisture in my underpants. I put my arm behind Tony's neck and rested my head on his shoulder. I wanted him but I was afraid.

"Wait a sec, Sam," Tony said. He started the car.

Thank God, I said to myself. I knew if we had kept going, I might not have been able to resist him, and that was not how my first time should be. He drove off the main street and stopped the car on a dark side road.

"What are ya doin', Tone?" I asked. "I gotta get home."

"In a minute. But right now, you listen to me. I wantya ta be my girl."

"Yeah, Tony," I said, taking his hand. "I want that, too."

"You're different from those other sluts," he said, squeezing my fingers. "You're innocent and pure and I don' want anybody else touching ya. The thought of it makes me so mad, I swear I'll kill anyone who comes near ya. All ya have to do is tell me. That's how much I care about ya."

I was speechless and my body tingled. Tony sounded like he meant what he was saying. He'd never looked more serious and I had seen his stone face at the feast and in the movie theater. He kissed me again as his hand slid under my skirt. I pushed him away.

"Jus' a little bit," he pleaded. "Please, baby. I just need to touch ya down there. I won' do it for long, I promise." His finger slipped into my underpants and I slumped against the seatback.

I was the last holdout among my girlfriends. I knew most of them had lost their virginity in cars and trucks and that Dara had lost hers at fourteen in a smoky basement when a friend of her father's lured her there, gave her wine, and took advantage of her. I had always imagined making love for the first time on a king-sized bed with lots of pillows in a luxurious place like the Pierre Hotel in New York City, with room service, a view of Central Park, and beautiful music piped in.

"Tony," I said, catching my breath. "Please, not like this." His hand lingered for a few moments before he slid it away. "You're right, Sam," he said. "You're much too special to do this in a car. But you're driving me crazy!"

I was relieved, and again pleased that he hadn't forced himself on me. Tony wanted me, I wanted him, but he obviously felt like I did—that it was definitely not the place or the time. I reached over and took his hand but he pulled it away. "Listen," he said. "I got somethin' really important to tell ya and I need ya to concentrate."

"Sure."

"Ya wanna be my girl?"

"Aw, Tony," I said. "I know I'm young and all, but I want that more than anything."

"Good. But I want ya to know there are certain rules ya hafta follow if we're gonna go out." He looked so serious it made me feel nervous. "First, I want ya home every night. School is the most important thing for you."

"'Cause I'm gonna be a writer."

"Don't interrupt," Tony said. "The thing is, I don' want ya hangin' out with your friends at night. They might steer you in the wrong direction and now ya got *my* family to hang out with.

"Number two, I need respect—for my friends and family and me—all the time, no matter what. Ya gotta problem, ya work it out with me privately. Ya never mouth off like Dara or discuss our stuff in front of our friends like that Janice did, and ya never tell your girlfriends what goes on between us. Ever. Got it?"

I didn't think that there had to be strict rules that went along with a relationship. I felt doubt, and I didn't want to feel doubt, but that's what was overshadowing me at this very moment. So what did I do? For the first time in my life, I ignored it and just passed it off as the way it was in Bensonhurst, and if that was the way it had to be with Tony, so be it, as long as I was with him. So I said, "Sure, Tone."

"Finally, most important, Sam, don' cheat on me. Ever. You unnerstan'? 'Cause that would be the worst mistake of your entire life." I knew that was a guy thing, that he needed to be sure I wouldn't make him look small in front of his friends. Grandma had told me the Brooklyn Boys were a pretty insecure bunch. Maybe Tony would grow out of it. Regardless, he didn't have to worry. I wouldn't cheat on any boyfriend I had. Tony exhaled slowly.

"You look like you're glad to get that talk over with," I said. "Was it scary?"

He laughed. "Yeah," he said, "real scary!" He growled and curled his fingers into monster hands. I pushed away from him toward the door on my side, pretending an attempt to escape. He pulled me by the hem of my skirt and stroked my bare leg.

I pushed him away. "Tony," I said, "I thought we decided to . . ."

"Just one touch. I need to feel your skin again." He bent his head down to the area on my thigh where he was stroking and inhaled deeply. I felt the heat between my legs once more. "Ya smell so sweet, Sam. Jus' like baby powder." Tony sat up and started the engine. "I mean it, Sam. You're killin' me," he said.

"I swear to God if another guy comes close to ya, he's a dead man." I shivered, but couldn't help feeling flattered as I had before. "That's how much I care about ya."

The ride home was silent. When we pulled up in front of my apartment house, Tony stopped the car and reached over to kiss me. His hand inched back up my skirt and he slid two fingers inside my panties. I tried to pull away but he stopped me with his soothing voice. "C'mon, Sam. Just a good-bye touch." He adjusted his crotch with his other hand. "You don't know how I get."

"I gotta go in, Tone," I said.

"I know," he said, accepting his frustration. He reached over and opened my door. "Ya better go now, Samantha Bonti, 'cause if you don', I might never let ya go."

I got out of the car and started toward the entrance but turned around when I thought of something else to say. I leaned forward and looked into the car. "Why don't ya call me when you get home?"

"I gotta go out and you're gonna be fast asleep, right?"

"Where ya goin'?" I asked.

"Never mind. Just remember, you're my girl now. Anythin' happens, you come to me. You're my girl."

Tony's girl watched as Tony drove away.

8

On Monday, I had a hard time concentrating on my school-work all day because the excitement of the previous week hadn't worn off. The anticipation of seeing Tony again height-ened as I left the school when classes had ended.

My head swiveled from side to side as I made my way to the curb. There was no telltale roar of a motorcycle that I half expected to hear and Tony was nowhere in sight. I took one last slow look around before hopping onto the bus that took me home.

"Did I get any messages?" I asked Mom before I dropped my schoolbag and took off my sweater. She sat in shadow on the frayed couch as the light from the window behind silhou-etted her frail upper body. An empty wine bottle and almost empty wineglass stood on the scuffed side table. A cigarette with a long ash dangled from her lips.

"Yeah," Mom muttered as she scanned the open newspaper in her lap. My eyes widened and my heart skipped a beat. "Janice called," Mom deadpanned as she raised her head to look at me. My face went blank and my shoulders slumped. "Whatsa mat-ter?" Mom asked with a smirk. "Ya was expectin' someone else?"

"No," I lied, and collected myself. "What'd she want?"

"She said she was going out and she'd call back."

I poked my head into the kitchen. "Where's Gram?"

"At bingo with Mabel," Mom said, her head lowering again. "It's just you and me tonight."

That prospect didn't thrill me. It was hard enough being around Mom when Grandma was there to keep the peace. Lord only knew what would transpire when she wasn't. Maybe Mom would just go to bed early, I hoped, and I wouldn't have to deal with her mercurial moods and her meddling. The last thing I wanted was to have her close by when Tony called. Regardless, I decided I'd make the best of it. "What's for dinner?" I asked.

"Whatever you make."

The way she said it didn't sound like a promising start to the evening. It seemed I would have to carry the load if we were to have a civil time together. I reminded myself that my mother was too far gone from her Woodstock days, from her glue-sniffing and drug use with her friends, from her sleeping around. I steeled my resolve. "No problem," I said as I went into the kitchen.

"So," Mom called out from the couch, "ya waitin' for a call from that boyfriend of yours?"

Maybe it would be better to talk from a distance, I thought. "Not really," I lied again over my shoulder as I put a pot of water on the stove. Pasta with broccoli instead of the grilled cheese that Mom would no doubt have made was just the thing to keep me in a positive frame of mind.

"Yeah, right," Mom said. "You're not foolin' anyone."

I hadn't been able to conceal how I felt about Tony over the last week. Not because of anything I had said—I hadn't mentioned a word to either Mom or Grandma. There was just a little more bounce to my step, I knew, and a perpetual posi-tive attitude about everything in the face of the usual carping Mom threw at me. Hell, right then I was still tingling from Tony's kisses two nights before. I was sure it had been obvious to Mom even in her haze. "So what if I am?" I shouted.

"I don' like the kinda guy that'll keep ya out all hours." Maybe she had heard me come in late the night I went to Platinum, I thought. "I know the type," Mom droned, "drinkin', whorin', and pickin' fights with everybody, especially his girlfriend." I bit my lip and thought about my father, and about the constant arguments and sometimes fights Mom had with her transient male suitors. And about the fights she herself picked all the time with the married man with three kids she had dated on and off since I was four years old. I'm headed for a different life, I said to myself. "Tony's not that kind of guy, Mom. He's real considerate."

"Says you," Mom said. "I won' have ya latchin' onta jus' any man who comes along."

"We just started goin' out, for Chrissakes."

"Watch your mouth!" Mom chastised. I said nothing, and Mom kept up her diatribe. "Before ya know it, ya won' know which end is up." The voice of experience, I thought. Mom met my father at eighteen, was pregnant with me by nineteen, and was divorced a year later. That was her experience; it wouldn't be mine, I vowed. Tony was different. She'd see, I was sure. And I wouldn't throw it in her face when the happiness that had eluded her was mine. "You don't know him, Mom," I said.

"And you do?"

"Yes."

"After one week."

"I just know," I said. Mom didn't respond, and I just knew something else. She'd be reaching for her wineglass. I decided to take my time preparing dinner.

Half an hour later, the pasta and broccoli with oil and garlic were just about done. "Dinner's ready," I called out as I emptied the pot into a strainer, but Mom didn't acknowledge my announcement and there was no sound from the living room. I mixed all the ingredients in a large, hand-painted serving bowl that we had gotten from Dominick's Italian import store on

Eighteenth Avenue. I set it on the table and then went to the doorway.

Mom was slumped on the couch, her head tilted all the way back on the rear cushion, and her breaths were low and irregular. Mom's arms were splayed beside her and the stem of the empty wineglass rested on an open palm.

It's not just the wine, I said to myself as I turned around and slipped into the kitchen. I filled a serving bowl and brought it to my room, where I would think about Tony and write while I waited for his call.

It never came that night.

I hadn't heard from him by Wednesday, so I decided to accept an invitation from a few of my classmates to go to Outer Skates after school. I was never interested in the silliness that was often exhibited by the girls who were my age and the clumsy attentions of the boys who followed them around like puppies. But I didn't have a lot of homework that day and was grateful to have something to do that would keep me away from home and away from my thoughts about Tony for a while.

It turned out that I had a better time than I had anticipated. The girls didn't engage in any petty gossip and the boys sprang for our skate rentals as usual and behaved themselves. We were having harmless fun and I felt a little guilty about the way I often thought about my contemporaries. Maybe I should give them more of a chance, I thought.

Nick, who had gotten skates for me, was a perfect gentleman who seemed to enjoy my company. We skated side by side in our group, which circled the polished wood floor, and talked casually across the railing when I took a break on the carpet that surrounded the rink. He appeared to be a nice guy. We skated to the Bee Gees. It was so thrilling.

I felt like a real girl and I could tell Nick was being extra nice to me.

We shared some innocent opinions and observations and I was pleasantly surprised by his honesty and intelligence. I giggled when he made fun of how Brooklyn Boys, himself included, behaved, preening themselves and strutting like cocks of the walk. Perhaps he deserved more of my time, I thought, and lost myself in our interplay for half an hour.

That was until Tony came.

"Who the fuck da ya think ya are?" Tony roared as he bumped me and grabbed Nick's shirt with both hands, raising him on the toes of his skates. "What the fuck are ya doin' with my girl?" he asked, eyes opened wide and saliva collecting at the corners of his mouth. My eyes were wide open, too, as was my mouth. But it was bone dry. I couldn't speak.

"Nuh . . . nuh . . . nu . . . thin'," Nick panted. Tony tightened his grip and pulled Nick closer.

"Duzzin't look like nuttin' ta me," Tony growled. Skaters slowed their pace around the rink and glided erect, with hands lightly clasped behind their backs, while keeping an eye on the scene. Patrons on benches nearby stopped whatever it was they were doing. Nick trembled.

"We wuz just talkin', Tone," I managed to say. Tony glared at me and then leaned toward Nick. "I see ya with her again, I'll break your face."

"I . . . swear . . . I didn't . . . know," Nick said.

"Now ya do," Tony said, and he thrust his arms forward, sending Nick flying. His legs pumped frantically to and fro as he tried to gain his balance, but it was futile. His skates came out from under him and he crashed on his back to the wood floor. No one moved as he moaned and rolled onto an elbow, head down.

Tony flexed his shoulders, put his hands on his hips, and smirked while eyeing the scene beneath him. "Get those fuckin' skates off and wait for me outside," he said without looking at me, and then headed toward the manager's office.

I made my way to a bench, changed my shoes in a hurry, and headed to the exit without making eye contact with anyone. I glanced back and saw Nick's buddies escorting him off the rink.

Tony's bike was on the sidewalk right outside the door. I considered leaving but stood next to it with my hands below my waist, holding the straps of my bag, and my head lowered. I didn't know what to think.

Tony strode out of the rink a couple of minutes later and lifted my chin with a finger. "I told ya not ta go hangin' around with friends," he said, and then gave me a peck on my lips.

I looked away. "Jeez, Tone, it was only skating," I said.

"That's how trouble starts."

I faced him. "There wasn't any trouble until you showed up."

He placed his hands on my shoulders and looked at me. "Are ya my girl, or ain't ya?" I hesitated, captivated once more by those damned azure eyes.

"I guess," I said as I looked down.

"What's that supposed ta mean?"

"I didn't hear from you for days, so I went out."

Tony crossed his arms. "Are ya or ain't ya? I gotta know."

I looked into his eyes again for a long moment. "Yes."

"Okay then," he said. "I want ya home soze I know where ta find ya."

"You didn't seem to have any trouble locating me."

"I told ya, I know people." He didn't have to tell me. I had seen it everywhere we had been together, at the feast, at Platinum, and at the movies, where an usher waved us in without our paying. Tony smiled and put an arm around my waist. "Now hop on. I'm takin' ya shoppin'." He swung a leg over the seat and I climbed behind him. "But I gotta make a quick stop first," Tony said as the bike roared to life.

Having been initiated previously, I was more comfortable on the motorcycle as Tony sped along the streets. I was also glad that we couldn't talk for a while; I wanted to put the incident behind me and collect myself. I felt real bad about what had happened to Nick and vowed that I wouldn't give any other guy an opening that would lead to harm. After a few minutes, the cool, stiff wind in my face blew my thoughts away and I was able to just enjoy the exhilarating ride until Tony pulled up in front of Café Sicily and shut the engine off. "Wait here," he said as he got off the bike. "I gotta see someone about sumthin'."

I remained straddled on the bike and crossed my arms. There was nothing else to do while I waited except think, and my vacant mind was soon filled with thoughts. Everyone knew Café Sicily was Tino Priganti's place, so it wasn't a stretch to figure Tony was meeting him or his son Vin there. That took care of the "someone" part of Tony's statement. The "sumthin'" part was another matter. It could be legitimate, I thought. Maybe it had to do with the construction union that Tony and his pals were part of. A moment later, when I took note of the two rotund men in black suits and slicked-black hair who were leaning against the tan stucco wall fifteen feet away, smoking cigarettes and taking turns talking into each other's ear, I started to think otherwise. When two more dark-suited, swarthy men with weathered, pockmarked faces got out of a Cadillac and entered the restaurant through its smoked-glass doors, I concluded Tony's meeting must have had something to do with the radio "business" he talked about at Platinum. And I thought about that next.

I figured if I were to go on with Tony, I would have to reconcile that with what he and his cohorts did that was outside of the law. His "business" probably included more than radios whose origin was suspect. I wrestled with what that meant—about Tony and about us. I didn't get a thrill like a lot of Bensonhurst girls did from being around hot merchandise and the men who trafficked in it. And I didn't necessarily approve of such low-level crime. But I came down on the side that Tony was just a product of his environment and of an upbringing that might have been more deficient than my own. At least I had Grandma to keep me motivated in the right direction, I thought. Neither of his parents had struck me as a winner and maybe Tony had no one. I felt that as long as he kept his "business" on the lower end of the crime spectrum, limited to the kinds of vices that almost everyone in Bensonhurst either ignored or participated in in some way, then I guessed I could live with it. And maybe when I got across that bridge I would, indeed, show Tony another way to rise above the Brooklyn streets.

To me, it always came back to the struggle to make something of oneself, and I was sure Tony felt the same. It was just that he was going about it another way, and who was I to judge? He was young, strong—not to mention gorgeous—and deserved a better life, too, and he was entitled to make his own decisions about how to get it. He had his faults, his rough edges, such as I witnessed that day, but upon reflection, I felt those would be overcome when he achieved the success he sought. Just as Nick would overcome his hurt pride, the only real injury he had suffered.

The two overweight men in dark suits had shot me a look once or twice as I sat atop the Harley but otherwise ignored me. I felt safe with them around. Protecting women and staying away from another Brooklyn Boy's girl was part of the Italian code that governed Bensonhurst. It might've been overdone at times, but the territoriality that such men exhibited struck me as quaint. A girl, particularly one with not much to her name, couldn't help being flattered by it, even though it might shock her from time to time.

I glanced at the smoked-glass doors that reflected the late-afternoon sunlight. I couldn't help thinking that all of us in Bensonhurst were a reflection of the neighborhood in one way or another. The nerds symbolized the buildings and social fabric that had been the same for generations; the wannabes stood for the striving that every immigrant group brought with them to America; the mobsters, despite their ways, represented the independent attitude that was required if one refused to be under someone else's thumb.

And what about me? I wondered then. What did I reflect? A little bit of everything, I concluded. Grandma had instilled tradition and propriety in me that I still respected, I strove to belong—not to the local crowd, but to another group that lived in the real world in Manhattan—and I sure as hell was independent, albeit in a different way than the mobsters were. So maybe I hadn't given Bensonhurst enough credit, I thought, just as I had thought earlier that I hadn't given my classmates enough of a chance. Maybe it's all part of growing up, I reasoned, just as having a real relationship was.

I glanced again at the restaurant doors. I couldn't wait for Tony to come out. The truth was, after I hadn't seen him for three days, my body tingled at the prospect of spending the rest of the evening with him. My heart skipped a beat when I saw him burst through the entrance.

I frowned when Tony neared and I saw his narrowed eyes and tight lips. He mounted the Harley without saying a word and I saw his biceps tense as he squeezed the handles with his powerful hands. He hesitated a moment. "Fuckin' bullshit," he said as he slammed a fist on the handlebars. The two men outside who had watched Tony when he came out smiled before turning away. Tony flexed his shoulders a couple of times before he turned the ignition key. The engine roared to life. I wrapped my arms around his waist and rested my chin on his shoulder.

"You all right?" I asked. Tony turned his head toward me.

"Yeah. I just didn't get everything I came for and then they stuck me with some more shit." I squeezed his midsection. "Let's get the hell outta here," he said, and we sped off.

My eyes widened and my heart raced when Tony pulled up to Sugar, took my hand, and led me to the door of the shoe store that I had never dared to enter. The prices on the imported Italian shoes were so exorbitant that I knew I couldn't afford even the least expensive pair. And I knew that if I went into the place I would have to try on a few pairs, would fall in love with all of them, and then would suffer the disappointment and embarrassment of walking out without buying anything. So why bother? I had resigned myself to the vicarious enjoyment, accompanied by a touch of envy, of seeing the kick-ass heels on Janice and the other girls whose boyfriends or parents favored them with such an extravagance.

"Summer Breeze" by Seals and Crofts played in the background as we entered, and Stella Mangioni, the striking woman who owned the store, came over to Tony. Her straight, thick, black hair with a cut that angled back from below her chin framed her face. There wasn't a strand out of place. Stella's lilac jumpsuit clung to her body as if it had been painted on, it was unzipped far enough to expose her ample cleavage, and its tight belt accentuated her nonexistent waist. She didn't need the heavy makeup she had on her face, I thought. She wore the four-inch black pumps with thin straps that were featured in the display window as the newest arrival.

Stella eyed me for an instant before resting a hand on Tony's upper arm. "What can I do for ya today, Tony?" Stella asked as she chewed gum, her face aglow.

"Let's start with what you're wearin'," Tony responded after his eyes traveled from her lips to her shoes. "This is my girl, Samantha."

"Pleased ta meet ya, doll," Stella said, her gum cracking. "Any friend a Tony's is a friend a mine. I'll have Lisa show ya all the latest." Stella turned back to Tony. "Can we get youse espresso or cappuccino?"

"Two espressos," Tony said, and then he led me to the

padded, chrome-framed chairs next to the front window. I wanted a cappuccino but didn't say anything as we sat down. Nothing was going to ruin the thrill, I decided, and I mouthed the words of the song as I waited.

> *Summer breeze makes me feel fine,*
> *Blowin' through the jasmine in my mind . . .*

I was in my glory as boxes that were prettier than any shoes I owned were set on the floor in front of me. The different pastel-colored papers that wrapped the shoes were like petals as Lisa unfolded them to reveal each pair, which sparkled in the store's overhead spotlights. When she showed me a pair of slate gray, closed-toe heels, I caressed the soft leather before Lisa slipped them on my feet. I stood and modeled them from every angle in the low mirror.

"They flatter you," Lisa said.

"They're a bit tight."

"I'll get you the next size," the perky salesgirl said as she sprang from her knees and headed for the stockroom. I sat, slipped the shoes off, and then leaned back with my arms stretched atop the armrests and inhaled the ambience that would stay with me for a long time. I curled my toes in the thick, purple carpet. Once more, I felt like a queen.

"This is better than some dumb skating party, huh?" Tony smirked. The events of an hour before had faded with all the excitement of what I had been doing.

"Sure," I said. "It beats anything else there is to do after school." Except maybe my writing, I reminded myself. But a girl could be forgiven if she was spending her time in Sugar.

Tony put an arm across the back of my chair and leaned close to my ear. "We'll see about that," he breathed. The tingling from Saturday night had yet to cease. I blushed.

"I meant things like cheerleading," I said as Tony rested

back in his chair. That was something I had always wanted to do but couldn't.

"I don' want no jocks puttin' moves on ya. You're either home or wid me. *Capisce?*"

"I understand, Tone. I can't afford the uniforms anyways and the time away from my schoolwork."

"Duzzint matter. Anyone even looks at ya, he wouldn't be able to play football or do much of anythin' else for a while."

I sighed. "I know, Tone. I got it," I said as Lisa returned.

I could have stopped after trying on ten pairs of shoes, but Tony wasn't satisfied until Lisa had shown me double that amount. When she was finished, I slumped in my chair. I never knew how exhausting shopping like that could be, the standing and sitting and the walking and posing. Not to mention trying to decide which pair I wanted most. It was overwhelming.

"Which one should I wrap up?" Lisa asked me, her hands resting on her thighs as she knelt before us.

"She'll wear the black number with just straps out of the store, and we'll take the ones Stella's wearin' and the dark gray pair," Tony said as he stood up and reached into his pants pocket. *Three* pairs! I exclaimed silently. Who cared if he made the decision for me? Tony pointed to the beat-up wedges I had come in with. "An' throw those out," he said.

Lisa slipped the new shoes on my feet and gathered the other selections as Tony peeled off six hundred-dollar bills from the wad in his hand with less hesitation than I would part with singles. He slipped the money into Lisa's hand as she stood. "Thanks for everythin'," he said, and then he tucked a folded fifty into the small, slanted pocket of her black mini-skirt. "That's a little sumthin' for ya," he added.

"You're the best, Tony," Lisa gushed before taking my shoes to the counter. I never took my eyes off the boxes as she slid them into a custom-made shopping bag.

"Ya like what ya bought?" Tony asked.

I hadn't bought a thing, I thought, but that's the way Brooklyn Boys were with their women. "You kidding? I can't wait to show them to Janice."

"You blow her away without them," Tony said. He slipped an arm around my waist and leaned toward my ear once more. "We'll hit Voga for a coupla pair of Sergio Valentes before I get ya home," he whispered.

"Tony!" I exclaimed.

"You can't be walkin' in them shoes wid doze ragged jeans a yours."

I smiled from ear to ear as I relished the thought of strolling the two blocks to the contemporary fashion store with the distinctive purple bag swaying by my side for all to see. I wouldn't have minded walking all the way home with a bag in each hand, I chuckled to myself. But I didn't want to take advantage of Tony's generosity. "You've done enough already, Tone," I said. Despite my best intentions, it didn't sound convincing, not that it would have mattered anyway.

"I'll tell ya when we're done."

"Okay, whatever you say." I really didn't mind agreeing with him. I had only one decent pair of jeans. I wore them every day at school and then washed them on Saturdays so they'd be ready for the following week. Mom had only bought me two pair, which I alternated from week to week.

"Ya better get useta this," Tony said. "It's how it's gonna be from now on."

And that's how it was.

9

I was invigorated the next day and threw myself into my schoolwork until lunchtime in the cafeteria, when I had a chance to reflect without splitting my attention.

Seeing Tony made everything right in my world again. I had my ambition and my drive and my writing, but it just seemed to me that he completed the picture. His attention was almost as intoxicating as he was and I found myself seeking more of it. I wouldn't neglect my work at the typewriter, I knew, but I couldn't deny, either, that a sexy, mysterious boyfriend interested me a great deal. I could still taste the long, deep kisses he gave me on the Harley when he dropped me off after shopping at Voga.

I rubbed the denim of my new blue jeans and stared through the cafeteria window. The fact that Tony had kissed me right under my apartment window, when the approaching dusk provided enough light to see what we were doing if anyone wanted to—and in Bensonhurst there were plenty of interested eyes peering between cracks in curtains and from the edges of blinds—told me he didn't care if the whole world knew what we had. It gave me goose bumps.

If Mom or Grandma had seen anything, neither said so. They had plenty to say, however, about the two shopping bags in my hands when I walked in, the usual cautions about Brooklyn Boys and their ways. I should not be taken in by the extravagances they shower their girlfriends with, they said. There was nothing said about the wonder of a new relationship that was real and exciting and promising. Grandma would have been more willing to share my enthusiasm if Tony were Jewish, but I knew Mom would have said the same things she did no matter who or what he was. Her bitterness wouldn't allow her to consider the possibility of a fulfilling relationship. As they were women, however, they couldn't resist pawing the merchandise from Sugar and Voga. I chuckled when I recalled that.

"I like that article on dating you're developing," Mr. Wainright said to me. I hadn't noticed his taking the adjacent seat. I turned toward him. His hands were clasped behind his neck as he leaned back in the plastic chair, and he had a broad smile on his face.

"Really?" I asked.

"Yup. Could be a whole series. But you'll have to give me more about what's going on in that heart of yours, not just your head."

"More of the agony and aching you've talked about?"

"You got it. Like Gene Fowler said, 'All you do is stare at a blank sheet of paper until drops of blood form on your forehead.'" Mr. Wainright slid his chair back. "That's when you know you got it right."

"I'll keep that in mind," I said, and then he stood up and surveyed the room before locating the next student he would counsel. I turned my attention to my garden salad and thought some more. I had plenty of new material to get my blood flowing.

The scene at Outer Skates replayed in my mind. There was no excuse for Tony's behavior but maybe there was a reasonable explanation for it. It just came back to the baggage one carried in Bensonhurst. I knew Tony was smart enough to unload it; it was just going to take a while. In the meantime, I reminded myself not to create any opportunities for him to flex his muscles—literally or figuratively. Over time, he'd adopt the more refined behavior of the real world across the bridge that the shoes he bought me represented.

I looked down at another old pair of shoes on my feet and wished I could have worn a kick-ass pair of new ones that just weren't appropriate there. I thought about Platinum and the other fancy places Tony was sure to bring me and I pictured myself gliding across dance floors and plush carpets in them. I imagined the dresses from Vittorio's I'd be wearing. And then I thought about Tony's wad of cash.

How did he have so much money? I wondered. But I knew the answer and I reminded myself I had already reckoned with it. He had told me just before he sped off that he had something real important to do with the guys. I knew there was no construction business at that hour, unless it was picking up equipment from locked work sites. I also knew that whatever it was must have had something to do with Tony's meeting at Café Sicily. I decided that his "business" would be just one more piece of baggage that would be flung over the railing as we crossed the span together.

The hope I felt then reminded me of Our Lady of Guadalupe. I decided I'd have enough time after school to drop by before heading over to Janice's for one of our hangout sessions.

The church looked as it always did when I stopped in, serene and almost empty, and I sat in the same last row. But my feelings were different, as they always were each time I entered the sanctuary. It was as if I could sense new growth of my spirit with each visit. I liked the way I felt in those surroundings and promised to make a better effort to show up more often. When I saw Father Rinaldi heading toward me, I swore I would.

"Nice to see you, Sam," he said as he leaned over from the aisle.

"You, too, Father."

"Slide over and we'll talk," Father Rinaldi said. I shifted along the polished wood and he sat next to me with one hand on the back of the pew in front of us and his other arm resting on the seat back behind me. "How are things?"

"Real good," I said, and wondered why it was that Father Rinaldi smelled so good. His inexpensive aftershave was distinctive and pleasant on him, and I savored it for an instant. Just before I continued speaking, I concluded that it was his purity inside that made it so. "I'm blessed."

"Happy to hear that. Mom and Grandma okay?"

"The same."

"I guess that's good as well. Grandma is still with us, and Mom could be worse. Right?"

"Yes, Father."

"How's the writing coming along?" I perked up as I always did whenever that topic was broached. "Better than ever," I said. I chose not to go into specifics about the new material and inspiration Tony was providing.

A white-haired, stooped woman acknowledged Father Rinaldi as she shuffled up a side aisle and he nodded toward her before continuing. "So. You have a new boyfriend," he said. I was sure it wasn't just my glow that gave me away. Father Rinaldi knew everyone and everything in our corner of Bensonhurst. He would have been in the mob if he hadn't chosen another path, I surmised as I looked into the priest's face.

"Tony," I said, wide-eyed.

"The strapping young blond man."

"Yes!"

"The same man who cuffed a boy around at Outer Skates yesterday."

I braced myself. "Yes."

"And that's the type of person you should be with, my child?"

"He's just like everybody else, Father. Only different, too. You'll see."

Father Rinaldi paused as he surveyed his domain. "I see a lot." I lowered my head and he shifted his arm behind me, placed his hand on my shoulder, and gently squeezed. I felt more secure then than I did on the Harley in front of Café Sicily the day before. That wasn't surprising to me. Not only was Father Rinaldi a man of God, but he had been born and raised in Bensonhurst. "And I hear even more," he continued. I decided I would be totally honest with him no matter what he asked. I had nothing to hide, anyway, I said to myself. "I don't know why you should be at a place like Café Sicily. There's nothing for you there."

I looked at the priest again. "We just stopped for a minute, Father."

"A minute can change someone's life. Remember Judas." I didn't know a lot about scripture, but I knew about Christ's traitor, who regretted his act a moment after he did it. "It cost him his soul," Father Rinaldi finished.

"He had to see someone there, is all," I offered. "Something about work."

Father Rinaldi glanced at my jeans. I was happy then that I didn't have on any new heels. "And what might that work be?" he asked.

"Construction."

"Nothing wrong with good, hard work, Samantha. Makes us better people. Christ Himself was a carpenter."

"I know, Father."

"And you sure labor over your typewriter, don't you?" Father Rinaldi asked.

He did know everything. I smiled to myself. "That's for sure," I said.

"But are you sure Tony isn't mixed up in easy money?" My honesty was being tested, I thought.

"I don't really know," I said. Which was the truth; I had seen and heard some things, but none of it had amounted to very much. Regardless, it didn't have anything to do with me.

We sat back in silence for a few moments. The stuff about radios might have been all bluster and boasting for all I really knew. Not an uncommon trait for many men in Bensonhurst. Even if Tony had his hands on hot merchandise now and then, that was just reality, I thought. It was what was and what had been for generations. Not my reality, not Manhattan reality, and certainly not Father Rinaldi's reality, but reality just the same. For a lot of Brooklyn Boys, that would be their reality until their dying days, and it would be passed on to their off-spring. Such boys didn't have God in close support as a priest did, nor the towers and cables that, at that moment, I thanked the Lord I had. Father Rinaldi would reach out to save as many as he could, I knew. That was his hard work. Mine was getting across a bridge and taking Tony with me.

Father Rinaldi turned toward me again. "I don't like a lot about what I hear," he said. "I don't want you to get hurt, Sam."

My eyes met his. "I won't, Father," I said. I was too smart for that, I knew.

"I have faith in you, child," Father Rinaldi said, and I followed his glance toward the statue of Mary far off in the front of the church. "And I have faith that our Blessed Mother will watch over you."

I knew, as well, that She would.

"You're percolating, Sam!" Janice said as we sat with legs tucked under us atop her bedspread.

"I guess it's been obvious to everyone," I replied.

"Nothing wrong with that. Enjoy."

"Well, I don't enjoy everything about Tony," I said.

"Yeah, I heard about the rink. Richie said that guy had it comin' to 'im."

"Not at all," I said, remembering Nick's bruised ego and body. "Christ, we were jus' talkin'."

"Then be careful who ya talk to," Janice said with a chuckle.

"I'm serious, Jan. There was nuthin' goin' on other than friendly conversation. Can't a girl have that?"

"Not with boys. If you're serious about Tony, that is."

"I found out about that. Big-time."

"Better get used to how you have to behave. It's not hard once you get the hang of it," Janice said, and then rubbed my jeans. "Just like it ain't hard to get used to having nice things."

We both chuckled. "Wait 'til you see the shoes!" I said, forgetting for a moment that Janice had a closet full of Sugar styles. "My God!"

"It's just the start, believe me. It seems like every time I see Richie he's got somethin' for me or gives me serious cash to shop."

I decided not to hurt my best friend's feelings by asking if her boyfriend was still trying to make up for the beating he gave her. I glanced around Janice's bedroom, which was half the size of my apartment. "I don't know where I'll keep the stuff," I said. "I share a closet with Grandma and we're out of space as it is."

"You'll figure something out," Janice said, and then twirled her new, diamond-chip-studded gold necklace. "Besides, jewelry fits anywhere."

"That kind of stuff is a long way off for me, I'm sure."

"I'm not," Janice said, and then shifted onto an elbow. "So how'd your mom react when she saw your swag?"

"With the usual skepticism," I said as I reclined on my side as well. "Gram was more neutral, but her frown made her feelings an open book." I decided I'd keep Father Rinaldi's comments to myself.

"Speaking of books, how's yours comin' along?"

"The new chapters are practically writing themselves," I said, and we laughed aloud together.

"I want to see them as much as your shoes," Janice said. "Ya really know what you're doin', Sam."

I perked up. "My school stuff's clicking, too."

"What are you working on?"

"A series on dating."

"Seems to me that'll write itself, too, huh?" Janice asked, and we giggled together once more as we had done for two years.

Janice was right, I thought, as I rode the subway home. There weren't any writing blocks for me over the previous couple of weeks. My hand had raced across my journal with all sorts of new material about Brooklyn Boys, about relationships, about the excitement of discovery . . . and about the thrills of melting in a man's arms. I couldn't wait for the next installment.

"Any calls?" I asked Mom and Grandma when I came through the door.

"What, no kiss?" Grandma asked, sitting on the couch with her feet in a tub of hot water.

"Sorry, Gram," I said, and leaned over to give her a quick buss on the cheek.

Mom sat on the other end of the couch and ran the fingers of both hands through her hair. She actually looked good for a change, wearing a short-sleeved white cotton blouse and three-quarter yellow slacks. And there was some life in her eyes, too. Grandma must have kept close tabs on her today, I thought.

Mom looked at my face and saw the want of an answer to my question. "That boyfriend of yours called," she droned, "but said there was no message."

I did my best to hide my disappointment. And then I was struck by the thought of how much Mom had talked to Tony. Did she try to pry? I wondered. Did she make any cracks? I decided I wouldn't go down that road. It wasn't worth it. "What's for dinner?" I asked, but what I really wanted to know was what Tony wanted.

"Blintzes and latkes," Grandma said.

I looked at her varicose veins and gnarled feet. "You didn't have to go through all that trouble," I said. "I would've cooked."

"Who knew when you'd be here," Mom cracked as she rose and headed for the kitchen.

Grandma gave me a wink. "She's always where she's supposed to be, isn't that right, my Samelah?"

"That's right, Gram," I said, and knelt in front of her. "And right now, I'm supposed to give your legs and feet a nice massage."

"Oh, no. I'm fine," Grandma said with no conviction in her voice.

"I know you are," I said as I grabbed a towel and started to dry her feet. "But we'll kill some time while Mom gets dinner on the table."

Grandma stroked my hair as I ministered to her. "You're so beautiful," she said. "It's no wonder every boy wants my granddaughter."

"I only want one, Gram."

"I know, I know. Don't worry, he'll call back."

"I know he will," I said.

Grandma leaned forward and whispered, "Remind me later to give you the money I won at bingo."

"You don't have to do that, Grandma."

"Hush, child. If you're gonna be out socializing, I want for you to have a few spare dollars in your pocketbook."

I hugged Grandma's legs and rested my cheek on her knees. "You're the best, Gram," I said.

Later, halfway through dinner at the kitchen table, the ringing phone jarred me. I resisted the urge to spring to the receiver. I let Mom pick it up. "Hello," she said, standing in the doorway, and listened while she lit a cigarette. "No," Mom started, taking a drag. "We can't do anything at this time," she finished, and then hung up.

"Who was it?" Grandma asked as Mom returned to her seat, beating me to the punch.

"The church," Mom said.

"What did they want?" Grandma asked. Who cares? I thought. If it wasn't Tony, it didn't matter to me.

"A donation," Mom said as she stubbed her cigarette.

"Typical," Grandma muttered.

"And the Jews are any different?" Mom asked.

I tuned them out for the next few minutes. That story was already written, I thought. The one with Tony was just beginning and my family had no idea that I passed the time as they bickered pondering my boyfriend. When their argument escalated, I was jolted from my reveries. "Can't we just have a peaceful meal?" I sighed as I put my fork down and looked from one to the other.

"We're just talking, Sammy," Grandma said. Sure, I said to myself. And I know what just talking can lead to. "Now finish your food before it gets cold."

"I will, so long as you two don't give me any agita," I said.

"We can't upset our baby's tummy now, can we, Joanie?" Grandma asked playfully with a nod toward her daughter. She always had a way to lighten the mood, and I was grateful to pass the rest of the meal with idle chatter. Then I rushed to do the dishes. I wanted to be finished before Tony called back and avoid the grief I'd be given because of an unfinished chore. Mom went into the living room with a box of hair dye while Grandma took her time standing up. "You'll watch some TV with us?" she asked.

"I've got some work to catch up on, Gram," I said as I started the hot water. "I'm on deadline."

"Then go," Grandma said as she shuffled toward the sink with stooped shoulders. "I'll clean up."

"You sit down," I said over my shoulder. "This won't take me long."

"God bless you, Sammy," Grandma said as she detoured to the living room.

I made quick work of the dishes and then went to my desk, which had been calling to me the whole time. Each key of the typewriter that I struck at my small desk moved both the piece I was writing and time along. When I took a break and checked the clock at eleven thirty, I couldn't believe how fast the evening had gone. Mom and Grandma must have fallen asleep on the couch, I supposed, which was why I hadn't been interrupted. Tony must have been tied up and couldn't phone back. As I put my papers away and straightened my desk, I regretted having missed his call earlier. I wanted to take his voice to bed with me.

10

I wasn't happy the next morning about not hearing from Tony, but I was more than satisfied with the dating article I turned in first thing at school. Satisfaction turned to thrill when Mr. Wainright came up to me during lunch and said it was good enough to show to a couple of his friends in magazine and book publishing. And I knew where those people would be—in the real world of Manhattan!

"Don't get overly excited, Samantha," he said after breaking the news. "You've got potential, but you'll have to produce a lot more, and get better every day."

"I'm willing to do whatever it takes," I replied.

"I trust you will."

"You can count on me, Mr. Wainright," I told him as he walked away. I was so excited and distracted with consideration of the possibilities that I couldn't take another bite of my usual salad. I positively floated through the rest of the school day.

By the time I burst out of the school doors I was bursting inside. I just couldn't wait to spread the news to Grandma and Janice. Even Tony would be proud of me, I thought as I skipped along the sidewalk to the curb. I couldn't help perking up my ears and scanning a wide area in search of him while

I located my school bus. When my hopes went unfulfilled, I headed toward the open yellow doors.

Two short honks in rapid succession attracted my attention. I stopped and checked the area once more, but couldn't identify the source of the horn among the usual array of sports cars and luxury sedans that awaited some of my more fortunate classmates. I started toward my bus once more.

When the honks repeated, something told me they were for me and I stopped again but with more determination. Wedged between two buses that were behind mine was a champagne-colored Eldorado convertible with its top up and I peered through the windshield. My heart skipped a beat when I saw Tony behind the wheel and my excitement doubled. I smiled and went to the passenger side, my lips widening with each step. I stooped to peer through the open window.

"Get in," Tony said through pursed lips as he stared straight ahead.

I decided to postpone telling him the news that all but sprang from my mouth. I wondered what was up as I kept my words in check, but that couldn't quell my bubbling inside. "This is a real treat, Tone," I said as I sank into the leather bucket seat. "Is this yours?"

Tony didn't answer right away. Instead, he poked his head out his window and jerked a U-turn onto Eighteenth Avenue just in front of oncoming cars that didn't honk or take any evasive action. And no curses or vulgarities emanated from any of them, either. U-turns and double-parking were common in Bensonhurst, as I and everyone else there knew, and no one thought twice about such violations. They were even invisible to cops, who looked the other way or would have felt ashamed if they ticketed anyone for such insignificant offenses. Cops in Bensonhurst were either on the mob payroll or in search of bigger prey.

"It's Vin's," Tony said in a monotone after the rocking

Cadillac settled on its course. I was dying to ask why he had the car, but those words were stillborn as well. Instead, I focused on the familiar buildings that were whizzing by.

"You in a hurry to get someplace?" I asked.

Tony's massive hands choked the padded, tan leather-wrapped steering wheel. "I've got to pick up my pain-in-the-ass sister from school and drop her at a friend's," Tony said without taking his eyes off the road. Which was a good thing, I thought as I angled my eyes and stole a glance at the speedometer.

I didn't know what I could do to calm Tony down. There was no stopping a Brooklyn Boy when he got his macho up. I wished the radio were on so some songs could dispel some of the thick air around me. I resigned myself to savoring Mr. Wainright's news by myself until whatever it was blew over, and I attempted some casual conversation instead. "What's her name?" I asked. Tony hadn't talked much about his family other than repeating that they were mine, too.

"Brat," Tony scoffed.

"C'mon," I said.

Tony wheeled into a narrow side street without applying the brakes. "You'll see," he said, oblivious to the startled, reproving faces of the old women on the sidewalks and stoops who were a blur as we sped by. "A typical spoiled twelve-year-old who does nuttin' but pout and complain," Tony continued. "Everyone just ignores the fat bitch."

I looked at my agitated boyfriend. "What's the matter, Tone? You all right?"

Tony tightened his grip on the wheel again. "The fact ya don' know makes it worse."

"What the hell are you talkin' about?" I asked as Tony screeched to a halt in front of a middle school, drawing more reproving snarls from mothers and crossing guards gathering in front. He slammed the gearshift into park and leaned toward me as he rested an elbow on the armrest. I recoiled against the door as I looked at his contorted face.

"I told ya I wanna know where you are, and the *next* fuckin' day ya disappear!"

My upbeat mood was deflated and my fanciful thoughts about writing that I had longed to share with Tony were dashed and in danger of drifting out of the open window behind me. How could he make me feel so good just a couple of days before, I wondered, and then torment me the next time I saw him? I lowered my head. "Christ, Tone," I said. "I didn't disappear. All I did was stop at Janice's." The small lie didn't bother me. Mentioning Father Rinaldi wasn't going to help matters. I searched his face for the softness I knew was buried somewhere in him. "I was home by dinner."

Tony sat back in his seat and looked over my shoulder, eying the stream of students exiting the school. "Ya jes' don' get it, do ya?" he asked as his gaze returned to me. "What it means to be my girl."

I did but I didn't want to. I do know what it means, I told myself. Something special that stirred me in my body and my mind. Being with Tony had become part of a future I had envisioned for myself. I had always struggled to keep my hopes and dreams alive; how much of a struggle was it going to be to keep a new dream alive that included him? I wondered. How long would it be until Tony would be ready to begin another life with me? "She's my best friend, Tony," I said, and thought about that for a second. "My only friend."

"Ya got me."

"She's a girl friend, Tone."

"All ya need is me."

"Look," I said as I squirmed in my seat. "You've got the guys, right?"

"That's diff'rent. You'll see Janice when everybody gets together."

I knew I'd do an awful lot for my relationship with Tony, but sacrificing Janice wasn't going to be part of it. "I like hangin' out with her, just the two of us. What's the harm us bein' close?"

"The harm is ya not where's ya supposeta be," Tony said, and then he pointed to a short girl with black, matted hair whose midsection rolls strained against her tight red polyester T-shirt. "There's Katrina. We'll finish this later."

Tony's sister ambled toward the Cadillac and bent over outside my window. "Jailbait" was written in glittered script across the front of her shirt. "Who's this?" Katrina scoffed.

"Jus' get in back," Tony ordered. Katrina opened the door and I leaned forward while she squeezed behind my seat. Tony eased the car away from the curb.

"Why do I haveta ride in the back?" Katrina moaned as she slumped into the leather, shoulders hunched.

"Shut the fuck up, willya?" Tony said. Katrina pouted and looked out her window.

Regardless of her attitude, I wanted to smooth the way. Hell, I thought, she was the first member of his family I had met and I was determined to get off on the right foot. I turned around to face her. "I'm Samantha," I said. "It's nice to meet you."

"Yeah, right," Katrina said without looking at me.

"How's school goin'?" I asked.

"What's it to ya?" Katrina snarled. I gave up and turned around.

"Be nice to my girl, Katrina," Tony said as he negotiated a turn.

"What for?" she responded. "You'll have a new one soon enough." Tony jerked the car to the side of the street and twisted toward his sister with his foot pressed against the brake pedal. "Behave yourself or you'll be hoofin' it to Becky's," Tony growled. "I mean it."

Katrina kept her gaze fixed outside the window. "Whatever," she muttered.

Tony turned around and pulled away. "Sam's a part of our family now," he said. Katrina turned her head toward the front.

"We'll see about that," she said. "Dad's too zoned out to care one way or the other, but Mom'll sure have something to say about it."

"Mom's gonna love Sam, Katrina," Tony said, "and ya can jus' keep your sour opinions ta yaself."

I wondered what had caused a bitter disposition in such a young girl. Over time, I felt, we'd grow closer and I'd find out, and maybe then she'd be more receptive to me. Maybe then I could help her.

Katrina's mentioning their parents led me to thinking about them. Janice had only met them briefly a couple of times when she and Richie stopped by to hook up with Tony. All she had said to me was that Philip Kroon seemed like a lost soul and Pamela was your typical middle-aged Bensonhurst wannabe who died her dark hair blond and wore tight-fitting clothes. I'd see for myself at some point, I reasoned.

Tony pulled up in front of a well-kept two-family house and leaned across me to open my door. Katrina pressed the back of my seat into me, causing me to hunch over almost to my knees, and exited without saying a word. She headed up the walkway and didn't look back as Tony gunned the motor and took off.

"She's just a typical teenager dealing with her hormones," I said.

"Pay her no mind," Tony said. "She ain't important."

I looked at him as he drove on. "She's your blood, Tone."

"Don't remind me," he said. "What's important is that you an' me are together." Tony glanced at me. "The way it's supposeta be."

I gazed through the windshield and squinted in the

late-afternoon sunlight as I thought about a lot of things that were supposed to be. I was supposed to have a father in my life and a normal relationship with my mother, be better off than I was, and have an uncomplicated relationship with a boyfriend. But I had none of those, and that was just how it was for me on the Brooklyn side of the bridge. I knew the only thing that was completely in my control was my station in life.

As we drove in silence I revived my glee about Mr. Wainright's news. I told myself that I could deal with anything at home or with Tony that came my way as long as I kept my feet moving forward toward the other side of the East River span. I looked through my side window and a tight smile came to my face as I contemplated anew that journey for a minute longer.

"So where we headed?" I asked, turning toward Tony once again.

"Sally's."

I thought that would be a good place for us to finish our earlier conversation. It had been great to be there with Janice, I thought, but it would be even better with Tony. "I love that place," I said.

"I'm meetin' the guys. Ya just get sumthin' ta eat and keep quiet about what we talked about. Save it for when we're alone."

"Sure, Tone," I said, looking at his profile. "You know I want to make you happy."

He grinned for the first time that afternoon. His soft side was returning and I melted. "Yeah, well," Tony said, "I've got some ideas 'bout how ya can do that."

He eased the Cadillac into a vacant space on Eighteenth Avenue and then ignored the meter as he strutted toward the diner. I let myself out and hurried to catch up, slipping an arm around his when I reached his side. Tony thrust the glass door open and headed for the last booth, where Vin Priganti and Richie Sparto were drinking coffee. Tony waited for me to slide into the vacant seat and then plopped beside me.

"Hey," Tony said to his friends with an extended fist.

"Hey," they responded in kind, then nodded toward me.

"Hi," I said.

"How's things?" Richie asked me. I didn't have to look toward Tony before replying. "Great," I said as I thought about Mr. Wainright.

Tony reached across me, grabbed two menus, and dropped one in front of me. "I'm not really hungry, Tone," I said.

"Order sumthin'," he said as he scanned a menu.

I wished I felt like eating as I viewed the selections that I had seldom had the opportunity to enjoy. "Okay," I said after a moment. "Just get me a fruit salad."

Tony closed his menu and slid it past me. "I'm havin' a burger and fries," he said, and looked across the table. "Youse eat already?"

"Sally's holdin' our order," Vin Priganti said. "That thing go okay so far?"

Tony clasped his hands and sat back. "Routine," he said.

Vin glanced at Richie and then faced Tony. "Good," he said as he slumped against the faux red leather. "You're movin' up in my family."

Tony beamed. I wondered what it was going to take to move up in Tony's family. Katrina hadn't been a promising start. "I appreciate that, Vin," Tony said.

Vin crossed his arms. "Everythin's fallin' inta place," he said. "Meet us at Rocco's after you're done." Tony nodded.

Rocco's, owned and run by Janice's father, was one of the neighborhood hangouts. Only for Italians of a certain persuasion, that is. Any nerd or Jew or black person soon found that out upon wandering into the bar. Janice had told me many times of Richie's carousing there. Tony didn't seem like much of a drinker to me, and I didn't know about Vin, but I pictured them puffing their chests in such environments.

"What's da latest with that DJ?" Richie asked Vin as he chewed on his hamburger after the food had arrived.

"Oh, dat *finocchio*? Don' look so good fa him," Vin scoffed, and the guys laughed.

"I haven't seen dat faggot lately," Tony said.

"Don' matter," Vin said. "Somone's gonna do a piece on 'im sooner or later."

The Brooklyn Boys continued talking as if I weren't there. I picked at my fruit until they had finished eating and then everyone stopped outside for a moment. The boys tapped closed fists and Tony and I went back to the Cadillac. I jumped in while he pulled a parking ticket from under the wiper blade. He crumpled it and tossed it into the street before sliding in behind the wheel. His scent wafted toward me.

Tony put the key into the ignition and turned to me before he switched it on. "Listen, Sam," he started, "I don' wanna make a big deal outta how it hasta be between me an' you. I jus' want ya ta do the right thing." He gazed into my eyes. "Unnerstand?"

"Sure, Tone," I said. "But I gotta be able to see Janice. It's not like she doesn't belong." Tony turned away, started the car, and held the wheel for a moment. I could see him thinking. "She dates your best friend, doesn't she?" I said.

Tony switched the radio on and eased the car from the curb. "Ya jus' gotta know how I feel about ya," he said with a measured cadence. "I gotta be able ta find ya when I gotta see ya or hear ya voice."

My eyes lingered on Tony for a moment before I responded. His passion was genuine and I melted once again. It felt good to be close to him. I knew we belonged together and decided we'd just have to get used to each other. Learn to get along like every couple had to. "I'll give you Janice's number. If I'm not there, I'll be home. Okay?"

Tony snapped his chin forward and back. "All right. But dat's it."

I reached for his shoulder. "I promise," I said.

Tony leaned toward me and moved his arm across the burl console. He rested his hand on my knee and squeezed. "I don' wanna hafta talk 'bout dis no more," he said. "Now I gotta drop ya off."

Tony kept his hand on my leg and I felt his touch through my new jeans as we made the short trip to my apartment. It was just a matter of time, I thought. It had only taken a couple of hours for Tony to calm down and for us to renew our connection. Imagine what a year would do, I asked myself. We would get closer and closer while we distanced ourselves from Bensonhurst. I was sure of that.

Tony put the gearshift in park and left the engine running in front of my home. He leaned his upper body across the console, slipped an arm behind my head, and pulled me to his lips. Dusk was still far off but I didn't care about any prying neighborhood eyes, even those belonging to my mother. She would have to deal with things just as I had to do all the time, I reasoned.

Tony locked his lips on mine and probed my mouth with his tongue. All reason left me then, and my legs parted slightly. He slid his left hand over my cotton blouse, spread his thumb and pinkie finger, and pressed them into my nipples. The bolt I felt was followed by a much bigger one when that hand slipped between my thighs. I moaned as our lips parted.

Tony buried his face in my hair and his tongue found my ear. I thrust my chest forward and writhed as he licked and probed. When he stopped, I went limp and felt the wetness left behind as his short breaths bathed my ear. He squeezed the V between my legs and then moved his hand to my thigh. "I . . . tellya . . . ," he groaned, "ya . . . don' know . . . whatya . . . do . . . ta me, Samantha Bonti." There was no mistaking the closeness between us then and I wanted more. A Chicago tune that emanated from the dashboard echoed the way I felt:

If you leave me now, you'll take away the very heart of me . . .

"Do you have to go?" I asked. "It's Friday."

Tony pulled away slowly and slumped in his seat with his eyes closed, his blond hair cradled in the headrest. "Yeah," he sighed. "Seeya later."

"What time?" I asked.

He opened his eyes and turned his head toward me. "I mean whenever."

"Oh," I said, and reached for the door handle. He sat up, grabbed my neck with his strong fingers, pulled me across the console, and held my mouth close to his. "Jus' one more for the road," he murmured. I locked my arms around his neck and my lips around his narrow smile.

I never wanted to let go. But the truth is, I was beginning to wonder why . . .

11

When I turned sixteen in early October, Tony took me to Angelo's in Little Italy and gave me a platinum bracelet—he said it would remind us always of the dance club by the same name. A day later, I took a job at a small bookstore on Eighteenth Avenue. Tony didn't like that and told me he'd give me all the money I needed, but I wanted to help out a little at home and squirrel away a few dollars for my own future.

My life settled into a comfortable routine over the two months that surrounded my birthday. I didn't mind the time I spent at school, where I received positive reinforcement for my writing efforts, and each day brought me closer to the graduation that would be the last step before taking the first one into Manhattan. I also didn't mind the hours after school in the bookstore. Its aura of history and creativity and the feel of a volume cradled in my hand never failed to kindle new reveries of my own future. During quiet moments at work, I'd look around and imagine where among the shelves and displays my book would be.

And I didn't mind, either, the impromptu shopping sprees Tony took me on to the shops on Eighteenth Avenue, and his insistence on my having a standing appointment at Salon D'Belezza, the chicest place in all of Bensonhurst, where Italian women idled away hours to look good for their men. It seemed that Tony took as much pleasure dropping me off there and basking in the admiring glances from the women in every corner as I did from the hours of pampering lavished upon me per his direction.

Other than the couple of times when Tony had made a date in advance, I never knew when I'd see him. He'd show up in his old Toyota or Vin's car at school or at work once in a while and we'd visit the usual haunts. I felt regal whenever I got into and rode in the Cadillac. But I didn't mind the beat-up car; Tony was paying his dues like I was. Besides, it made me feel less embarrassed whenever he was in my welfare apartment.

Tony called most days, but most of the time our conversations were brief. More often than not, he had something or other to do with Vin and Richie and I got to see him maybe two or three times a week. We became regulars at Platinum and other clubs, where he showed the new me off to everyone. It was fantastic to belong to his inner circle and to receive attention from people I hardly knew because of the respect they had for Tony. The times we had not only thrilled me, they supplied fresh material about people and places and relationships, and about how life worked in Bensonhurst. I wished I saw Tony more often, but I had plenty of the usual things to fill my time.

First and foremost was my writing. With each pat on the back I got from Mr. Wainright, on top of the unflagging praise from Janice, my confidence increased and the words seemed to flow from me without difficulty. Alone in my apartment one Friday night in mid-November, I sat back at my desk after a couple of hours of work to ponder things. Grandma had dragged Mom to the movies before Tony had called to inform me during another short conversation that we wouldn't be getting together that evening. We were on for Saturday, however. Tony said he had something to celebrate.

I thought about that in front of my old Smith-Corona. Our special occasions, other than my birthday, had revolved around something in his life such as a nice score or a pat on the back from Vin. I hadn't celebrated once with Tony my hard-fought advancement in writing. When I did bring it up every couple of weeks, he didn't probe or show joy. He did, however, remind me about his friend in publishing a couple of times. I didn't press him for more information about that and I was reluctant to toot my own horn, so I remained content to savor my progress within whenever I was with him.

Although I most wanted to share my writing passion with Tony, I was blessed to have others who took almost as much pleasure in my advancing steps as I did. Grandma was right behind Janice and Mr. Wainright with support, and often gave me a gentle pat on my behind with her words of encouragement. Father Rinaldi always mentioned my blossoming career when we sat in the pew together. I suspected he received regular updates about it from Mr. Wainright when he dropped by for a Saturday confession. I had been an observer at baptisms and First Holy Communions when I chanced upon them at Our Lady of Guadalupe, and although my interest in the Catholic faith kept growing, formal rites such as confession remained beyond my personal experience; my sins, I thought, would be voiced through my writing.

I didn't know if I'd ever be baptized but I did know I'd maintain my connection to the Blessed Mother. That's what I found in Father Rinaldi's church every time I was there, and I intended to keep Her with me always. Father Rinaldi never failed to direct his gaze at the statue of my patron saint at some point during our conversations. The Blessed Mother's hand in my life, I knew, was as real and as close to me as the ones of those dear to me who touched me in my daily life.

I looked at the half-filled page in my typewriter. My dating series had progressed to my satisfaction and had fed my writing passion, with all manner of topics from what to wear and what to say, to what to think and what to feel. But the words on the paper that night were only for my book. They were about the other passion in my life, the one that blossomed every time I was in Tony's arms. My body's responses to his attentions were the physical representation of the stirring I had in my soul. I was a writer, I knew, but I was also a young woman and Tony helped me to know what that felt like.

Sexual contact was a part of every date I had had with him, from a couple of minutes kissing to prolonged petting. I was grateful that Tony hadn't forced the issue of consummation with me and let me set some boundaries. There were a lot of things I wanted him to leave behind, but his respect wasn't one of them. Nor was the softness that his deference bespoke. That's what gave me hope that he was the type of guy who belonged with me on the other side of the river. His business and his irregular hours would be a thing of the past then.

As I gathered my thoughts to write some more that night, I couldn't help but sense the feeling of accomplishment growing inside me, and I marveled about how I had felt differently about some things in only a few short months. My attachment to Tony made my distance from my mother easier to take, and I was more tolerant of her shortcomings. Maybe she sensed my growing independence and its inevitability, too, I thought. And my new life had made me recognize how old my grandma was and how much more I should cherish my time with her. Serious writers always confronted mortality head-on; it was part of the bleeding they had to do, Mr. Wainright had told me. I knew my time with Grandma wouldn't last forever and I vowed to get as much of it on the page as I could.

I had different feelings about writing, too. The satisfaction with my work and the acknowledgment of its merit I received from people who mattered became more important than the material things my career might provide. I had had some fancy meals and expensive gifts bestowed on me by Tony, but they never seemed to mean as much to me as my work did.

I hovered over my typewriter and then thought about the feelings that had remained the same as time went on. Father Rinaldi would never be other than what he was, pure as the halo around the Blessed Mother. And Janice was a constant throughout. We caught up all the time on the phone, and met at Sally's or huddled on her bedspread. Janice and I shared the latest developments and the giggles and hugs that always accompanied them. She took great pleasure in my blossoming as a woman and I didn't know what I'd do without her in my life. Grandma, Mr. Wainright, and Father Rinaldi were wonderful, but it was only with Janice that I could reveal intimate details of my throes of passion, and only she could read the words describing the stirrings within me that Tony engendered.

Despite the occasional volatility in their relationship, Janice and Richie remained connected. They were much farther along as a couple than Tony and I were. I hadn't got past the feeling of dating yet with Tony and it seemed I learned something new from her every time I was with my best friend. That helped me to develop my relationship—and my writing. Janice was far ahead of me with her sexual activity, too, as were most of the Brooklyn girls who were my own age, but she never looked down upon my limited experience and halting steps in that area. Janice said my descriptions of what was going on inside me reminded her of how she had felt when she first started having serious physical contact with a boyfriend. Her tales of intercourse and shared orgasms—things I could only contemplate—showed me how much more growing up I had to do and stirred my imagination about what awaited me.

My fingers edged toward the keyboard and then flitted with renewed zeal from letter to letter as I poured my heart onto the page before me.

✦ ✦ ✦

On Saturday night, I sat in the living room with Mom and Grandma while I waited for Tony to pick me up. When I heard the toot of a familiar horn, I sprang up, grabbed my pocket-book and new leather jacket, and bolted for the door.

"Now he doesn't even bother coming up," Mom snarled, cigarette dangling from her lips. I ignored the crack as my freedom neared, just as I had ignored just about everything she said and did recently. Mom raised her voice. "Why should he? Everyone knows he's turning you into a *puttana*," she said, "right in front of our home."

I kept my thoughts about who was the whore in our family to myself and turned the knob in my hand. "Bye, you two," I said over my shoulder.

"Have fun, *bubelah*," I heard Grandma shout as the door closed behind me. I skipped down the stairs and couldn't help thinking that the chapter of my life that was on the other side of that door was just about closed, too. I jumped into Vin's Cadillac and into Tony's waiting arms. He pulled me to him and embraced me as Van Morrison held my heart in his voice. Tony brushed my hair aside with his fingers and kissed my neck. I felt goose bumps rising all over my body.

Making love in the green grass
Behind the stadium with you
My brown-eyed girl

"Ya smell so good, Samantha Bonti," Tony moaned into my ear. I buried my face in his chest and his own scent enveloped me, sending me adrift as he traced kisses down my neck and back. Tony grabbed my hair and brought my lips to his, and I drank from the well that sustained me when I wasn't with him.

"So what're we celebratin'?" I asked when we pulled away.

"Jus' a little sumthin' I picked up the other day," Tony

said. He was aglow, and it wasn't just from our greeting. "Wait'll ya see."

I couldn't imagine what it could be. Like all Brooklyn Boys, Tony was full of surprises and took pride in showering his girl with extravagant gifts and having them flashed in front of anybody and everybody. But his self-satisfaction that night told me it had nothing to do with me, and I was okay with that. The enjoyment I had seeing him get what he wanted was as much as the pleasure I took in my own attainments, in which Tony didn't show much interest. I knew he would celebrate my fulfillment after he got where he wanted to go.

Tony headed north on Ocean Parkway and then worked his way over to the Red Hook industrial section near the water that separated Brooklyn from Manhattan. "Jus' a quick stop," he said as he turned into a dark street bordered by low warehouses, "and then we'll have the rest of the night to ourselves." I looked forward to the rest of my life with him.

Flashing red and blue lights and sirens pierced the darkness as a police car appeared, seemingly from nowhere, on our bumper and another one sped up the block in front of us to cut us off. Tony veered to the curb, slammed on the brakes, and cut off the ignition. "Don' say nuttin'," he barked as he slumped in his seat and stared straight ahead.

A loudspeaker atop the squad car behind us crackled. "Put your hands on the wheel and don't make a move." I shook as Tony complied.

Two uniformed cops got out of the car in front of us and stood beside it with their guns drawn. The two from the rear car edged along each side of the Cadillac to the windows behind Tony and me. In the side-view mirror I could see an officer leaning forward with a hand on his holster. The one on Tony's side tapped his window with a nightstick. Tony's hand moved slowly to the window switch. "What's this all about, Officer?" he asked as the glass disappeared.

"Shuddup and get outta the car," the cop replied, adjusting his grip on his holstered gun. "Real slow." Tony opened his door and slid out of the Cadillac. "You, too, Miss," the cop on my side said. My moist, wavering hand pulled the door handle and I almost fell onto the sidewalk when my foot caught the doorjamb as I exited. I stood, trembling, beside the cop and looked across the car at Tony. Father Rinaldi's words echoed in my mind. *And that's the type of person you should be with, my child?*

The officers in front of the Cadillac came forward and searched the vehicle, running their hands under the dashboard, inspecting every storage pocket and rifling through the contents of the glove compartment. When they were finished, the officer on the driver's side popped the trunk and joined his partner at the rear of the Cadillac. "What do we have here?" he announced. He looked around the trunk lid at Tony. "You have a receipt for these, of course," he cracked. Tony didn't respond. "Let's take 'em in," the cop said as he slammed the lid down. The cop next to Tony shoved him against the Cadillac and reached for his cuffs.

"Please turn around, Miss," the cop beside me said with one hand on my shoulder and his other on his handcuffs. On the verge of tears, I lowered my head and did as I was told.

"Let her go, willya?" Tony asked over his shoulder. "She's got nuthin' ta do with this."

"I told ya ta shuddup," the cop behind him said. He slapped the cuffs on Tony's wrists and then Tony and I were led to separate squad cars.

The stale air in the rear seat reeked from years of others who had been there, handcuffed as I was. And if the metal constraints on my wrists weren't clear enough, the locked doors and the heavy metal mesh partition right in front of me told me I was farther from that bridge than ever before.

I never once looked up when I was led from the banged-up blue and white squad car to the front desk at the police station.

Tony was brought in right behind me, and we only had one moment to look into each other's eyes before I was escorted to a small room and then uncuffed by a plainclothes detective. "I'm Detective Quinn," he said as he closed the door. "Take a seat."

I shuffled to a wood chair at a gray metal table. He removed his jacket, slipped it over the back of his chair, rolled up his sleeves, and faced me. Light-colored crew-cut hair sat atop Detective Quinn's round head and splotched, round face. A wrinkled white shirt strained against his midsection and a gun that protruded from a leather holster flapped under his left arm as he placed his hands on the chair back. "Mr. Kroon is being booked and we can keep you here for quite a while," he said.

"I was . . . just . . . on a date," I quivered.

Detective Quinn smiled, straightened, and sat down. "We know that," he said. "We know all about you, Miss Bonti." My brow furrowed as I looked at him. "We've been following Mr. Kroon and his crew for a while. We saw you with him at the feast."

"That's when I met him."

"That's right," Detective Quinn said. He clasped his hands and leaned on the table toward me. "What else can you tell us about Tony and his friends?"

I could have told him a lot about that. About Bensonhurst and Brooklyn Boys, and about the reality of a culture that was sometimes just over the legal line. But I didn't. "Not much," I lied, "we only dated a couple of times."

"Ever see 'im with Richie Sparto or . . ." Detective Quinn started and then leaned close to me. "Vin Priganti?"

I squirmed in my seat. "At Platinum," I said. Dectective Quinn raised an eyebrow. "I didn't drink," I added.

"We'll overlook that for the moment," he said. "They mention anything about their 'Midnight Auto Sales'?"

"I don't know what that is, Detective."

"Traffickin' in stolen parts. Do you have any idea how much was in that trunk?"

I paused for a moment. "No, I don't know anything about that," I said.

"You're sure."

I nodded. "We just hung out and danced, is all," I said.

Detective Quinn stared at me as I shifted in my seat. "We saw you with Father Rinaldi, too," he began after a minute. "Perhaps you should spend more time wid him than wid the likes a Tony Kroon." He slid his chair back and rose. "We'll have a squad car take you home."

Carrying on in a Cadillac in front of my apartment was one thing. Showing up in a police car was another. "Can't I take the subway?" I asked.

Detective Quinn crossed his arms and narrowed his eyebrows. "Yeah, now get outta here."

"Thank you, sir."

"Maybe you should start choosing your boyfriends more wisely. Next time you won't be so lucky."

The express train lights kept making my already red eyes blink tears of fear. There was no denying that Tony, my Tony, might've been not just some Brooklyn Boy, but rather an up-and-coming criminal. But I was not ready to believe such a thing, no way. The thought of it left my mind quickly but still engulfed my heart.

No one was in the living room at home when I entered after eleven. Thank God, I said to myself. I had had enough questions for one night. I wished I could call Janice but didn't want to run the risk of being overheard. Besides, I said to myself, she was probably still out with Richie. I tiptoed down the hallway to my room and undressed in darkness before crawling into bed.

I hadn't stopped thinking about Tony since I left the police station. I stared at the ceiling as I listened to Grandma's low, strained breathing. Her struggle for air, I thought, mirrored the one I had for my future. And Tony's, too. He hadn't had much of a start in life and chose the only one that made sense to him. I had chosen to be with him and had chosen to show him how the baggage that came with his life could be unloaded. That was the way it was, I thought, and turned over on my pillow. I grasped the rosary under it and closed my eyes. Everything's going to be all right, I said to myself.

I was just kidding myself.

12

I awoke before Mom and Grandma early Sunday morning with a pit in my stomach. I got out of bed and went to the kitchen without making any noise, and then dialed Janice's number.

"Janice, it's me," I said when she answered her private line.

"Sam?" she started groggily. "What da fuck time is it?"

"Seven thirty. Sorry I woke you."

"That's okay," Janice said, and I heard her shifting in her bed. "Whatsa matter?"

"You hear what happened last night?"

"No. Richie never showed up."

"The cops busted me and Tony."

"You?!"

"Yeah. Pulled us over in Vin's Cadillac and then took us to the precinct."

"Where'd this happen?"

"Red Hook."

Janice was silent for a moment. "Where are ya now?" she asked.

"Home. They let me go."

"What about Tony?"

"They said they were booking him."

"What for?"

"Stolen auto parts. That's all I know, which is why I called. To see if you knew anything."

Janice paused for a long minute. "I wish I did," she said.

"This ever happen to you?" I asked.

"Yeah," Janice said. "Once. Richie got caught with some hot radios. No big deal."

I knew better. This *was* a big deal. It was apparent that we weren't dating boys who read at the local library, but who robbed, deceived, and did God knows what else. I would keep quiet and shove it under the rug. No matter how stupid it sounded. That seemed to be what I was doing these days.

How serious could it really be? There didn't seem to have been any impact on their lives, as Richie was out and about with the boys and he and Janice did whatever they wanted to do and went wherever they wanted to go. Business as usual in Bensonhurst, I concluded. I wanted to be able to be so calm about such things, as she was, but this was all new to me. The pit in my stomach was still there and my palms were sweaty. "I wish I knew how Tony was," I said.

"Let me make some calls and I'll get back to ya."

"Hurry, willya?"

"Sure," Janice said. "And Sam?"

"What?"

"Don't worry. This is just normal bullshit."

We hung up and I tried to follow her advice. I guessed that what had happened was normal, but normal for who? I figured it was all part of the baggage that would be left behind soon enough. Still, the thought of Tony in a cell troubled me. I occupied myself with putting on a pot of coffee, and when an idea for my next dating article struck me, I pulled out a notepad while I sat at the kitchen table and jotted some tidbits that I would flesh out on my typewriter. When I heard shuffling footsteps half an hour later, I tore the sheets from the pad and slipped them into my robe pocket. No way Mom was up at this hour, I said to myself as I reached for my coffee cup. It had to be Grandma.

"Up so early, Samelah?" she asked at the doorway.

"Yeah," I said as I stood up, then went to hold my grandmother close. I rested my cheek on her shoulder as we hugged. "I wanted to make breakfast today," I said. Grandma stroked the top of my head and then held me at arm's length as she scanned my face. "What's troubling you?" she asked.

"Nothing, Gram," I said with a peck on her cheek.

"You just get me a cup of coffee," Grandma said as she headed for her chair. "Then we'll talk."

I opened a cabinet and brought a cup and saucer to the table with the pot of coffee. I filled my cup, filled Grandma's, and then returned the pot to the counter while she flopped into her seat and started to massage her legs. As I sat down, I glanced at her stockings, which were rolled below her knees, and then at the frail hands that kneaded her calves.

"*Oy gevalt,*" Grandma moaned as she rubbed. "Don't get old."

I stared at the pink scalp that showed through her white hair. "I want you to get a lot older right before my eyes, Gram," I said.

Grandma reached for her coffee and sat back. "So," she started, and then took a sip, "what's Tony done to my granddaughter?"

"Nothing, Gram."

Grandma scanned my face again. "Your heart is heavy, no?"

"No," I said as my hands clasped my coffee cup.

"Well, it's something," she said.

I rotated the cup in my hands for a moment. "Even great relationships aren't always smooth, are they, Grandma?"

"*Acch!*" Grandma said, throwing her arms aloft. "There's no such thing."

"I didn't think so, 'specially with young Italian boys."

"Not even for the Jews." Grandma shrugged. "So, you're having problems?"

"Nothing abnormal," I said, then glanced at the wall phone. "Tony's dealing with guy stuff."

Grandma leaned her arms on the table and looked into my eyes. "That doesn't concern me as long as he doesn't hurt my Sammy."

"I'm fine, Gram," I said. "Really."

"*Gut*," Grandma said as she sat back once more. "Now get Grandma some matzoh for dunking while we wait for your mother. And then you can cook for us like you said."

Janice called back during breakfast to tell me she didn't have any news. Richie hadn't answered the phone in his room, and none of his and Tony's associates whom she had spoken to knew anything. She promised to call again when she had any updates.

The pit in my stomach still hadn't been removed, but there wasn't much I could do about it. I channeled my nervous energy into writing at my desk until late afternoon, and then took a walk alone to church.

Later that evening, I tore myself away from my desk and went to the kitchen for something to drink. When the phone rang, I leapt to grab it. "Richie's brother called back," Janice said. "The cops picked Richie and a coupla others up at the warehouse the same time they took you in." Mom and Grandma were watching TV in the living room as I cradled the phone in both hands. "What's gonna happen to them?" I whispered.

"Nick said it's all taken care of. A suit will be there first thing tomorrow to get them out."

"They're gonna get off so soon?"

"Nah, just bail. The case will come up later."

It appeared my worries had only just begun. "How's that gonna come out?"

"Who knows? I seen guys who done worse get off with just a slap on the wrist." That was hard for me to imagine. But Janice knew more about such things. I just couldn't understand how she was blowing this off as an "okay" event. It wasn't, it just wasn't. My mind kept telling me, my heart kept denying. "Just keep your shirt on," she continued. "At least until you see Tony." We hung up.

I walked into the living room and headed for my bedroom. "Won't you sit with us awhile?" Grandma asked. I didn't want to expose myself to Mom's prying and Grandma's sixth sense. Besides, my typewriter had been sizzling all evening. "I want to finish what I'm working on," I said as I neared the rear hall.

Mom grunted. "She doesn't have time for us anymore, Mom," she said without looking away from the television.

"She's a good girl, my Samelah," I heard Grandma reply as I left the living room. "Leave her be."

"Your piece on loyalty was outstanding," Mr. Wainright said to me as I closed my locker just before leaving school on Monday. I had forgotten about the article I turned in that morning and hadn't thought about anything except Tony all day. "I like how you balanced commitment to a boyfriend with the need to be true to yourself."

"I bled enough for you?" I chuckled as I secured the lock and turned to face him.

"It was all over my hands," he said, and his ear-to-ear smile made me forget everything except my quest to cross the Brooklyn Bridge. Grandma's words a couple of months before flashed into my mind and I smiled. I was writing myself out of one story and into another, I said to myself. And I'd be writing Tony out of his, I thought. I looked up into Mr. Wainright's face and beamed. "Geez, thanks, Mr. Wainright," I said. He placed a hand on my shoulder. "I'm serious, Sam. This one goes in the clip file."

I clutched my book bag against my chest as I watched him disappear among the students milling in the hall. Good people who support me come and go, I thought, and it would be my responsibility to secure their cables within me so I could make it across that East River span to the real world and my future.

I felt good about myself as I floated out the doors. I was ecstatic when I saw Tony leaning against a silver Porsche with his arms crossed, a broad grin plastering his face. I hurried over to him and dropped my bag. "Tony!" I exclaimed. I fell into his open arms and rested my cheek against his broad chest as I hugged him. We were alone in our own world as sights and sounds of the scores of people who were coming and going or milling about faded away. Tony lifted me off my feet and we kissed. I'm going to tie down this cable for sure, I said to myself as we parted.

"Youse wuzn't worried, wuz ya?" Tony asked.

"Nah," I lied. "Jus' some stuff you hafta deal with."

He put an arm across my shoulders. "That's my girl," he said, and then he waved the arm over the Porsche. "Now lemme take ya for a spin."

My eyes widened. "Is this yours?" I asked.

"I told ya I had sumthin' to celebrate." Tony grabbed the passenger-side handle and opened the door. "Get in," he said with a wave of an arm.

"Jesus, Tone, this is unbelievable," I said as we pulled away from the curb and the staring eyes in the front schoolyard. In the midst and surprise of seeing this new car, I neglected to focus on what had happened and continued in the moment. My moment. Unfortunately I knew it would be the beginning of more lies.

"Well, believe it," he said. I melted into the leather bucket seat as Tony glanced my way. "I toldya ya gotta get useta things."

I rested my head and closed my eyes. "It's not hard," I breathed.

"Yeah, well, everythin's not easy," Tony said as he worked the gearshift. I opened my eyes and turned toward him.

"You in a lot of trouble?"

"Nah. I don' have no serious priors. The lawyer said I might not hafta do any real time." I contemplated any time apart from him. It wouldn't be easy, but nothing in my life was, I knew. It would just make everything taste sweeter down the road. "Anyways," Tony continued, "nothin's gonna happen for a while. Postponements are all parta da game." I wished Tony didn't have to be in such a high-risk one but figured he wouldn't be playing it forever if I had anything to say about it. Andy Gibb warbled on the radio,

Darling, for so long
You and me been finding each other for so long

and I marveled how others' writing could speak to me, how it could encapsulate my life. I wanted to have people feel that way about my writing.

Tony spun the wheel as he negotiated the streets until we stopped at a traffic light. He turned toward me as we waited. "Ya handled yourself pretty good," he started. "That means sumthin' ta me."

My entire body felt a rush and I looked into his eyes. "It wasn't anything," I said.

"Ya didn't start bawlin' all over the place and ya kept ya mouth shut when it went down."

"I gotta admit, Tone, I was shakin' a bit."

"Don' matter. Ya did the right thing." The light turned green and Tony coaxed the Porsche into gear. "Ya didn't say anythin' later, didya?" he asked.

"'Course not," I said. "What could I tell them, anyway?"

"Nuthin'. No matter what."

"You got it," I said as Andy Gibb sang on:

I want you laying in the love I have to bring
I'd do anything to be your everything

Tony turned into a side street and pulled up to a two-family brick house. "Where are we?" I asked.

"My grandmother's," Tony said as he switched off the ignition. "My mom is inside. I wanna show my mother da ride."

I looked at my jeans and the tight shirt I wore under the leather jacket. "I woulda put on something nice the first time if I knew," I said.

Tony grabbed my neck and pulled me to him. "Ya look great no matter whatcha wearin', Sam," he said, and then he kissed me full on the lips. "It's time ol' Pamela met my girl."

Tony's mother opened the house door as we reached the top of the stoop. A massive hair clip held her bleached-blond hair in a high pile atop her head, and she wore a tight-fitting buttoned blouse and stretch pants that hugged her legs all the way to her ankles. She looked me up and down before pushing on the screen door and waving us in. Red toenails that matched the long ones on her hands were squeezed together in the front of her slip-on high heels. "So that's the big surprise, huh?" Pamela said to Tony, snapping her chewing gum as she looked at the gleaming car at the curb.

"Yeah, she's a real beaut', huh?" Tony said as we stood in the vestibule.

"You'll take me out in it later," Pamela said, then looked me up and down again.

"This is Samantha Bonti, who I told ya about, Mom," Tony said. "She's a real beaut', too, doncha think?"

Pamela didn't answer her son and offered her hand to me slowly, palm down. "Nice ta meetya," she said.

I reached for her outstretched fingers. "Likewise, Mrs. Kroon," I said.

"You jus' call me Pamela like we wuz old friends, sweetie."

"Sure thing, Mrs. . . . Pamela," I said.

She turned toward her son. "You settle that nonsense okay?"

"It's all under control," he replied. "Where's Grandma?"

Pamela replied with attitude, "She's sleeping. Your father and I are staying here tonight." Pamela ushered us down a short hallway. "The cops don' have much," she said as we reached the living room. "They didn't find anythin' here yesterday 'cept your father, sittin' jus' like he is now." Philip Kroon, in a wrinkled dress shirt and stained slacks, was sprawled in a large armchair. "Honey," Pamela said, "this is Tony's new girlfriend, Samantha." Mr. Kroon looked at me with heavy lids over his eyes and nodded.

"Glad to meet you," I said. As I studied his blank face, I saw that it was obvious where Tony got his electric blue eyes and rugged, handsome Dutch face. I also saw Philip's expression of sadness and disappointment. I don't know why it was there, but it just was. Maybe it had something to do with his tour in Vietnam. Tony had hinted to me that Philip had had more than his share of revolting experiences there.

Tony once told me he loved his father but knew he was weak, not the man he had been before he left for Southeast Asia. When Philip Kroon returned home, he was unable to hold down a steady job, Janice had told me. He relied on burglaries to provide for his wife, his son, and his ungrateful daughter, Katrina. He got caught and did a six-year stint in prison and by the time he'd gotten released he was pretty much good for nothing. By then, his son was making the kind of money that Philip had dreamed about making. Tony had told me that his father sat down on that leather chair one day, and except for eating, drinking, and running an errand or two when he needed cigarettes or a bad novel to read, he seldom got up from it.

Janice told me that she thought Philip was resigned to being the father of a wannabe and husband to the woman popularly known, she had said, as a "witch on wheels" who stashed money and contraband for her son until he could use it without getting caught. Philip stayed close to home except when he joined the neighborhood beat cops for the weekly poker game under the church. He was a compulsive gambler, but because his wife doled out his weekly money from what she collected from her son, Philip did not have the potential to ruin the family with his debts.

Pamela put an arm around Tony's waist and looked at me. "Let's all sit down soze we can get ta know ya," she said.

"That'd be nice," I said. Tony took my hand and led me to the couch. Pamela sat across from her husband in another armchair. "So," she said to me, "Tony tells me you're graduatin' soon, huh?"

My eyes widened. "Well, it's a year and a half away. But I can't wait."

Pamela eyed me up and down. "Tony's had them younger," she said. "And they all couldn't wait for him to come around." I flinched but kept a sunny disposition. Maybe a sour mother was something else Tony and I had in common, I thought. He looked at his mother and crossed his eyes. "Samantha's special, Mom," he said.

"Sure, sure," she said. "I'm just makin' small talk."

"She's makin' sumthin' of herself," Tony said. I beamed the instant he said that.

Pamela looked at me. "Of course she is. Isn't she nice, Philip?" Her husband grunted and didn't respond.

I looked toward Mr. Kroon. "Tony tells me you were in Vietnam," I said.

"Lotta good that did me," he deadpanned.

"You just do what ya hafta do ta get better, honey," Pamela said. "We've got Tony to take care of things now." She reached out an arm and put her hand on her son's knee. "You jus' lay low for a while until this all blows over, and then things will get back ta like they was."

"Nuthin's gonna change, Ma," Tony said. I begged to differ but didn't share my opinion at that moment. He reached across my shoulders and pulled me close. "It's me an' Sam, just like this no matter what." I slumped into Tony's side and looked up at him. That was something I totally agreed with. As long as we were together, I felt anything was possible for us. I just knew he would outgrow this stage, get a real job, and be a provider.

Pamela stood up and looked at Tony and me. "Why don' we drink to you two, then? That all right for you, Samantha?"

"It's fine," I said.

"Then we gotta go, Ma," Tony said.

Pamela brought a tray with a bottle of red wine and some glasses to the cocktail table and Tony did the pouring. His mother made a flowery toast, and I sipped as she engaged in talk about the usual things women in her circle concerned themselves with. Who bought what, who wore what, who drove what, who went where and with whom, and the like. I smiled and nodded at appropriate times, but couldn't have cared less about such inconsequential matters. All I cared about was Tony and me and our future.

The pit in my stomach had left the moment I saw him earlier and a warm feeling from the alcohol took its place as I listened to Pamela go on and on. Philip gulped his wine and motioned to Tony for a refill as soon as his glass was empty. It was the most animation I saw in him the whole time I was in the Kroon home.

When I had finished my glass, Tony drained his second and stood up. He took my hand and led me to the front door.

"Remember what I said about stayin' outta trouble," Pamela said to her son through the screen door as we started down the steps. "Good-bye, Samantha," she called out to me. "We'll be sure ta have your folks ova for the holidays."

"That'll be nice, Mrs. . . . Pamela," I said over my shoulder. "Bye."

Tony and I jumped into the Porsche and I stole a glance at his mother, who remained at the front door. "She loves ya, Sam," Tony said, and then the car screeched as he pulled away.

"I don't know," I replied.

"I do. You'll see. She's a great gal."

The bucket seat embraced me again and it didn't matter to me how his mother felt. It would be nice to get along great with her, but all that really mattered, I thought as Donna Summer belted out a song, was how Tony and I felt about each other.

Put all the other things aside, there's only you and me
Believe in us, we were always meant to be

I looked at Tony as he mastered the powerful machine and I felt again that everything was going to be all right.

Me for you and you for me, 'til eternity

Tony hummed along with the lyrics. "That's not a bad song," he said as he turned onto Eighteenth Avenue. "We'll hafta find one that's ours." We'll find everything together, I thought.

Tony cruised through town, waving or nodding to a few people who recognized him at the wheel, and then pulled into the Café Sicily parking lot. Two different men in dark suits standing adjacent to the entrance took note of our arrival before returning to their conversation. "You gonna be long?" I asked as Tony switched the ignition off.

"You're comin' wid me," he said as he hopped out, and then

he sprang to my side of the Porsche. I swung my door open and he grabbed my hand and helped me out of the car. "I'm takin' ya ta dinner." Another missed meal at home, I thought, but decided Mom and Grandma would have to get used to a lot of things, as I had to all the time.

The feeling of royalty revisited me as we strolled into the dimly lit restaurant. "Right this way, Tony," the maître d' said. He led us past the bar, where a couple more men in dark suits sat on stools, to a table covered in a red-and-white-checkered cloth. The maître d' pulled a chair out for me and then opened menus in front of us. "The lobster fra diavolo special is excellent tonight," he said. I felt as if I belonged.

Time always seemed to be suspended whenever I was with Tony, and the next hour passed as if it were only a couple of minutes. We ate and talked and sprinkled our conversation with a few laughs. No one in the busy dining room paid any attention to us; everyone there knew how to mind his own business, I thought. I liked that, and liked the feeling I had in that environment with Tony. Saturday night seemed like a bad dream.

When a noticeable hush came over the room, Tony and I stopped talking and looked around. Our eyes settled, as had everyone's, on the rotund man who had strolled through the swinging kitchen doors. His black suit and tie matched his plastered hair and he smiled at everyone and patted a couple of men on the shoulder as he made his way through the dining room. He seemed to be headed directly for Tony and me.

Tony grabbed his wineglass. "That's Tino Priganti," he said, and kept his eyes on the boss as he sipped. Tino Priganti's pockmarked face and bulbous nose loomed as he approached.

"I know," I said as I looked down and shifted in my chair. "I've seen him before."

The massive man stopped at our table and placed his massive hands on our table. "*Buona sera,*" he said, and turned toward Tony. "Dis da girl who wuz widya Saturday night?" he asked.

"Yes, sir, Mr. Priganti," Tony said. "Samantha."

"She gotta last name?"

"Bonti."

"I like that," Tino said, and slid his meaty fingers under my chin. "Lemme have a look at ya," he said as he lifted my face gently and locked his eyes on mine.

"She's the best, Mr. Priganti," Tony said, beaming.

Tino Priganti stood straight, looked at Tony, and slapped a palm on his shoulder. "Ya ain't so bad yaself," he said, then turned toward me. "Ya boy here is a big earner." I smiled and Tino locked his eyes on mine. "Ya deserve nuttin' but the best, Tony," he said. "She looks like a keeper ta me." Tony beamed as Tino Priganti addressed me again. "Your food okay?" he asked.

"Fantastic, Mr. Priganti," I said.

A thin smile appeared on Tino's face and he nodded. "I'm glad youse like it," he said, and squeezed Tony's shoulder while he kept his eyes on me. "I betcha didn' like being sweated in da precinct, huh?" he asked me before breaking into a hearty laugh.

Tony smiled. "She handled it like she wuz one a us, Mr. Priganti," he said.

"Good," Tino said, and his face went blank as it remained fixed on mine. "If youse do nuttin' wrong, youse got nuttin' ta worry about. Ain't that right Tony."

"Yes sir, Mr. Priganti." Tino leaned over and whispered for a minute into Tony's ear. "Yes, sir, Mr. Priganti," Tony said again when Tino had finished.

Tino patted Tony's shoulder once more and stood straight. He motioned with his hand to a waiter in a crisp white jacket and addressed him when he came over to the table. "His money's no good tonight, Sal," he said with a nod toward Tony. "It's with me."

"Yes sir, Mr. Priganti," the waiter said before taking his leave.

Tino stooped and reached for my hand, and it disappeared when he held it between both of his. Our eyes locked once more. "Looks like a real keeper ta me, Tony," he said without looking away.

"Think what ya wan' 'bout my mother," Tony said as he pulled up to my apartment at midnight and left the car running, "but Tino sure as hell liked you."

He had seemed genuine to me, but then what did I know? I asked myself. Brooklyn Boys all had charm, and the one at the top of the heap would have the most, I reasoned. "I'm sure he likes all the girls," I said.

"And they all like him," Tony said. "Whadya think?"

"He seemed nice," I said, and then I looked up at the living room light that was still on. "What did he whisper to you?" I couldn't stop myself from asking.

Tony stiffened. "Union shit," he said flatly. "Some black coalition fuckin' wid a window job site in Clinton Hill." Tony pulled me across the console. "But that don' matter right now. Lemme show ya how no one's as nice as I am," he said, and he sucked my neck to the sounds of Joni Mitchell:

Help me I think I'm falling in love again
When I get that crazy feeling I know I'm in trouble again . . .

Abruptly I was interrupted by his voice and a small duffel bag being shoved in my lap. "Listen, can you hold this for me, put it on your fire escape until I ask for it back, don't show anyone."

Now that piqued my curiosity.

"What is it?"

"Don't ask so many questions, just do it. It's not a big deal, it's Vin's. I'd rather you keep it for me, okay?" I was hesitant, I had no idea what this could be, yet I took the bag and that was that.

"I gotta go, Tone," I sighed as I dragged myself away from him, taking the duffel bag with me.

"I know," he said, "but sumday, you'll never hafta leave."

I took my heels off outside the apartment door and closed it gently, hiding the duffel bag by my side, but when cigarette smoke assaulted my nostrils I knew my precautions were pointless. Mom was wide awake and slumped on the couch behind a huge gift basket on the coffee table that was wrapped in translucent yellow cellophane. I could see two wine bottles encased with straw and all sorts of Italian delicacies that were nestled in shredded green paper.

"So," Mom snarled, "he's finished with ya for the night?"

"Mom, please," I said as I dropped my schoolbag onto the tattered area rug, "not now."

"It's bad enough ya miss dinner"—she ignored my plea—"but no call? What kinda respect is that?" Mom covered her mouth with a fist and coughed.

I looked at her lined, ashen face and shrunken body but opted not to comment about respect. "I just got caught up in things, is all," I said. "Sorry."

"You're sorry. I'm sorry what we been tellin' ya all these years hasn't sunk in."

It wasn't the time to explain to her how different we were, and how much different I was from almost everyone in Bensonhurst. I pointed to the basket. "What's that?" I asked.

"As if you don' know," Mom harrumphed.

"No, I don't," I said, and then smiled. "Is it from Tony?"

Mom tore the card from the plastic wrapping and held it in front of her eyes as she read the inscription. " 'With appreciation', it says, and it's signed 'The Prigantis'." She looked at me and her eyes were overflowing with judgment. "What for, you and God only know."

"Tony musta said something about me and him gettin' serious," I said, and regretted the words as soon as they left my mouth. Revealing my heart to Grandma was never a problem, but it was way too soon to tell Mom how I was starting to feel about Tony. She would just hassle me no end, I knew. It would be better to fill her in much farther down the road, maybe even after I crossed that bridge.

Mom raised an eyebrow. "What's serious is the kinda shit this leads ta."

Saturday night returned to my consciousness when she said that. "It's no big deal," I said as I took off my jacket, "and now we have some nice treats for Thanksgiving."

Why would Tino send me a basket? Who was I kidding, I knew why, but it felt wrong. There was a part of me that felt like a big shot, the girl that everyone talked about, but it still didn't seem right. Oh well, I guess I would send him a thank-you; that's what Grandma would do.

I went into my bedroom, opened the window, and placed the duffel bag in my hiding place under the planter. That's what Tony asked me to do, so I did it. I hoped that whatever Tony gave me would stay safe out there. I was tempted to look inside but got distracted by Mom's yelling.

"I'll be thankful when I get you away from this neighborhood," Mom said as she reached for another cigarette.

She had no idea how far away I intended that to be or what would happen to me before I got there.

13

The next few weeks flew by with schoolwork, hours at the bookstore, get-togethers with Janice, pounding away at my typewriter, and sporadic dates with Tony. Most of those included Richie and Janice and Vin and Dara, at either a restaurant or a nightclub. Other than one or two comments about how much their lawyer was costing them, the three guys seemed unaffected by their criminal case, which was proceeding at a snail's pace. It seemed to consist primarily of postponements and faded into the background. Tony's references to our life together, at just the right time every other week when my concern peaked, to a house and kids and fine things, kept it there. My worry about him going away for a stretch seemed unwarranted.

My time alone with Tony was for the most part confined to heated, clawing moments in his Porsche or heavy petting in his bedroom—even when his mother was at home a few times—as Playboy bunnies looked down on us from wall posters. I found it ironic every time I was in Tony's room that he wouldn't hear of me hanging photos of rock and movie stars in my room.

With each makeout session, I came closer to the point of no return. I had no illusions that Tony wasn't very experienced with sexual consummation; not only did he know exactly what he was doing as his hands and mouth traversed my body, but the knowing glances and smiles he got from the guys and so many women told me plain as day that I was far from his first conquest. I marveled at his restraint, at his not forcing the issue with me. It could only mean, I reasoned, that he held me in high regard, that what we had was, indeed, special. I knew that when I crossed the line and went all the way with him, that would be special, too.

On Christmas morning, I sat on a brown, tattered armchair in my apartment and looked forward to that moment. My eyes rested on the worn, faded emerald green area rug at my feet, and I focused on a darker border thread that twisted with another and seemed to go on without end. I'm looking forward to an entire life with Tony, I said to myself. I couldn't wait to see him later that afternoon.

I hadn't been with him on Thanksgiving; he had said he had to do something with Vin but that he didn't know exactly when it would be, and he didn't want to leave me stranded at his house or drop me back at mine after a short time together. I had been disappointed, but at least Mom and Grandma were happy to have me to themselves for a change.

It had turned out to be a pleasant holiday. Mom was in rare form and managed to get through an entire day without any of her usual sarcasm or vitriol. It was both a surprise and a relief not to feel like I had to walk on eggshells around her. Spontaneous smiles and laughter punctuated the kind of girl talk that had been all too lacking in our home. For once, we were just three women sharing an attachment and a good time.

A miniature Christmas tree, what I called a Charlie Brown tree because it was so small and had only a few stray red balls and no tinsel on it, stood humbly on the faux mantelpiece in the Bonti living room beside a brass menorah in full flame. That prized possession of Grandma's had been in the family for years, and she was in the habit of lighting all the candles each night after the Christmas tree arrived—accentuating the battle between the two religions that had remained after my father left when Mom was eight months pregnant with me. I recalled how Grandma always harped on the fact that I was born a Jew because I came out of a Jewish vagina, and how the religious conflict that had become Mom's badge was something Grandma grieved over almost every day. On Christmas, I hoped that peace would prevail as it had on Thanksgiving.

As I stared at the flickering lights on the Christmas tree and the menorah ablaze, I wished as I had many times before that Mom and I had had a more normal life. But she had continued on her path of self-destruction ever since I was a toddler. When things had gotten worse for us financially, her destructive habits had gotten even worse and then her health deteriorated, too. She had even resorted to taking things out of Grandma's jewelry box and pawning them. I recalled the time when she made me shoplift that expensive shampoo and conditioner she loved at the drugstore. I was only twelve at the time. Then of course it escalated into shirts and pants and anything else she would want off the avenue, until we got caught. No charges were ever filed. By thirteen I would have been getting charged for theft. Thank God she had the sense to stop. Once again she returned to the church with a vengence to repent for what she made me do as well as for herself. I often wondered why she couldn't just get a job, but she claimed she was way too sick to work, the welfare was fine, and I had to deal with it. I had always had other plans.

I knew Mom had been ill for a long time, but I felt that her lack of positive energy and her negative attitude were what kept her from getting well. No wonder she hadn't had any stable men and drifted from one lowlife to another, I thought. I swore I would not wind up with any man just for the hell of it and I would make my own money as a writer. I would never give up. Besides Tony, that was all I had, a dream, my dream.

I glanced at the book in my lap, *Understanding Shakespeare,* which I'd picked up in the library but with which I was not making a great deal of headway. My mother was of no help with such things, of course, so I had read and reread the lyrical phrases to myself, enjoying the swell of the phrases, trying to understand the words, while Mom sat on the couch and smoked a cigarette. I was distracted watching my mother pull the smoke into her mouth and send it back out in perfect white rings that traveled across the room, lost their shapes, and disappeared. Didn't she know how bad smoking was for her? I always asked myself. It just never seemed to matter to her. Almost every morning since I was about fourteen she had spit up horrible mucus that was bloody sometimes. How could she do that to herself? I wondered. My poor grandma and I just never knew what to do about Mom's behavior. Every year that passed I knew that her demons were getting to her more and more. Sometimes I felt as though it wasn't her, my beautiful mother from my birth, but rather a beaten-down, worn-out woman who didn't care about anything, never mind her health.

I knew that when she saw me with Tony all she could see was a reflection of herself with my father and her countless beatings. She didn't want that for me and no matter how much I reassured her, she never trusted it and sometimes I didn't either.

It was the first Christmas since Mom had converted to Catholicism that we Bontis were not cooking dinner in our small kitchen. Pamela had made good on her promise and had invited us to spend the holiday at her house. Mom and Grandma had agreed and decided to have a breakfast of cheese blintzes and applesauce and then exchange presents in the living room before we left for the Kroon residence.

When Grandma walked into the living room, she wrinkled her nose. "Put that out, willya?" she said to her daughter. "It's one thing if you want to keep smoking and kill yourself, but Sam has a good long life ahead of her. She needs a working pair of lungs."

Mom rolled her eyes, took two long pulls on her Marlboro, coughed, and stubbed it out in the ashtray. I put my book down and got up to hug Grandma. "Merry Christmas, Grandma," I said.

"Same to you, honey," she said, and then frowned at the Christmas tree. "Even if it *is* about things I don't believe in." She smiled beatifically at the menorah before nodding her head and sitting beside her daughter.

"Let's just open our gifts, Ma," Mom said. She'd heard it all before, over and over again. "Then I need a little nap before the party."

"Here," I said as I picked up a large package. "Let's start with this. It's from Tony for all of us." I placed the present on their laps.

"It's so heavy," Grandma said.

I giggled and set the gift on the floor as I knelt in front of them and opened it myself. Inside the professionally wrapped department store box was a red and black Oriental rug, a runner that would fit perfectly in the short entrance hall. I was delighted when I saw my grandmother smiling.

"Isn't it beautiful, Mom?" I asked.

Mom's eyes narrowed. "Why would Tony give us a rug?" she scoffed. I pursed my lips. It looks like she's going to be her usual bitter self, I thought, instead of the pleasant, regular person she had been a month before. Mom poked the box away with her foot. "What does he think, that we can't afford one ourselves?"

"We can't," Grandma said.

"Well, we can't keep it," Mom said.

Leave it to her to have an attitude about a rug she knew damn well she couldn't afford. I steamed. "Why not, Mom?" I barked. "I think it's a wonderful gift. Of course we'll keep it."

"Don' get fuckin' loud with me," Mom said.

"Hey, no swearing," Grandma chided. "It's a holiday."

Mom screwed her face. "Yeah, but not your holiday."

"That doesn't matter," Grandma said. "At least he remembered us."

"I remembered you, too," I said. I jumped up and grabbed two small square gifts, nudged Mom and Grandma apart, and snuggled into the space between them. "Make room for Santa," I said with a big smile. I handed a box to my mother. "This is for you, Mom," I said, and pecked her cheek. "Merry Christmas."

"Oh, Sam, it's wrapped so pretty!" Mom said, and pulled the paper off the black velvet box. She opened the lid, looked down, and took the beautiful silver cross into her hand. "It's so beautiful," Mom said. She thought for a second and then her face darkened as she looked at me. "Tony gave ya the money for this, didn't he?" I said nothing as my head and shoulders slumped.

"The boy's serious about her," Grandma jumped in. "He's courting her."

"Courting, my ass," Mom said. "That's how her father started with me." I fought back tears, got up, and ran out of the living room.

Grandma found me on my bed, crying. She sat beside me and gave me a hug. "Why is she so mean to me?" I asked through my tears. "Tony is a nice guy."

She took a hand-embroidered handkerchief out of her housecoat pocket and wiped my eyes. Then Grandma held it on my nose and said, "Blow." I did as I was told and forced a smile.

"That's what I like to see," Grandma said. "You got a smile that could stop traffic. Now where's my gift?"

I was still clutching the second box. I straightened the orange bow and handed it over. "Happy Chanukah," I said.

Grandma opened the gift and saw a silver Star of David on a thin silver chain. "Just what I wanted," she said. "Now help me put it on."

I clasped the chain around Grandma's craggy neck. "Do you really like it?" I asked.

"Oh *bubelah,* it's so pretty. Your old granny never had anything so nice."

"Really?" I asked.

"I would never lie to my little Sammy."

"It's just so hard, Gram. You get a star, Mom gets a cross, and I get all the *tsuris* when you two are fighting about religion."

"Faith isn't something to get aggravated about, Sammy."

I thought of the Blessed Mother and knew Grandma was right. "Faith is a good thing, Grandma, but I also believe in myself. In case you want to know, I didn't get the money from Tony. I saved some of my pay and I paid for the gifts myself."

"Why didn't you tell your mother that?"

I blew my nose again. "'Cause she'd never believe me."

"Your mom knows you're no liar," Grandma said. She caressed my forehead and stroked my hair. "Do you want your gift now or should we wait?" she asked.

My face brightened. "Now, please," I said.

Grandma went to her side of the room, opened the middle drawer of her dresser, and took out a large package that she gave to me. I sat up, opened the box, and beamed when I saw a classic trilogy by Robert Louis Stevenson that she had bought for me.

"Now, no more crying," Grandma said. "That was my last clean hankie. You'd better shower and get dressed while your mother rests. We have a party to go to at your nice boyfriend's house, right?"

I smiled. "Right."

"Good. What are you wearing?"

"I haven't decided yet."

Grandma kissed my forehead, left our room, and left me alone with my thoughts. I was nervous, but it had nothing to do with my mother or what I was about to wear. It was all about Tony's mother and the rest of his family. I hardly knew Pamela and Philip, Katrina hadn't wanted any part of me, and I'd never met any of his other relatives. I prayed we would all get along and that my family wouldn't embarrass me. Most of all, I didn't want to embarrass myself.

I thought about why I was so afraid of the Kroons as I took my time in the bathroom and got dressed for the party. They were not pure-blooded Italians any more than the Bontis were, but they had so much more money and lived a hell of a lot better than my family did. Tony had reassured me that his mother would make my family feel welcome but I was not convinced, especially when I thought about how loud my grandmother talked and recalled that Janice had told me that Richie said Pamela did not like Jews.

I put on a wool skirt that wasn't too short and matched it with a sweater that my mother had bought for me at Filene's Basement. I pulled the sweater down to make sure it covered my waist and turned to see how it looked from behind before I rejoined Mom and Grandma in the living room. We headed out the door to a waiting cab—a rare convenience but one I had treated us to that day.

My anxiety increased when we arrived at the Kroon home and found it decked out like a Hallmark Christmas card. Large, humanlike statues on the front lawn evoked a Charles Dickens tale. Hundreds of tiny white lights lined the walkway to the front door and climbed the front steps, while a multitude of red and green bows surrounded the windows. When we entered their home, my oh my! It was like a fairy tale.

The tree almost touched the ceiling and filled an entire corner of the living room where it stood. It was decorated so meticulously, so perfectly, and an abundance of gifts beneath it covered the plush pile carpet. They were all professionally wrapped with silver-speckled red and green bows. Mouthwatering aromas of ham, roasted turkey, freshly baked bread, and steaming lasagna—without which no Bensonhurst Christmas was complete—finished off the perfect holiday scene. How could they afford it all? I asked myself.

I placed my gifts among the others under the tree. I had wrapped them in newspaper and had fashioned bows from swatches from Grandma's old red housecoat. All in all, they looked pretty damn creative, I thought, but it sure showed off my lack of funds. And although the gifts inside were humble, I felt guilty that I had spent more money on the Kroon family than I had on my own.

When Tony smiled and came over to hug me, however, I felt better. He was acting like the host with the most when he greeted Mom and Grandma as if they were long-lost members of his family. Pamela joined in the act, sidling up to us in her gold lamé jumpsuit with a rope belt that was much too tight. Large reindeer earrings dangled beneath her high, teased hair. Pamela's figure had seen better days, and her clothing accentuated every curve and the extra pounds she had put on. But I could see that she must have been a real looker when she was younger.

Pamela extended a hand and greeted us graciously, then pulled me in for a hug as if we were best friends. I yielded and played the game, hugging her back, but it was all a ruse, because Pamela had never seemed happy to see me. When she shook Mom's hand, however, and pretended not to be flustered by Grandma yelling hello in the background, I was grateful. At least Pamela put up a good front, I thought.

Tony looked toward Mom and Grandma. "Lemme get youse some wine," he offered. "It's homemade."

"Oh yes," Pamela added, "sit and enjoy." She gestured to an empty couch. "My husband will get youse sumthin' ta eat." Grandma winced and began to mumble under her breath about Pamela's heavy Brooklyn accent, which matched her son's. "He loves a house full of people," Pamela finished.

The three of us occupied the couch and looked over at Philip Kroon, who was sitting in his green leather armchair, talking to no one, his eyes on the floor. I tried not to stare at the painfully thin, salt-and-pepper-haired war hero. If I didn't know better, I would have thought he was sleeping. Whatever he was or wasn't doing, he didn't look like he was anxious to serve anyone or enjoying a house full of people at all. In fact, if Pamela hadn't pointed him out, I might have mistaken him for someone at the wrong party. I had never met anyone quite like Philip, but like his wife, when he got up and shook hands, at least he was making an effort to welcome us into his home.

Grandma offered a bakery box she had been holding to Pamela. "This is for you," Grandma said. "A nice sponge cake."

I cringed. Sponge cakes were so Jewish, usually for Passover.

"Well, Grandma Ruth, thank ya so much," Pamela said as she bent over to take the white box, which made her bloodred fingernails stand out even more. "And don't worry, the people here'll eat anything I give 'em, even if it's Jewish."

I was speechless while Grandma muttered a Yiddish expression under her breath. Actually, I didn't blame her for doing that.

Tony reappeared with two filled wineglasses and handed them to Mom and Grandma. Then he turned to introduce his sister, who had come over from the dining room, where she had finished setting the table.

I stood and greeted the sour-looking, overweight girl who had just turned eleven. Katrina did nothing to hide the fact that she did not appreciate having outside guests for Christmas dinner. "The table's not big enough," she whined to Tony. "I don't want ta eat at the foldin' table wid cousins I don' know."

"They're family," Pamela said.

"Yeah, well, not everybody here is," Katrina almost shouted. "Anyways, those cousins are so go-shay!"

I leaned toward Tony and whispered, "What does that mean, Tone?"

He pretended to box Katrina's ears when he answered loudly enough for everyone to hear. "She means 'gauche.'" Tony looked directly at his sister. "Shuddup, Katrina. Ya sound like a real idiot," he said before taking the cake box from his mother and heading back to the kitchen. His sister stuck out her bottom lip.

I sat next to Grandma again and glanced at Katrina. She looked toady to me, bloated and overweight for an eleven-year-old, with badly permed stringy dark hair, a doughy face, and angry gray eyes. She hardly had a chance to be much different, I supposed, considering her father's isolation and her mother's pushiness and fawning over Tony. But the young girl's negative demeanor and her penchant for whining made the decidedly unattractive preteen look worse. It had to be tough with a brother like Tony, who had the personality and the looks in the family, and it had become clear to me over the preceding months, as it must have been to Katrina her entire life, that he was his mother's favorite. To me, Pamela seemed obsessed with Tony.

Grandma leaned toward me. "Did you see how that Pamela stares at her son?" she whispered. I supposed it was obvious to everyone. "You'll never get this one away from his mother." I didn't respond. No matter how Pamela felt or acted, I knew Tony was his own man.

Dara walked through the front door with Vin, both of them dressed in their Christmas best. They had probably gotten whole new wardrobes, I thought. Dara, in a bright red skintight jumpsuit, made her way over to me as Vin searched for Tony.

"Hey, Dara," I said.

"Hey, Sam." Dara glanced at Mom and Grandma on the couch. "Your family?"

"Yeah," I said, and made the introductions.

"Vin didn't bother to invite mine. Must be nice," Dara said, and then she went away. Probably to give Vin an attitude, I worried. Dara was famous for such antics and the holiday would be no exception for her. Man, she was a piece of work, just like all the guys said, but I felt it wasn't really her fault. Like me, she hadn't had much of a life, but unlike me, she certainly didn't fantasize about a better one. After the distant cousins—a sad-looking, eccentric couple and two shy children who sat near Philip and kept to themselves—arrived, everyone engaged in easy conversation and laughter. Katrina had changed her attitude somewhat when she saw the unwelcome guests place a gift under the tree for her, and all was peaceful as the group drank eggnog, wine, and cocktails; munched on ricotta salata and mozzarella cheese, crackers and miniature meatballs; and exchanged neighborhood stories and gossip.

After an hour, Pamela made an announcement after one of her many trips to the kitchen. "It's ready. Let's *mangia*!"

"More freakin' food," Mom said to me in a low voice when we got up from the couch. "All we been doin' is eatin'."

"Shush, Mom. Not now," I pleaded as I had too many times before.

"Reminds me of your father's family, and look where that got me."

I turned to my mother with red eyes. "I'll never be you, Mom. *Never*." It was how I felt and my mother had to know. Mom swallowed hard and went to the table. I hesitated and felt sorry for her, but at that moment I wasn't taking back my words. I had become so sick and tired of my mother putting me down. It was only when she was in a rare good mood that she would tell me that I was pretty or smart. She had never read a word I wrote, and what did that say about Mom and our relationship? I asked myself. At least I had Tony, I thought, and went to his side.

Katrina sat down first, and everyone looked for his or her name on the tags that were placed on the red and green cloth place mats. I was relieved to be seated next to Tony. Grandma sat on my right, and my mother sat on Tony's other side. Philip muttered something about saying grace but no one bothered as Katrina started stabbing turkey slices with her fork. "Grace," she scoffed, and giggled as she piled ham onto her plate along with spoonfuls of buttery mashed potatoes, green beans with bread crumbs, and, of course, piping-hot, cheesy lasagna.

It seemed the meal was over quickly and everyone got up and went to sit near the tree. It was time to open gifts, and at last, Katrina looked happy and excited. She unbuttoned the top button of her pants, exhaled loudly, and crawled around under the tree, grabbing the gifts with her name tags and shoving other presents to the side. I had bought her a jacket that cost more than I could afford, but Tony had slipped me some extra cash when I told him I was going shopping for his family. "Here's a coupla C-notes," he had said as he peeled off five bills from the thick roll he always seemed to have. "Pick out sumthin' nice." That was what all the Brooklyn Boys told their girls, I knew.

"Careful there," Philip warned his daughter in a low voice, one of the few things he had uttered all day.

Katrina paid no attention and everyone left her alone. When she got to the present I bought her, she thanked me quickly and pushed the jacket away. Why had I bothered? I wondered to myself.

Pamela walked over and handed me a gift. "For me?" I asked. I was surprised but shouldn't have been. I had been so afraid of buying the wrong things for the Kroons that I'd almost forgotten I would be getting gifts, too. I took the large box from Pamela and gave her a small one in return.

Pamela opened it immediately and squealed with delight.

"Uh, thanks, Sam," she said after she turned the eighteen-karat gold-filled pin over in her fingers.

Tony smiled and looked at me. "Let's see what Mom got ya," he said. I felt so on display. I lowered my eyes, smiled without parting my lips, and opened my gift. The sweater, one that must have cost five times as much as the one I was wearing, had my initials engraved on the right side and perfect pink and blue stitching along the edges.

"Thank you so much, Pamela," I said, and gave my boyfriend's mother a hug.

"You're welcome, dear," she said, "but you need to thank Philip and Katrina, too. It's from all of us."

"Thank you," I said to the others. I glanced at my mom and Grandma, who were overwhelmed as they opened their gifts. Pamela had bought a beautiful cut crystal bowl for Mom that would easily be the most expensive accessory in our home, and a pair of antique lace handkerchiefs for Grandma. After the cousins exchanged gifts and Philip had opened his present from me, a burgundy wallet, Pamela put on the coffee and brought out dessert trays filled with pastries and pies. The Kroons really knew how to do Christmas, I thought.

Tony sat beside me and I handed him a present. "This is for you, Tone." He smiled, kissed me quickly, and opened his gift. It was a pair of black leather half gloves for his Harley. "Thanks," he said as he tossed them on the coffee table, "but I don' need gifts from ya. We'll take a ride later for yours."

"That'll be great," I said.

"You know what's great?" Tony asked. "Jus' havin' you here with my family and all. Its like bein' on TV or sumthin'. You know, the lights and food and everybody bein' happy. We're practically the Nelsons." Tony looked over at his dad, who was listening to Grandma while she shouted a story. She was actually making him laugh, something Tony hadn't seen his father do in many years.

Tony looked into my eyes with a vulnerability I hadn't seen before. I reached over and hugged him and didn't care who saw it. It was Christmas and I was so happy.

At seven o'clock, Tony borrowed his mother's Lincoln and we dropped Mom and Grandma off in front of our apartment building. After hugs all around on the sidewalk, the women headed inside. "I'll have her home early," Tony promised, and then we got back into the car and took off down the street.

I shivered beside him. It was a freezing cold night and I snuggled close to Tony. "Damn! It's cold," I said. "The wind-chill factor must be zero or something. Maybe I should go back home and get a warmer coat."

"No time," he said. "I gotta meet a guy. Just stick close to me."

Tony drove to the center of Bensonhurst and stopped on Eighteenth Avenue in front of Coppo's Jewelers. "Wait here," he said. "I'll be right back." Tony left the car running and hurried into the store. I sat in the car wondering what the hell he was doing as I watched him through the storefront. It's Christmas night, for God's sake, I said to myself. Why would it be open now? I shivered again even though the heater was on. I was ready for some hot chocolate back at his house with all those crazy people.

I watched as Tony talked and gesticulated with an elderly man and a younger one who must have been his son. The Coppos, as Tony referred to them, cowered and the older man handed Tony a small box. Tony nodded, turned around, and came back to the car.

"Son of a bitch," he said with a malevolent grin on his face. "He thought I was a pushover. At least his dad had some sense." He handed me a velvet box. "I got this for ya."

I scrunched my eyebrows and looked at Tony. What had he just been doing? I wondered, but didn't dare ask, although I so wanted to. Instead, I opened the box in my hand and stared at what was inside.

"Merry Christmas," Tony said as he reached for the sparkling gold bracelet with a heart-shaped diamond charm. He polished it against his jacket and put it on my wrist.

"This is for me?" I asked. "Are you sure? I mean, are these really diamonds?"

"Yeah. 'Course they are. Those guys owed me."

"Ooh," I said. "I love hearts and this is the first time I got diamonds for a present."

Tony smirked. "There'll be a first time for everything."

"Oh, thank you, thank you," I blurted, and reached over to tousle Tony's hair. He flinched and pulled back. "Hey, watch the hair," he said, checking his blond coif in the mirror. Carly Simon's song "You're So Vain" flashed into my consciousness, but I overlooked his moment of vanity. I had been getting used to letting it pass. I looked at the heart again and then I hugged and kissed him. "How can I ever thank you enough?" I asked.

"I gotta few ideas," he said as he squeezed my breasts. That bothered me. I knew he wanted me to have a different feeling but I was put off by his coming on so strong at such a tender moment. I nudged him away. "Cut it out, Tony," I said as I collected myself and slipped the bracelet onto my wrist. I sat back in my seat and as I stared into the diamonds, I couldn't help but wonder where they came from. I wouldn't dare say anything to Tony, but why didn't I get a wrapped box like everyone else did?

Tony beamed as he drove away. "A good guess. I think Mom got jealous when I told her I was gettin' ya one," he said with a laugh. I didn't think that was funny. Pamela always acted as if I was taking away her Tony. With an added resentment like this gift, I thought, it could only get worse. Was Tony deliberately trying to upset his mother or was it just the way things were? I wondered. "Looks good on you, Sam," Tony said. "I guess I got real good taste."

"You sure do," I said, looking forward to showing it off wherever we ended up next. But in a few minutes we were back in front of my apartment building. "What are we doin' here, Tone?" I asked. "I want to go show off my present."

"Show your mom. I gotta do a thing wid Vin."

"Oh, Tony, not tonight. Please. It's Christmas. I don't have school tomorrow and I can stay out late. My mom won't care. Honest."

Tony's eyes narrowed. "What did I just say? I gotta go out and you gotta go home. That's the way it is." I slumped against my seat and tucked my chin into my chest. Tony looked at me for a moment and then softened his tone. "Ya gonna wear that for New Year's?" he asked.

"Of course," I mumbled as I twirled the bracelet. I didn't want him to leave but decided I would be happy to go in and wait until I could tell Janice about it. Besides, Tony and I would be together on New Year's Eve and that was exciting. I didn't want to ruin it by not appearing grateful.

As he drove away, I thought it strange how all the guys would leave their girlfriends alone no matter what night it happened to be. I found myself perched to Tony's every word, and when he wanted to see me, I jumped.

I made a vow to myself Christmas night that the New Year would be different. I would *make* it so.

14

"That's some bracelet!" Janice exclaimed the next afternoon when we sat across from each other at Sally's. "I toldya you'd better get used ta that kinda treatment."

I looked at my wrist and thought about how Tony had dropped me off when I wanted to stay out with him. "I guess I'll have to get used to being left flat, too," I said, my head still lowered.

"It's worth it. The Young Turks are movin' up on the Mustache Petes in Bensonhurst."

I looked up at my best friend. "I'm not interested in Bensonhurst," I said.

"I know, I know. It's Manhattan ya want to conquer."

"With Tone right beside me."

Janice looked out the window and I followed her gaze. Bustling Eighteenth Avenue was filled with women wearing fur coats, spike heels, and teased coifs, and men with slicked-back hair who shuffled along looking side to side with their hands in leather jackets. "I gotta be honest, Sam. I don' know if he'll ever fit into that world," she said, and then we faced each other again.

"He has to," I said. "'Cause that's where I'm gonna be."

"Did you tell him you'd be with me now?" Janice asked.

"Of course. On the telephone this morning, right after he mentioned about everyone going to Platinum tonight."

"Isn't it great? We get to spend almost the whole day together."

My eyes drifted again to the scene outside the diner. "Yeah," I said, and wondered where in the neighborhood Tony was at that moment.

For Tony, as I found out later, a great deal was changing that Christmas week.

I always used to think that Vin had a secret crush on me, and God, I would never even breathe that out loud. But every time I was around Vin, he would always try to show off about his family and their business. He talked a lot. He would say things a girl like me, well, should just not hear. But there he was this one time, blabbering away about a bunch of shit I wasn't supposed to know about. I pretended not to pay attention, but I listened to everything.

Around the same time, Tony and Vin had become inseparable, and Tony had become Vin's "come with" guy when he was out doing business. Vin liked Tony's easy manner and his willingness to follow directions, and for him to be Vin's eyes and ears around town. In fact, he became so valuable to the Prigantis, they invited him to a local meeting with the Teamsters.

The union president and Tino were in negotiations, as Vin wanted a piece of their action and the Teamsters needed protection from the local cops. Tony was helpful at that meeting with his easy manner and lighthearted banter, which worked out so well, they all raised a glass at the end of the evening, satisfied that each side had gotten what they wanted.

At the same time, Tony was included in a high-level meeting with Vin and a guy named Andrew LaCocca, a multimillionaire who was planning a scheme to rip off a well-established banking institution. "And you boys would each get a hundred grand for this one. Providin' there are no fuckups. *Capisce*?"

"My good friend Tino said you guys have balls," said LaCocca, "but I don't know. They better be made of steel for the job I'm planning."

The threesome were sitting at Vittorio's Pizza Palace in the center of Bensonhurst, where the rushing traffic sounds drowned out their conversation.

"We won't disappoint you," said Vin coolly. He was taking to his role as future boss, staring down this wealthy, cocky guy who went nowhere without a bodyguard.

"Does that mean you guys are in?" LaCocca asked, suddenly standing. His bodyguard, nearly as thick as he was tall, grunted and stood also, his hand resting inside his jacket pocket.

"We're in," said Vin.

Tony nodded.

LaCocca and his man walked to the door and slipped into the moving crowd, passing pedestrians on the street. Vin and Tony exchanged glances. They were ready for this one, as if all their years of petty thievery and violence were preparation for the score they were about to make.

"Shit," said Tony. "Did he just say a hundred grand?"

"Yeah," agreed Vin, "apiece. For each of us. Let's get outta here."

It didn't make much sense to me at the time, but it did later.

After I left Janice, there was still time before dinner that I had planned to have at home, so I detoured to Our Lady of Guadalupe. The musty air with a faint hint of incense embraced me as I entered and sat in my usual seat for some quiet contemplation.

Surrounded by icons, I thought about what I had told Grandma on Christmas Day. A spiritual attachment to the Blessed Mother was a big part of me and that would always be so. The rites and customs associated with religious observance, on the other hand, were still foreign to me and I didn't know if that would ever change, either. I decided that that wasn't what was important. Just like what Tony did to survive wasn't important, either. What was important, I knew, were the feelings I had about the Blessed Mother and those between my boyfriend and me, and my faith in myself.

I prayed for a few minutes in the informal manner that was my own and then stole a final glance at the statue of Mary before dipping a finger into the holy water. I made the sign of the cross and then pushed on one of the two heavy wood doors at the rear of the church. As I skipped down the concrete steps, a familiar voice called out. "Stopped in for some inspiration, Samantha?"

I turned in the direction of Father Rinaldi, who was approaching, and my smile matched his. "I can always use some," I said as I joined him on the sidewalk.

Father Rinaldi placed a tender hand on my shoulder. "It's there for the taking, my child," he said. "What's important is how you use it."

"It restores me, Father. Makes me feel that anything's possible."

"As long as you keep the faith," he said.

My conviction about belief a few minutes before in the pew came back to me as I looked into the priest's eyes. "I will, Father," I said.

Father Rinaldi crossed his arms. "Bear in mind that you must keep your faith with those who also believe," he said. I thought about Tony and it seemed Father Rinaldi was reading my mind. "I'm not so sure Tony Kroon is one of them."

"He's no worse than any of the other guys around here," I said.

"Maybe in that group he runs with. But remember, Sam, Christ is our model and there are those who strive to be more like him every day. Maybe you're not seeing everybody."

I thought about Nick at Outer Skates, and about the nerds in school who stimulated my mind with their interests but didn't stir my budding womanhood. "I've seen a lot, Father," I said.

He glanced at my bracelet and his face tightened as he looked me in the eyes. "Including the inside of a precinct."

I lowered my head. "What he did wasn't all that bad," I said. A cold burst of wind swept the avenue and buffeted the naked branches above us and my own limbs. I shivered. Father Rinaldi spread his arm and his warmth across my shoulder.

"There are no degrees of wrong, Samantha," he said softly. "What's wrong is wrong."

I looked again into his face, which had turned beatific. He's shielding me in more ways than one, I said to myself. But, I thought, in the arms of the church as he was, he didn't have to reach out in the neighborhood. Tony and the rest of his guys did. They stuck together and used their connections to get somewhere. They lived in the real world, I thought, even if it was different than the one I was headed for. I believed in Tony, too, I decided, even if Father Rinaldi didn't. We were doing the best we could in the Bensonhurst outside the church's walls.

"I always try to do what's right, Father," I said.

His strong arm hugged me close. "I believe you, Sam." His eyes pierced my soul.

"Thanks, Father," I said. "You restore me, too."

"God does that, child. Remember his forgiveness always."

There was a mob of young people behind a red velvet rope at Platinum as Tony steered the Porsche to the curb in front of the club entrance. He got out and tossed the keys to a valet and I hurried to catch up to him at the smoked glass doors. Tony shared the usual laugh with his bouncer friend as he waved us through. A chorus of grumbles from those shivering on line was muted when the door closed behind us.

Tony grabbed my hand and pulled me through the packed club to the bar, where patrons stood three deep waiting for drinks. He caught the eye of a bartender and then jostled the young men in front of him as he reached toward the bar to put some money down.

"Who the fuck do ya think ya are?" one of the guys asked.

"Whatsit to ya?" Tony snarled as he wedged closer to the bar to wait for his drinks.

"Maybe ya should wait like everyone else," the guy said.

"And maybe ya should jus' shut the fuck up," Tony growled as he shoved the guy's upper body with a forearm. If it weren't for the others packed in around him, the guy might have gone sprawling, I thought. I stepped back as the guy steadied himself and started his hands toward Tony's chest. Tony thrust his hands and parted the guy's arms before they reached their target, and grabbed the guy's shirt near the collar. He jerked the guy close, popping two of his buttons, and got into his face. "Whoya with?" Tony growled.

The guy nodded toward his friends next to him. "Just these ... guys ... here," he stammered.

Tony tightened his grip. "I mean, whoya with?" he growled again. The guy's eyes narrowed and he didn't respond. "That's what I thought." Tony laughed and shoved him away. "Ya better watch yaself, then, if ya know what's good for ya." Tony picked up two drinks from the bar with one hand as he kept his eyes on the guy. He smirked as one of the guy's friends grabbed his arm and they all backed away and melted into the crowd.

"Fuckin' assholes," Tony muttered, and headed for the tables in the rear to find his friends. I followed close behind on the edge of the packed dance floor, where partiers gyrated to Al Wilson blaring from speakers that rocked the club:

Whoa, oh, oh, oh show and tell just a game I play
When I wanna say "I love you"

I may have to drag Tony with me across that bridge, I thought as we joined the foursome of our friends at a round table.

"Christ," Tony said when we sat down. "What a guy hasta go through jus' to get a fuckin' drink." He took a long swig from his scotch and water. Vin and Richie smiled broadly.

"Problems, Tone?" Richie asked.

"I almost hadda give some *stronzo* a beatdown," Tony said.

"There are dickheads everywhere," Vin said. "Ya gotta do what ya gotta do." The guys laughed as I exchanged fast hellos with Janice and Dara. I took a sip of my drink and winced. I wasn't accustomed to scotch.

"Whatsa matter?" Tony asked. "Too strong for ya?"

"A little."

"Well, I hadda get sumthin' in a hurry."

"It's okay," I said.

Vin waved to a waitress. "I'll get some more champagne," he said as he pointed to the empty bottle on the table and held up a flute. "Connie's a good girl. She'll be right over."

"Ya should know," Tony said, and the guys chuckled. Dara rolled her eyes. Tony downed his drink and grabbed another waitress as she walked by. "Bring me a coupla scotch and waters, honey, willya?" he said, his arm around her waist and his cheek inches from her breast.

"Sure thing, Tony," the girl said with a wide smile.

"Veronica's not bad, either," Tony cracked when she left. I frowned but didn't say anything. I may have to corral him, I thought, before I can drag him anywhere.

"Ya tryin' to catch up in a hurry, Tone?" Richie asked.

"Nah, deez glasses are like thimbles," Tony said. "Besides, the drinks are watered-down in this fuckin' place."

The guys traded comments and jokes as they polished off a couple of rounds of drinks. With their boisterous behavior and the loud music that shook the floor, it was impossible for the girls to trade much talk. I spent the time toying with my flute and looking at everyone on the dance floor having fun as they contorted to the sounds that bounced off the walls.

I tugged Tony's arm after half an hour. "Can we dance?" I asked.

"Later," he said without looking at me, and he continued his conversation with Vin. "So what's up with the lawyer?"

"That hard-on with a suitcase? He's worse than a loanshark. Gonna take our lungs."

"I thought your father was takin' care of it," Tony said.

"Yeah, he said he would," Vin said. "But we gotta take the weight ourselves."

Tony shook his head from side to side. "Ya sure?" he asked.

"I'll show 'im I can handle things."

"How?" Richie asked.

Vin turned toward Richie. "I got it all figured out," he said. "Doze punks won' know what hit 'em." Vin looked at Tony. "We'll talk aboudit later."

"Okay by me," Tony said, and then he stood up. "Gotta *pisciare*. Be right back."

"Don' stand next to any *finocchios* who might try'n grab your best friend," Vin cracked. Richie roared as Tony made his way to the men's room.

Vin put his arm on the back of my chair and leaned toward me. "So, ya met my father, huh?" he asked. I could smell the liquor on his breath.

"Yes. At his restaurant."

"He liked you."

My forehead wrinkled. "I didn't really talk to him that much," I replied.

"That's what he liked," Vin said with a smile, "'sides ya bein' a looker an' all." He glanced at Dara and turned back to me. "We like women who can keep quiet. Ain't that right, Richie?"

Richie pulled Janice close and breathed into her face. "'Cept when we're on top of 'em, huh, baby?" Janice blushed and

Richie finished his thought with a chuckle. "Then they can scream all they want."

Vin chuckled and reached for my wrist with his other hand. "Lemme see what my *compare* got ya for Christmas," he said as he raised my arm and eyed the bracelet. "Hmm, not bad. Coppo has some fine stuff, no?"

"I love it," I said.

Richie sat back and nodded toward the rock above Dara's cleavage. "Just the start of your collection," he said to me, "if you're good to 'im."

"She's good, period," Janice chimed in.

Vin eyed me up and down. "I'll bet she is," he said. I blushed, shifted in my seat, and then searched the room for Tony. I was glad when I saw that he was on his way back to the table. As he edged along the dance floor, a blond and brunette who were wriggling together reached out and pulled him onto the dance floor. My eyes widened and the Bee Gees reverberated in my ears:

What you doing on your back, aah,
What you doing on your back, aah,
You should be dancing, yeah
Dancing, yeah

Tony's hands pumped the air and his eyes never left the two young girls with tight bodies. Spotlights reflected off his teeth, which were exposed in a perpetual smile, as the girls pawed his open shirt. I shifted in my seat again, looked away, and caught Janice staring at me. I lowered my head, reached for my flute, and gulped some champagne until the song ended.

"Everythin' come out okay?" Vin cracked when Tony sat down at our table. I returned my gaze to the dance floor.

Tony grinned from ear to ear, beads of perspiration on his forehead. "Almost," he said.

"I've got to go to the ladies' room," I blurted as I slid my chair back.

Janice jumped up. "I'll go with you," she said, and came around the table to join me as I headed into the crowd.

"What the fuck was that?!" I blurted when the bathroom door closed behind us. The thump of the music and muffled lyrics provided a backdrop. "Geez," I said as I thrust my hair back with my fingers.

"Ignore him," Janice said. "It's all part of their bullshit."

"How can you say that?"

Janice grabbed my shoulders. "It's jus' them bein' macho, Sam. You'll get useta it."

"I'm not sure I ever will," I replied. "Or want to, for that matter."

Janice's hand moved to my wrist and she elevated it in front of my face. "Listen," she said. "It's you who he buys stuff for, and you who's goin' home with him. That's what matters."

I had definitive ideas about what mattered, but it was neither the time nor the place to go into them. "If you say so," I said.

"Good. Now let's go back out there and act like nothin's wrong."

We went back to the table and sat down. The guys didn't acknowledge our return as they kept up their animated conversation. Dara said nothing and she continued chewing gum as her head swiveled, seemingly bored with everything.

A few songs later, Tony grabbed my arm. "We gotta go," he said, and then we stood up. "Seeya around," Tony said to Vin and Richie, and then we weaved our way through the crowd again to the exit.

"Didya have a good time?" Tony asked as we pulled away.

"I guess," I said with a low voice.

Tony looked over at me and then at the road ahead. "Whatsa matter?" he asked. "It was fun, wasn't it?"

"I wanted to dance with you," I murmured as I stared through the windshield and wondered where we were headed.

"C'mon, the guys and me wuz jus' gettin' it on."

"That's not all you were getting on with."

Tony flicked a hand. "What? That jailbait? That wuz nuttin'."

"You didn't look like you disapproved," I said.

"Geez, Sam. What coulda I done? They practically raped me!"

"Sure, Tone."

He drove for a minute before he broke the heavy silence. "I'm tellin' ya, Sam, it wuz nuttin'."

Father Rinaldi leapt into my mind. "Just like your case is nothing," I said.

"Total bullshit," Tony sputtered, and he turned toward me again. "Besides, that's my bizness, not yours."

But it would soon be mine, too.

15

In the week between Christmas and New Year's, Pamela had taken off for a few days to visit her sister upstate, and on Friday night, Philip was out playing poker and Katrina was sleeping over at a friend's house. Tony and I had the Kroon home to ourselves.

We snuggled together on his parents' bed under a Blessed Mother statue that hung on the wall directly above us, and we were at peace in each other's arms, watching *The Maltese Falcon*. I thought Peter Lorre looked soft and timid, especially next to Humphrey Bogart, who made everyone look weak. "I love the old movies, Sam," Tony said. "Don't you?"

"Sure do," I lied. I preferred contemporary films, but if I could spend the time cuddling with Tony, I really didn't care what we watched. I thought for a moment about my novel being turned into a movie, and how cool that would be. Someday, I thought . . . someday.

"Yeah," Tony said as the movie ended and the credits ran, "they jus' don' make 'em like they useta."

"You sound like an old man," I said with a good-natured smile. "You know, the kids today are no good and all the rest of it."

"Ya think I'm an old man?" Tony asked, twisting my arm

behind me. He wrestled me underneath him and then pinned my arms above my head. I laughed and tried to wriggle away. "Take it back," he said.

"Uh-uh," I said, struggling to get loose.

"Man, you're a feisty one," Tony said, and strengthened his grip. "I said, take it back."

"No chance."

"Then pay the price," he said, easily holding my two hands in his one as he began to sneak his fingers up my short vinyl skirt.

Ripples of excitement charged through my body as I squirmed to get away from him, but truth be told, I wasn't trying all that hard. "Okay, okay," I acquiesced, "I take it back."

"Too late," he said, continuing to push his fingers inside my panties.

"C'mon, Tony," I said. "That feels good . . . but I really don't think I'm ready."

"You're soaking wet, Sam," he said, focusing on touching me just right. "You're ready, believe me." He continued to hold my hands over my head as he began licking down the center of my chest. With his free hand, he ripped off my blouse.

"Watch it, Tone," I said in the midst of my pleasure. "My grandma gave me that. And she can't afford a new one."

"We'll just hafta buy ya another, then, won't we?" he said as he rolled on top of me, parting my legs with his knee. "Sam, tell me you need me. Right now. Tell me, 'cause I need ya so bad, baby!" He pulled my bra down, grabbed my nipple with his thumb and index finger, and squeezed.

"Ooooh," I moaned in response. Tony relaxed his grip on my hands as his tongue traced an areola. I had never felt such burning pleasure in all my life, both on my breasts and between my legs. When he bit my nipple, I pulled his head away from my chest. "Ow!" I said. "That hurt."

"I didn't mean ta hurt ya, Sam," he moaned in my ear.

Sweat had formed on his forehead and temples. This time it's for me, I thought. "It's jus' that ya get me so hot, I lose it." Tony lowered his head and nibbled at my breasts gently. I threw my head back, moaned again, and wondered about the huge bulge in his pants. I wanted to touch it, but I was just so afraid that if I did, there would be no going back, and I still wasn't sure I was ready.

Tony stared into my eyes as if to hypnotize me. Then he took off my skirt and pulled down my panties. I arched my back instinctively as Tony's fingers took control, playing me like a finely tuned piano that put sound to the way I was reeling. I had never felt anything like it, and then he stopped. Panting, and groggy as if awakening from a dream, I looked at Tony, whose eyes were fixated between my legs.

Self-conscious, I giggled. "So how's the view?"

"Don' make fun, Sam." He ripped off his jeans to reveal his throbbing penis. My eyes opened wide. It was bigger than I had ever imagined one to be. It looked strange, but I had never seen one before so I guessed it was normal. "Meet my best friend, Sam," Tony said with a twisted grin. "I know he's big but don' worry. He really likes you." More than his mother does, I thought as Tony stroked my thighs. It didn't seem to matter where he touched me; I felt it all in the soft, wet tissue between my legs. I sank into the pillow and closed my wondering eyes. I couldn't think anymore.

Tony spread my legs wider with his elbows and kneaded my bottom cheeks with his powerful hands while he brought me to a shuddering climax with his tongue. The giant between his legs seemed to have grown, if that was possible, and just as I was about to speak Tony placed the tip of his erection against my softest place.

My eyes popped open and I saw the Blessed Mother above me. I didn't know if what I was doing then was right and that frightened me. I inhaled sharply and felt a staggering pressure at my vagina, which opened to receive a man's lust for the first time. I knew then that I wasn't dreaming. The pain was so intense I thought I might pass out, but the pleasure that accompanied it soon after made me ache for more, an ache I knew would find its way onto the page. It was all so complicated to understand.

I shortened my breaths and tried to accommodate his size as Tony began to thrust with everything he had in him. I felt as though I were in a car that was racing at full speed and couldn't stop. I didn't know if I could take any more pain and pleasure, but I held on and he let out a moan so deep and demanding that I surged my hips forward to meet his passion. He threw his arms around me as we rocked back and forth together, sounds coming out of both of us the likes of which I had never heard before. And then the car crashed at last when Tony climaxed inside of me.

It was over so, so fast that I asked myself why there was such a big fuss about it. I had thought it would last a lot longer; that's what Janice had told me. There was this big buildup to it, which was better than the actual intercourse, I thought. Tony slumped his entire weight on me and I tried to inhale. "I can't breathe, Tony," I said. He propped himself on his arms. "You'll get used to it. You're lucky I don' weigh as much as Richie. Janice has some damned thick thighs ta support him, though, huh?" Tony slid off of me and turned over on his back.

"You shouldn't be talkin' about Janice like that," I said. "She's my best friend and she's really trying to lose some weight."

"Right," said Tony. He stared at my nakedness. "Go to the bathroom, Sam," he said, "and bring back some toilet paper."

"Why?"

"Jesus Christ, just do it," he said. "And come right back. Don't even pee." I shook my head and got out of bed. My eye caught the Blessed Mother again above the bed and it seemed She was staring at me. I got a weird feeling in my stomach as I went into the bathroom, and then I stopped for a moment to stare into the mirror. I was not a virgin anymore. Did it show on my face? I wondered.

"What the hell are ya doin'?" Tony asked after less than a minute.

"I'll be right there," I called out, and wondered what the hell he wanted as I brought a long strand of toilet paper to the bedside. "What do you want me to do with this?" I asked. "Wear it on my head?"

"Wipe yourself down there," he directed, "and show it to me."

"What the hell is the matter with you, Tone?"

"Just do it," he said.

I exhaled and swiped the toilet paper across my swollen vaginal lips. I winced and closed my eyes for a moment. When I brought the tissue back up and we looked at it, I was shocked to find blood on the paper. I was alarmed, but I was even more shocked when Tony smiled. "Okay," he said. "Good."

"What do you mean 'good'?" I asked. "I'm bleeding."

Tony laughed. "It's just your cherry, dummy. It was supposeta break. I swear to God, if you'd been lyin' to me, I don' know what I woulda done." I fumed as I stared at him, naked, my vagina still burning as the Blessed Mother still looked down at me. "What's wrong now?" Tony asked as he got up, tied a towel around his waist, and strutted toward the bathroom.

"I can't believe you thought I was lying to you," I said. "I feel humiliated."

"Jus' try ta stay mad," he said as he closed the bathroom door. I had a bitter taste in my mouth but decided to let it go. Now that he knew he was my first, I thought, maybe he'd become more manageable. I slumped onto the bed and pulled the covers over me.

When Tony had finished in the bathroom, he raised the sheet and slid in next to me. He touched between my legs again and I cried out. "It hurts down there, Tony," I said.

"That's 'cause I'm built like a horse," he said. "Ask any-one. But don' worry, you'll get useta it." He leaned toward me and inhaled. "I swear to God, ya smell so good. I never thought a girl could get to me like this." He kissed me on the back of the hand and got back on top of me. I didn't want to do it, but he forced himself on me. I felt like I was being raped, but I didn't want to disappoint him. It hurt so much, I hated it, I truly did. How could I love him so but hate having him inside me?

"Ya take a rest and I'll make ya the best damned refried rigatonis youse ever ate. Mom's recipe," Tony said. I flinched at the mention of his mother as he got out of bed and headed for the kitchen.

My mind drifted while Tony cooked. So I was no longer a virgin, I thought. It had to happen sooner or later, and why not with a guy who put me on a pedestal? I felt like I had finally matured and that made me think about growing up with my mom and grandmother. Would they know? I asked myself. I decided I'd have to get home after they went to sleep so they wouldn't see me walking funny.

My vagina was just so sore. Could he have been gentler? I wondered. I'd check with Janice, but I didn't remember her complaining about when she had been deflowered. Maybe I'm different that way, too, I said to myself, and I got up to dress. I rummaged around for my panties, put on my skirt, and had to tie my blouse because some buttons were missing. I'll be sewing these back on, I said to myself. No way Grandma is going to see this blouse, I vowed.

Tony turned toward me when I joined him in the kitchen. "You'll always be my little virgin," he said, and then returned his attention to the stove. He looked so funny, shirtless and cooking, dressed only in a towel. I laughed to myself as Tony went on. "If anybody so much as thinks about ya wrong, I swear he'll pay." There was nothing funny about that, I thought. "Hope ya like rigatonis," Tony said over his shoulder. "It's my favorite pasta."

I sighed and went into the living room to wait. Angel hair was my favorite, oh well. I wondered how long I would really be his "little virgin" now.

16

On New Year's Eve, I checked myself in my bedroom mirror. I could have worn something that Tony had bought for me, but instead I straightened the skirt of the dress that Grandma had altered for me just for the occasion. We might not have had enough money to buy something off the rack, but Grandma was a whiz with the sewing machine and she had transformed my old, dowdy black sheath into an elegant little party dress with a fitted bodice. After I put on the pearl earrings and neck-lace that Grandma lent to me and the diamond and platinum bracelets Tony had given me, I felt that I looked sensational. I went to greet him when I heard his booming voice shortly after nine o'clock.

Tony was finishing a round of polite kisses and hugs as I entered the living room. He commented on how lovely my mother looked, gave chocolates to Grandma and a bottle of champagne to Mom as she stood stiffly, and then flattered the hell out of me. I couldn't have been more proud to be his girlfriend. I grabbed my coat and Tony escorted me out of the apartment with his arm affixed to my waist.

I was buoyant as he made a big show of treating me like a lady when he opened the car door for me, once again knowing that we were being watched from the window that overlooked the street. But by the time we got to the corner, he was trying to get his hands under my dress. I shoved him away. "Stop it, Tone," I said. "You only think about one thing."

"Ya just look so damned hot, Sam, I can hardly control myself." His advances, though crude, nonetheless flattered me and his rugged looks made me melt.

"You don't look so bad yourself," I said. His white shirt was unbuttoned nearly to the waist and he was wearing an extra gold necklace over the others that were usually wrapped around his neck. "Looks like you got a new chain."

Tony laughed. "Dem Coppos are still payin' off their debt," he said. He reached under my dress again, but I shoved his hand away once more.

"I told ya to cut it out. I gotta stay neat and make a good impression on your mom," I said. I looked at my wrist where Tony's Christmas present sparkled as we passed each streetlight. "I still don't think I should be wearing this. You told me yourself it made your mom jealous."

"Ya jus' keep it on. I need ta show it off. What the hell did I get it for?" Tony grunted. "Besides, my mom loves you."

"I'm not that naive, Tony," I said. "I could tell how she felt."

"Well, she better get useta ya," he said, "'cause I wan' ya wid me. She has ta like ya." Tony squeezed the steering wheel. "I'll make her."

I lowered my eyes. "I don't think it works that way, Tone."

"It works like I say it will. Just hold that wrist out when ya meet people—like this." Tony thrust his wrist close to my eyes and laughed.

I shoved it away as I chuckled. "I don't want to blind anybody," I said. "Especially your mother."

"My mom is a good ol' girl. Ya just need to learn how ta manage her," Tony said as he pulled up to his house. "C'mon. Watch what I do."

The party was in full swing in the living room when Tony

and I arrived, and he made a big show of hugging his mother. Unfortunately, I had been right about the bracelet. After a fast greeting, Pamela glared at the diamond heart that glinted on my wrist. She said nothing more and walked away.

I did my best to avoid the hostess of the party, the mother of my steady boyfriend who was as jealous as if she were his girlfriend herself. It was very uncomfortable to be around that woman, but I convinced myself I had to adjust.

Katrina pouted when she saw me, said a fast hello, and then walked away just as her mother had done. I saw her sneak a beer and head for the rear hall but I didn't bother telling anyone. If the alcohol would change her nasty expression and her negative attitude, I was all for it, but I doubted that the drink would make a bit of difference.

I sipped from a champagne flute and Tony introduced me to his aunt Tessie and Uncle Nicky, Philip Kroon's brother, and I met close family friends such as Gilda and Mikey Coravano. Tony told me to mingle while he made a phone call.

The only person I didn't approach was a beautiful young woman with long legs and blond hair who never got up from the stuffed leather armchair in the center of the room, as if she were holding court. Her looks were striking and I watched as people came and went, bringing her food and drink. She just looked so damned self-assured, as if she couldn't care less who else was there as long as they hovered over her.

"Didya meet everybody?" Tony asked me when he came back.

"I think so," I said. I cast a glance in the blond woman's direction. "Mostly."

"Good," Tony said. "You're makin' a big splash, Sam. They all love ya, I just know it. Make sure they see the bracelet. Ya know, flash it around."

"Sure, Tony, whatever you say." Tony took my empty flute. "Let me freshen up your glass," he said, and headed for the bar. He stopped on the way to kiss the blond woman on her cheek.

She looked up at him with heavy eyelids and smiled, and her hand lingered on his arm when he walked away. Who the hell was she? I wondered.

I scanned the room but Janice and Richie hadn't arrived yet. Vin and Richie worked the stereo equipment and Frankie Valli sang out,

> *No woman's worth crawling on the earth*
> *Just walk like a man, my son*

Someone tapped my arm and grabbed my elbow. I turned and saw Pamela Kroon next to me. "Hi, S-a-a-am," she said. A few drinks must have improved her friendliness, I thought.

"Great party, Pamela," I said. "It's nice to be here."

Pamela took a healthy sip from her glass. "Where elsh wouldya be? After all, we're almost related." She looked down at my empty hands. "Go get s-shumethin' ta drink," she said.

"Tony's getting me one," I answered.

"Isn't my Tony s-sumthin'?" she gushed.

I looked around for him but he was still out of the room. "He's the best," I said. My eyes rested again on the seated blond.

"She's s-sum beauty, huh?" Pamela asked.

"Yes, she is. Who is she?" I asked, but regretted showing interest in her.

"Oh, no one," Pamela said with a glint in her eye. "Jus' an ol' frien' a Tony's." She scooted away as Tony returned with a Long Island iced tea for me. I thought I shouldn't mix drinks but I didn't say anything.

"Ya know sumthin', Sam?" Tony asked. "You're so beauti-ful, ya make me want to throw ya down right here and have my way with ya."

"Not with all these people here!" I giggled.

"Yeah, they might get in the way," he cracked, his face flushed.

"I'm thinking they might not like it," I said. "Your mother sure wouldn't."

"And I'm thinkin' I don't give a fuck," Tony said. He pulled me close and gulped his highball. "I gotta go talk ta Vin. Mingle some more, okay? Everybody here loves ya," Tony said once more, and then slipped away. I knew that wasn't true no matter how many times he said it, and wished he would just stay with me. I wandered over to Aunt Tessie, who had an inviting manner.

"Hello, Samantha," Tessie called out with a warm smile as I approached. "What a beautiful dress!"

"It was specially designed," I said.

"I can tell," Tessie said.

"You look real nice, too," I said.

Tessie chuckled. "This old thing? I wear it every year." She leaned in close to me. "I really come for the food," Tessie whispered. "Have you tried the crab balls? They're ta die for."

"Everything's great," I said, and my eyes returned to the blond on display in the center of the room. She flipped her luxurious hair back from her face.

"That's Rochelle," Aunt Tessie said. "Damned pity, isn't it?"

"What?" I asked. I couldn't imagine why that girl should be pitied.

"You didn't hear about the car accident? She's so young. What a shame. She was something before it happened. But you could hardly blame Tony for not wanting to be with her anymore. He's so strong and virile. He needs someone who can keep up with him, the little egotistical bastard that he is." Tessie winked. "You should know, right?" I was shocked. Did all their family members speak about one another in that manner? I wondered. I smiled but was confused about Rochelle. She used to be Tony's girlfriend? Why hadn't he mentioned that? And why would she be there, anyway? "Nice of the family to still include her, after what he did to her, don't you think?" Tessie asked.

I was shocked by her response but wouldn't dare pry further. It was obvious this girl being here was Tony's penance. "After all, this was the only way she would stop the nasty lawsuit and drag them all through the mud," Tessie laughed. I didn't even want to know; besides, I had a different opinion about that, but nodded anyway. I watched Rochelle smile at Vin, who handed her a plate of hors d'oeuvres that he had brought to her. When she shifted her position to take the food, I saw the ends of heavy metal braces on her legs that had been hidden under her long plaid skirt. She was what young, callous locals called a gimp. My annoyance and simmering anger about Tony's beautiful former girlfriend being there were replaced by the pity that Aunt Tessie had mentioned.

Tony came out of the kitchen and joined Vin at Rochelle's side and tousled her hair. They bantered with her for a couple of minutes and then Tony walked over to me. "Lookit," he said, "Vin and me are goin' outside for a few minutes."

I nodded in Rochelle's direction. "Why didn't you tell me about her?"

"'Cause she's no one."

Pity for her couldn't subdue a pang of jealousy. "It doesn't look that way to me," I said.

"Fuhgeddaboud Rochelle. She's got nothin' to do with you."

I screwed my eyes and my lips tightened. "That's not how I feel," I said.

Tony twisted my arm with his massive hand and pulled me close to him. Everyone in the room looked at us. "I tol' ya never to air our stuff in public," he grunted. "When I tell you to forget sumthin', I expect ya ta fuhgedit." His voice rose. "Now get outta my face!" he said, and slapped me with the back of his hand. My jaw dropped and I gasped for air. I thought my teeth had come out of my mouth. All around me felt surreal.

Pamela couldn't hold back a grin. It seemed as though she had been counting the moments and knew it was bound to happen. Tony nodded at Vin and they stopped at the bar to grab beers before going out the back door.

I ran to the bathroom.

I glared with disbelief at my red cheek in the mirror and then heard a knock at the door. "Samantha, please let me in, honey." I recognized Aunt Tessie's voice. I opened the door and saw her standing there, shaking her head. She came into the bathroom and shut the door behind her. "Let me see," she said as she turned my chin toward her. "It ain't so bad, is it," she said.

"How could he do this to me?" I sobbed. "That son of a bitch!"

"Better not let him hear ya say that," Tessie warned. She sat on the closed toilet seat.

I stood over the sink, looking at my face. "Are you saying he had the right to do that to me?"

"Of course not, Sam. No one has the right to hit anybody, but that doesn't mean he won't. There are ways to make sure these things don't happen. Like never start stuff in front of anyone."

"I didn't start it," I protested. "He did."

"That's beside the point," said Tessie. "I'm telling ya, no arguin', no complainin', and absolutely no jealous rages. These guys like to make their women jealous; it makes them feel like more of a man. But if we complain in front of others, they think it makes them look weak, like they can't take care a their woman. It only pisses him off if he can't control you."

I wiped my eyes with a tissue. "Well, he can't," I said.

"But ya hafta make him *think* he can. That's the name of the game. I do it all the time with Nicky." Tessie got up and put an arm across my shoulder. "It's good to learn this while you're still young. It's not the end of the world." She gave me a fast tug. "C'mon, let's go back out there together," Tessie said. "Smile. Okay?"

I forced a smile, although I knew Tony's behavior was wrong. Very wrong, and no amount of explaining could change that. The last thing I wanted was to be stuck like Janice was. That would never happen to me. What happened to my mother—that could never happen to me, either. Never, I vowed. Then an even smaller voice said something to me: "It just did." The words went on and on in my head as I followed Tessie back to the living room. I knew that I should have left but I was afraid that if I did, the repercussions would be enormous. I did not like feeling that way.

I dreaded facing anyone, so I walked across the room without making eye contact and took a seat by myself on a folding chair while Tessie joined her husband. Was she glad she'd married Nicky? I wondered. She looked like she was, but how could she be? I was different from these people, I thought. Sure, I wanted to be in love with Tony, but I had bigger and better things to do than placate a macho asshole with lies and strokes so he wouldn't smack me. Maybe Tony and I should call it quits, I considered. But I had given myself to him. Didn't that mean anything?

"Hey," Tony said. In my simmering rage, I hadn't seen him come in. I looked up for a moment and then turned away and lowered my eyes. "Hey," I said in a flat voice.

"Can I sit?"

"Your house, your chair," I said.

"Look, baby," Tony said as he took a seat, "I guess I lost it for a moment there." I said nothing. "Ya givin' me the silent treatment? Don' bother, 'cause it ain't gonna work."

I stared straight ahead but felt his eyes on me. "How could you do that to me?" I asked. "I thought you loved me."

Tony touched my arm. "I toldya, Sam, I lost it. Rochelle don' mean nuttin' ta me."

I turned toward him. "Oh, yeah? Well, she meant enough for you to belt me one."

"No," he said, his voice low. "I'm tellin' ya. It was the way ya talked to me in front of my friends and family." He squeezed my arm. "I warned ya."

I squirmed, trying to loosen his grip. "I wouldn't worry about your mother," I said. "She looked happy when you hit me. Probably wanted to join in."

"That's nuts, Sam."

"Like mother, like son," I said. "I didn't do anything 'cept ask you a question."

His anger bubbled up again. "Ya made me look like a fool. It ain't right. I told ya it wasn't allowed. No guy wants to look pussy-whipped. I'da told you about her. Just not right then, ya know?" I grunted. He never said he shouldn't have done it, but he had apologized in his own lame way, hadn't he? I asked myself. At least he cared enough to try, I thought. I was hurt but didn't want to break up with Tony, I decided. All couples had problems, I reasoned. Even Grandma had said so. Maybe we could work it out.

"It's almost midnight, Sam," Tony said. "Don' ya wanna get a kiss for New Year's?" he purred. "'Specially since I'm goin' out later and all."

"When?" I asked.

"Right after midnight. Vin and I were supposeta leave earlier but I told him I hadda be with my girl when the ball goes down. See?" he asked, and glanced at Rochelle, who was still in her chair and had kept her eyes focused on us. "I'd rather be with you any day than a gimp who can't walk. No matter how good she looks," he added before turning his eyes back to me. I didn't know what to say to that. Tony leaned close. "Tell me ya love me," he whispered in my ear, and teased my earlobe between his teeth.

I leaned away from him. "Don't ever do that again, Tony," I said.

"Tell me ya love me," Tony repeated as he squeezed my arm again. "I mean it."

I hesitated for a long moment. Midnight was seconds away and I didn't want to contemplate not being with the man who had taken my virginity. "I do, Tone," I said.

The ball in Times Square hit bottom and lit up. Tony and I kissed as Pamela shuffled by. "The lovers are at it again," she said.

Fifteen minutes later, Tony and Vin gave each other the eye. Vin gave Dara a peck on her cheek and headed over to us. "I gotta go now, Sam," Tony said.

I frowned. "I thought we could spend some time . . . you know."

"It's tradition, Sam," Tony said as he stood up next to Vin. "We been goin' out every New Year's Eve since forever," he said to Vin. "Right?" Vin nodded, his face blank. "You don' expect me to break tradition, do ya?" Tony asked. It was something harmless that they always did, I reasoned. Just some stupid thing the guys did to make them feel like guys. Nothing worth getting into another fight over.

"'Course not, Tony." I said. I stood and gave him a fast hug as Vin headed for the door.

"Better not have a long face or my mom'll think ya didn't like her party," Tony said. "Janice and you can go home together when she gets here."

I scanned the room looking for my friend, who was very late. I hoped she was all right. "What about Richie?" I asked. "Isn't he goin', too?"

Tony grabbed both of my arms. "What the hell have I been tellin' ya, Sam? Don' ask me about my business." I lowered my face. Tony put his fingers under my chin, pressed his thumb under my lip, and forced me to look into his eyes. "Smile for me, Sam," he said. "I need ya ta support me. We talked about that, too. Remember?" Once more, I forced a smile. "Good,"

Tony said. "That's my girl." He let go of my chin. "I'll see ya around," Tony said, and then he caught up to Vin and left.

I didn't know when that would be. And I didn't know how long I could stay in his house without him.

I felt like my mother. I felt like her mirror.

17

The ringing telephone beside my bed jarred me for a second time late New Year's morning. I had decided to sleep in and intended to stay right where I was—huddled under my quilt that was pulled up to my ears—as long as I could. I heard footsteps in the hall, and I knew it had to be my grandmother. Mom's still unconscious, I thought.

After a low knock, Grandma opened the door and peeked in. I kept my head on the pillow, with the cheek that had been slapped resting on it, and I looked toward her. "It's Janice, Samelah. I told her you were still in bed, but it's the second time she's called." Thank God, I thought; she hadn't shown up at Tony's house. After I'd waited another fifteen minutes, most of it spent during another visit to the bathroom, I split because I couldn't stand the eyes and small talk from Tony's family any longer. "Do you want for me to tell her you'll call back?" Grandma asked in her sweet voice.

"No," I murmured, "that's all right, Grandma." I stretched a hand to the phone. "I'll take it. Thanks."

"Happy New Year, Sammy," Grandma said.

"You, too," I said as she closed the door. I picked up the extension and then rolled over and stared at the ceiling.

"Sam?" Janice said when she heard the click on the line. "You all right?"

"Yeah," I replied, as I cleared the cobwebs. "I was worried, too. Christ, where were you?"

"I couldn't tear Richie away from Rocco's."

I paused for a second. "And I couldn't keep Tony with me," I said.

"The annual tradition with Vin."

"Right."

"Did he call this morning?"

"Nope," I replied, and thought about the last time I had heard his voice. "I asked him when he split why Richie wasn't with them."

"That's why he got drunk. He's always sayin' how he introduced Tony to Vin an' all, but he ain't included on everything."

"Why?"

"Fuck if I know. Richie doesn't, either, but he makes like it's no big deal."

"Those guys, Janice," I sighed.

"I know," she said, then paused. "Who drove ya home?"

"I took the subway."

"At that hour? Wid all da bums?"

"It wasn't as bad as some other things."

There was a longer pause before she spoke again. "I heard about the slap. Dara called me first thing. Couldn't wait ta blab."

I ran my fingers over the cheek that had met Tony's hand. "I didn't do nothin'," I sighed.

"Ya know I know," Janice said. "Listen. I gotta go have brunch with my family."

"Yeah. Tradition."

"Meet me at Sally's at three, okay?"

Any excuse to get out of the apartment was fine by me. I'd hibernate another hour and then hurry out the door. Grandma wouldn't mind, and, with any luck, Mom wouldn't have stirred yet. And she might not be coherent even if she had, I thought. "I'll be there," I said, and we hung up.

Sally's was packed with hungover diners huddled over coffee cups and some solid food when we met there. The usual buzz of conversation was missing as almost everyone kept to himself. If it weren't for the clink of glasses, dishware, and utensils, the place would be as quiet as my church, I thought. Janice and I saved our conversation while we waited a few minutes for a booth.

"Eat sumthin'," Janice said when we sat down. "I'm stuffed."

"No problem," I said as I grabbed a menu. "I hardly ate anything at Pamela's party and skipped breakfast."

"Not up for a cross-examination, huh?" Janice chuckled.

"You know it."

"Well, at least they wouldn't have asked about your cheek. It looks fine, Sam."

"Yeah, I checked it out in the mirror first thing. But I'm still steamed."

"It's no fun, that's for sure," Janice said, "especially in public an' all."

"It's not just that," I said. "Tony dancin' right in front of me and droppin' me off early all the time . . . I don't know, Jan."

"You're too motivated to let that get to ya, or stop ya from gettin' where you're headed."

"It's hard enough," I sighed. "I don't need the extra baggage."

"Don' let it weigh ya down."

I thought about how the next New Year would bring my graduation from high school. "I won't," I said, and looked my best friend in the eyes. "Know what's weird? I miss him already."

"Tell me aboudit," Janice said. "I've given up tryin' ta figga it out." I placed our order for a Greek omelet and two coffees and then continued the conversation.

"Speaking of baggage," I started, "how's Richie?"

"Ya think I know? Probably still holed up in bed."

"That's where I'd still be if you hadn't called."

"Nah, Grandma Ruth woulda dragged ya out." We laughed together and it felt good. Janice leaned on the table toward me. "Listen," she started, her voice lowered, "now that ya been wit' Tony a while, I figure I can share some shit I got from Richie." Janice looked quickly around the diner.

"He tells you stuff?" I asked.

She chuckled. "Yeah, when he's blotto. Swear ya won' tell a soul." That word, "swear," made me think of Father Rinaldi once more. There was no way I'd breathe a word of anything she said about what went on with the Brooklyn Boys to anyone I knew. Especially the beatific priest.

"Who am I gonna tell?" I said.

"Vin's determined to pay the lawyer. Won't hear of leanin' on his father for the millionth time," Janice said. "They're desperate for money."

After a long pause that seemed interminable, I said, "So?"

Janice looked around again before she strained to get closer. "Richie said sumthin's goin' down," she said softly. "Sumthin' big."

My eyes widened. "While their case is still going on?"

"Don' ask me. I jus' listened," she said, and then she stiffened and slid back against her seat. Her eyes were focused over my shoulder. I turned around to follow her gaze and saw Richie striding toward us before I faced Janice again. She whispered, "My father musta told 'im where he could find me."

"Hey," Richie said to me as he nudged Janice over and sat down in the booth. His round face sported a two-day growth.

"Happy New Year," I said.

"Yeah," he responded. "Youse eat yet?" His speech was labored.

"Sam's waiting for her order," Janice said. "I had brunch at home. Wish you coulda been there."

Richie ran both hands through his disheveled hair. "My fuckin' head's still poundin'," he said. He didn't see Janice's narrow smile as he perused a menu. "Don' know what the fuck I feel like havin'."

"Stomach okay?" Janice asked.

"Fuck no," Richie replied. "Prayed to the porcelain god all night and it's still rumblin'." He missed both of our smiles after he said that. "I'll just get a double order a toast and some coffee," Richie said as he closed his menu and looked up. "What're youse two talkin' about?"

Janice's eyes met mine. "Nuthin'," she said. "Girl stuff."

"Sorry I missed it," Richie cracked. "Where's Tone?" he asked me.

"No idea," I said.

"Seein' him later?"

"Your guess is as good as mine."

"Well, I'm seein' 'im an' Vin in an hour. Wanna send a message?"

"Just tell him I said hi, and that I'll be at home."

Janice turned toward her boyfriend. "Willya be long?" she asked.

"Don' know," Richie said, and then he smiled. "Vin said he's got sumthin' for me."

Janice and I caught each other's eyes again. "That's great," she said. "We gonna hook up after?"

"Don' count on it."

"Okay. I'll be home, too," Janice said, and then looked at me. "Ya wanna hang at my place?"

"Can't," I said. "I got homework. School starts tomorrow."

Respect was the topic as I pounded away on my Smith-Corona that evening. Over a couple of pages, exploration of that theme led to expanding it to include acknowledgment of oneself. You can't respect someone else, I wrote, if you don't respect yourself. I wrestled with where one should draw the line, and counseled that one should pay attention to what the head is saying while also listening to the heart.

I sat back and took my own advice for a few minutes. I had to deal with what Tony had done. While there may not have been any outward signs on my cheek, the sting remained with me. The thought that he had crossed my own line nagged at me. And then I thought about my mother.

Although it hadn't been physical abuse at home, I'd put up with a lot more from her, I reasoned. Was it just because of a blood tie? I wondered. Did Grandma's deflecting of some of the shit that came my way help me to maintain my dignity? Regardless, I concluded, I wouldn't have to deal with it too much longer. I was headed for the real world, which would bestow enough affirmation to remove me from Bensonhurst and insulate me from the slings at home . . . and from Tony's. I decided I wouldn't let him cross that line again.

My fingers moved once more to the keyboard. He always talked about respect, but it can't be one-sided, I wrote. It can't be just about the other person. And it can't be just about two people, either. There were others, such as my grandma and Father Rinaldi, whose feelings needed consideration, and times with those such as Mom and Pamela when accommodation had to be sought. You may not be as close to them, but you had to give them their space as you fought to establish your own.

I finished the article and slipped it into my bookcase. It's a good start to the year, I said to myself. I rose from my desk, straightened my hair, and took another look at my face in the mirror even though neither Mom nor Grandma had said anything about it during dinner. When I had assured myself that an unpleasant chapter in my life couldn't be read on my face, I shut off the light and opened my bedroom door. As I headed down the short hallway, Lawrence Welk's familiar "an' a one, an' a two, an' a three" reached my ears. Grandma sure held sway over her space, I chuckled to myself.

New Keiser High School was abuzz the next morning. Everyone was upbeat despite the vacation being over, showing off some of their presents and trading tales of holiday revelry. I fit right in; more than a few girls remarked about the bracelet that jangled on my wrist. A gift like that said a lot to my peers, as did getting picked up at school with a Harley or a Porsche. The grapevine had already spread the news about me and Tony, and I garnered more interest from the girls, who probed me for some juicy details about a local hunk. The word "respect" popped into my head again as we chatted in the hallways and stairwells. Did they sense how close Tony and I had gotten on Friday night? I wondered. Did my passage into womanhood and the hard-won confidence that came with it show on my face? Regardless, pieces of the article that I had turned in came to me along with the girls' questions, and I gave them just enough to confirm my standing with Tony without violating my relationship with him.

As I headed to a conference with Mr. Wainright at the end of the day, I wondered, too, if Tony respected me. I had given myself to him; did that lessen me in his eyes? I asked myself but dismissed that thought right away. If nothing else, Tony sure had a powerful regard for my virginity, I said to myself as I recalled the scene in the bedroom after he had taken it. But would he be able to respect the line I had drawn? I pondered as I turned the knob outside Mr. Wainright's office and entered.

The cramped room was filled with bookcases and a small, worn couch that was against the wall opposite Mr. Wainright's desk. I sat on a wood armchair across from him. Dust particles were suspended in the rays of light that pierced the multiple panes of a tall window behind him. The room smelled and felt like the bookstore.

"Well," Mr. Wainright began, my pages in his hand, "I see it wasn't just partying for you over the last week."

"No, sir. Writers write . . . right?" I smiled at my play on words.

Mr. Wainright's face was expressionless. "It's nice to see you so upbeat, Sam."

"The whole place is," I said.

"I'm not talking about holiday cheer," he said. I scrunched my eyebrows. Mr. Wainright placed the pages on his desk and looked me in the eye. "Writers write what they know, too, Sam," he said. "I can read between the lines, too." I sat back in my chair and he continued after a downward glance. "There's some heavy stuff in there."

"Too much bleeding?"

"No, realism brings people into a story. Makes them relate. Makes for good writing." Mr. Wainright sat back in his large swivel chair and clasped his hands behind his head as was his wont. He raised an eyebrow. "I have some concerns about *your* reality."

"I can only write about my life," I said.

"That's the point, Sam," he said, and then rested his arms on his desk. "I know all about what goes on in the neighborhood streets. I don't want to see you get sidetracked."

"You know me, Mr. Wainright," I said with smiling eyes. "I'm just passin' through."

"I hope so. But don't hesitate to come to me—or someone else you trust who has your best interests in mind." I nodded as he grabbed the pages and stood. He squeezed around his desk and put a hand on my shoulder. "Now, let's get this published," Mr. Wainright said.

✧ ✧ ✧

I did my best to concentrate on my work at the bookstore—had to, returns were still pouring in—but that had become increasingly harder to do over the previous weeks. My life and my writing demanded more and more of my attention, and I found myself easily distracted, as I was on that Monday. I just couldn't get Tony or the people who made reference to who he was out of my mind.

I hadn't heard from him since he had dropped me off, and he wasn't outside the school that day to drive me to work. Not that I looked that hard at the usual gathering of vehicles at the curb; I didn't really expect him to be there after hearing the way Richie talked about a meeting that seemed pressing and exciting to him. Tony and Vin would no doubt be worked up about it, too, I thought.

I was glad when closing time came and I bolted out the door. I only gave a cursory glance to the vehicles outside before huddling under my coat and heading for the subway. I knew Tony wouldn't be there, either.

I didn't make any detours that day on the way to my apartment because I didn't want to miss his call. I waited as long as I could after arriving there before asking Mom and Grandma if I had any messages. When told there were none, I threw myself into dinner preparations and decided that I would enjoy another evening at home. When life deals you lemons, make lemonade, I reminded myself. I chuckled inside as I thought that I had sure been handed enough of that yellow citrus.

"First day back go okay?" Grandma asked as we worked at the kitchen counter, side by side. Mom had shown no interest in making it a threesome and had remained on the living room couch, wrapped tightly in her robe.

"Great," I said. "Writing's going better than expected."

"We didn't have much of a chance to talk about New Year's. That Pamela behave herself?"

"She was fine. Why do you ask?"

"I saw how she barely tolerates you. She lives for that son of hers."

"Like I don't?" I chuckled.

Grandma let go of her mixing spoon and turned to me. "That's fine, Samelah, as long as you live for each other."

I gave her a quick hug. "I'm the one writing the story, Gram, remember?" I said.

I was startled after school the following day when I found Janice waiting for me outside her Camaro at the curb, and was concerned the instant I approached her and saw her dark face. She barely said hello before waving me into the front seat.

Shock is the only word to describe my reaction when Janice dumped the reason for her unannounced appearance as soon as her door closed. "Richie's been shot!" she shouted, on the verge of tears. From the looks of her eyes, it seemed like she'd been bawling for a while.

"Jesus Christ! Jan," I exclaimed as I reached for her across the console. "Is he okay?"

She started to sob. "No, Sam, he's in Methodist," she said, her chest heaving, "and . . . he . . . might not . . . make it!" The floodgates opened and Janice wept bitterly. I held her for a couple of minutes until her shaking body calmed down.

"What the fuck happened?"

"Haven't ya seen the *News*?" Janice asked, and reached for the paper on the rear seat. I hadn't; that daily, for the most part, reflected Brooklyn. I had always made it a point to scan the *Times* instead, in the school library. It described the world I was headed for, even if I didn't know half the words and spent as much time with the dictionary as I did with the broadsheet.

"No," I said as Janice spread the paper on the dashboard. I wondered for the first time whether circumstances would keep me stuck on the wrong side of the bridge.

A drug deal gone bad was spread all over page four. A

photo of a covered body on a sidewalk dominated the adjacent story. My eyes flew over the article. "I don't see his name anywhere," I said.

"That's a black coke dealer there in the picture. Cops found a gun and said it was fired three times."

"So?"

"Aldo said they took three slugs out of Richie last night."

"Did his brother say it was connected?"

"Didn't hafta. What else would anyone think?"

"Listen, Jan," I said as I stroked her tousled hair. "There's a lot of shootings in this godforsaken borough."

"Do the math, Sam," she grunted.

"Okay, even if Richie was there, maybe it was self-defense," I said, and shuddered as I thought that maybe he wasn't the only one who had to defend himself. "Were Vin and Tony with him?"

"Nobody knows," Janice said, "or is sayin' anythin' if they do. Aldo couldn't reach out to either of them." She began to sob and shake again. "What am I gonna do if he dies, Sam?"

"He'll pull through. I just know it," I lied. I had no idea how this unplanned chapter was going to work itself out. I opened the glove box and pulled out a few tissues that I stuffed into her hand.

"I've . . . got . . . to go . . . see . . . him," Janice said with labored breathing. She wiped her eyes and pulled herself together as best she could.

"Want me to drive?" I asked, though the thought scared me. I had gotten a license but had driven only a couple of times since my road test.

"No, but can you come with me? I'm so scared, Sam."

I hugged my best friend again. "Of course," I said. I was plenty scared, too. And not just about Richie, though that was more than enough. I pictured Tony in some cell again or, worse, holed up bleeding somewhere, and I was afraid all of this was becoming too much for me to handle, too much to carry across the bridge that was in walking distance from the hospital where we were headed. But I forced my worries into the recesses of my mind; my friend needed me then.

Richie's family was gathered in the small waiting room adjacent to the CCU. Their grave faces told me how critical his condition was. I let go of Janice's hand and stood near the doorway because I didn't know Richie's family well and wasn't comfortable enough to approach them. Janice hugged everyone as she sobbed anew. I fidgeted near the door for a long minute and then decided to go back downstairs to the small chapel off the main lobby.

A peaceful feeling enveloped me as I knelt in silent prayer, alone in the bosom of a facility that had been constructed decades ago. It seemed I was far away from the torment that was being endured only a few floors above that I was powerless to alleviate, and my lifelong goal seemed to be slipping from my grasp in the Bensonhurst world that was all too real that day. I bowed my head, closed my eyes, and sought the Blessed Mother.

Ten minutes later, I looked up at the chapel's large wood cross. The suffering all around me, I knew, paled in comparison to Christ's. I vowed to endure my own, and to do whatever I could to help others do likewise. I bowed my head again, made the sign of the cross, and clasped my hands for a moment longer on the pew in front of me.

I left the chapel and headed for the elevators, where I saw the back of a priest who was waiting. That wouldn't be unlikely, I thought, in a hospital with a religious affiliation. But I knew who he was, and that seemed appropriate to me, too. "It's good to see you, Father," I said as I reached his side.

Father Rinaldi turned toward me. His face was all business. "'Twould be better if I saw you and those upstairs in my parish."

I glanced at the descending lights above the elevator door.

"I suppose saving souls can happen anywhere," I said, and turned my head back to him.

Father Rinaldi's face brightened. "Out of the mouths of babes." He smiled as the elevator chimed.

On the subway an hour later, I knew I'd be hunching over my Smith-Corona for a long time that night. Still no word from Tony; was he involved, was he on the lam, was I insane having these absurd thoughts? I just didn't know anything at the moment. I had sat with Janice in the corner of the waiting room until she had had a chance to see Richie. She came back after a two-minute visit at his bedside and moaned about the tubes coming out from all over him. It made me think about how some connections were really tough to sever. And that, in turn, made me think about Tony again. In the swaying train, I decided I'd call his house as soon as I could steal away to my room after dinner. The clanging wheels beneath me marked the passing time until I reached the stop near my home.

Mom and Grandma were in the living room, sitting on the couch, when I arrived. Grandma's socks were rolled beneath the simple, faded housedress she always wore and Mom was wrapped in her robe, whose random stains had never come completely out in the wash. The *News* was spread open on the coffee table.

"Nice crowd ya hang with," Mom said through a haze of cigarette smoke.

"You should talk," I murmured as I headed for the kitchen.

"What was that?" she called after me.

"Nothin'," I said as I disappeared. She couldn't wait to say I told you so. Then the unexpected came from her.

"Whatever I did in my life you do exactly the opposite! Look at me. You know why I'm sick and poor, because I abused myself. Going out with the wrong guys, drinking too much. Finding myself in situations I wasn't very proud of. This is what happens when you wind up with the wrong man. If I can tell you one thing and one thing only, that's it." My mother exhausted herself with her words, yet continued on. I could see it within her red swollen eyes. "Do you think I like being on welfare? Having to walk around with those fuckin' food stamps? It's a horror."

"Mom, I understand," I blurted out to her.

"No, you don't, and hopefully you never will! Now go and get me another box of cigarettes."

Her talk was genuine; however, it seemed to revert back to self-destruction, and cigarettes were a part of that. So I got them for her; sometimes I felt that was all she had left. My heart ached for my mother.

Grandma sat quietly. I knew that at this moment there was a bigger issue: Richie fighting for his life.

That struggle served as the start of the next chapter that I felt I had to get on the page as soon as I entered my bedroom, before I made that call to the Kroon residence. The later the better, anyway, I reasoned. There would be more of a chance to catch Tony there.

At my desk, I felt that Richie's struggle trumped my own and I filled pages with my ruminations about perspective. In the scope of things, how important was my quest to reach the other side of the river? I wondered. Did it matter, and did it matter if Tony was with me? Would not making it across make any difference in either of the two worlds that I was straddling? Would crossing it even change anything?

Thoughts raced through my mind as I questioned everything. An hour later, I had sorted it out in my mind and on the pages advancing in my typewriter. It came down to building something, brick by brick, cable by cable, until it was finished. So what if it wasn't easy? I asked myself. The struggle for life never was, I felt. Even those born with a lot more than I was given had their battles. The movie stars and rock stars, whose posters Tony wouldn't let me hang in my bedroom, carried their own crosses. Everyone had to fight to get somewhere, I reasoned, and use every means of support, whether it was fans or family money. Or the loved ones I had, I thought as I wrote. I decided that my towers and my roped wire were as real as the life that was waiting for me.

I spun the last filled page from the carriage and clipped it to the rest before reaching for the phone. Pamela answered.

"Oh . . . hi, Sam," she said after my greeting.

"Is Tony there?" I asked. Please, God, I said to myself.

"No."

"Do you know when he'll be home?"

"He said not to wait up," Pamela deadpanned. At least she'd talked to him, I thought. "So ya's don' know where he is, huh?" she scoffed.

"Will you tell him I called?" I asked.

The phone went dead.

18

Katrina Kroon's afternoon birthday party in early February was starting in thirty minutes and Tony was late. I set my hand mirror on the dresser and looked into the full-length one on the inside of my bedroom door as I assessed both my appearance and the events of the weeks that had followed New Year's.

Tony had finally showed up at school two days after Janice and I visited Ritchie in the hospital. He swore the lump above a blackened eye was the result of a "discussion" that had taken place at Cue Ball. I didn't mention days later that Janice had been unable to confirm his story with information from her father, who alternated between his pool hall and Rocco's below. Not that he would be likely to blab, anyway, I had thought, not even to his own daughter.

I knew that Tony wouldn't be any more forthcoming than Mr. Caputo and I didn't want to add to the stress he always appeared to be under, but I needed to know what happened. Richie had taken a turn for the better and was out of danger. Maybe I can create a story, I thought when I eyed myself up and down and recalled that frantic episode in Janice's Camaro.

I knew that Tony was on his way because he was obligated to be at his sister's family celebration and his mother would never forgive him if he didn't show up. It seemed like he had been busy more often than not since New Year's, and distracted every time I saw him, which hadn't been often. I had asked him numerous times about this drug thing; I mean it made the papers and television. Still, I got no response, not even his usual bad temper. I felt that something was brewing, something that even I couldn't get out of. For once I was beginning to actually feel trapped. I'd be with him for only a few hours, but when the sex was finished he dropped me off at home and told me he had to meet the guys. His phone calls were abrupt and he always said he'd call back but usually didn't. Was his business consuming him, I wondered? Even though the usual wad of C-notes was ever present in his pocket or his hand. What business? I wondered more. Were the legal proceedings against him and the visits from cops for questioning about Richie's incident, which he let slip once to me, getting to him? Or was Tony losing interest in me? Was there someone else? I wondered.

That whack across my face still gnawed at me. Janice had suggested I forget it but I couldn't. It seemed like all the girls overlooked their guys' bad behaviors because one wrong word or glance would cost the women plenty. Like it had for me. Those girls didn't want to lose their Bensonhurst world, but I desperately wanted to lose mine. I didn't want to follow in my mother's footsteps and end up sick and bitter from trying to find happiness with a batterer and philanderer. I needed to keep myself fresh and creative, not only to make it to Manhattan but to stay there. It was waiting for me, I knew. I could see my name in bookstores and I wanted everything to work out with Tony so he'd be by my side when success hit.

It seemed like Tony "knew a guy" just about everywhere and I thought that maybe he really did have contacts in publishing. But that wasn't the only reason I wanted to keep seeing him. He was handsome, strong, confident . . . and had taken my virginity. I loved the guy and wanted him to be proud of me, but I made a vow to myself: if he ever hurt me again, I would dump him. I would tell him that, too, and if he didn't like it, that was too damned bad.

With weeks of time on my hands, I worked on myself. My job at the bookstore allowed me to read more and learn more about the publishing business. The store owner gave me books for free now and then and I was in heaven. I suspected Tony wouldn't like it since it had nothing to do with him, and I decided I would only tell him if I felt like it. After all, he had *his* private life with the guys. Why shouldn't I have my own?

Now, when the doorbell rang, I went to the living room to greet Tony. I caught my breath when he waltzed in. He looked as good as I'd ever seen him, his soft hair just so, his wonderful physique exaggerated by tight pants and a shirt that was tucked in to reveal his narrow waist. What a looker! I beamed. Just like that, any bad memories and doubts I had about our relationship faded away. How could love banish all the bad? I just wasn't strong enough to turn him away. That was my problem.

Tony waved at Mom and Grandma and complimented me in front of them before taking my hand. "C'mon, Sam," he said as the others looked on without saying a word. "I don' want ya makin' us late for my sister's party."

I fought the urge to scoff. Who had kept whom waiting? I asked myself. He sure knew how to kill a mood, I thought. I grabbed my pocketbook and gave Mom a kiss on the cheek. She snarled under her breath. I know she just wanted to scream at him, "Stay away from my daughter, you loser," but she didn't; frankly, she just didn't have the strength. That was all she did after New Year's Day when Tony was around or was mentioned. She must have seen something on my face then, some little clue, I thought, or her own experience as a battered woman helped her interpret my body language and mood. Or maybe it was just her convictions about who Tony was and the neighborhood he came from, I thought. Whatever the reason, Mom had refused to talk about Tony Kroon. She had made up her mind that he was no good for her daughter, and she would continue to hold her ground. She'd tried to prevent me from ever seeing him again until Grandma reminded her that Grandma herself had tried the same thing before her daughter had gotten married. The resistance had done no good at all then, and wouldn't work with me, either, Grandma had said. Besides, I was too smart and would be able to handle myself.

Mom lit a cigarette as I kissed Grandma's soft face. "Do I look okay, Grandma?" I asked.

"You're my little beauty, *bubelah,*" she said with a smile, and stroked my cheek. "You have a good time." She looked at Tony and her smile disappeared. "You be good to my granddaughter," she ordered in her usual raised voice.

"Yes, ma'am," Tony said without shame. "Always."

Despite my family's misgivings, and my own concerns, I was happy to leave with Tony and felt as good as I had before when he opened the Porsche's door for me, even though that only happened in front of my apartment building. We were silent as he drove a few blocks and then he pulled over to the side of the road. Tony looked me over and smiled.

"What're ya doin', Tone?" I asked. "We're already late."

"I got sumthin' for ya," he said. Tony reached into his pocket, pulled out diamond earrings, and dropped them into my hand. They glistened in the daylight.

"Oh my God," I said. I rotated them in my palm and rainbows danced around the car's interior. "They're so beautiful."

"Damned right they are," Tony said, and then he put them on my ears. He sat back and smiled. "What do ya think of your boyfriend now?" he asked. "Maybe this'll show your mother how serious I am about ya."

My mother would not be impressed at all by him trying to make up for violent and still unknown criminal behavior with jewels. I knew better, too, but this was a moment, my moment, so I went with it. I looked from Tony to my ears in the rearview mirror. He hadn't apologized for any of his behavior, but weren't the earrings the next best thing? I pondered. The words "I'm sorry" were not in Tony's vocabulary, but didn't an expensive gift prove how much he cared? Wasn't it a sign of how things would be someday? But as happy as I was at that moment, I considered telling him that if he ever hit me again, he'd be saying good-bye, just like I'd planned. I decided not to ruin the mood. He might think I wasn't grateful, and I was. And I was sure that his inattention to our relationship was because of his struggle, and the smack that night had to be a fluke. He was still young and he just needed to learn a little self-control. Isn't that what he was trying to say with the earrings? I constantly found myself in my very own war of contradiction. My brain would say one thing and my body would do another.

Tony looked calmly over my shoulder through the window and then back at me. He eyed me up and down. "Take off your clothes," he said.

I was appalled. Once again, he had spoiled things for me, I thought, right after I had taken pains not to dampen his mood. "No, Tony," I said softly, "there'll be plenty of time for that after the party. You don't want to disappoint your sister, do you? She really looks up to you," I said. "If we don't make it, she'll be devastated. And so will your mom." Mad as hell, too, no doubt. And she'd blame me, I knew . . . He cut me off abruptly.

"I don' give a shit about my fat sister. I need ya right now, Sam. It's been too long."

I resisted until Tony gave up. It reminded me of the times he had done that before we'd gone all the way. He started the car and didn't look in my direction or say another word the rest of the way. We arrived late and Pamela was so upset that she ignored Tony. He whispered to me that he wished his mom would just lighten up. He didn't see what the big deal was all about.

Philip nodded to Tony and me with a half smile. I wondered if he felt proud of his daughter, and how he really felt about taking a backseat to Tony, whether he minded how Pamela fawned over their son. But even though I tried to know and fit in better with Tony's family for his sake, I felt detached from them. My mind wandered. I looked forward to my high school graduation and associating with a different group of people. I could hardly wait to get away and start my real life with those who had broader ideas and visions. I thought it ironic that with all our differences, there was one thing—getting out of Bensonhurst—that Mom and I had in common. I took Tony's hand and he squeezed mine.

For the first time it occurred to me that Tony could never come with me. I, on the other hand, was plenty determined.

Katrina pranced around the living room, showing off the low-cut ruffled dress she'd bought at what the locals called the "Mafia Princess Shop," a glitzy boutique named Amore, on Eighteenth Avenue. If Katrina really cared how she looked, I thought, maybe she could try losing a few pounds. I felt it was hard to like Tony's sister but promised myself I would do my best because Tony wanted me to consider his family as my own.

The celebration was an elaborate affair. If Pamela knew how to do anything, hosting a party was at the top of the list. A local Italian restaurant, Monti's, had catered the birthday celebration right down to a sumptuous white cake with cannoli filling and yellow frosting from the Luigi Alba pastry shop, which was a Brooklyn landmark. Tony nearly gagged when he read the cake's inscription: *To the prettiest, smartest, kindest daughter.* "They must have been talking about someone else," he muttered to me—not his mean-spirited sister, who only had bad things to say about everyone. His mother was happy, though, and his dad was, too—a rare occurrence in the Kroon household—so Tony refrained from offering his opinions to anyone else. That was rare, too.

When the party ended Tony and I left and got back into his Porsche, which was parked at the end of a dead-end street. I primped my hair in the rearview mirror and waited for him to start the engine. I felt good. We had been a relaxed couple in his family's house, comfortable and natural together. Tony had behaved himself and I had to admit that I'd gotten satisfaction from flashing around my diamond earrings. Tony was turning over a new leaf, he had to be. I had believed in him from the day we met, and I decided I wouldn't stop then when he was sagging under the weight of his own crosses. I knew that with my help he could grow into the powerful, successful-but-loving man that he was meant to be. I recalled the expression "Behind every great man is an even greater woman, encouraging him to succeed." I reset the rearview mirror and turned to Tony. "Why aren't we going?" I asked.

"I've waited long enough, Sam. Get in the backseat."

"Now? Can't we wait until . . . ?"

"No," Tony said, and he glanced at the earrings.

I sighed, opened my door, and got out of the car and into the cramped rear. I scrunched into the corner, reached up under my skirt, pulled down my panties, and dropped them on the floor. Tony wedged in next to me. I was not up for sex, but I knew that if I didn't take care of my guy, he'd go elsewhere. Tony ripped off my top and pawed my breasts. "Jesus, Tone," I said, "that hurts. They're not goin' anywhere."

He seemed distracted, as if he were in a trance. "They're mine . . ." he breathed. "All mine."

It was over in record time, and I ran my hand over the floor to find my panties. I felt something metallic. I picked up a silver lipstick tube that puzzled me for a few seconds. "What the hell is this?" I asked. He was ruining everything, I thought. Again.

"Stop lookin' at my stuff," Tony said.

"Your stuff?" I scoffed. "You wearin' makeup now?" He stared at me for a moment and then at the lipstick case.

"Give it to me," he said.

I flung it out the window. "Ya want your stuff, you jerk," I said, "ya better go chase it." There was fire in Tony's eyes but he said nothing.

I labored to get dressed and then returned to the front. I slammed my door as Tony got behind the wheel. My breath was short and my heart ached. Hot tears burned my eyes and I tried to hold them back. I'd been so ready to believe in Tony but my mother was right. He was no good and I had no business being with him.

Tony put the key into the ignition and turned to me. "Look, Sam," he said. "Ya need ta—"

"Look yourself," I said through clenched teeth. "I've had enough of this. All I ever wanted was for you and me to be together and now look what you've done." He reached for my hand but I pulled it back. "No!" I shouted. "Don't you touch me or talk to me. Don't even breathe on me."

Tony reddened. "Give me a break, Miss Fancy Pants. Like you're the only woman who ever found a tube of lipstick in her boyfriend's car," he said. I stared through the windshield as Tony rambled on. "I don' know where it came from. It might be Katrina's, or maybe it's even your mother's. She was in the car that night when I took you all to Monti's."

"We were in your mother's car that night," I said.

"Whatever," Tony replied. "Anybody coulda dropped that fuckin' lipstick." He scanned me from head to toe. "Just look at yourself. Freakin' out like a goddamned idiot. Looks like I hit a nerve. Maybe you're the one who's cheatin'."

I turned to him and my fiery eyes narrowed. "Tony Kroon, you're not getting out of this one so fast," I said. "You know I don't believe in cheatin' and I thought you didn't either. But I guess I was wrong . . . about a lot of things."

"C'mon, Sam," Tony prodded, turning on the magnetism. "I'll take ya to Spades. Ya always wanted ta go there." I knew that Tony and the guys never took their steadies to a club where they hung out alone, but desperate measures were in order for Tony right then. He would have some explaining to do to them if I showed up at Spades, but I wasn't buying his pitch, anyway.

"You wanna take me to a place where you pick up your whores? No, thank you." Tony's face contorted but I didn't care. "You know what else?" I said as I stared into those blue eyes that faded with my every word. "I don't ever want to see you again."

"Ya don' mean that."

"Yes, I do," I said, gathering courage. "You can get one of your whores to take care of your dick 'cause I don't ever want to see that disgusting thing again, either."

Tony grabbed me by the hair and slammed my head against the dashboard two times in rapid succession. He let go and watched me sit up and touch my face, tears and blood streaming down my cheeks as I screamed out in fear. He then leaned in and opened his glove compartment to reveal a handgun. I didn't know what size it was. I just knew it was a gun. He took it out and waved it at me. And placed it by my cheek, hard. My life flashed in a way I never knew before. I was consumed with fear.

"Is this what you want me to do. 'Cause I will."

At this point I didn't know what he was capable of or how much. I reached into my purse to get some tissues and pressed them against my forehead. For a moment, Tony looked as stunned as I was. "Oh shit," he said in a soft voice. "I don' wanna hurt ya, but don' ever say sumthin' like that again, Sam. I love ya, baby. I really do. I mean it," he said in rapid succession. "I don' hit girls but ya make me so crazy, I can't control myself. It's 'cause I love ya." Tony ran a fist across his mouth. "Ya ain't *never* goin' ta leave me, Sam. Never. You're mine until the day ya die." His words were not of love, rather of obsession.

The tone of his voice and the saliva in the corners of his mouth frightened me. When he tried to put his arms around me, I pushed him away and cowered against the door. "Just take me home," I said. "Right now."

"Sure ya don' wanna go out?"

I glared at him. "I need to go home."

"Ya sure, Sam?"

I turned away from him and looked out the window. "I'm sure."

When he pulled up to the curb in front of my apartment, I bolted from the car with Tony close behind. He grabbed me around the waist before I had gotten very far and I froze. I felt unseen eyes on my body and I moved a hand to my damaged face.

"This'll never happen again, Sam," Tony pleaded in a gentle voice. "I swear it. I just lost it for a second but it's cuz I love ya so much. Not many women can say their guy loves them that much." I knew I would never be able to trust him again. I said nothing and waited for him to let me go so I could escape to the safety of my crazy Jewish-Italian home. At least I never got physical abuse there, I thought. "Say we're okay, Sam," Tony continued. He sounded so pathetic, I might have taken pity on him if not for the dried blood on my forehead. He kissed me and I held my breath.

"I gotta go now," I said, desperate to get away.

"But we're okay, right?"

"Sure, Tone," I nodded, just to get rid of him. "We're okay."

"That means we're still together, baby, right?"

"It means whatever you want it to mean," I said. "Will you please leave now? I have some explaining to do."

"Can I walk ya ta the door?" I shook my head and cringed when Tony kissed me again. I turned around and tottered to the steps of my building. I exhaled when the door closed behind me. I had gotten away from him but my anguish wasn't over. I had to face my mother and grandmother. I shivered when I realized that Tony had actually thought he could fix the trouble between us. I knew better. No amount of fixing could ever make it right again. Hit me once, your fault. Hit me again, my fault. I shuffled up the stairs with another bruise and a broken heart.

Mom and Grandma rushed to me and skipped the hellos. "We were on the expressway," I explained in answer to their frantic queries, "and some idiot stopped right in front of us. Tony slammed on the brakes just in time and my face plowed into the dash. Of course, you know me, not wearing a seat belt and all. Good thing nobody got killed."

No matter how many times I swore that my banged-up face had been caused by a tailgating accident, Mom didn't buy it. Grandma did. Unless she was in denial that the same thing that happened two decades earlier to her daughter could happen again to her smart granddaughter. I couldn't look her in the eyes.

"I never thought you were the type of girl not to use precaution," Grandma said. Mom just shook her head and helped me with my wounds.

"I was there myself, you know, more than once. And you know something, Sam, I knew every excuse in the book." Mom's tired red eyes pierced me as if she saw right through me. She knew all too well that I had come home with a battered face and a broken spirit. "How many times I pretended to fall down the stairs or walk into a door. Shit, let me fuckin' count."

"Don't swear again." Grandma added her two cents.

"Oh please, Ma, as if she doesn't curse by now."

There would be no changing Mom's opinion about moving us out of Bensonhurst to Bay Ridge, which she had more than hinted at for months. Maybe, just maybe, it was a good thing.

Bay Ridge was a historical neighborhood that was sleepy in comparison to ours. It was proud to have been the home of such personages as Robert E. Lee and Stonewall Jackson, and its old stone houses mixed with newly built shopping centers and eight-lane intersections made people there feel like they were straddling two unrelated worlds, as I always felt wherever I was in Brooklyn.

Grandma and I saw a resolve in Mom that we hadn't seen in years. After what had happened to me she made up her mind that I was heading in a bad direction, the die was cast, and it would be better to move sooner rather than later. Even though Bay Ridge was only three miles from our place on Seventy-third Street, mom thought it would make a world of difference to be in an area that was filled with a mixture of religions and cultures.

I knew she hoped Tony wouldn't come to see me there but that was stupid, I thought. Ridiculous. Picking up and moving to a different location in Brooklyn wouldn't stop someone like Tony.

It would be up to me to do that, or, at this point, God.

19

Sooner came a couple of days later. Mom's friend from high school, Cynthia, her husband, Fred, and their young daughter, Justine, lived a few blocks away from where Mom planned to move. Although Mom and Cynthia hadn't always gotten along when they were growing up, Mom was grateful to her for a job minding Cynthia's baby and her loan of nine hundred dollars on short notice for the move to Bay Ridge. Mom's conviction remained unchanged that the multicultural atmosphere there, as opposed to the homogeneous Italian neighborhood where she thought I was hanging out with the wrong people, would be a chance for us to have a better life.

I was worried. I had felt a sadness about leaving and wasn't as convinced that a relocation would solve the problems of the world. There was evil everywhere, I knew. It was just a matter of who a person was . . . and whom she associated with, like Father Rinaldi had said. But once Mom had made up her mind, she refused to reconsider. She was determined to snatch me away from Tony, who she thought was a raging lunatic who would continue to harm her daughter. Mom wanted to take me away from the type of man she had married, the type of man who could ruin a life. We would be living in a quaint three-bedroom with a peaceful elderly couple renting out the other side. With Cynthia close by and a nicer place to live, I tried to be hopeful about the move. If it weren't for the fact that Janice would no longer be close by and I'd have a helluva commute to school because there was no way I was going to make a switch, I might have even felt excited about the whole thing. But Janice and I weren't going to be that far away from each other and I knew we would make the effort to see each other every chance we could. No matter what our different futures might turn out to be, she and I would spend them together. We had often talked about the possibility of sharing a place after I turned eighteen. I hoped, too, that that might become a reality someday, but wondered if Janice would be living with Richie before we had a chance to do so.

It was hard for a teenager to deal with any major change, and Mom did what she could over the next few days to help me accept the upcoming move. "Just think, Sam," she had said, "you'll have some privacy. Ya never had your own room before. Grandma's will be right next to you. And it's going to be good for me, too. Watching little Justine will give me something productive to do. I'll even stop smokin'. How does that sound?" I didn't believe Mom would, or could, change anything about herself. Regardless, I knew I couldn't change her mind.

On the day we packed for the move, I passed my hand over the wallpaper in the old bedroom I shared with Grandma. The violets had faded until you couldn't tell the difference between the leaves and the flowers. I would miss that place, but I had to admit that the previous few weeks had crushed me and maybe it would be best to get as far away from Tony as I could. I hadn't seen him since the head bashing but his words continued to echo in my mind: *Ya ain't never goin' ta leave me, Sam. Never. You're mine until the day ya die.*

I had gone numb right after Tony had claimed me as his personal possession—as if I were a Raggedy Ann doll. I was a real person, an individual with likes and dislikes and feelings that could be hurt. I had dreams and goals for my future that no longer had anything to do with him. His saying those words tore at my heart. Tony wouldn't understand that. Well, maybe he'd get it when he realized that I was being swept away because my mother considered him dangerous. I knew that word traveled fast in Bensonhurst; he was bound to hear about it all soon enough.

Janice was sad when I called to tell her I was moving and why. "When did it happen?" she had asked.

"The decision to move or the head bashing?"

"Both."

"He got me after Katrina's party and Mom made up her mind the same day."

"It's probably the best thing for you, Sam," Janice said. I could hear her resignation over the phone line. I assured my friend we would still see each other regularly. "No wonder ya didn't wanna meet me at Sally's."

"I never want to run into him again," I said.

There was a long pause before Janice continued. "Ya can hardly blame your mom. Looks like she's finally doing something right by you."

"I don't. And you wanna know something? I'm exhausted from all this. I loved Tony but ever since he beat me up, I can't get the feelings back. I don't even want to try. I swear to God, I never saw it coming. I didn't do a damned thing and the next thing I knew . . ."

"It's always the same story," Janice said. "One time Richie gave me a black eye becuz I answered the phone when he was in the shower. It was some girl callin' and when I asked him who she was, he belted me right across the face. It's so weird; I was the one who was supposeta get mad but he beat me to it." Janice paused. "Literally." She paused again. "And he never said he was sorry. I ended up apologizin' instead."

"What is it with these guys?" I fumed. "What gives them the right?"

Janice lowered her voice. "*We* do."

I went silent for a moment. I knew Janice was right. The guys continued to abuse their women because the women let them get away with it. They didn't know any other way; the women were too afraid of losing their men to defend themselves. Janice continued, "It's some kinda age-old tradition. 'Keep the women in line *before* they do anything.' It's all about their stupid egos. They act like such wise guys, like they can do no wrong and everythin's our fault." Janice sighed then. "What's crazy, Sam, is in his own way, Tony really loves ya."

"What's crazy is him slammin' my face inta the dashboard."

Janice chuckled. "Hey," she said, "if that's not love, what is?"

I knew she was trying to lighten the mood, but that only made me more determined to get out of there, even if I preferred right then not to leave the neighborhood where I had grown up. But I had to go, and leave Tony and everything bad behind. My life was too precious, and he hadn't even made an effort to say he was sorry, even if that wouldn't have changed things. He probably didn't think he had anything to apologize for, anyway, I thought. No phone calls, no flowers, no gifts. There would be no Tony anymore, I knew.

When Janice and I hung up after swearing to meet soon, I wandered into our tiny kitchen, where everything was already packed in boxes. The empty shelves looked sad and the entire kitchen needed a fresh coat of paint. I sat on the floor a moment, inhaled the old cooking aromas that had been permanently infused into the walls, and thought about life in Bensonhurst. Was Tony's violence a part of a man that every woman had to rise above? I wondered. Or was he just an asshole, a batterer, and not good enough to buckle my Sugars, which he had bought with tainted money? Janice had always hoped Richie would change, but he never demonstrated any signs of that in the years they'd dated. She'd probably end up marrying the guy and having a miserable life with a brood of overweight kids, I thought. That was exactly what my mother had told me time and again I needed to avoid. Why couldn't I hold out for a nice boy? She echoed Grandma's advice many times.

Having no father in the house when I was growing up was probably a good thing because he had hurt my mother so much, but I was unfamiliar with men and the ways that they thought and acted, good or bad. But I had to admit to myself that I had read about and seen good men, and was writing for the world they inhabited. I knew how a woman should be treated, no matter what the circumstance. "Nice boys don't hit girls," my mother had told me ever since I was a little girl, confirming what had always been in my heart. The striking of a man's hand on any part of her body is abuse, plain and simple. And that was plainly wrong.

I returned to my bedroom, where I had always found my solitude with the typewriter that Grandma had given me so many years before. She had used it sometimes, too, to write her poems, and I thought she must have found a similar peace of mind when she did that. That room was where I wrote night after night with depth and honesty about growing up in Bensonhurst, and I knew I wasn't finished.

I sat down at my small wood desk and began clicking away. The typewriter was so worn that I had to hold the ribbon in place sometimes as I typed. I looked forward to the day when I would get a brand-new professional model. My words seemed to come out faster than my little fingers could move, but when the last ones were on the page and I stopped to read what I had just created, my eyes filled with delight and then melancholy touched my heart. I realized it would be the last time I fashioned words in the apartment where I grew up.

Writing would be the only priority in my life from then on, I decided. Nothing was going to get in the way. I was so fulfilled doing it and I couldn't wait to share this joy with the world. Someday, I thought as I covered the Smith-Corona. I stood and then taped the boxes that held my few possessions and threw the last of my clothes into two suitcases.

That's when I remembered the duffel bag on the fire escape. My heart sank deep within my chest and all of that past Tony anxiety came forward like a rush of hot air. I rushed over to my bedroom window and opened it. The bag was still hidden perfectly under the planter and was completely drenched from the rain. I pulled it in and this time had no hesitation as to what the contents were. I unzipped it to find a plastic bag, and inside of that was a dried-up bloody police shirt, badge and all. I was startled. Someone must have gotten hurt from one of his unruly scores or God knows what else he may have done to this innocent person. I knew one thing, I wanted nothing to do with it. I had held on to this mess for way too long and had to release it. How dare he make me hold this; what was this, who was this, and why was there blood? I put it all back, zipped it up, and was ready to throw it in the garbage with the rest of the junk I was getting rid of when I stopped. There had to be a better place to discard this bag for good . . . My mind flirted with ideas and then it hit me.

I knew I was probably throwing away evidence of some kind and I couldn't have cared less. That's when I remembered the night he and the boys were out late and I had fallen asleep on my sofa, when he came honking the horn at God knows what hour and he asked me to take a ride to get burgers and shakes at the local diner. Tony, the guys, and me, all shoved in the booth with the quarter jukebox playing in my ear. I had no idea why I had to be there, but I was. They all went on and on about how they beat up this cop, knocked him out cold, took his clothes, and placed their clothes on him instead. And of course robbed some store in the process. Great, I thought to myself as I sipped my milkshake, my stomach turning as I listened to the violence creep though their veins and out of their vulgar mouths.

I so wanted to be rid of Tony.

I knew I had about an hour of time to kill as I waited for a friend of Mom's to arrive with his old, crusty van, and for the next chapter of my life that was yet to be written.

So I did the unthinkable, even for a girl like me. I took the duffel bag from the planter on the fire escape, added some rocks to the bottom of it, jumped on the R train, did some transferring to other trains that I had never taken before, and headed to the Brooklyn Bridge. I got out and walked slowly toward it, admiring the cables in all their glory, and started my descent upon it, duffel bag in hand. I managed to get to the middle of the bridge and, with no one looking, dropped it. I never even watched it fall. Who cared? I was rid of it. That was all that mattered at this point. Rid of its history and the Tony that went along with it.

The phone rang the next day while we were unpacking in our new home. "I'm comin' over," Janice gushed. "I gotta see ya."

I cleared a small area on my bed and sat down. "We're up to our asses in boxes here," I exhaled. "I just wanna get done and then crash."

"Help is on the way," Janice announced. "We'll talk while we work." I didn't have the energy to argue with my best friend so I hung up. I knew there wasn't any point to it, anyway. She was going to show up no matter what I said.

I found myself looking forward to seeing her. I was already feeling the first pangs of separation from my old neighborhood, and it was reassuring that attachment to its good parts would always remain. I glanced around the first room that I would have to myself. It wasn't much, but it was mine. I looked forward to the first conversation Janice and I would have there.

I unpacked the items for my desk and took my time setting

it up, and was grateful that there was more space around it for my files and reference books. Even though there was much left to be done with Mom and Grandma to set up our new home, I couldn't resist sitting at the desk the moment my typewriter case was unzipped.

I banged away on the keys. There had been plenty to make me bitter in the recent past and my fingers struggled to keep up with my thoughts. The detachment instead of progressive closeness with Tony when we were a couple, the macho strutting instead of genuine consideration of the Brooklyn Boys, the senseless violence visited upon Richie and so many others instead of the spread of peace, the loss of my virginity that had been humiliating instead of something to be cherished—all of that spilled onto a few pages. But all of it served as a counterpoint to the gratefulness I felt in my new room, for there was a lot more than some more space to be thankful for.

I still had my best friend, there was a chance—however slim—that Mom could still salvage her life, Grandma and others, like Janice, had never stopped rooting for me, and I had hundreds of pages written, with more on the way, that validated their support and my hopes. All of that found its way onto pages as well.

Forty-five minutes later, I heard the commotion outside my room when Janice arrived. I sprang from my chair to the door with a smile on my face. I was happy about seeing her, but also pleased with the healthy chunk of my novel that I was leaving behind as I went to greet her.

Janice and I embraced. "Things are lookin' up," she said to the three of us after we separated. "I'm so happy for you." I wondered if she knew how much of a part my manuscript played in what she had just said. I grabbed her hand and gave her the fifty-cent tour before we ended up in my bedroom, where we shared the small space atop my bed.

"What's the latest with Richie?" I asked.

"Unbelievable," she said. "Must be the Sicilian in him. Tough as nails."

"Have you seen him much?"

"Yeah. He's home recouping. Needless to say, he won' be smackin' me or anyone else around for a while." I didn't ask if she had run into Tony. Janice's face turned serious, as if she had read my mind. "Listen, Sam," she started, "about Tony an' all. I'm kinda sorry now I introduced ya to him."

"You don't need to apologize, Jan," I said, and saw the Smith-Corona out of the corner of my eye. "It's my life."

Janice shook her head. "I shoulda realized that my life was never goin' ta be yours." Her hands touched my shoulders. "So how are ya? Really."

"I've been queasy the last coupla days."

"No wonder. Ya been turned upside down this past week." Janice put her fingers on my chin and gave my face a once-over. "Almost totally healed," she said. "You're 'bout ready ta come out again."

I glanced at my desk and pictured myself sitting in a Greenwich Village café. "I'm through with men for a while," I said. "It's all about my work right now."

Janice put her hands on my shoulders and beamed. "That's why I'm here!" she yelled, and gave me a fast hug. "I have to cut back my hours at Dani's 'cause Richie's gettin' funny about it. Ya know, he wants me to be at home and all." God, did I know that all too well. "I asked her if I could have my girlfriend help me on Wednesday and Friday afternoons and she said yes." Janice beamed. "That's you, Sam! You can save more money for that move to New York." That small typewriter is the biggest thing in my room, I thought when my eye caught sight of it again before Janice continued. "I might even move in with ya like we talked about."

I thought for a moment. "What will she pay?"

"Decent money, the shop is always busy, and it's under the

table. And the tips!" Janice exclaimed. "They add up, 'specially if ya get good at doin' nails, and I know ya will. You're real smart. Then ya get regular clients that ask for ya. Oh, Sam, I jus' know it's gonna be great."

"Who's gonna train me?"

"That's the best part! *I* will. All ya have ta do at the start is greet people and send 'em ta the diff'rent stations. They got a cosmetician there, too, and she can teach us all about makeup. When you learn to do that and can consult with people, then ya make real dough."

There was nothing to say but yes to her offer. I had wanted another job to add to my bookstore earnings but I was always afraid that Tony wouldn't like it. That no longer mattered; I could do whatever I wanted and right then, I wanted to make more money. So, Wednesday and Friday I would be at the nail salon and I'd work three days at the bookstore. Not bad, I thought. I would be saving a lot and learning the right way to do makeup. The girls in the old neighborhood overdid their faces with so much rouge and lipstick, they looked more like sluts than high school girls.

I wanted to look sophisticated so I would feel like I belonged in that real world when I stepped off that bridge.

20

Over the next two months in Bay Ridge I really started to like my new job. Janice was a good teacher and I took to it right away, answering phones, making appointments, getting to know the ins and outs of the business while I kept things running smoothly. The best part was learning about makeup and colors, and all my purchases were discounted so I could try out different shades and combinations of shadows and lipsticks. My sadness about Tony faded over time, and although Janice and I were living farther apart, we saw each other more than before because we were working in the same place. Truth be told, I was amazed that Tony did not reach out to me.

On the afternoons when Janice left early to placate Richie, I worked by myself, happy that no one was telling me what to do or how to live. I really had had no idea how much pressure I'd been under, worrying what Tony thought and where he was and whom he was messing around with. That wasn't a concern any longer; he could see whomever he wished and I didn't have to know about it or find lipstick or anything else in his car.

Janice sensed that I didn't want to hear much about Bensonhurst, but she had dropped a few tidbits about what was going on with the Brooklyn Boys. They couldn't get away from the reality that the murder case was a much bigger deal than the stolen auto parts were. She told me that when she was with Richie, he always looked behind him as if expecting a tail, and when he was drunk on a few occasions he bemoaned the legal troubles that nagged his crew. She felt as though they were up to something again, but no possible future trouble could stop them from gearing up for yet another score. However, I was more interested in the updates Janice provided about her and Richie. He had become surlier, more distant, and more detached when they were together. I knew from her face that there were more shoves, more slaps, more fists, and more bruises that had healed.

One Friday afternoon when Janice was getting ready to leave the salon, we took a coffee break together. We sat in the back room and chatted while Janice checked her watch a couple of times. "You got an appointment?" I asked.

"Nah. Richie wants me to be home by now, in case he calls. But you know something? It seems like if I stay here, he'll call, but if I go home, he won't. Sometimes I think he has somebody tailin' me."

"I wouldn't put it past him," I cracked.

Janice sighed. "Yeah," she said, "these guys are tough, aren't they? But I guess it's worth it." Even though she had had some tough times with Richie, it wasn't often that she sounded unsure about him as she had then.

"Are you two having more problems?" I asked. "I mean, if you don't mind telling me."

"It didn't take him long ta get back to his usual ways when he got outta the hospital," Janice said. "But you know what? With all his shit, I love him, Sam. It's just that sometimes I get the feelin' I'm not enough for him." Janice looked down at her body and then at me. "Do ya think maybe I should lose a few pounds?"

I reached for her hand. "Stop this," I said. "You're a knockout just the way you are. Don't allow a man to dictate that."

"Yeah, well, I don' know if I knock Richie out any more. Remember I told ya if I caught him cheating, I'd look the other way?"

"How could I forget that?"

"Well, I jus' don' know anymore. I'm almost twenty-one and I want sumthin' real," Janice said, and then paused for a long moment before looking me in the eyes. "It ain't real if he's cheatin', is it?" It wasn't, I knew, but I didn't say anything. My best friend had already come to her own conclusion. Janice went on. "It's the company he keeps besides Vin and Tony. Like those two guys, Sal and Joe. They're like human trash cans, full of filth, spitting out foulness, and holding on to garbage—the biggest sluts in Bensonhurst. Richie says he never looks at other girls when I'm not there, but I don' believe 'im anymore." Janice lowered her head and paused. "Ya know, I thought you and Tone were forever and look what happened. How can I be sure about Richie?"

"I had no idea you were so upset with him."

Janice grabbed her pocketbook and stood up. "Maybe I'm not, really," she said. "I think I'm about to get my period and I'm just blowin' off some steam with ya. I mean, what are friends for? Right?"

I watched as my friend left the salon and headed off down the street. I felt bad for Janice, especially since my life was on course for the river. I felt like I was really coming into my own. My new job was going well and I was writing like crazy. After all, it was the only therapy I had. I sometimes felt it saved me. Grandma and Mr. Wainright were proud of me, and my zest for life was returning. Father Rinaldi had obviously kept his fingers on the grapevine and shared my animation with smiles on the less frequent occasions when I went well out of my way to visit his church. Mom had been right and had done the right thing, I thought. The move had been good for us.

"Write what you know," Mr. Wainright always told the

class. I knew the boys of Bensonhurst better than anything—
their vices, their abusive ways, their constant ego trips—so
why not write about them? I knew all too well about rebellion
and bad marriages and self-destructive behavior through my
mother, and Jewish faith and Jewish cooking and Jewish men
through Grandma. I knew quite a bit and had a lot to write
about.

I finished my shift and when I left the salon, I was greeted
by the fragrant air and waning sun of a perfect early spring
evening. I decided to make the detour to Our Lady of Guadalupe for a fast prayer. I felt I had a lot to be thankful for. When
I arrived at the church that never failed to comfort me, I knelt
under the large crucifix outside its entrance. When I finished, I
made the sign of the cross with my index finger and then continued on to Eighteenth Avenue to catch the bus to the subway
that would take me home.

By the time I arrived home, I was tired and happy after a
long day. Fridays and Saturdays were the busiest days in the
salon, but they were also the days when the most money could
be made. When I moved my key toward the door, I noticed
that the mailbox door was wide-open and our mail was strewn
across the front porch.

That's odd, I thought. I considered the possibility that the
mailman had taken off running from a dog and I smiled when
I pictured that in my mind. I gathered the scattered mail and
checked my watch. It was seven thirty. Grandma went with
Mom to a late-afternoon appointment at her doctor's office
and they'll be getting back soon, I said to myself. Maybe I'll
surprise them and make one of Mom's favorite dishes—tuna
fish casserole with crumbled potato chips on top. My mouth
watered in anticipation and I decided that that was what I'd do.
I fit the key into the lock and opened the door.

I dropped my purse and the mail on the floor and stared
into the living room with my eyes and mouth wide open. The

couch had been slashed, the matching lamps were broken, and the contents of my mother's storage trunk were strewn on the floor. My grandma's things that my grandfather had brought home from the war were all over the place. I ran to see if his cuff links were still in the box; they weren't, they were gone, too. Poor Grandma, those stained gold elephant cuff links were all she had left of his memory.

I rushed to my bedroom and found my dresser drawers open, my clothing dumped on the floor, and my journal pages torn out and scattered on the bed. I burst into tears and stood there, sobbing, for a few minutes. How had anyone gotten in when the doors and windows were locked? I wondered. And why would someone tear my journals? When I entered my mother's room, I had my answer. Shattered glass covered the carpet below her window and her clothes were similarly scattered.

For some reason, Grandma's room had been left undisturbed, but I checked the jewelry box that was on her dresser. One of the few things with any value in the house—Grandma's wedding ring with its diamond chips that were worth little but meant so much to her—was still there. I thanked God for that and, after I had finished a fast survey, for the fact that the only thing that seemed to be missing was a carton of orange juice from the refrigerator. Was it a homeless person who was hungry? I wondered. If it was, why would he ransack some areas and leave others alone, and tear my journals apart? Why hadn't he taken Grandma's ring? I couldn't help but recall the nights I would look out of my bedroom window and see the local boys breaking into the storefronts or into cars. Petty crimes, but this was way too personal for me.

I called the police and then shuffled back to my room. I grabbed my stomach and sat on the floor, sickened by the idea of a stranger who might have read my most intimate thoughts before ripping the pages apart. What kind of person would do such a thing, and why? I racked my mind. And then I panicked when I thought about my work in progress. I reached under the area rug where I hid a small brass key and bolted to the metal box that I kept stashed under the tall steam radiator. My book was my toll for Manhattan and I felt certain that when I finished, I would make it to the other side. My heart raced as I fumbled with the key. I exhaled when I looked inside—my manuscript was still there, as was the diamond heart bracelet that Tony had given me.

I waited for the police in the living room, sobbing again as I clutched my manuscript to my chest. What would I have done if it were missing? I fretted. I pushed the thought out of my mind but it was immediately replaced by another. What would the break-in do to my mother? Despite my doubts before the move, she had been doing better in our new place, but with her fragile mind, I thought the incident might send her on a drug and drinking binge and back to bed. I wiped my eyes and took a deep breath, pulling myself together to face the cops.

"You shoulda called us from a neighbor's phone, Miss, as soon as you opened the door," said the older of the two uniformed officers when they arrived. "Whoever it was mighta still been inside."

"I wasn't thinking, Officer," I said.

"Let's have a look around," he said. We ended up back in the living room after a quick pass through the apartment. "So you say nothin's missing?" the older cop asked.

"Nothing," I said, and then I remembered the orange juice. "Other than maybe some juice." The cops glanced at each other with slight smiles. The older one turned to me. "Looks like some random mischief here," he said. "Kids."

"That's it?" I asked.

"Happens all the time."

"What about drug addicts?"

"I doubt it. If it was, anythin' an' everythin' that could be sold, for any amount, would have been taken outta here," the cop said, and then he pointed. "Like that old TV there, or the portable radio in the kitchen, not to mention your typewriter and Grandma's ring."

I looked up at the cop's lined face. "Do you think you'll catch whoever did this?"

The cops glanced at each other again and then at me with tight lips. "With nothing stolen, there's not a lot to go on. Probably not much anyone can do about it," the older cop said.

I had a different idea about what could be done, and as soon as they had left I summoned the nerve to make a phone call and then braced myself to speak to Tony. I prayed that Pamela wouldn't answer the ring.

"Yo," Tony said.

"T-Tony?" I hadn't been prepared for the old feelings that stirred in me.

"Sam? Is that you?"

"Yeah . . . it's me. Am I botherin' ya?"

"Nah. I'm busy, but that's okay."

Even though I was bursting to get to the reason for my call, I tried to make some small talk to break the ice. "What's new?"

"Nuttin'."

"Jeez, Tone. We haven't talked in months. Somethin' must be new."

"Sure," he said, "a lot's new."

"Like what?" I asked.

"Nuttin'." That was going nowhere, so I decided to get to the point.

"Listen, I need to talk to ya. We had some trouble here and I wanted you to check into it—that is, if you feel like it."

"Like I said, I'm pretty busy with work and all."

"The cops just left," I said.

"Cops? Why were *rats* at your house?"

"Somethin' awful. Our place got broken into."

"Too bad," he said. "What did they make off with?"

"Nothing. We have nothing. That's what's so weird."

"Ya got lucky, then. So what do ya wan' me ta do aboudit?"

"I thought you could look into it for me. You know everybody and maybe you could find somethin' out for me."

"People break into houses all the time, Sam. Petty shit. Not much anyone can do."

I didn't mention that the cops had said the same thing. I had been hoping for more from Tony, and then the conversation with Janice about how we gave Tony and Richie the right to control our lives popped into my head. I regretted making the call. "Well, I shouldn'ta bothered ya, Tony. Sorry."

"Don' be. I'm just glad you're okay, Sam. Now I gotta go do sumthin' with my mom."

"Sure," I replied.

"See ya," he said, and we hung up.

When I got to the salon after school the following Wednesday, I found out that Janice hadn't shown up for work and hadn't called in. I telephoned her and when I got the machine I left a message to call me right away.

It wasn't like Janice to disappear, I knew. She was too responsible and it just wasn't her way. I felt it had to be something serious with her family . . . or with Richie. I wanted to leave right away and go to her house but the salon was busy. I couldn't leave them doubly short-staffed if I wanted to keep the job that was helping me to save money for a new life. I pushed thoughts of Janice to the back of my mind and forced myself to focus on my work.

Time dragged as I painted the nails of the carefree women on my schedule. They must have known that my mind wasn't on the brushes in my hand because I had to redo my work more than once. I was relieved when closing time mercifully arrived four hours later. I couldn't wait to get home and get some news about my best friend. After I bolted out the door and started hurrying down the street, I heard a familiar voice behind me.

"Yo, Sam."

My heart skipped a beat. I stopped and turned around and my stomach fluttered. Tony, wearing a powder blue T-shirt and black jeans, stood with his arms crossed. My heart raced. The dick, I said to myself. He just had to wear blue, didn't he? It had always made his eyes more vivid and they came back to life that day. I noticed that his hair was darker—gelled back, just like a real Italian, I thought, and that turned me off somewhat. What had happened to his soft hair that had always set him apart from the other guys? "What are you doin' here?" I asked.

"I wanna talk ta ya."

"You didn't care much about talkin' when I called last week."

"I was busy, Sam. You shouldn'ta expected me to drop everythin' when you call outta nowhere."

"I shoulda known better," I said, and looked away. "Let's just forget it, Tony."

"No, it's all right. I was jus' taken by surprise, is all."

I faced him. "Listen. I can't talk now," I said, and started to turn away. "I gotta go do somethin'."

"Wait, baby," he said as he grabbed my arm and moved closer. "I ain't gonna bite." I crossed my arms. Damn! I said to myself. What is it with us Brooklyn Girls? I chastised myself. I couldn't deny that he looked good, even with his gelled-up hair. "I did some thinkin'," Tony continued, "about ya gettin' broke inta and all. I bet it was your neighbors."

"That's real dumb, Tony," I said. "They're harmless old people and keep to themselves. They even brought us some cannolis when we moved in."

"Old people do weird shit. Look at my mom—she took a cruise to Italy to go look for her dead ancestors." A devilish grin spread on his face. "Which means I got the house to myself for a while."

Was he coming on to me, I wondered, after months without any contact at all? Without even an attempt at an apology? No calls, no gifts? Nothing? I regretted again making that call after the break-in. I had opened the door, I guess. But it was just like him to go after what he wanted with no consideration for my feelings or for how badly he'd treated me. I tapped my foot. "What are you doin' here?" I asked. "Really."

All hints of playfulness disappeared from his face and he gazed into my eyes. "I'm dyin' without ya, Sam."

"I told ya we were over, Tone."

"We're never over," he said through clenched teeth. "We were meant for each other right from the start."

I recalled in an instant the early days on Eighteenth Avenue, the Santa Rosalia feast where we had met and the good times we'd had after that. Were they really real, I wondered, and were they gone forever? And then I thought about the other, hurtful things that had happened. They were real enough, I knew. I fought back the tears I didn't want him to see. "I can't be with someone who messes around all the time," I said. Once you eat the poison, I thought, you crave it forever.

"I've changed, Sam. I mean it." I wanted to believe him but doubted that enough time had passed for that to happen.

"It's too soon, Tone," I said.

"Okay, then we'll start slow. How 'bout a pizza?" I was worried about Janice and couldn't deal with anything else right then.

"Not now. I gotta get home," I said, and started to turn away from him again. He jumped next to me and put his arm around my waist. I inhaled his familiar scent—the poison that I had craved. My resolve slipped. Damn! I said to myself once more.

"Hey, Sam, let's make a run for it!" Tony shouted. He took off and I ran after him without hesitating. What was I doing?

I asked myself as I struggled to catch up. We were like a couple of carefree kids in a playground, cavorting and laughing like a genuine couple, and it sure felt good. But it felt wrong, too.

When Tony got to the end of the block, he stopped and turned to face me. I ran to him with a big smile on my face and a bigger question in my heart. He caught me in his arms and we looked at each other with happy eyes. "Sam," he said, "I got a present for ya." He reached into his jeans pocket and slipped something that sparkled into my hand.

I stared down at three white diamonds set in a platinum ring embedded with diamond chips. "This has to be worth a fortune," I said. "Was this off a truck, too?"

Tony glared at first but then smiled and made light of it. "Bizness has been good lately," he said, and then lowered his eyes. "I got no one to share my success with," he said.

"No lipstick buddies?" I cracked.

"Not a one," he said as he looked up at me. That sounded genuine to me. He'd never show up in Father Rinaldi's confessional, I knew, but maybe he had been doing penance in my absence, I thought. "I keep tellin' ya," Tony continued, "that lipstick belonged to somebody I don' know." How could I believe him? As I looked down at this ring I wondered who suffered at his hand for him to get it. As reluctant as I was, I still believed him.

I felt that Tony was better than the typical Brooklyn guys. They were more crude and more ignorant, not to mention less attractive. But then Tony's dashboard slammed into my consciousness as it had my face and I thought differently. "This is too expensive," I said. I handed the ring back to him.

Tony looked crushed. He put the ring back into his pocket. "Okay, Sam. I get it. You wan' me ta work for ya, don'tya? Fine. I'll do whatever it takes. The ring'll be waitin' for ya." He put his hand on my shoulder for a moment. "Let me take ya home. Ya ain't livin' near here no more, ya know."

There wasn't any harm in that, I felt. Besides, the sooner I got home, the better. I didn't want to miss a call from Janice. "Okay, thanks," I said.

We didn't hold hands when I walked beside Tony to the Porsche and on our way to my new neighborhood. I had to admit, though, that it felt good to be with him. I even felt okay about Tony's new hair. I supposed it was inevitable that he'd start looking like the other Brooklyn Boys. At least it was still blond and those blue eyes still set him apart.

When we reached the corner of my street Tony pulled over and I said good-bye. He tried to pull me in for a kiss but I rebuffed his approach. I felt I wasn't ready to take him back, and probably never would be. Too much water under the bridge, I felt. There would be no hugs, no kisses, and no walking me to the door, either.

Tony didn't protest. I supposed he knew that we had gone as far as we were going to go and that he wasn't ready to confront Mom and Grandma, anyway. I could relate to that; I didn't relish the repercussions if I ever sprung our getting back together on them. I decided that if Tony and I ever did, I would have to break it to them gently and give them some time to accept it before they saw him again.

On Friday afternoon, I still hadn't seen or heard from Janice, although Mrs. Caputo had returned my message the day before and told me she was in New Jersey visiting a cousin. But I was very excited that afternoon and had to talk to my best friend, so I tried another call from the salon. "Is Janice there?" I asked her mother when she answered the phone.

"I'm sorry, Sam," Mrs. Caputo said, "but she's in New Jersey like I told you."

"I miss her a lot and need to talk to her."

"She's taking a break from that idiot boy, and I hope she stays away for good." Mrs. Caputo sounded angry and resolved.

I shuddered as I imagined what Richie had done. He must have really screwed up, I thought.

"She just quit her job and didn't tell me anything," I said. "I'm worried."

"I'll tell her you called," Mrs. Caputo promised.

"Please tell her to phone me as soon as she can," I said, and hung up, frustrated. For some reason, Mrs. Caputo wouldn't give me a number where Janice could be reached and insisted on relaying my messages. I wasn't so sure my girlfriend was getting them. I figured Mrs. Caputo must have wanted to cut off any association with Bensonhurst for a while. I hoped that wouldn't include me for long.

Life was lonely without Janice, my confidante, and I wished I could at least understand why she was away. I wanted to share with her how happy and fulfilled I was with my new life. I enjoyed my job at the salon and without a steady boyfriend, my spare time was all about finishing my novel and contributing to the school newspaper. Something special happened that day that had thrilled me and I was busting to tell my friend all about it.

Mr. Wainright stopped me in the hallway that day after an editorial meeting. "Great addition to the series this week, Sam," he had started. "You really nailed the pressures of dating. I'm sure everyone can relate to the demands you described. Keep going." I had felt proud and intended to do as he advised. All the way to Manhattan.

Throwing myself into that assignment had come naturally. After all, I had dated someone who had given me an awful lot of stress. I knew how it felt to deal with sexual demands and to suspect that a boyfriend had been cheating. Finding the lipstick fueled my passionate approach to, and honesty about, the topic. It had been difficult to admit in writing that I still had some feelings for a guy who had not only cheated on me but who had raised his hand to me, too.

But Mr. Wainright's affirmation wasn't the only reason for

my excitement. While we were talking, a gentleman dressed in an expensive navy suit and print tie joined us. "Professor Greenburg," Mr. Wainright said with a smile, "I want you to meet Samantha Bonti." I shook hands with him and gave my favorite teacher a puzzled look. "Professor Greenburg is the faculty supervisor for New York University," Mr. Wainright continued, and my heart raced. He was talking about a famous university not far from where the Brooklyn Bridge touched down on the other side of the river. It was one of the best and it was . . . in Manhattan!

"I've read all of your articles to date," Professor Greenburg started, "and I must say I was impressed." My pride went into overdrive and it was written all over my face. "Did you ever think of turning those articles into on-air material and talking live about each of the issues?"

"God no," I said. The possibility had excited me but it made me quiver for a moment, too. "What about my Brooklyn accent, Professor? I'm not sure people would like the way I sound even if they cared about what I had to say."

"I don't think that will matter to our listeners, who don't always find it easy to express how they feel about social issues, and aren't always comfortable asking questions that they're dying to ask," Professor Greenburg replied. "You seem to have answers and I feel you should share them." I was in my glory, which I was sure was shining on my face, just as Mr. Greenburg's bald head was shining in the sterile lighting of the hallway. "Give it a try. If you absolutely hate it—which I know you won't—then we'll shut it down. Fair deal?" I smiled broadly. "Is that a *yes*?" Professor Greenburg asked with a smile that matched mine and the one that had been on Mr. Wainright's face the whole time.

I nodded slowly. "Uh-huh," I said.

"Excellent. You won't mind traveling to Manhattan, will you?"

"I don't think so," I gushed. How could I? I had thought. I'd pictured myself doing just that my whole life. "When is it?" I inquired, and Professor Greenburg then went over the details. The first show would be recorded in a month, with installments every week until the end of the school year. If things worked out well, I could continue with the show in the fall no matter what else I was doing. "Of course," Professor Greenburg had said near the end of our conversation, "we'd want you to matriculate at our university. From what Mr. Wainright tells me, your grades won't be an issue." But money certainly would be, I thought as I frowned. Mr. Wainright put a hand on my shoulder then. "I took the liberty of looking into scholarships and grants there, Sam. Financial aid won't be an issue, either," he offered.

I was overwhelmed. "Radio!" I blurted.

"It's only a local college broadcast, Ms. Bonti," Professor Greenburg cautioned. "Barely enough watts to get the signal across the East River." It was sufficiently strong to pull me over to the real world, I thought.

"It's plenty powerful for me, Professor," I responded. He promised he would contact me when he and the host started developing the initial segment. I could hardly believe my ears—producers and segments and all the rest of it.

When I had left the school, I felt as if I'd won the lottery. I hadn't applied to any of the big schools in Manhattan, let alone out of state, where the costs would be doubled. I assumed I'd enroll in a community college and then try to get into a better place later. I wanted to run home to tell Mom and Grandma the good news but I had to work at the salon. On the way to the shop, I remembered that they wouldn't be home, anyway. They planned to go to the movies and then have some Chinese food. They'd be home late. Damn, I thought. I really wanted to share my news with someone I cared about and without Janice around, there wasn't anyone else to talk to except

Father Rinaldi, but there was no time for another detour to Our Lady of Guadalupe.

When I got home after work my excitement was still high and I felt inspired. I pulled out my manuscript and was typing feverishly when the phone rang. I ran to answer it, hoping Janice was on the line.

"Hey, Sam," Tony said.

My shoulders slumped. "Hey," I said flatly. There was silence on his end for a long moment. "What's goin' on, Tony? I'm kinda busy." He laughed, but it was obvious that he was nervous. "What's so funny?" I asked.

"You bein' busy," he said. "So watcha doin'?"

"Writin'."

"'Bout me?"

"You'll have to buy the book," I said. I had the upper hand for a change and it felt good. My excitement bubbled over and I couldn't resist telling him my news. "Guess what? I'm gonna be on the radio!"

Tony hesitated. "Well, that's real good . . . I guess."

"You better believe it," I gushed, and then calmed myself, skipping the subject. "So why'd ya call?"

"I wanted ta know if they caught the asshole which broke inta ya place," Tony said. That dredged up unpleasant feelings that had been buried for a while. "What did the cops find out?"

"They never got back to me so I called them. They said that since nothing was stolen there was no point pursuing it any further."

"That's good then, Sam."

What the hell did that mean? I wondered. What was good about it? Didn't Tony know how much it bothered me? Someone had broken into my house and he was telling me that it was good that nothing happened? That the police never found the piece of shit who did it was okay with him? I didn't get it. "Why'd ya call, Tony? For real."

"The thing is," he said, "I'm kinda lonely here since my mom's away. It's a big house, the TV broke, and the guys are busy."

"Where's your dad?"

"Down the street at the local dive."

"So you called me as a last resort?"

"No, no," he said. "It's not like that. I really miss ya. I mean it. Come over. I'll make ya some spaghetti." If I agreed to go over, wouldn't it open a can of worms? I worried. Had enough time elapsed to effect real change in him? "I don't know, Tone," I said.

"C'mon, Sam. Just dinner. I promise. I'm dyin' ta see ya."

He had had the power of persuasion over me, and it seemed like it was working again. I worried some more. Had enough time elapsed to effect change in me? Could my feelings of despisement toward him ever be totally erased? I wondered. I decided I was getting too far ahead of myself. It was only dinner, I reasoned. What harm could it do? Besides, I was dying to celebrate! "Okay," I said. "Just some spaghetti."

"I'll be so good, ya won' recognize me."

I found out when I arrived that Tony had been telling me the truth; I didn't recognize him. He was running around like a suburban housewife, tidying the living room, wearing an apron decorated with apples, cherries, and bananas and a tall, white chef's hat that he must have gotten from Café Sicily. I laughed and Tony didn't take offense. Maybe he had changed, I thought. He gave me a hug and I didn't resist—I felt there was no harm in that, either. His male scent, however, stirred the desire that had been buried, and there was no doubt about how dangerous that was. And no doubt that I'd have to be on my guard.

We went into the kitchen. Tony took two wineglasses from the cabinet and filled them from a bottle of Chianti he'd uncorked and allowed to breathe. "To friendship," he said, clinking my glass.

"To friendship," I agreed, and tasted the wine. It was as smooth as silk. This wasn't so bad after all, I thought, and continued to drink while Tony stirred the sauce. Maybe we could get along like normal people after all, I supposed.

Tony served dinner and more wine at the dining room table while we talked about old times—only the good ones. I tried to show concern about his legal case two or three times but he brushed it off as if it didn't bother him at all. The whole time we ate, I was dying to steer the conversation to what had happened with Professor Greenburg. However, I was again reluctant to draw attention to myself and decided it would be better, anyway, if Tony brought it up. But he never said a thing about it at the table.

When we had finished eating, we sat on the living room couch. Tony refilled my glass and then opened another bottle. Maybe he was going to toast my success then, I thought. I felt giddy. "I've had enough, Tony," I said. I hadn't felt that way in a long time. It felt good, but then the questions about whether I should have been with him forced their way into my mind once more. And then a different question popped into my head. "What happened between Janis and Richie?" I asked. I couldn't stifle a giggle and felt bad about that.

Tony topped off my glass. "She went nuts is what happened," he said. "Richie don' even know where she is. Ya'd never disappear like that, Sam, wouldya?"

I didn't know what had happened and so I couldn't say what I would have done. I was having trouble thinking straight about anything right then. Tony leaned in and grazed my lips with his. He took me by surprise, like he had done before, and my body got chills up and down as it had before. I hesitated because I felt I should have backed off, but I was so relaxed, I kissed him back.

"Ya kiss so good, Sam," Tony breathed. He sprawled on top of me and I felt a familiar bulge in his pants and ripples of pleasure when he rubbed my breasts on top of my blouse. In an instant, my buttons were open and his kisses traced along my bra.

"I think you better stop," I said.

"Whatever ya say," Tony said, but his mouth continued to tease and suck, from my breasts to my navel. My voice hadn't fooled me, so why would Tony take my protest seriously? I asked myself. "Oh, Tony," I moaned as he slipped a hand under my jeans.

I didn't remember moving from the couch to Tony's bed. We got lost in a swirl of white sheets and body parts, and made love as if it was the first time. When Tony was finished and he had gotten up to go to the bathroom, I hugged the sheets. I was sure he still loved me and I had to admit to myself that I still had strong feelings for him. Despite it all, call me an idiot, but I did. No matter what he had done, I guessed I still loved him. Maybe Janice had been right, I thought, as I recalled what she had said on my bed, that Tony loved me in his own crazy way. Tony and I just loved differently, I reasoned, and showed it in different ways. We could work out our differences together.

I smiled and pulled the sheets up over my head. I wanted to look like an Egyptian mummy, so I stretched my legs all the way to the bottom of the bed. I loved to play the clown and intended to make Tony laugh when he got back. My foot bumped into something frilly that was crumpled under the sheets. My underwear must have gotten lost in the bedclothes, I thought.

I giggled and reached under the covers. The panties were pink, and they weren't mine! Someone else had been with him! I fumed. And maybe it had even been that same day, I thought with revulsion. My stomach churned. God, when would I learn? I admonished myself. How much more did I have to see before I would wake up?

I knew I had to get out of there as fast and as far away as possible. I sobbed as I got out of bed and gathered my clothes.

Tony swaggered back into the room with a smile that turned into a frown when he saw my face. "Whatsa matter, Sam? You sick?" I burst into tears and flung the panties across the room. They landed at his feet. "What's that?" he asked.

"You tell me," I said, sniffling.

"Ain't they yours?"

"No, Tony . . . they're not. Like you don't know."

"I'm gonna kill that Vin," Tony said. "Every time he uses my room, his girl leaves somethin'. I told him—"

"It's always someone else," I interrupted, humiliated again in his presence, "isn't it, Tony? I can't believe you tricked me again." I breathed deeply and tried to pull myself together as best I could while I started to dress.

"I didn't do nuttin'," Tony snapped.

"Sure, Tone," I said as I fumbled with my blouse. "Whatever you say."

"You're so jealous, Sam. I have no idea how they got there. Where were they, anyway?"

"Buried in your sheets!" I shouted.

"I'm tellin' ya, Sam," Tony said. "Vin uses my bed a lot."

"To cheat on Dara?" I scoffed. "That's just plain disgusting."

"As a matter of fact, yeah. He's that kinda guy. I keep tellin' him not to. And the lousy bastard doesn't have the decency ta change the sheets. I told him—"

"Give it a rest, Tony. This is my fault for bein' here. I thought you were lonely for me but all you were was horny." I tucked my blouse into my jeans.

"I swear it wasn't me, Sam," Tony said, and he grabbed the telephone. "Jus' wait while I get Vin. He'll tell ya what happened."

"No he won't, 'cause I'm outta here. My life was going just fine before I let you back in. How could I be so stupid?" I put my heels on and started past him on my way out of the room. "So long," I said as I wiped my eyes. "You're no damn good."

"I'm not as bad as ya said I was," Tony blurted. "Ya said I didn't give a shit aboud anybody but me. It ain't true. How could you write that kinda stuff?" I stopped in my tracks. A terrible time had just gotten far worse and I couldn't get a line from a Bee Gees song out of my head until it had repeated itself a few times: *Tragedy, when the feeling's gone and you can't go on, it's tragedy*. Misery wafted over me then and I faced him with rage in my watery eyes.

"You lowlife!" I screamed. "You broke into my house! Were you ever gonna tell me, or did you think it was okay for me to be scared for the rest of my life?"

"C'mon, Sam," Tony pleaded. "It's jus' that I love ya so much, I wanted to read what ya wuz writin' so I could call my publishin' friend an' tell him how great it was."

"You're a liar, Tony. A thief. A cheater," I said. "You violated me and my family!" I gritted my teeth and started for the door. "I can't fuckin' believe I just slept with you." He reached for me but I brushed him aside. I should go to the cops, I thought. He bolted for me and grabbed my arms so hard I thought I I they were going to come out of their sockets. Somehow, with the help of prayer and seeing the Blessed Mother's face in front of me, I managed to get out of his powerful lock.

"Sam . . . ," he called out as I left the room.

I didn't hear anything after that other than my own voice telling me I needed to get home and get his scent off me under a hot shower.

21

I hadn't told my mother or grandmother what happened with Tony when I had gotten home Friday night. When they had asked me why I was in a bad mood, I told them I had PMS and to just leave me alone. I couldn't tell them that I had let Tony hurt me again, that I was pining for an honest, loving relationship. And I couldn't breathe a word that Tony was the one who had broken into our house. My mother would have been livid. After all, she'd moved me to Bay Ridge to get away from the guy. What would she do next? I wondered. Have Grandma send me away to Hebrew school?

No, I couldn't bear to undergo my mom's wrath nor give her something else that she would hold over my head for the foreseeable future and use as a weapon whenever the mood struck. But I reconsidered confiding in Grandma the next day. It would have been comforting for me because she was much more broad-minded and forgiving than Mom, but I knew, even though Grandma wouldn't come right out and say it, that she would have been hurt by what she heard. Anyway, I was so ashamed of myself, I decided to let the incident fade away. Besides, I was about to appear on my first radio show and I wanted to do well. I needed to focus on what lay ahead.

Over the next two weeks, I attended a couple of meetings

in Manhattan with Mr. Greenburg. Each time I got on the subway, I felt like it was my birthday. I didn't think about Tony once, as my mind was preoccupied with things that were more important to me. I was so grateful for the opportunity to get on with my life and to put him behind me once and for all.

One afternoon when I'd come home from class exhausted, I sprawled on the couch while my mother started preparing her Kraft macaroni and cheese and eggs in the kitchen. When someone knocked on the door, she went to answer it because she was expecting Cynthia, who would be picking up her baby.

"Janice Caputo!" Mom announced, and I jumped up.

"You're a sight for sore eyes, Sam," Janice said as I threw my arms around her.

Tears welled in my eyes. "Jesus, Janice, where the hell have you been?"

"That's a damned long story," she said. She smiled at Mom and gestured toward my bedroom.

We sprawled on my bed, our favorite place to talk, and Janice began with an apology. "I'm so sorry, Sam. I hated ta leave ya in the dark, but I was afraid if I talked to ya, Richie would find me."

I frowned. "That's ridiculous. Don't you trust me?"

"More'n anybody," Janice said. "But I don' trust Tony. I know how he can turn the screws when he wants ta know sumthin'. I didn't wantya ta know where I was so you wouldn't get tricked into spilling the beans. The last thing I needed was an angry visit from Richie." Janice knew all about the tricks the guys pulled, and her words reminded me of Tony's treachery.

"What happened?" I asked. "Tony told me Richie said you'd lost your mind and they sent you to a nuthouse."

"What a joke! Richie was cheating again and used my face like a speed bag when I busted him on it. I couldn't stand it no more, Sam."

"I was worried that's what it was."

"Never again," Janice swore.

I reached for her hand. "I'm glad, Janice."

"What about you and Tone?" she asked.

I skipped the details about Tony's latest betrayal. "He's just like Richie and the rest of them," I said. "We're through." Janice smiled from ear to ear, but I sensed there was more to her satisfaction than what I had just said. Her eyes were lively and it looked like she'd lost some weight. "There's something else, isn't there?" I asked.

"How did you know?" she bubbled.

"It's all over your face," I said. "You're in love, Janice Caputo, aren't you?"

Janice squeezed my hand. "For real this time," she said.

"Huh?"

"A guy named Roberto Gianotta. He owns a garment business and he's loaded. Ya should see him! He's distinguished, and treats me like a princess. His wife divorced him a couple of months ago and my aunt had him over for dinner. He's the perfect guy. I swear, the wife should have her head examined. He has this big house about a mile from here, with his own housekeeper. Her name is Linda and she told me she didn't like the wife at all. Too demanding."

I was so happy for her but it sounded too good to be true after such a short period of time. And then I thought that maybe good things are always right in front of us and we just had to see them, as Father Rinaldi had said. Regardless, I was thrilled to have my best friend back and shared the joy that she continued to express.

"I tell ya, Sam, legit is the only way to go. This guy is so fine. He thinks I am, too. And guess what? He asked me to marry him and I said yes!"

"What?" I exclaimed. Falling in love so fast was one thing, I thought. Getting married was something else. "You're so young, and you hardly know him!"

"I know this guy's the real thing and I'm getting married. Well, not right away. But we're getting engaged."

"Jeez, Janice. What did your mother say?"

"Guess," Janice said, grinning. "As long as his name ain't Richie Sparto and he ain't from Bensonhurst, she'd let me marry just about anybody. Can ya believe it, Sam?"

Maybe that was the way it was supposed to be, I thought. Maybe after enough hard lessons it was easy to know exactly what was right and what should be done. And maybe Janice was teaching me again. My face broke into a huge smile and I hugged my best friend. "Just promise you won't disappear again."

"I swear. After all, I gotta stay close ta my maid of honor." We shared a trademark giggle.

"When do I get to meet him?" I asked.

"As soon as ya want." A tight smile came to my face. "What's wrong?" Janice asked. "Ain't ya happy for me?"

"'Course I am," I said, and then I couldn't resist unloading my recent baggage. "But something happened and I couldn't tell anybody else."

"It's Tony, isn't it? Didya run into his fist? I swear ta God, if he hurt ya, I'll call Roberto. He knows everybody and—"

"He didn't beat me up," I interrupted. "But two weeks ago . . ." I told Janice everything about the panties in the bed and my discovery about the break-in. "He said they belonged to some girl Vin was screwin'," I said, and Janice remained silent. It was a relief to share it all with someone I trusted. "I've had an ache in my chest ever since, because I allowed him once again to put a dagger in my heart."

Janice threw her arms around me. "I'm so sorry that asshole broke your heart again."

"I never want to see him," I said, and then hesitated for a moment. "But it's kinda confusin'."

"Ya miss him, anyway," Janice said.

"No, just why it took me so long to get it."

"It's understandable, Sam," Janice said. "He was your first. But he sure ain't gonna be your last. Forget Tony, cuz he's no good."

"I found that out the hard way."

Janice grabbed my hand with both of hers. "I'm gonna see if Roberto knows a nice guy you can date. Then we can be a foursome, just like the old days."

"I think I'd like to forget those, too," I said. "And I really don't want to date anybody right now." I filled Janice in about the radio show. She bubbled.

"I knew it, Sam. You're the most talented person I ever met. You're gonna be somebody."

"Do you really think so?" I asked.

"It's as sure as that bridge is across town."

"Thanks, Jan. Every time Tony shows up in my life, bad things happen and I forget who I am and who I'm supposed to be. It's like I lose my mind. Maybe *I* belong in the nuthouse."

Janice shook my arms. "Ya belong right here. Ya jus' hafta stay away from that blond heartbreaker. I tellya, my mom's right." I knew she was right and she continued. "Them guys think they're God's gift. And, really, they're nothin' but trouble. That's why I had ta get away." Janice looked down. "I got sick of having my own heart broken."

It was my turn to hold her arms. "Well," I said, "things have sure changed for you now."

Janice's face brightened. "How does the name Mrs. Janice Gianotta sound?" she asked.

I thought about how sweet it would be to hook up with a real guy, a gentleman in every sense of the word, who would care for me and support everything I wanted to do. "Sounds beautiful," I said. It felt so good to have Janice back, I thought. I felt my resolve strengthen to let the Dutchman go and embrace my life without him.

"Didya tell your mom that Tony busted inta your place?" Janice asked in a hushed voice.

"God, no," I said. "I was afraid of what she'd do."

"Well, it's behind ya now," Janice said. We talked some more and shared a few more giggles. Just like old times.

I awakened on the day of my radio show feeling nauseated. I had gotten accustomed to the periodic fluctuations in my stomach from the roller-coaster ride I had been on, but I was not prepared for how frightened I felt. What if I blew it? I worried. But I was heartened by the fact that Janice was going to go with me and that I wouldn't have to deal with Tony no matter how it turned out. I steeled myself and concentrated on what I had to do to get ready.

After I put on my best skirt and blouse, I applied some makeup, thankful that I had learned how to do that properly, and then filled my favorite bag with what I would need: two books on dating and my newspaper articles.

My stomach churned. I looked at my watch, breathed deeply, and waited for Janice to show up. We would be taking the subway to Manhattan and when the show was over, Janice had promised to take me to a Greenwich Village café for lunch, compliments of her new boyfriend's credit card.

I didn't tell my mother I was so afraid that I felt sick. She might have forbidden me to go, telling me I was too young, too frightened, or too something. But I was too determined.

When Janice arrived, I grabbed my bag and hugged my mother and grandmother on the way out. The moment we got out onto the street, my stomach settled, and with each step we took toward the subway station I knew I was getting closer to where I wanted to go.

I did such a great job with the radio show that a celebration was exactly what was called for. Janice and I sat at a sidewalk table and she told me to order anything I wanted. It felt good not worrying about how much something cost, and not worrying about the person picking up the check and how he had gotten the money. And it felt even better to have a lot worth talking about. I was a writer, that was concrete, and that day I was a girl who had a radio spot.

Janice flashed Roberto's gold credit card with a giggle, and I loved that she had found a man outside the circle. Life was better in the real world, that was for sure. Janice had found someone out there, I was finding myself there, and maybe I would find the right kind of man there, too, I hoped. She raised a glass. "Here's to you," she said, and took a long, cool drink of lemonade. "Ya did it, Sam. Ya was great."

"Was I really?" I asked, needing to hear it again. Maybe that's what all creative people need, I thought, and I made a mental note to work that out on my Smith-Corona. "It felt like I started and then it was over. I can't even remember what happened in between. Do you think Mr. Greenburg was happy?"

Janice smiled from ear to ear. "I think he was ecstatic," she said. "I can hardly wait for it to be aired. Wait'll everyone hears ya. You're a natural, Sam." I took a deep breath as a waiter brought our grilled chicken salads. Maybe I had done well enough to gain a foothold across the river, I thought. "I'm so proud of you," Janice said. I was proud of myself, too. I had dumped Tony, my best friend was back, and I was almost at my goal.

Janice and I ate with gusto and then ordered dessert and coffee. We had talked the whole time about our good fortune. As I looked at her, seated across from me, Father Rinaldi's words about seeing everything echoed in my mind. I only saw good right then, and knew that I'd be writing a lot more about that, too.

When I got home, I burst 'through the front door and dashed into the kitchen to find Mom seated with a beer and a cigarette in her hand and Grandma having Entenmann's coffee cake. She swore by Entenmann's, no other, even if he did pack a lot of sugar in his cakes. After all, Grandma felt, he was a Jew.

"I did it!" I cried out. "I was wonderful today." When I got little reaction from my family, I was surprised and disappointed. "What the hell happened here?" I asked. "Did somebody die?"

Mom looked at me through her thick, wrinkled lids with vacant eyes that used to be big, beautiful green cat eyes. "Didya look in the living room?" she asked.

"No, I just came right in here to see you. I thought you'd be happy for me."

"We are, *bubelah*," Grandma said. "Real proud." When my mother would not look me in the eye, I walked out of the kitchen and into the living room. On the coffee table was a white box filled with a dozen long-stemmed red roses that were visible through the clear cover. I picked up the card. "Sam," the envelope read, and I opened it:

How are you? I guess you must be doing really good out there. I hope your writing and that radio thing went real good. I haven't called because it seems like you really did lose your love for me. I just want you to know that it wasn't my fault. But I guess it was real easy for you to just walk away after all the time we spent together.

Don't get scared. I'm not trying to get you back. I just want you to know how much I loved you, even when you thought I didn't love you back. I really should have made an effort to get along with your mom better. All I want to say is, please don't go with anyone else. I really couldn't stand that. If you get lonely, call me and I promise we can just have a calzone together, just like the good old days.

—Tony

I dropped the card. What a stretch Tony was making, I thought. From hitting me in the face, breaking into my home, and sleeping with other women to sending me roses and telling me not to sleep with anyone else. What did he think? I scoffed to myself. That I would turn into a nun so he could "stand it"? What a fool he was, I thought. What a fool *I* had been to put up with him for such a long time.

I began to sob. I had put Tony out of my life but he was forcing his way in again. I had waited for him to say "I love you" the whole time we'd dated, but he was too macho to express his love to a girl. Now that we had separated, it was like he was torturing me with his words, the very words I had prayed to hear.

Grandma came to my side and hugged me. *"Oy vey iz meir!"* she exclaimed. "What's going on?" It felt so good being held by her, secure in her bosom. Once again, I felt blessed to have her close to me. I forced a smile. "I'm okay, Grandma," I said, and then looked up at her. "He ruins everything. I was feeling so good when I got home. I swear to God, I don't ever want to hear his name again."

"I know, Sammy. I know," Grandma sighed. "Those damned Italians. Listen to me, *bubelah*. My voice is tired, but my words are strong. I tell you good things of faith like my mother and my mother's mother told me. Everything you need to break this bad cycle has to come from within you."

Grandma glanced at Mom walking toward her bedroom, cigarettes in her hand, before she turned back to me. "Please don't become the apple that didn't fall far from the tree. It's not your destiny to be like her. Get away from this life. Go, *bubelah*."

22

Three weeks later, I awakened sick to my stomach as I had for the previous three days. I had missed my last period and I went to the doctor to confirm what I already knew. I would have rather died than have this baby, his baby.

Two days after that devastating one, I gathered my courage to make a call. When the phone rang in the Kroon residence, Katrina answered and didn't bother to talk when she heard me on the line. "Tony," she shouted, "it's that girl you broke up with." I cringed.

It seemed like forever before Tony picked up the phone. "Sam," he said in an upbeat voice. "Did you get the flowers? I heard you were on the radio and I want—"

"I'm pregnant, Tony." Dead silence was all I heard for a moment.

"Well," he said, "it ain't mine." The ice in his words chilled me.

"Oh, really?" I was still. "Now that's the answer I needed to hear." Tears welled in my eyes. Damn! I kicked myself and struggled to stay calm. I didn't want to break down in front of him ever again. "Then it must be another immaculate conception, 'cause you're the only guy I slept with."

"How do I know that?"

I gritted my teeth. "'Cause I'm tellin' ya. Anyway, I don't care what you think. I know."

Tony raised his voice. "You can't have a baby, Sam."

"I can if I want to," I said. "But I don't. Not like this." I wanted a career and a new man to love me and be with me for a lifetime.

"So take care of it," Tony said.

"I need money," I said. "Three hundred. Janice knows a guy."

"Cash don't just fall in my lap, Sam."

No matter how it had gotten there, his lap had always been full of cash. I'd seen that too many times to count. But I didn't go there. "You'd rather I had the baby?" I asked. I pictured him mulling things over while I waited for his response.

"I still don't think it's mine," he deadpanned.

I wanted to scream out "Fuck you!" over the phone, but I didn't go there, either. "It's yours, Tony, and you know it. Do you want to pay support for eighteen years?"

"I don't know, Sam. I just hit up Vin last night."

I couldn't believe that the big shot in the neighborhood who did all kinds of big deals and collected money from every establishment this side of the street didn't want to part with a lousy three hundred bucks. He and the guys flashed their rolls of dough around town all the time. I'd seen Tony throw C-notes around as if they were singles. He even had a new car, a freakin' Porsche! I shouted to myelf. But that wasn't the time to throw it all up to him. I needed the money and I had to get my condition over with and soon. "I don't have the money, Tony."

"What, with *two* fuckin' jobs?" he scoffed. The grapevine was still alive and well in Bensonhurst, I thought. That figured. But it was none of his business that I had been throwing more into the pot at home and squirreling away deposit money for NYU.

"I need the money," I repeated.

He hesitated again. I could almost hear the wheels turning in that dense head of his. I knew he'd never suggest selling my bracelets to get the money, and I hadn't considered that because if he had found out I did, he would have a reason to confront me. I knew the day would come when I would get rid of them—maybe I'd toss them off the Brooklyn Bridge, I had thought—but it hadn't arrived yet. Tony broke the long silence. "I'll see what I can do."

"You better, 'cause this is serious."

"Okay, okay," Tony muttered. "Come over to the house in a coupla hours."

My already queasy stomach did flip-flops when I showed up at Tony's door. I knocked and Philip answered. I gazed at his sad face. With his scruffy beard and bloodshot eyes, he didn't look too good, as usual. "Is Tony here?" I asked.

"He hadda go out," Philip said. I was about to cry again. "Did he leave somethin' for me?" I blurted. And then rage started to build within me. How could Tony put me in this position? I wondered. Having to ask for the money from his father. I was pregnant and didn't want to see much of anybody, least of all someone in Tony's family. It was hard enough to explain to Mom and Grandma why I was crying so much. I had never been a liar growing up and I hated having to lie again as I had for months. A lot about me had changed since I'd met Tony, I thought. I had to change back to the person I was before, I vowed. But I had to get past my crisis first.

Philip reached into his pants pocket and took out a wrinkled envelope. He handed it to me and I took it with trembling fingers. "Do you want to come in for some iced tea?" he asked. His gesture struck me as sad, and for a moment I felt sorry for him. His world, probably the only one he'd ever know, was confined to a leather armchair, dark bars, and smoke-filled card rooms. But I never wanted to see or be inside that house again. "No, thanks," I said, stuffing the envelope into my purse.

"Do you have a message for Tony?" Philip asked.

"No, I don't," I lied once more. I resented what Tony had just put me through. He was such a coward, I thought. He couldn't even face me but I just wanted to be rid of everything that had anything to do with him. I wanted to tell him that but I turned around and walked away. I was relieved it was over.

I headed for the subway and when I sat down on a molded plastic seat, something told me to open the envelope. The distress about what I had faced came right back when I found one hundred dollars in it. My rage returned then—how could Tony be such a creep? I asked myself. How? And how would I get over my ordeal? I decided I had no choice but to ask Janice if she could loan the rest of the money to me.

On the way home, I had an overwhelming urge to light a candle. I took a familiar detour to Our Lady of Guadalupe.

I looked up at the cross outside the church as I always did, but went to the pew in front because I wanted to be closer to the Blessed Mother. I knelt before Her statue and prayed as I had never done before. The last time I had looked at Her, I recalled, was after Tony had taken my virginity in his parents' bed. The thought of that in church made me want to die inside. I adored the Blessed Mother and believed in Her, and felt ashamed about my recent past and my current condition. But I knew that She would help me and answer my prayers.

When I had finished asking Her for guidance, I went to light a candle for my family and my troubles and for the horrific decision that confronted me. Father Rinaldi came into the sanctuary and walked over when he saw me lighting a match. As always, he looked wonderful. "Hello, Father," I said.

"Hello, Samantha. Isn't it nicer here than in a hospital?" he asked.

"Sure is, Father."

"How are you, child?"

I turned away from him and my hand shook as I lit a

candle. "Everything's good," I said, and then admonished myself. How dare I lie in church! And to the purest of men! Hadn't I sinned enough already? I decided if I was going to change, I had to start right there. I blew out the match and turned back to the priest. "Father, I need to talk with you . . . about . . . my condition."

"What condition?"

I was afraid and felt as if the entire world was listening to me at that very moment. I cast my eyes down to the marble floor. "Father . . . I'm pregnant. And I don't want to be. I never wanted to get rid of something more in my life." I looked into his face and knew I had said something terrible to that holy man.

Father Rinaldi pursed his lips and put his sure hand on my shoulder. "Let's talk by our Blessed Mother," he said. "She will guide us." He took my hand and led me back to the pew across from the statue. His voice and his touch soothed me.

"Is Tony Kroon the father?" the priest asked when we had sat down.

"Yes."

"Do you love him?"

"Not anymore. I was crazy to ever get mixed up with him."

"The church and I will help you and your child." He offered assistance, I thought, instead of reminding me that he had told me to stay away from Tony. He's so good, I said to myself. I wanted to be more like him—honest and pure and selfless. But I also knew that no matter how wrong an abortion was, I could not have a baby, least of all one with a crippled soul like Tony's. I just could not. I squirmed in my seat. "Has he hurt you?" Father Rinaldi asked.

I looked away. "Yes, Father. In many ways. I've been wronged and done wrong and that's why I know I can't keep it, not under these circumstances; besides, who will take care of my sick mother and grandmother? They need me more than this baby. I just want to make this a bad memory and go on with my life . . . I need the money to get rid of it, you're my only hope at this point." I could tell that Father Rinaldi was beside himself, caught up in his own fear of me even asking such a thing.

"Samantha, the church . . . me . . . I cannot give you money for an abortion. It would be unethical. I mean the mere word can strike me dead. It is not our belief."

I just frantically hung on to his sleeve. "Well, it's the only belief I have, Father, will you help me? I beg of you . . . I have to be rid of this and the life that I once had with this person. I've been hurt way too much."

"Samantha, you are straining me so here. My heart bleeds for you and your thoughts. Do you hear what you are asking of me, as a holy man of the most highest? We must do confession immediately. These horrible thoughts have to leave you."

"I don't care about confession, I just want to be rid of this baby, I am sorry . . . so sorry." I had cried so much I couldn't feel my eyes any longer. I was so desperate.

"An abortion is a mortal sin, Samantha," Father Rinaldi said. "The Church cannot condone that." He squeezed my hand. "That's not the answer, child. You must seek strength from our Holy Mother." I turned back to him and to those eyes that had never lost their luster. "She will help you with what it is you must do," Father Rinaldi said, and he guided my head to his shoulder. I clutched his black sleeve tighter as my tears of desperation and humiliation fell upon it.

We stood in front of Mary for over an hour, but who was thinking about time when I was consumed with a way out of this? I never stopped begging him to help me. Finally, in my last breath of hope and despair, I gazed upon him one last time.

"Wait here." Father Rinaldi left to go to the rectory and, after what felt like an eternity, slowly came back with a look of death and despair covering his face. He leaned into me, grabbing me with all of his might, and placed something into my pocket. I looked at him knowingly and ran out of the church as fast as I could. A poor man was left clenching his fists in his heart and falling to his knees in front of Mary.

I had no time to think of what I had done.

It was a gloomy day and dark clouds filled the skies when Janice and I came up from the subway on Third Avenue in downtown Brooklyn, a stone's throw from the bridge that seemed to be collapsing before me. I was so ashamed that I had even thought of asking Father Rinaldi, but by then Janice knew everything, and she had given me the last two hundred dollars.

We had forgotten an umbrella and the skies opened up after we had walked the few blocks to the abortion clinic and stood facing the all-white brick building on Thirty-ninth Street. A group of picketers held up signs proclaiming death for the abortion doctors. There was an array of detailed photos carried by these protesters with sayings such as "Don't kill your baby" and "Let us help." Yeah, right, I thought. Everyone was going to help me. I was in my own hell and had already chosen what I was going to do to put out the fire. At no point did I ever intend to keep this child. As religious as I was, Mother Mary would somehow have to forgive this sin. I could not raise Tony's child; I would have hated the child and what I would eventually become. I knew this for sure.

> *When I find myself in times of trouble, Mother Mary comes to me*
> *Speaking words of wisdom, let it be . . .*

I pushed my way through the crowd with Janice following close behind as the words of the Beatles song swirled in my head, trying to keep me calm.

"Don't be a murderer!" a woman screamed when I approached the door to the clinic. The door opened and I took the hand of a clinic worker who pulled me inside.

Someone handed us towels to dry off before we took seats in the crowded waiting room. By the traumatized look on all the faces, I assumed the pressure of the picketers outside must have gotten to everyone. Most of them were slumped in their chairs, staring blankly straight ahead.

"Wilson," a nurse called out. A skinny black girl who couldn't have been older than thirteen stood up and looked as if she'd have found a firing squad preferable to what she was facing. She disappeared behind a door as I took a clipboard from the unsmiling receptionist. "Fill in both sides," the gray-haired woman told me. "Do you have cash?"

I nodded. "Do you want it now?"

The nurse reached a hand under the glass window as I pulled the three hundred-dollar bills from a wrinkled envelope. Tony's comment at the racetrack months before about milk money bubbled up from my memory as I handed over the precious bills that could have been spent on better things. I tossed the empty envelope into a trash receptacle and went to a seat with Janice to fill out the questionnaire and waiver forms. I was grateful for the distraction; I didn't think I could handle any conversation. I felt so afraid and ashamed of myself, I thought I'd burst into tears if she tried to console me.

I returned the forms to the receptionist and the woman motioned me through a door. After a wistful glance at Janice, who gave me a tentative thumbs-up sign, I walked into a back room where they took my blood and checked my blood pressure. Then I went to the ladies' room to give them a urine sample so they could make sure I was pregnant. Afterward, I went back out to sit beside Janice, praying that it was all a mistake, that I had gotten a false positive and that the nausea had been caused by the upheaval in my life. But no such luck.

"Bonti," a woman called out with a Spanish accent half an hour later. I hugged Janice and got up to cross a bridge of a different kind.

Janice pulled my arm. "It's almost over and you can start again," she whispered. "You're gonna be okay, Sam."

I choked back tears as I joined a nurse in a consultation room, awaiting a counseling session that never came. Instead, she recited instructions in a monotone voice. "Here's the key to your locker, number sixteen. We'll be giving you some gas . . ." The nurse quickly corrected herself. "I . . . mean sodium pento-thal." "Gas" made me think of Grandma's stories about Auschwitz. "I wouldn't think about driving anywhere right after," the nurse continued. "Is someone here who can help you?"

"My friend is waiting for me," I said. What if I were alone then? I wondered. Thank God for Janice, I thought. The nurse gathered some papers and opened the door. "Will it hurt?" I managed to squeak out.

"Oh, not much," the nurse said. "You'll probably have a lit-tle discomfort, but I wouldn't worry about it." I wouldn't either if I were standing where you are, I thought. I'd heard doctors talk about discomfort before, a softer word for the shitload of pain I was expecting. But didn't it serve me right? I chastised myself. How dumb had I been to get myself into this position?

The nurse directed me to an elevator and I went up one floor to a hallway of lockers. The walls were dingy, the metal lockers were scratched with unintelligible graffiti, and mine had what looked like pink Teaberry chewing gum stuck around its lock. I fought a powerful urge to cut and run.

I didn't want to kill a baby, my baby. I believed it was a sin. But what other choice did I have? I tormented myself.

Several women were doing what I was doing—fumbling in front of an assigned locker and avoiding looking at anyone. They were alone with their thoughts, which probably included the men who were waiting in comfort while they suffered. That didn't seem fair to me. I saw Tony's face in my mind's eye, the father of the seed that was growing inside me. He was already the worst boyfriend in the world, not really caring for me at all.

It was all about him, I knew. He didn't and couldn't love anyone. I knew he would make a terrible parent.

I took off my white T-shirt and peach-colored pants, folded my clothes with care, and placed them in the locker. I removed the blessed mother I always wore around my neck, kissed it, and put it in my purse, which I then placed on the shelf. My throat felt thick and I trembled as I put on a thin, honeycombed blue robe and paper slippers and dropped the key into a pocket.

Another nurse appeared and ushered me down the hall to a small, cold room in a row of rooms that probably looked the same and had the same purpose. I felt weak and hopeless as I looked around. I wished I were getting ready for a facial instead of a revolting procedure. It appeared that all the girls were lined up, like an assembly line. It had to be the most degrading thing I ever had endured. The ominous steel table with stirrups waiting for my feet dominated the room, and the instrument packets and needles on metal stands glowed in the harsh overhead lights. I shivered.

The nurse left and I took off my robe, put on the paper skirt and torso cover she had handed to me, sat on the table, legs dangling over the side, and faced the door. It had been left ajar, and I caught glimpses of clinic personnel and heard them rushing in and out of doors like the White Rabbit in *Alice in Wonderland*. But I knew I wasn't in some fairy tale.

The nurse who had brought me to the room came back and prepared me for the procedure without saying much. With curt commands, she instructed me to lie down and put my feet in the stirrups. "The doctor will see you now," she said when she had finished, and she left the cold room.

She returned a moment later with a young, good-looking man with short, brown hair and a white coat who stood over me without an introduction. "Relax and breathe." He tapped my arm for a fresh vein and inserted the sodium pentothal. I so wanted to see my grandmother, the woman who had loved and nurtured me so much, standing in the corner of the procedure room. I wanted to tell her I was sorry.

I gritted my teeth as I contemplated all that I had done over the previous months, the mess I had made of things. My mind raced, flitting wildly from one heartache to another, and then for some reason it settled on Psalm 23. I had first discovered it when I was thirteen in a Bible at church. This felt right. *The LORD is my shepherd; I shall not be in want. He makes me lie down in green pastures, he leads me beside quiet waters, he restores my soul. He guides me in paths of righteousness for his name's sake. Even though I walk through the valley of the shadow of death . . .*

I had a hard time opening my eyes. Was something wrong? I wondered. Had they decided I was too young for an abortion? My memory of my mother's words when she was trying to scare me had all come true: Lifebuoy soap and a wire hanger my mother had used for her first two abortions on a kitchen table and a few hot towels. She was lucky to still be alive. I guess it was only fair that history would repeat itself and bestow that ungratefulness upon me. Would I have to face my mother and grandmother and tell them the truth? I tried to clear the fog that filled my head. I needed to find a button to contact the nurse and explain to her that I *had* to have an abortion, and then I felt a searing pain below.

As I made sense of what had happened, I was wheeled into recovery. I wasn't pregnant anymore. It was over, but I sure as hell still felt terrible. I sat up too fast and vomited all over my scrubs. My stomach roiled and I had a putrid taste in my mouth. I really wanted a drink of water but that wasn't permitted. The nurse changed me quickly and left the room. A thin stream of blood ran down my leg.

I wiped the blood and changed my sanitary pad with a new one the nurse had left for me. I felt dizzy, weak, and very cold. All I wanted to do was get the hell out of there and stand under a warm shower but my head was spinning. Take it easy, I told myself, and I took my time lying down on the cold, hard surface.

I wondered how long they would leave me there. When would someone come back? What if I passed out? What if I bled to death? I fretted. It was a possibility, I reasoned, because the clinic was so busy.

Forty-five minutes later, I couldn't bear the torment any longer and decided to leave. I took my time sitting up and putting on my robe and slippers, and then I moved on shaky legs out of the room and down the hall. I leaned against my locker for a moment and wished it were the one at New Keiser High.

"Who said you could get up?" barked a nurse who had come up behind me.

"No . . . one . . . was . . . around," I said as I turned to her. "I really . . . didn't know . . ."

The nurse eyed me up and down. "As long as you're here, get your clothes on and check out, then," she said, and brushed by me. "We'll see you out front."

I got dressed and shuffled like a piece of cattle to the elevator and went down to the main floor. As I took a sheet of recovery instructions from the receptionist, Janice ran up to hug me. I couldn't look her in the eye.

It was still raining when we got outside and we pushed through the boisterous crowd of protesters that castigated me with screams of baby-killer and murderer. If Janice hadn't been with me, I would have collapsed in tears right there on the sidewalk.

As soon as we were out of sight down the street, I fell into her arms, sobbing.

When I got home, I stood, sopping wet, in the hallway, and was grateful for the rain that had drenched my hair and plastered it on my wet face. It disguised my swollen eyes.

"Is that you, Samelah?" Grandma called out from the kitchen.

"Yeah, it's me. I'm soaked."

Grandma came out of the kitchen and hugged me. "*Oy vey!* Go change, *bubelah*," she said as she squeezed me in her arms. I could have burst into tears, but took strength from Grandma as she let go of me. "You'll catch your death."

"Where's Mom?"

"She's been in bed all day." Thank God for small favors, I thought. "I need to get some rest, too, Grandma," I said without looking her in the eye. I took off my wet jacket and headed for my room. "I'm beat."

"I love you, Sam," Grandma said.

"I love you, too, Grandma," I said over my shoulder.

I closed my bedroom door, got out of my wet clothes, and crawled into bed. I clutched the red beads of the rosary with which I'd taught myself to pray by reading a pamphlet when I was a little girl. As I held them to my chest, I wished that I were still that innocent child.

I then prayed for the forgiveness that Father Rinaldi said would be there for me. But, what if?

23

My body recovered over the ensuing weeks, but my mind couldn't escape the ravage at the abortion clinic and the added torment from losing sight of my dreams. I made more detours and more purposeful visits to Father Rinaldi's church, said more fervent prayers to the Blessed Mother, and lit more candles with the hope that She would still light the way for me.

Memories of my sins dulled over the summer but I knew their sting would never disappear. I intended to keep them locked away until I had acquired the perspective to sort them out on the page. Constant reminders of my past, however, thwarted me as I attempted to distance myself from it.

My clients at Danni's salon evoked Bensonhurst in their dress and in their speech. The ladies prattled on about the kind of men and the kind of things I yearned to forget. Headlines in the *Daily News* and its regular "Gangster" series titillated readers with graphic coverage of the goings-on that had been all too real to me. I could no longer ignore that paper with the large, bold type that screamed to me as I walked past newsstands.

The paper found its way onto my stack of reading material in my room and we found ourselves talking about it there or on the "tar beach" atop my apartment house while we tanned. Janice and I pored over the pages that described people and places we knew and wanted to forget. We couldn't avoid picking at the scabs of wounds that hadn't healed nor at our visible and invisible scars. One in particular that I just couldn't get over kept circling inside my head. The rumors, the thoughts of what really did happen that day at Sommer Bank.

Janice told me all that she had heard. And I wrote it all into a story . . .

Sommer Bank, the building with the double glass doors, was located in the center of Bensonhurst, across from the outdoor meat market. Tony chugged back his black espresso in a paper cup, unaccustomed to stirring in the morning unless he was still up from the night before. With each sip of coffee, he fantasized a future in which he held all the cards. It would be his world, his way, with enviable wealth and women throwing themselves at him.

It all felt great except for a hole, right in the middle of his chest. I was supposed to be there to enjoy the products of his labor, his illegal labor, but I was gone now. "Screw her!" he thought to himself. I was too impatient. All he wanted was to sow some wild oats before he settled down with me, but I had blown it. Well, there were plenty of other fish in the sea, beautiful fish who would get to share the spoils of his most impressive robbery to date. I guess he always had the robbing in him. After all, his father had done a stint in jail, so why not let history repeat itself? Pamela was no help anyway. In fact, she just cheered on Tony's actions. God even seemed to help at times. Who would have thought that amazing family at Christmas was all a farce, all a sham, all off a truck?

Tony sat in the car with Vin, who sipped his own coffee, quietly watching the empty street begin to stir with activity. It was 9:30 a.m. and the locals were opening their storefronts on a Friday morning, all a bit weary from the week but not discouraged. Friday was always more hopeful for the Bensonhurst store owners, since the weekend was near and the customers spent more money right after they got paid. It was the best day for commerce, everyone agreed, and Vin and Tony sat in the car, watching the vendors chatting and comparing neighborhood stories while they opened their doors and washed down the sidewalks.

"We got it together, Tone," said Vin. "Right?"

"Yeah, yeah," said Tony. "I still think we could have used Richie's help, though."

"You know my dad won't let me work with him anymore. We've been over this again and again. He's out. Nothin' personal. He's part of another family. Just concentrate. Okay?"

"Okay," said Tony, reviewing what was about to happen. The old blue Oldsmobile in which they sat had been payment to Vin for a debt owed, and as run-down and ugly as it looked, it was the perfect getaway car since it was built for speed.

Those bastards should watch the gambling, thought Vin, *with no conscience about taking the car from people he'd known his whole life. What did they think, that he'd overlook what they owed after a bad poker night? Nothing doin',* Vin had warned the guys on his drug corners. *If they gambled their debts away and they wanted to keep their arms and legs, they better have trading material.* That was the way things were, the way things had always been in the Priganti clan.

"That teller, the Spanish chick, leaves at ten fifteen for her coffee break," Vin said, going over their plan out loud. "It's only that one other woman teller and Thatcher."

He was referring to the security guard, Frederico Thatcher, a white-haired man in his sixties wearing a brass badge. He was too old to be of any danger to them, and even though he carried a gun, no one had ever seen him use it. He was practically a fixture at the bank and the guys had no plans to hurt him—unless he got in their way. A gentle shove or two would show him they meant business and it would be all theirs after that.

Tony grabbed hold of the ski mask he was hiding under the seat. Vin kept talking: "In and out in eleven minutes. Leave the car running. Did you remove the plates? I forgot to look."

"Done," said Tony. For him, this was the culmination of years of working with Vin and courting his family. He thought back to the jobs he had done, the drug corner pickups, the beatings that he'd given people *at the request of Tino. It had been hard at first; he'd had to go against his own grain. But soon enough, he'd become anesthetized to the blood and screams of his victims. It was all about an eye for an eye. It had not been easy work getting into the good graces of the Prigantis but he had accomplished it.*

Vin smirked. "Who expects a break-in in the middle of the morning?" he said. "This'll really get some press." He started going over the plan again.

Vin's voice was like a drone in Tony's ear right now. He wasn't really listening because they had gone over this, time and again. Now, in a few minutes, his life was about to change as he and Vin got to split the LaCocca take that was way beyond their wildest dreams. And if all went well, it would only be the beginning . . .

Tony put on his black ski mask and gloves with unsteady hands. He and Vin emerged from the car at exactly 10:18, three minutes after they saw the Spanish teller leave her post. Tony felt for his gun. It was tucked snugly into his belt, making him feel secure. Who needed a girlfriend when a gun could open the door to women and wealth all over the world? Tony looked over at Vin, his partner in crime. It was ironic that Vin, not as smart or as good-looking as Tony, was calling the shots. It was all about where a guy was born, how much money he had at his disposal, and who his friends were. Life wasn't fair but Tony had done the best he could with what he had and it had made him stronger. Now, if all went according to plan, he was about to get the big reward.

Tony walked through the front door, turned to face Thatcher, and before he could reach for his gun, Tony whacked him on the head with the butt of his own gun. Blood started to squirt from the poor old guy's head. Tony looked down to see it all over his shirt; that sure annoyed him— after all, it was designer studs. Thatcher went down and didn't move as Vin rushed into the bank. The process had begun. It was only a matter of a few minutes and it would be all over . . .

Tony grabbed his reward as well, the gun from Thatcher's holster. He still didn't move. Tony touched the man on the throat. No pulse. Jesus Christ! Was Thatcher dead? Tony couldn't stop to deal with it right now as he shouted to the seven or eight customers in the bank, "Everybody get on the floor and stay there until we leave. Or else!" No one but Tony knew that Thatcher wasn't breathing, and he would not be telling Vin until they were on their way out of there, richer for their trouble. Collateral damage was not something on which they had counted but what was done was done.

People cowered in the corners of the bank, terrified of the men in ski masks who just knocked down sweet old Mr. Thatcher. Everybody liked Thatcher, he was a relic in the neighborhood. Tony and Vin approached the teller on duty, a young, skinny woman who had just gotten this job about a month prior. Her forehead was sweating and she looked like she was about to become hysterical. Tony pointed his gun at her chest.

"You keep it together or I'll shoot you. Do you understand?" Tony demanded.

She nodded. Her ponytail bounced at the back of her head.

"Good," he said. "Now load the money into that bag. Fuck up or touch the alarm and you're dead. Got it?"

"Yes," she whispered. "Please don't hurt me."

She filled the bag with the cash in her drawer and walked slowly to the next station as Tony instructed her. She took whatever cash was in that drawer and continued with all the teller's stations. They had just loaded up with hundreds and Tony practically salivated at the money. But what about Thatcher? He put it out of his mind for the moment.

Vin stood behind Tony, his gun on the terrified people. He stopped a moment to wave at the security camera and then he shot it. Glass fell to the floor and people screamed in fear. "Shut up or I'll turn this gun on you," he threatened, the adrenaline making him feel indestructible. Why had they waited so long to rob a bank? Vin wondered. It made all their other petty crimes pale in comparison. A guy could get used to this . . .

The sound of cop car sirens sounded in the distance as Vin and Tony were driving away in their getaway car with their take. They frantically made their way to Tony's house, where of course Pamela was waiting with bated breath to find out how much shopping she could do *this week. She sat fondling the gun in diamonds that hung from her neck on a thick gold chain. A gift she had given to herself when Tony started to make money. I mean, who wears a gun in diamonds around her neck? What does that mean? Who was this woman? What was she thinking?*

Tony and Vin entered around back. Katrina and Pamela sat at the kitchen table. Katrina was busy filing her nails. "What, did ya kill somebody?"

Tony looked at his sister with disgust.

Tony dumped a bag of stolen money onto the table. Katrina dropped her nail file and grabbed onto the money. Pamela threw her hands into the air, "Oh, my God! Look at yous! What happened?"

A dumbfounded Vin replied, "Mrs. Kroon . . ."

Pamela jumped into action; after all, this was the moment she'd lived for. "Never mind, not now! All that blood, Tony! Jesus! Give me those clothes. We gotta get rid of them."

Pamela moved abruptly about the house. "Come on. What are you, stupid? We can't waste time. Katrina, get me a T-shirt from the laundry room."

Katrina rolled her eyes and went to get it. Tony removed his bloodstained shirt and gave it to Pamela. Pamela cut it into small pieces and threw it down the sink disposal.

She'd done this before.

Moments later Katrina threw Tony a T-shirt. "You boys better go and clean your hands, since you've been playing with guns. Get the Ajax! It'll remove the gunpowder."

Pamela looked at Tony with cold eyes and started to give harsh orders. "Fuck! All right, let's all stay calm. Look, Tony, this place will be swarming with cops in no time. I want you to put that car in the garage and take mine. You hear me, Vin?"

Vin nodded his head yes. "Thanks, Mom."

Tony kissed his mother on the cheek and the boys exited through the back.

They assumed that someone had tripped the alarm and the cops had been on their tail ever since they left the bank. No sooner did they get in the car than the cops were on their tail.

Tony stared at Vin, who seemed to have lost his mind, as he kept his gun out and cocked by his side. Several cops flew onto Vin's car, took him out, and struggled Vin to the ground. Tony stood there, allowing himself to be pushed to the ground beside Vin. They did not look at each other. In a flash, the handcuffs were on, and the light caught the silver as Tony was led to the police car. He was no longer in control of what would happen next.

Tony had killed Thatcher. He couldn't believe it. Murder was not in the plans, but apparently he had hit the elderly man with the butt of his gun in such a way that Thatcher had died on impact. Nothing had gone right, and when he heard how they'd gotten caught, he wanted to kick himself, but he figured Tino Priganti would take care of that.

No one had tripped the alarm. The cops had been waiting, tipped off by a big-busted woman named Nancy, a woman Tony had screwed a few times who turned out to be an undercover cop. He had a loose tongue on one of those nights, mentioning something about the bank job. He thought he hadn't been specific, but he wasn't really sure. When a girl gave a blowjob like Nancy did, it was easy to forget exactly what you said and didn't say. Besides, she acted so excited and conspiratorial. How was he supposed to know she was wearing a goddamned wire? Tony had gotten too cocky for his own good, and now both he and Vin were about to pay the price.

Tino paid the bail money for Vin and Tony, and now he was giving Tony hell. "First, you hit an old man in the head so hard, he dies on you," he admonished his son's best friend. "Thatcher has been a friend of this family for years. I can't believe you were so fucking stupid! If you can't keep your mouth shut, then you better keep your zipper up, you idiot. You're ruining our family." Tino smacked Tony and Vin each across the face. Then he called a family meeting.

What happened next sealed Tony's fate. Vin was ushered into the meeting room. They slammed the doors shut behind him, right in Tony's face. Blood was thicker than water, Tony had always known that, and *he sat outside the door, isolated and miserable. There was no chance for him now, as he waited until the door opened again. Vin left the room and walked straight past Tony without a glance. Tony knew he was screwed, with no money and no one to vouch for him.*

It wasn't supposed to end this way.

But now he had killed someone.

He was trying to keep his legendary cool, but inside he was hot as steaming lava. He had always believed that his loyalty would pay off, that Priganti would help him out and protect him. But when he saw the witness list for his upcoming trial, he seethed inside, mostly at himself. Fucking Nancy, the woman with the big tits who went all the way with him on the first date, was a mole. A rat. She was his enemy, not his friend, and because of his dick, he had been duped. How could he have been so stupid? he asked himself over and over. Tino was right to shove him out, even though the death of Thatcher was a mistake.

Tony had abandoned his best friend, Richie, for Vin, who was a higher-up and offered Tony big payoffs. But getting caught red-handed was more payoff than he'd dreamed. Richie had always been smarter than Vin, and Tony had an urge to call him and apologize, but he thought better of it. Why should Richie bother with him now? He'd walked out on his friend, and now he was nothing more than a bank robber and a murderer, facing a stiff prison sentence along with everything else.

"It's fuckin' unbelievable, Sam." Janice finished her story. She settled into her woven-plastic-tubes lounge chair and closed her eyes. "Ta think that wuz our life." Switching from the bank to the current headline gave me a headache full of fear and disappointment. The current headline burned into my eyes again.

DJ's mutilated body had been found in a Dumpster. "Will we ever be able to leave it behind?" I asked. Will it ever rub off? I wondered as I reached for the mixture of baby and olive oils and massaged it into my exposed skin.

"That poor DJ," Janice sighed. "They offed him jus' becuz he wuz a fag."

"You think Vin and his crew had anything to do with it?"

"I doubt Richie did," Janice said. "He's in enough trouble already." Richie Sparto had been linked in a previous exposé to the drug dealer's murder; the slugs that had been removed from Richie had matched the dealer's gun. "I don' know if he'll beat that rap," Janice finished.

I wondered how much involvement Tony had had with that execution, and the one where they found Sal and Joe riddled with bullets in the front seat of a Cadillac that had been splashed across the pages of the *News*. I'd seen his name in the stories as a "person of interest" in those awful crimes. I couldn't imagine that; I had known of his contraband exploits, and he had been violent with me, but murder? I shuddered in the warm sun and hoped it would stop my skin from crawling.

As I soaked up the beneficial rays on the rooftop, I thought as I had for days about the baptism I had happened upon at Our Lady of Guadalupe. An unfinished page for an article I was writing on purification and rebirth rested in my Smith-Corona. Could I wash away my sins, I wondered, just as a woman could cleanse herself in the ritual bath I was describing thereon? What rituals were required to cleanse one's soul? Was there enough forgiveness to purify me? I fretted as I glanced at my best friend, who appeared to be at peace.

Janice was engaged now and was on her way to a new life. She'd be caught up in preparations for her wedding and for a different future with Roberto, I knew. She escaped from Bensonhurst without leaving Brooklyn. Good for her, I said to myself. I closed my eyes and my thoughts turned to the goodness that Father Rinaldi had spoken about.

When I had seen him recently, he welcomed me with his open arms and appeared the same as he always had, even though he could tell I wasn't pregnant any longer. The priest's hands and words soothed me then as they had before, and the Blessed Mother still called to me when I had knelt before Her statue afterward. "Forgiveness is there for the taking," Father Rinaldi often said.

As I recalled those words on a lazy summer afternoon with Janice, I decided the path to my new life would go through Our Lady of Guadalupe. I would take her forgiveness and find forgiveness in those who had hurt me in the past. I would be able to move on with my own dignity and not by the hand of a man any longer, who had controlled me for so long.

24

I spent the rest of the summer working at my jobs and writing at home. Although Mom had felt good that I wasn't with Tony anymore, her health worsened and dragged her down. Her coughing became more persistent and more loathsome. Coughing up blood became a daily ritual, yet she would never go to a doctor. She just told me I was stupid and to pay attention to my *own* life, all this while her bad moods prevailed. Despite my dogged progress toward renewal, she couldn't overcome the bitterness that had taken root long before. Grandma maintained her cheery disposition even though she seemed to be slowing down more every day.

Tony might have been history to my family, but I often worried that he would find some excuse to force his way into my life again. I found myself looking over my shoulder as I walked on Eighteenth Avenue to the bookstore, and flinching every now and then when the phone rang. I dreaded a confrontation with Tony and the times he evoked. It was bad enough that detectives had surprised me twice in front of my home to ask me what I knew about his activities. I couldn't tell them much, but I wondered, with a pang of guilt, if I would've come clean if I had known anything that would help them make a case. They seemed pleased when I had told them I wasn't with Tony any longer.

When my senior year rolled around after Labor Day and I hadn't seen or heard from him, my heart was lifted. Without the baggage Tony represented, I threw myself into my writing and my radio show. I interspersed serious topics with lighter ones such as makeup tips and the foibles of men I overheard at the salon when the ladies gossiped. Whether I covered matters large or small, it was always about a woman's ability to tap her own strength to become what she wanted.

Professor Greenburg cheered me on and Mr. Wainright remained steadfast in his support. They confirmed my feeling that the towers and cables in my life were still strong enough to get me where I had to go. Late in the year, Mr. Wainright introduced me to his publishing friend. I knew then who had told the truth and who had been a liar. The editor I met was generous in her coaching and we made steady progress together toward the completion of the roadbed I needed to reach the other side of the East River.

When graduation day arrived at last in June, I brushed my hands down the pink taffeta dress that Grandma had bought for ten dollars at our local thrift shop. Stains and all, there was nothing bleach and Grandma couldn't get clean. She had altered it to fit me. The bodice hugged my torso, the shiny pink ribbon that Grandma had sewn as trim was pressed, and the hem hit my legs in exactly the right place. A black robe draped over my dress and a cap with a tassel sat atop my head. I had to admit that I looked beautiful.

I looked down the row of students who were graduating with me and my thoughts wandered. My classmates all looked as excited as I did, but there was one big difference. They were leaving school to assume their assigned roles in the Bensonhurst world; I had fashioned a different life for a different world and I could hardly wait to get out of school and out of Brooklyn to fulfill it. Whichever direction my writing took me in, I was on my way across that bridge. I felt that Brooklyn would soon become a place of the past, the place where Mom and Grandma lived and where I would visit once I had established myself outside of it. I only wanted to make them proud, and growing up in Brooklyn gave me each and every word to write in order to do so.

Soon enough, I knew, I would hand Mom and Grandma enough money to buy a place of their own. When that happened, I was sure my mother would finally heal from her ravaged life. I imagined my mother feeling so well that one day she would meet a wonderful man who would adore her and treat her with respect. How wonderful it would be if my mom and I fell in love with good men! I thought. Grandma would be so happy, I knew. I believed that her constant and unqualified support had kept such dreams alive and I knew I never would have gotten to graduation day without it. She deserved the peace it would bring to see her daughter and granddaughter realize bright futures. Her strength had kept us together, had anchored the cables on one side of the bridge so that I could make it across.

I scanned the audience from my seat on the stage. The wood-paneled high school auditorium was filled to capacity with graduates and their proud families and friends. I managed to find Mom's and Grandma's faces in the crowd, glowing with excitement. They smiled at me and my heart filled with pride. All except a small place that felt empty. I had always intended to have Tony with me on that day. When we had dated, there was no way to imagine this scene, the culmination of all that I had worked for, without him. He was supposed to be sitting beside my family, cheering me on, making that phone call to his publishing friend. But that no longer mattered, I thought. I would fill that empty space with something better, something good, something that was real. I'd cross that bridge without him.

The keynote speaker finished his speech and stepped away as the audience applauded. I missed everything he said, but that moment was the culmination of so many struggles and I was thinking about the ending of my book I was going to write soon, the closing of a hard chapter in my life. I thought about Tony's abuse, the robberies, the abortion, and, most haunting, keeping that dark secret from Mom and Grandma. My face turned red with shame, but I was glad that it looked like excitement to everybody else. I recalled Tony's lying and the nights when I'd found the lipstick in his car and the panties in his bed. And how he broke into my house. My thoughts then turned to those who had helped me through it all—Grandma, Janice, Mr. Wainright, and Father Rinaldi. They were the stone and steel in my life, I knew.

I had worked every chance I could with my English teacher to polish my manuscript. There was still a lot of work to be done on it, but with every change I had made, I felt my own transformation within.

The principal started to announce the graduating class and the closer he got to my name, the farther away I felt from the pain of my past and the baggage that I was ready to leave behind. "Samantha Bonti," he called out, and I stood up. I felt Mom's and Grandma's eyes on me as I made it to the end of the row. All of the arguments at home over religion and Tony had only made me stronger and they faded away with each step I took. I glanced at my two-hundred-dollar black high heels, one of the pairs Tony had bought for me with fanfare. I knew I could have chosen to spend the rest of my days pining for him and love lost, allowing life to drain out of me. But I chose to let it all go. It was time to step toward the podium and a new life.

The black robe swished as I strode to receive my diploma. When the parchment was in my hand, I shifted the tassel on my cap from one side to the other. The diamond bracelet that Tony had given me caught the overhead lights. I hadn't sold it yet, but I decided it would be the last time I would wear it. I smiled proudly and returned to my seat as Mom and Grandma sprang up and clapped.

When the ceremony concluded, the graduates left the stage and the women I loved rushed toward me. I hugged them each tightly. "You did it, *bubelah!*" Grandma yelled, swiping at her eyes. She and Mom were crying with joy for a change and I joined in.

"We're making a special dinner for you, honey," Mom said.

Janice pushed through the crowd milling about. Roberto stood quietly beside her as she and I embraced. I smiled and felt my heart fill with love. These were the people who mattered to me most, I thought, the loved ones who cared about me and wanted only good things for me. They represented all that was hopeful and possible in this world. That was where I belonged, I knew.

I sat in my room after graduation and reminisced while I waited for Janice to arrive. I had changed into a pair of black slacks and a white blouse while Mom was busy preparing her part of a minifeast—pasta and the stuffed peppers from an old family recipe, one of the few good things that had come out of her marriage to my father. Grandma was napping, but she had made her famous potato pancakes and chopped liver salad the night before. All she had to do when she got out of bed was add the sour cream and applesauce for dipping.

I felt—maybe for the first time since I'd met Tony—that my life was falling into some kind of order. I had graduated and I had been accepted for admission to NYU.

I was amused when I recalled Janice telling me that Tony had heard me on the radio when he started scanning stations after he had finished having sex with one of the many girls whose hearts he was busy breaking. He flipped out, his latest conquest told Janice, and screamed about "his girl" being on the radio and who did she think she was, giving advice to anyone? When the woman had told Tony to get over it, he smacked her across the face and sent her out the door without her coat. I just shook my head. The Brooklyn world would never change.

I looked in the mirror to see if I looked different. I did—confident and peaceful. That was how I was supposed to feel all the time, and that's the way it would be from then on, I decided. I smiled when I thought about Janice being a fixture in my life as she had always been. That was the way it was supposed to be, too. And I was going to be her maid of honor! I screamed inside and wondered what her dress would look like.

The doorbell rang and I ran down the stairs to answer it. Janice brushed through the door. "Roberto said he's sorry. He's got some work to take care of," she said.

"That's okay, as long as you're here," I replied, and gave her a hug. "He said you should come over for dinner real soon," Janice said, and then lowered her voice as she grabbed my arm. "I have a chef now who'll make us anything we want."

"Wow, a chef! Are you kidding me?"

"Roberto said there's nothin' I won't have," Janice said. Her head swiveled as she inhaled. "Everythin' smells great! Do I detect a cake in the oven?" she asked, her eyes twinkling. It was only Duncan Hines from a box, but it would do. "Yup," I said, and then we hurried up to the kitchen and kept Mom company while she made the final preparations for our meal.

"We're almost ready," Mom said a couple of minutes later. She coughed violently and then looked me in the eye. "I'm goin' to stop smoking," Mom swore as she tamped a cigarette out, "in honor of your graduation, honey. Now go get your grandmother."

I sprinted down the hall and knocked on Grandma's door. When there was no answer, I called her name a few times but still got no response. She'd been sleeping pretty heavily in recent months, I remembered. I would have to wake her up as I'd often done.

I opened the door and went to her bedside. Her arm dangled over the edge and her pocketbook was open on the floor. She must have been looking for something, I supposed, and then caught sight of a check sticking out from under the bed. I picked it up and saw that it was made out to me for thirty dollars. My graduation gift, no doubt, I thought. I couldn't wait to thank Grandma and celebrate with her. I shook Grandma but she remained motionless, and when she didn't move after I shook her a second time I screamed. "Mom! Janice! Hurry! It's Grandma!"

My mother rushed into the room with Janice right behind her. Mom placed her head on her mother's chest and listened, and then fell to her knees at the side of the bed and started bawling while clutching her mother. Tears poured onto Grandma's nightgown as Mom kept her head on her mother's chest and wailed.

Janice held me as I collapsed into her arms and burst into tears, unable to believe what had happened. I had been hugging Grandma only two hours earlier at the graduation. She had complained of being tired, but she was often tired, especially after the kind of excitement we had just had. I wasn't ready to let Grandma go. I still needed her.

Grandma must have been a lot sicker than she had let on, I thought as I sobbed. Was she waiting for me to graduate? I wondered. Maybe that was all that had been keeping her alive, I supposed. I dropped to my knees and rested my head on my mother's back. Janice picked up the phone and called the ambulance while I contemplated life without Grandma, the matriarch and calming force of our family.

People lost their lives building that famous bridge, I recalled. Did a piece of me have to die as well before I could finally cross it?

I never liked the inside of hospital emergency rooms much, but that was where I had to be at that very moment. As they rushed Grandma in, I knew in my heart she was only biding time. She saw me graduate, she saw me making a new life for myself, and she saw me writing. She knew that my mom would always be the same and she knew if anyone could save her, well, that would have to be me.

When I saw Grandma on a gurney and hooked up to three different machines, I was devasted. Mom and Janice sat by her side while I just looked on, knowing that for every leap of faith there were always ten obstacles to be reckoned with. That's how life was for me at present, and I was accepting every sad inch of it. When the bald, bulgy-eyed doctor approached us, we knew by the looks of his gloomy face that it wasn't good. "I'm afraid she needs a triple bypass. She is scheduled for surgery now."

You had to see my mother's face. Full of devastation and more fear. Not only of how we would be paying for this operation, but of what would be the outcome. I was elated that Grandma even had a chance. My mother grabbed onto me with all her might and for the first time, I felt so badly for her. I felt as though a child were crying in my arms.

As Mom cried and hours passed as we awaited Grandma's fate, I engaged in a solid stare at the pasty white walls, which were starting to close in on me. Just then the doctor came out of surgery in his operating greens. His walk was slow and calm, yet had a sense of urgency in every step. I knew, I always knew the bad news when it came. And this time it was certain. "I am so so sorry, we did all we could, her heart was very strong, but her will just wasn't."

Yes, I knew all too well that Grandma's heart was strong, as strong as a bull. It was her time to leave and in a strange, sad way I was actually happy for her. She got out of this mess and now I was the one who was biding my time. I knew I had to be there for my mother, now more than ever. Grandma was a vision, a vision that I never wanted to see, yet there it was. Covered in tubes, deceased.

"Sam, what is going to happen to us now?" I held my mother close.

"God will provide, he always does. You told me that." This time in my young life I felt as though I really were the parent. "Ma, don't worry, we'll make it work. I'll get a job, a good job, you'll see. Things will happen."

"Ms. Bonti, I'm so sorry. I'm so terribly sorry. If there's anything I can do . . ." Janice tried her hardest to be there for us, but what could she do. I knew I would hear those words one day, but not like this. Not now; I still needed her one more day. I needed her support, I needed her to read my pages, I just needed her, but I had to stop being selfish and realize that God needed her as well, another angel. I bent over and lay my head on Grandma's soft chest and kissed her lips good-bye.

June 1982

Tony's judgment day in the Brooklyn courthouse arrived a year after Grandma's passing. His trial exposed the mob family he was connected to and made more headlines. So much had been covered up. The papers claimed that Tony himself had been responsible for some of those horrible murders Janice and I had wondered about. I was still incredulous, and yet that—and burglary and drug conspiracy—was what he had been on trial for the previous three weeks. My God, who would have thought it could come to this, all this crime and hatred. For what? The almighty dollar? I could hear Pamela's words echoing through my mind. Money and greed, that's all it was. I wanted nothing to do with it.

Shortly after my graduation and Grandma's passing, Mom was diagnosed with lung cancer, and that explained the early-morning, wrenching coughing. Together with spitting up blood in the kitchen sink, which had gone untended for years. It turned out to be an inoperable tumor enlarged within the walls of her jugular. Years of smoking packs a day finally caught up with her and her self-destructive behavior. Her voice now would truly be silenced. In other words, there was no way out. It was yet another cross I had to bear, but hey, no one was counting anymore. My mother needed me and no matter what, she was still my mother, who brought me into this world, and I did love her. From diagnosis to death, it became a constant battle for me. My mother never talked much, just feeding me with guilts beyond all forms that my poor imagination could bear. She was of nasty mind during her last stages and who could blame her; she was miserable, miserable about her life and mad that she would die lonely. She had become a bitter woman, a young woman who had made a ton of mistakes.

But what about me, her daughter? I thought I was the most precious gift, the gift of life that God had given her. I needed her, too, though sometimes I thought not. Well, it wasn't until the end that she was telling all the nurses at the hospice how much she loved me and how proud she was of me and my work. My work. She never read a word. What did she know about my writing? It reminded me of when I was ten years old and everyone in my class received an award except me. My mother in all her born craziness swore I was discriminated against because I was poor and the half Jew. And with what I think at the time was bright red hair, she marched right into the classroom the next day wearing skin tight leopard pants and a tube top. She walked right up to the teacher and ripped her a new ass. I got my attendance award the very next day; shiny gold star and all. Who knows what they thought of her, and who cared? That was the one thing she taught me through the years—who cares about what others think of you? I mean, this is the same woman who wouldn't give me a compliment but seemed to always protect her child, even if it was behind my back and even if she did wear tight leopard pants. She was my mom.

It brought me back to her dying day when I would sit and watch her moan with tubes in her arms, the endless morphine drip that somehow would try to deaden the horrible cancer pain. I knew her time was nearing. I could actually feel her pain as it washed her soul slowly away. I wanted her to be released from this world, she needed to move on. She needed to go. To become another one of God's angels.

Maybe she could help me more from up there, where she could make peace with herself and with me. I knew that every night when I traveled to Calvary Hospice in the Bronx. It was the only place that accepted her, and me for that matter, not having any money to pay for it. At times it became so hard for me. Working all day, then traveling to see her at night.

The one night I didn't go was the night she passed. I was devastated. I don't think she wanted me to say good-bye. That was the night I was busy making funeral plans and filing for Medicaid and Medicare, and to my surprise both accepted her. I had not a bill after she died. Talk about faith and manifesting a miracle! I was free.

Well, almost.

After a year of nursing Mom at hospice and giving her a funeral with borrowed money, I was completely alone. I thought burying Grandma was the hardest thing I ever had to do, but by far my mother's death proved that indeed this would be my worst. She was all I had, besides Grandma. God knows my deadbeat father never stepped up to the plate.

But even at the end, as she lay in her casket in her red dress, she couldn't help but discomfort me one more time. A friend from my childhood named Julia showed up at her wake. God, it had been years. Her nickname was Jules in the neighborhood, and she always looked like a drag queen. I later found out that my mom would party with her behind my back, since Jules supplied and Mom couldn't afford. When she died, Jules placed a small bag of cocaine into her casket along with a joint. Midway through the wake I saw Jules reach into the casket and take a tiny plastic bag out, then she went to the bathroom in the funeral parlor and proceeded to snort a line. The sick bitch.

She came back in and placed the plastic bag back into Mom's casket. Who does that? I just sat there looking without saying a word. My tears suddenly turned to laughter. That was my mom. In a funny way her craziness was what I wanted to remember her as, to cherish; it was all I had. She belonged to me, she was my mother.

She would always be my crazy Joan.

I thought about that when I had stopped at the cemetery on the way to the courthouse. If she had only hooked up with a decent man like the pharmacist who cashed her welfare checks, she wouldn't have been in the ground and I wouldn't have been standing there. After all, could a man really save you from your fate? But then I thought about how everything happens for a reason, be it fate or God or whatever, and maybe if I hadn't had the life I'd had, I wouldn't have had the determination and drive to better myself. That survival instinct.

I asked Mom once again to accept my flaws as I reconciled with hers. I looked upon the grave where she had been buried with her mother, upon a headstone that had both a cross and a Jewish star engraved upon it. Even in their death they still clashed. Somehow I felt my grandmother standing with me as I made peace with the past and my mother. God knows she tried. She couldn't help herself, how on earth was she to help me become a woman? That I learned from the cards I was dealt. And I thanked God that Mom and I made some sort of peace while she was on her deathbed.

I awaited my last cross, Tony's verdict, in the back of the imposing courtroom. "I knew from the moment you were born you were special, and destined for something more than what I had become," Mom had once said, repeating the words she must have said to others at the nursing home who told me of her praise when I visited. "But I'm so sorry I never gave you the love you deserved. I watched you grow and I envied what you'd become—a beautiful, smart woman. I had wanted that for myself but instead I got pregnant and had you and had to do things I am not proud of to survive. I'm so sorry, Sammy. I always loved you, you were and are my life. Always know that you are a chosen one." All that was left from my home then was my spirit.

Amid the courtroom buzz, I hoped my prayers would be answered in Manhattan when the trial was over. The bailiff opened the jury room door and twelve people from Brooklyn took their seats in the jury box. Their faces were somber, and a hush settled over the room.

"All rise," the bailiff commanded. "The Honorable Justice Henry Clayton Evans presiding."

An austere, white-haired man in a black robe strode into the room and climbed the steps of his platform. He sat, and then everyone present did likewise as the judge whispered to the bailiff. Judge Evans shuffled some papers on his bench, scanned one for a moment with half-spectacles, and then addressed the jury foreman. "Has the jury reached a verdict?"

The foreman stood. "We have, Your Honor," he said, and handed a piece of paper to the bailiff, who delivered it to the judge.

Tony turned around and smiled thinly when he saw me. He looked like a stranger to me. He had lost twenty pounds, his face was sunken, and his blond hair looked thin around the temples. But I still recognized those blue eyes. The ones that had captured me, the ones I had looked into when I lost my virginity, the ones that had belied who he really was.

The hands. Oh yes, let's not forget those. The ones that years earlier had slapped my face in his lawyer's office, knocking me off the chair because I would not commit purgery on his behalf for his pending case. Blame another and never be accountable.

The sex drive. That was off the charts. Begging his mother to take me to the correctional facility he was occupying.

Feeling guilt-ridden, I went, only to find out that the hour visit had more to do with me locking myself in a bathroom with him, illegally, and jerking him off, which made me sick, but Pamela insisted I'd please her son. I thought for years how stupid I was to do that, and only to get caught by the correctional officer, photographed, and kicked out, as if I were the criminal. My dignity had disappeared and for what? A stolen moment with Tony, who cared more about getting off than about me. Pamela should have serviced him. It would have pleased us both.

Tony was a man with a troubled soul. And I had my share of troubled souls. I was done. I don't generally believe our parents can really destroy us, but in Tony's case they certainly did destroy him.

He'd called and asked me to be there when the jury gave its verdict. What he didn't know was that I was there only for myself.

When Tony turned back around, I looked at my watch. I would make my appointment in Manhattan that afternoon. But if Tony was declared innocent, would he come looking for me? I wondered. Would he understand that he couldn't do anything to stop me?

In the courtroom that was as silent as a church, Judge Evans looked at the jury. "In the case of New York versus Anthony Kroon, how do you find the defendant?"

"*Guilty,* Your Honor." The foreman read the counts. "Two counts of murder. One count of conspiracy. Two counts of felony. One count of drug and money laundering . . ." The foreman went on and on, his voice slowly fading away inside my head.

Pamela jumped up, wailed, and then collapsed in her seat. Reporters with microphones and photographers brandishing cameras rushed the railing. I knew the Priganti name would figure prominently in the next day's *Daily News, Post,* and all the papers.

Tony dropped his head into his hands. His lawyer looked embarrassed and he tried to whisper something in his ear. As he placed his hand around Tony's shoulder, he exposed the cuff on his shirt only to reveal *my grandfather's gold elephant cuff links*. There they were. Oh my God! I acually had to rub my eyes to make certain. Stolen from my house that horrible evening. When I thought back to how I had to console poor Grandma. Everything made sense to me now. My journals being ripped apart. My house being robbed. My life being torn to shreds. For what? For this? My coming today to this unforsaken courtroom—this was no mistake, this was fate. The fate that has led me here and the fate that will take me out. Starting now.

Tony shoved him away as the bailiff approached the defendant's table. He took his thick necklace that held a glorified gold medallion of an engraved face of Christ. Something he wore the day we met, amongst the cross which still hung on his neck with pride as he ripped it off and threw it onto the cold wooden desk. He bitterly stared into the eyes of the twelve jurors who'd decided his fate, and he knew all too well where he was headed. Twenty-five years to life.

Tony was guilty of everything, I thought, including stealing four years of my life. Mom's instincts about him had been proven right, after all, I thought. It wasn't her bitterness toward men in general or her envy of my having a relationship that had been responsible for her harping. I was sorry I hadn't seen that through the cigarette haze and her gruff exterior. It was true that I was better than she was in some ways, but it had also been true that I had been worse, too, when it counted most. I had gotten pregnant at a younger age than she had, and hadn't gone to term as she had done, to give someone a chance at life.

I should have listened to my first instincts; I tormented myself as I rose from my seat. I had seen firsthand some of the things that everybody in the neighborhood knew went on. From my first white lie and the subsequent black ones that had come all too easily, to Tony's brutality at the skating rink and in Platinum, the signs were as plain to see as were the good things that Father Rinaldi had mentioned time and time again. I frowned when I thought about how I should have run from Janice's bedroom that day when her bruised face made me sick to my stomach. I should have run and not look back until I was standing on the other side of the Brooklyn Bridge.

Maybe I wasn't better than anyone, I considered. Maybe I was just different from everybody and from a mother who maybe had done the best she could with the awful cards that had been dealt to her. And maybe I was no better than Tony, either; I shuddered as I rose from my seat. I was guilty, too, I knew. On all counts, I concluded, as the bill of particulars ran through my mind.

Guilty of letting him.

Guilty of compromising my integrity.

Guilty of lies, silence, and deliberate blindness to the truth.

Guilty of not heeding Father Rinaldi's guidance.

Guilty of sin . . . and of taking a life.

I started to swoon, but the Blessed Mother came to me and I was buttressed by the strength that had enabled Her to endure the humble birth of Her Son and to witness His brutal death. I remembered again God's forgiveness, which Father Rinaldi had told me never to forget, and I vowed to atone for all of my transgressions and to never stray so far again.

When the bailiff clamped the handcuffs on Tony's wrists, he turned around and spotted me again, as if there were no one else in the room but the two of us. There was a long moment when, from far across the room between the surrounding chaos, our eyes finally met for the last time . . . and I slipped out the door.

I emerged from the courthouse into the sunshine. My life was spread before me and nothing would stop me. I picked up my pace and when I reached the subway, I sprang down the staircase. I slid the bracelets off my wrist and startled a homeless man when I tossed them to him. Everything except my rosary, Grandma's ring, my books, and my typewriter would be left behind, I knew. The flashy cars, clothes, and jewelry and the trappings in the Kroon house on Christmas that had wowed me weren't what was real. What was real was what was in my heart and on the pages in the handbag I carried.

I squeezed into a crowded train that was headed for the real world. As I stood holding a metal pole that still shined after years of wear and tear, I thought about how someone endures. I knew, but it's what's inside a person that matters most of all, I realized. The sound of the doors closing was music to my ears, the screech of wheels on the rails below a ballad that sang my praises. I swayed with the shifting train, and thought of Grandma as the car I was in headed to Manhattan.

"Go, *bubelah*," I heard her say. "Go."

Acknowledgments

The one thing I know is that I am a survivor and was extremely determined to have my story told. I began writing it down at the tender age of seventeen and before I knew it I had over three hundred pages of "Life." Twenty-one years and over twenty-one drafts later, here I am today with a book deal that I dreamed of as a child growing up in Brooklyn. My mental and physical abuse, my financial hardship, my day-to-day struggle. It was by far some of the best things that have happened to me because it gave me the sense of urgency daily, to live to get out. This dysfunctional life allowed me to dream, to swallow as much faith as I could and to believe that hope is a good thing, it can never die unless you allow it to, and in my world hope was all I had. I knew in my heart that my story was worth hearing because there are so many young girls and women living similar lives that don't understand it's possible to free themselves. That the strength comes from within, and that they are equipped with the strength they need at birth. No one or no man can take that away from you! It's just circumstance and environment that shape our lives along the way and with enough negative influence it's easy to lose sight of what's good and bad. It is difficult to work the process and enjoy the fruit of your labor when all you see and hear are negative, derogatory remarks and responses, as well as fists that come out at you from all different angles. Then, miraculously you see a light. For me it was a Bridge. The lights of the Brooklyn Bridge, my entrée to freedom. A way out. However, I did not get out alone, although for most of my journey I felt that I was . . . all alone.

With no real family growing up to ever call my own, except Mom and Grandma. My friends have filled me with such joy and hope throughout my years I now have a chance to tell them just how much. Here are some of the most important people that held my hand and took me over. For that I am eternally grateful.

Maureen Regan, thank you so for getting me my first book deal. So ironic that I worked as a temp over twenty years ago at Simon & Schuster and what I wanted more than anything was to be published by them, and now I'm living the dream. I have met some magical people there. Mitchell Ivers, my amazing, honest editor. The coolest publishers on the planet, Louise Burke and Jen Bergstrom. You three are a genuine and brilliant group. And of course, Jessica Webb, who never says no. I could not have asked for a better beginning. Jennifer Robinson and Kristin Dwyer of publicity. Felice Javit who made legal pleasurable. Lisa Litwack for a kick ass cover and Esther Paradelo for design. And of course the entire sales force at Simon & Schuster—by far the best in the business.

Anthony Corso, thank you for stopping me on the street that day. My life was in complete disarray until you came in. I will always appreciate and love who you are and your love for me. (Softspot). Cynthia Savino my loyal, valued friend. Thank you for always understanding me, when others did not. Marie Seaquist, you are a trusted friend. Gump loves you. Marta Alen, my surprising Spanish sister. Our days at Trinity Church and Archangel Michael by our side to guide us, will never be replaced. I thank you so. Who do we bother? Franco D'Alessandro and Michael Casieri, my gay, fierce brothers. You have both helped me so much with your constant love, support and laughter. No words! Extra crispy! Ginda! D! Your Auntie Mame loves you! Patty Cleary, oh chardonnay you are a friend indeed. For my dear friends Olympia Dukakis, Lorraine Bracco, Armand Assante, and of course Craig DiBona for believing in this story, my story, and guiding me through the years it took to finally get it out there. You were more helpful than you know. See you on the SET!

The biggest blessing of my life to date, my daughter Samantha Rose, I did it right with that one. Samantha is the real gift in the scheme of it all. I have stopped the generational abuse when she was born; you will never know what its like to have a man ever tell you what to do! And learn from your mom's mishaps. Go forth and become the woman you are chosen to be, may this book be your bible to that knowledge.

Of course to all of the people back in Brooklyn. I have never forgotten any of you for one moment. You were always in my head and my heart and my words. I truly do pray that you are all doing well and are at peace with your lives. My life has been nothing short of a miraculous journey. As it unfolded I was presented with some other individuals who took me through to the next phase of each step of my life, and certainly had a hand in this story, either in its conception days, its writing days, its completion days and its afterlife! To those people who shall remain nameless; Gratitude *143td*.

Brooklyn Story

Suzanne Corso

INTRODUCTION

Brooklyn Story is the engaging coming-of-age story about Samantha Bonti, a teenage girl growing up in 1970s Brooklyn. An aspiring writer with dreams to someday leave her Bensonhurst community and dysfunctional home life for a new life in Manhattan, Samantha struggles to stay true to herself when she begins a relationship with Anthony Kroon, a "Brooklyn Boy" trying to break into the Brooklyn mafia scene. The devilishly handsome Tony sweeps Samantha off her feet—and into his world of violence, lies, and crime. As her relationship with Tony grows increasingly volatile, Samantha struggles to stay true to her beliefs until her writing can finally pull her across the East River and away from her tumultuous past.

TOPICS AND QUESTIONS FOR DISCUSSION

1. *Brooklyn Story* opens with a Sunnata Vagga quote about coming to peace with abuse by letting go of anger, which says, "Fury will never end fury, it will just ricochet on and on. Only putting it down will end such an abysmal state." Do you agree with the passage's message? Was Samantha able to truly let go of her anger and move on?

2. One of the recurring tropes throughout the story is crossing bridges, either physical or metaphorical. Can you think of any bridges you've had to cross in your own life? Could the transition from adolescence into adulthood, with all its trials, be considered one such universal bridge?

3. Samantha begins her story by stating, "Some people lived in the real world and others lived in Brooklyn." Where do you think Samantha considers is the "real" world? Do you agree with her?

4. Early on in the novel, Samantha's grandma instructs her to "Write yourself out of this story and into a better one" (p. 30). Do you think Samantha accomplishes this by its end? Does leaving for Manhattan begin a completely new story for Sam, or does it start a new chapter in the same tale?

5. At one point, Samantha tells the reader that "Surviving takes its toll, but makes you strong, I learned" (p. 58). Do you agree with her belief that survival fosters strength? Does surviving her ordeals make Samantha strong, or is she only able to survive due to an inherent strength she has, regardless of circumstance?

6. One of the main topics throughout the book is the influence neighborhoods have on their communities. Samantha remarks that "I couldn't help thinking that all of us in Bensonhurst were a reflection of the neighborhood in one way or another" (p. 115). Discuss the dynamic relationship neighborhoods and their residents have. How much does a neighborhood shape its people, and vice versa?

7. From gender roles to class status symbols, the effects of deeply rooted cultural and socioeconomic roles are prevalent throughout *Brooklyn Story*. Do you think such strict social systems are unique to urban communities or are they prevalent throughout other landscapes? Discuss.

8. Religious conflict between Samantha's Catholic mom and Jewish grandmother arises throughout the novel, constantly creating tension at home. After both women pass away, they share a gravestone with both a cross and Star of David on it, which Samantha considers emblematic of their ever-clashing views. Do you agree with Sam's viewpoint, or do you view the joint headstone differently, perhaps as a truce of sorts?

9. Samantha's relationship with her troubled mother is diametrically different from the one she has with her grandmother. After reading about Samantha's journey, who do you think had a greater influence on her actions, her mother or her grandmother? Discuss the ways both women shaped Samantha's actions and beliefs.

10. In addition to the role models in her life, Samantha's faith is an important anchor for her. She says, "The Blessed Mother's hand in my life, I knew, was as real and as close to me as the ones of those dear to me in my daily life who touched me" (p. 150). How much of her faith in herself and strength of character do you think she derives from her spiritual faith? Do you think she would have been able to find that strength to overcome all her adversities without such strong religious convictions?

11. On page 141, Samantha reflects on her relationship with Tony, saying "that was just how it was for me on the Brooklyn side of the bridge. The only thing that was completely in my control was my station in life." Samantha placed a great emphasis on leaving the physical space of Brooklyn in order to change her station. Do you agree with her that physically leaving Brooklyn and crossing that bridge was the only way she could change her station? How much of that bridge between the two worlds was Samantha's state of mind?

12. There are several instances of physical and emotional abuse, something Samantha feels very strongly about. After Tony hit her face into the dashboard, Samantha fumes to her best friend, Janice, about what gives men the idea that they can abuse women, to which Janice replies, "We do." Do you agree with Janice that the women in the story perpetuate the men's behavior by staying with them despite abusive acts? Explain why or why not.

ENHANCE YOUR BOOK CLUB

1. Visit the author's website: www.suzannecorso.com.
2. Bring New York to you! Enjoy some quintessential New York treats like pizza, bagels, and New York—style cheesecake during your discussion.
3. Brooklyn and its rich cultural history play a prominent role in the novel. Learn about your hometown's history, whether through internet searches or visiting your local library!

You opened the novel with a very moving Sunnata Vagga quote. How did you choose that specific passage to open *Brooklyn Story*? Is there a particular line from the passage that most resonates with you?

I came across it one day. I believe it was online and then I got *The Pocket Buddah* and to my surprise here was a quote that described my past and I knew from the moment I read it, it had to open my book. I felt as though it was written for me and I can only imagine how many other women felt the same way when they stumbled upon it.

Brooklyn Story is a partial parallel of your experiences growing up in Brooklyn. How much of your own life did you draw on to create Samantha's story?

Plenty. I absorbed so much growing up in Brooklyn and was so privy to the goings-on and the individuals within my neighborhood that I would just create characters from that and just write. It was therapy to me and the writing became my salvation. Writing came to me at the most crucial time in my childhood, a time when there was no therapy or happy pills to keep you sane. I had my words and they have helped me through; they still do tremendously to this day.

Did you find it challenging to separate your story from Samantha's? If so, how did you maintain that separation?

YES! It was the hardest thing to do. Every time I sat down to write all I could think about was Suzanne instead of Samantha. It became hard to separate us, however this enabled me to draw upon my past even deeper and write things that I normally would not have. So, I think it was a blessing in disguise drawing so much from me as a person to infuse it into my character. I maintained the separation only when I would look up and see that the name Samantha was on the paper that I was typing, not mine.

You quote a variety of songs throughout Brooklyn Story. Are you a music fan, personally? If so, are your favorite artists similar to the ones Samantha connects with?

My mother was a Woodstock child. She loved the '70s music; I was so young at the time, and that was all I heard. I love it to this day so much. Every time I listen to '70s music my heart fills with joy as well as some sadness over a life I no longer have. For me it's memories, both good and bad, and yes, I love music. It is part of meditation for me, I think it's one of the greatest silencers we have, just to listen to the music.

Throughout the novel, Samantha finds support and guidance from figures such as Mr. Wainright and Father Rinaldi. Did you have a similar mentor growing up? If so, who?

The truth, no. No one physical that is. My mentor would have to be the Blessed Mother. She guided me when no one else did. There were people here and there, but no one came close to her influence on me. When my mother was always falling apart, when my grandmother took ill and when I was being abused by my boyfriend and I had nowhere to turn, I would go to my spiritual guidance. That always helped me through. Sometimes the physical beings didn't understand or get it or me for that matter. I think now they do, I sure hope.

If there is one lesson you'd like readers to take away from Samantha's story, what would it be? Why?

To always pay attention to who you are getting involved with. For me it was a man, for others it could be any relationship. I guess the bottom line for me would be, do not let any man abuse you. Abuse comes in many forms. It just sneaks up on you and, by the time you are aware of it, you're so far engulfed in his world, you cannot escape. Abuse can be emotional, physical, mental, etc. . . . Once they do it one time, they will definitely repeat it again, trust me. A man controlling you is not normal. You need to remove yourself from the situation and have faith. Faith will take you exactly where you are supposed to go. Trust the process, it never fails.

You've written a variety of works, from screenplays to a children's book. How does writing an adult novel differ from the other projects? Did you find any challenges unique to the novel-writing process?

You know what is so funny, and I highly doubt any author will admit this, I truly think everything I have written before has had no significant impact the way that *Brooklyn Story* does for me. It is my success, my peace with me. It is the greatest accomplishment for me as a writer. Revealing oneself in words and sharing with others in the desire to help is an achievement which is so great with love and a higher purpose.

When I wrote poetry or children's books I think it was just my stepping stone to get me where I am supposed to be today a novelist and a screenwriter. And no, I love the novel-writing process the best. It is certainly for me the most rewarding because you can go on and on and never stop.

In *Brooklyn Story*, Samantha's writing mentor, Mr. Wainright, quotes Gene Fowler's description of the writing process as one where "All you do is stare at a blank sheet of paper until drops of blood form on your forehead" (p. 122). Samantha spends the novel "bleeding" into her work and pouring herself into her stories. If you had to choose, which piece from your own writing would you say you most connect with?

I am torn between my relationship with my mother and my boyfriend in *Brooklyn Story*. With my mother I could not get. She stayed inside my head as she remains to this day; my boyfriend is gone and so are his evil ways. There is the difference. Every chapter I wrote I would face different feelings. My most "bleeding" onto the page would have to be for her. It was very hard the life with her. I didn't know which way to turn. I could have very easily taken her path of self destruction but instead chose another with the help of a higher power.

Are there any plans underway for a movie adaptation of *Brooklyn Story*?

Yes. I have written the screenplay and will be a producer on this project. I have wonderful people already attached—an Oscar winner and an Oscar nominee—so I am thrilled. We are in the process of finding its proper home now.

Besides the film, what future projects do you have planned?

Brooklyn Story (Over the Bridge) the sequel, which I am writing now, and there will be a third book. Depends how far Samantha wants to go!